"Never Will I Belong To You!"

When the heavy door slammed shut, the room suddenly seemed unnaturally quiet and Judith was achingly aware of the man beside her. At this moment, Gavin remembered nothing of a quarrel. Nor had he any thoughts of love. He knew only that he was in bed with a desirable woman. He moved his hand to touch her shoulder and to see if the skin was as smooth as it looked.

Judith drew sharply away from him. "Do not touch me!" she said through clenched teeth.

He looked at her in surprise. There was hatred in her golden eyes, her cheeks flushed red. His hand went around her neck, his thumb digging into the soft flesh. "You are my wife," he said in a low voice. "You are mine!"

She resisted him with all her strength, but easily he pulled her face to his. "Never will I belong to you!" she spat at him before his lips closed on hers.

the church? Only when a man has many daughters does he allow that."

Also published by POCKET BOOKS/RICHARD GALLEN

The Golden Sky
  by Kristin James

Some Distant Shore
  by Margaret Pemberton

The Sun Dancers
  by Barbara Faith

The Velvet Promise

JUDE DEVERAUX

PUBLISHED BY RICHARD GALLEN BOOKS
Distributed by POCKET BOOKS

A RICHARD GALLEN BOOKS *Original* publication

Distributed by
POCKET BOOKS, a Simon & Schuster division of
GULF & WESTERN CORPORATION
1230 Avenue of the Americas, New York, N.Y. 10020

ISBN: 0-671-41785-1

First Pocket Books printing April, 1981

10 9 8 7 6 5 4 3 2 1

RICHARD GALLEN and colophon are trademarks
of Simon & Schuster and Richard Gallen & Co., Inc.

Printed in the U.S.A.

To Jennifer
for melting wax and double Fridays

The Velvet Promise

Prologue

JUDITH REVEDOUNE LOOKED ACROSS THE LEDGER AT HER father. Her mother, Helen, was beside her. Judith felt no fear of the man in spite of all he'd done over the years to make her fear him. His eyes were red with deep circles beneath them. She knew his ravaged face was due to his grief at the loss of his beloved sons; two ignorant, cruel men who were exact replicas of their father.

Judith studied Robert Revedoune with a vague sense of curiosity. He didn't usually bother with his only daughter. He had no use for women since his first wife died and his second, a frightened woman, had merely given him a girl. "What do you want?" Judith asked calmly.

Robert looked at his daughter as if seeing her for the first time. Actually, the girl had been kept hidden most of her life, buried with her mother in their own apartments amid their books and ledgers. He noticed with satisfaction that she looked like Helen had at that age. Judith had those odd golden eyes that some men raved about, but which he found unsettling. Her hair was a rich auburn. Her forehead broad and strong, as was her chin, her nose straight, her mouth generous. Yes, she would do, he thought. He could use her beauty to his advantage.

"You're the only one I have left," Robert said, his

1

voice heavy with disgust. "You will marry and give me grandsons."

Judith stared at him in shock. All her life she had been trained by Helen for life in a nunnery. Not a pious education of prayers and chanting, but one of high practicality, leading to the only career open to a noblewoman. She could become a prioress before she turned thirty. A prioress was as different from the average woman as a king from a serf. A prioress ruled lands, estates, villages, knights; she bought and sold according to her own judgment; she was sought by men and women alike for her wisdom. A prioress ruled and was ruled by no one.

Judith could keep books for a large estate, could make fair judgments in disputes, and knew how much wheat to grow to feed how many people. She could read and write, manage a reception for a king, run a hospital; everything she would need to know had been taught her.

And now she was expected to throw all of this away and become the servant of some man?

"I will not." The voice was quiet, but the few words could not have been louder if they'd been shouted from the slate rooftop.

For a moment, Robert Revedoune was bewildered. No female had ever defied him with such a firm look before. In fact, if he didn't know she was a woman, her expression would have been that of a man. When he recovered from his shock, he hit Judith, knocking her halfway across the little room. Even as she lay there, a trickle of blood running from the corner of her mouth, she stared up at him with absolutely no fear in her eyes, merely disgust and a touch of hatred. His breath caught for a moment at what he saw. In a way, the girl almost frightened him.

Helen was over her daughter in minutes and, as she crouched there, she drew her eating dagger from her side.

Looking at the primitive scene, Robert's momentary

nervousness left him. His wife was a woman he could understand. For all her outward look of an angry animal, he saw weakness deep in her eyes. In seconds he grabbed her arm, the knife flying across the room. He smiled at his daughter as he held his wife's forearm in his powerful hands and snapped the bones as one would break a twig.

Helen never said a word, only crumpled at his feet.

Robert looked back at his daughter where she still lay, not yet able to comprehend his brutality. "Now what is your answer, girl? Do you marry or not?"

Judith nodded briefly before she turned to aid her unconscious mother.

Chapter One

THE MOON CAST LONG SHADOWS OVER THE OLD STONE tower which rose three stories high and seemed to scowl down, in a tired way, at the broken and crumbling wall that surrounded it. The tower had been built two hundred years before this wet April night in 1501. Now was a time of peace, a time when stone fortresses were no longer needed; but this was not the home of an industrious man. His great-grandfather had lived in the tower when such fortifications were needed, and Nicolas Valence thought, if he sobered long enough to think, that the tower was good enough for him and future generations.

A massive gatehouse looked over the disintegrating walls and the old tower. Here one lone guard slept, his arm curled around a half-empty skin of wine. Inside the tower, the ground floor was littered with sleeping dogs and knights. Their armor was piled against the walls in a jumbled, rusty heap, tangled with the dirty rushes that covered the oak plank floor.

This was the Valence estate; a poor, disreputable, old-fashioned castle that was the butt of jokes throughout England. It was said that if the fortifications were as strong as the wine, Nicolas Valence could hold off all of England. But no one attacked. There was no reason to attack. Many years ago, most of Nicolas's land had been taken from him by young, eager, penniless knights who had just earned their spurs. All that remained was the ancient tower, which everyone agreed should have been torn down, and a few outlying farms that supported the Valence family.

There was a light in the window of the top floor. Inside, the room was cold and damp—a dampness that never left the walls even in the driest summer weather. Moss grew between the cracks of the stone, and little crawling things constantly scurried across the floor. But in this room, all the wealth of the castle sat before a mirror.

Alice Valence leaned toward the mirror and applied a darkener to her short, pale lashes. The cosmetic was imported from France. Alice leaned back and studied herself critically. She was objective about her looks and knew what she had and how to use it to its best advantage.

She saw a small oval face with delicate features, a little rosebud mouth, a slim, straight nose. Her long almond eyes of a brilliant blue were her best feature. Her hair was blonde, which she constantly rinsed in lemon juice and vinegar. Her maid, Ela, pulled a pale yellow strand across her mistress's forehead then set a French hood on Alice's head. The hood was of a heavy brocade, trimmed in a wide cuff of orange velvet.

Alice opened her little mouth to once again look at her teeth. They were her worst feature, crooked and a bit protruding. Over the years she had learned to keep them hidden, to smile with her lips closed, to speak softly, her head slightly lowered. This mannerism was an advantage, for it intrigued men. It gave them the idea that she did not know how beautiful she was. They imagined awakening this shy flower to all the delights of the world.

Alice stood and smoothed her gown over her slim body. There were few curves to it. Her small breasts rested on a straight frame with no hips, no indentation to her waist. She liked her body. It seemed clean and neat compared to other women's.

Her clothes were lush, seeming out of place in the dingy room. Close to her body she wore a linen chemise, so fine it was almost gauze. Over this was a luscious gown of the same heavy brocade as the hood. It had a deep, square neck, the bodice fitting very tightly to her thin frame. The skirt was a gentle, graceful bell. The blue brocade was trimmed with white rabbit fur; a deep border along the hem, and wide cuffs around the hanging sleeves. About her waist was a belt of blue leather set with large garnets, emeralds and rubies.

Alice continued studying herself as Ela slipped a rabbit-lined brocade cloak about her mistress's shoulders.

"My lady, you cannot go to him. Not when you are—"

"To marry another?" Alice asked as she fastened the heavy cloak about her shoulders. She turned to gaze at herself, pleased with the result. The orange and blue was striking. She would not go unnoticed in such an outfit. "And what has my marriage to do with what I do now?"

"You know it's a sin. You cannot meet a man who isn't your husband."

Alice gave a short laugh as she adjusted the folds of the heavy mantle. "Do you want me to ride out to meet my intended? Dear Edmund?" she asked with great sarcasm. Before Ela could reply she continued. "You needn't go with me. I know the way and, for what Gavin and I do, we need no one else."

Ela had been with Alice for too long to be shocked. Alice did what she wanted when she wanted. "No, I will go. But only to see that you come to no harm."

Alice ignored the elderly woman as she had all her life. She took a candle from the heavy metal holder by her bed and went to the iron-banded oak door. "Quiet, then," she said over her shoulder as she eased the door back on its well-oiled hinges. She gathered the brocade gown in her hand and threw it over her arm. She

couldn't help but think that in a few short weeks she
would leave this decrepit keep and live in a house—the
Chatworth manor house, a building of stone and wood
surrounded by high, protective walls.

"Quiet!" she commanded Ela as she threw an arm
across the woman's soft stomach and pressed them
both against the damp wall of the dark stairwell. One of
her father's guards walked clumsily past the foot of the
stairs, retied his hose, and made his way back to his
straw pallet. Alice hastily snuffed the candle and hoped
the man did not hear Ela's gasp as the pure black
stillness of the old castle surrounded them.

"Come," Alice whispered, having neither the time
nor the inclination to listen to Ela's protestations.

The night was clear and cool, and, as Alice knew
they would be, two horses waited for her and her maid.
Alice smiled as she threw herself into the saddle on the
dark stallion. Later, she would reward the stableboy
who took such good and proper care of his lady.

"My lady!" Ela whined in desperation.

But Alice did not turn because she knew that Ela was
too fat to mount the horse by herself. Alice would not
waste even one of her precious minutes on an aged and
useless woman—not when Gavin waited for her.

The river door in the wall had been left open for her.
It had rained earlier and the ground was wet, yet there
was a touch of spring in the air. And with it came a
sense of promise—and passion.

When she was sure the horse's hooves would not be
heard, she leaned forward and whispered to him. "Go,
my black devil. Take me to my lover." The stallion
pranced to show he understood, then stretched his
front legs long and straight. It knew the way and ate up
ground at a tremendous rate.

Alice shook her head, letting the air blow against her
face as she gave herself over to the power and strength
of the magnificent animal. Gavin. Gavin. Gavin, the
hooves seemed to say as they thundered on the
hard-packed road. There were many ways that the

muscle of a horse between her thighs reminded her of Gavin. His strong hands on her body, the strength of him that made her weak with desire. His face, the moonlight glinting on his cheekbones, his eyes bright even on the darkest night.

"Ah, my sweet, careful now," Alice said lightly as she pulled back on the reins. Now that she was nearing the trysting place, she began to remember what she had so carefully tried to forget. This time Gavin would have heard of her impending marriage, and he would be angry with her.

She turned her face to catch the wind directly. She blinked rapidly until the tears began to form. Tears would help. Gavin always hated tears, so she had used them carefully during the last two years. Only when she desperately wanted something did she resort to the trick; thus it did not grow thin from overuse.

Alice sighed. Why couldn't she speak honestly to Gavin? Why must men always be treated so gently? He loved her, therefore he should love what she did, however disagreeable to him. It was a useless hope and she knew it. If she told Gavin the truth, she would lose him. Then where would she find another lover?

The memory of his body, hard and demanding, made Alice push the heels of her soft shoes into the horse's side. Oh yes, she would use tears or whatever else was needed to keep Gavin Montgomery, a knight of renown, a fighter without equal . . . and hers, all hers!

Suddenly, she could almost hear Ela's needling questions. If Alice wanted Gavin, why then was she promising herself to Edmund Chatworth, a man with skin the color of a fish's belly, with fat, soft hands and an ugly little mouth that formed a perfect circle?

Because Edmund was an earl. He owned land from one end of England to the other, estates in Ireland, Wales, Scotland, and, it was rumored, in France as well. Of course Alice could not know exactly the extent of his wealth, but she would. Oh yes, when she was his wife, she would know. Edmund's mind was as weak as his body, and it would not be long before she controlled him as well as his property. She would keep him happy with a few whores and tend to the estates herself, unhampered by any man's interfering demands and commands.

Alice had a passion for the handsome Gavin but that did not cloud her judgment. Who was Gavin Montgomery? A minor baron—not rich, but poor. A brilliant fighter, a strong, handsome man, but he had no wealth—not compared to Edmund. And what would life with Gavin be? The nights would be nights of passion and ecstasy, but Alice knew well that no woman would ever control Gavin. If she married Gavin, he would expect her to stay home and do women's work. No, no woman would ever control Gavin Montgomery. He would be as demanding a husband as he was a lover.

She pushed the horse forward. She wanted it all— Edmund's fortune and position and Gavin's passion. She smiled as she straightened the gold brooches, one on either shoulder, that held the flamboyant mantle in place. He loved her—Alice was confident he did—and she would not lose his love. How could she? What woman came close to her in beauty?

Alice began blinking rapidly. A few tears and he would understand that she was being *forced* to marry Edmund. Gavin was a man of honor. He would understand that she must uphold her father's agreement with Edmund. Yes, if she were cautious, she would have them both; Gavin for the nights, Edmund's wealth for the day.

Gavin stood silently—waiting. The only part of him that moved was a muscle in his jaw, flexing and unflexing. The silver moonlight glinted off his cheekbones until they looked like knife blades. His straight, firm mouth was drawn into a severe line above a cleft chin. His gray eyes were black with anger, almost as black as the hair that curled about the neck of the wool jacket.

Only long years of strenuous training as a knight allowed him such rigid outward control. Inside, he was seething. This morning he'd heard that the woman he loved was to marry another; to bed with another man, her children belonging to him. His first impulse had been to ride straight to the Valence keep and demand that she deny what he'd heard. But his pride held him back. This meeting with her had been arranged weeks ago, so he forced himself to wait until he could see her again, hold her again and hear her tell him, from her own sweet lips, what he wanted to hear. She would marry no one but him. Of that he was sure.

He stared across the emptiness of the night, listening for the sound of hoofbeats; but the countryside was silent, a mass of darkness broken only by the darker shadows. A dog skulked from one tree to the next, eyeing Gavin, wary of the silent, still man. The night brought back memories of the first time he and Alice had met in this clearing, a wind-sheltered place open to the sky. In the day a man could ride past it and not notice it, but at night the shadows transformed it into a black velvet box, only big enough to hold a jewel.

Gavin had met Alice at the wedding of one of her sisters. Althought the Montgomeries and the Valences were neighbors, they rarely saw each other. Alice's father was a drunkard. He cared little for his estates; he lived—and forced his wife and five daughters to live—as poorly as some serfs. It was out of a sense of duty that Gavin attended a wedding there, as a representative of his family actually, his three brothers having refused to go.

Out of the dung heap of filth and neglect, Gavin saw Alice—his beautiful, innocent Alice. He could not at first believe she was one of the family of fat, plain daughters. Her clothes were of the richest materials, her manners delicate and refined, and her beauty . . .

He'd sat and stared at her, as several of the other young men did. She was perfect; blonde hair, blue eyes, a little mouth that he ached to make smile. Right then, before he'd even spoken to her, he'd become infatuated with her. Later, he had to plow his way through men to get to her side. His violence seemed to shock Alice and her lowered eyes, her soft voice had mesmerized him further. She was so shy, so reticent that she could hardly answer his questions. Alice was all and more than he could hope for—virginal yet womanly.

That night, he asked her to marry him. She gave him a startled look, her eyes like sapphires for a moment. Then she lowered her head and murmured something about needing to ask her father.

The next day Gavin went to the drunkard and asked for Alice, but the man gave him some nonsense about the girl's mother needing her. His words were strangely halting, as if he'd been coached and spoke a memorized speech. Nothing Gavin said could make Valence change his mind.

Gavin left in disgust, furious at being thwarted from having the woman he wanted. He had not ridden far when he saw her. Her hair was uncovered, the setting sun making it glow, the rich blue velvet of her gown reflecting her eyes. She was anxious to hear what her father's answer was. Gavin told her, angrily, and then he'd seen her tears. Alice tried to hide them, but he could feel them as well as see them. In minutes, he was off his horse, pulling her from hers. He didn't remember how it happened. One minute he was comforting her. The next, they were here, in this secret place, their clothes removed and in the throes of passion. He did not know whether to apologize or rejoice. Sweet Alice was no serf to tumble in the hay; she was a lady, someday to be his lady. And she was a virgin. Of that he was sure when he saw the two drops of blood on her slim thighs.

Two years! Two years ago that had been. If he had not spent most of the time in Scotland, patrolling the borders, he would have demanded her father give Alice to him. Now that he'd returned, he planned to do just that. In fact, if need be, he would go to the king with his plea. Valence was unreasonable. Alice told Gavin of her talks with her father, of her begging and pleading with him, but to no avail. Once she showed him a bruise she received for pressing Gavin's suit. Gavin had been insane then. He'd grabbed his sword and would have gone after the man if Alice hadn't clung to him, tears in her eyes, and begged him please not to harm her father. He could refuse her tears nothing, so he sheathed his sword and promised her he would wait. Alice reassured him that her father would eventually see reason.

So they had continued to meet secretly, like wayward children—a situation that disgusted Gavin. Yet Alice begged him not to see her father, to allow her to persuade him.

Gavin shifted his stance now and listened again. Still there was only silence. This morning he'd heard Alice was to marry that piece of water-slime, Edmund Chatworth. Chatworth paid the king an enormous fee so that he would not be called upon to fight in any wars. He was not a man, Gavin thought. Chatworth did not deserve the title of earl. To think of Alice married to such as that was beyond imagination.

Suddenly all Gavin's senses came alert as he heard the muffled sounds of the horse's hooves on the damp ground. He was beside Alice instantly and she fell into his arms.

"Gavin," she whispered, "my sweet Gavin." She clung to him, almost as if in terror.

He tried to pull her away so he could see her face but she held him with such desperation that he dared not to. He felt the wetness of her tears on his neck and all the rage he'd felt during the day left him. He held her close to him, murmuring endearments in her little ear, stroking her hair. "Tell me, what is it? What has hurt you so?"

She moved away so she could look at him, secure in the knowledge that the night could not betray the lack of redness in her eyes. "It's too awful," Alice whispered hoarsely. "It is too much to bear."

Gavin stiffened somewhat as he remembered what he'd heard about her marriage. "Is it true then?"

She sniffed delicately, touched a finger to the corner of her eye and looked up at him through her lashes. "My father cannot be persuaded. I even refused food to make him change his mind, but he had one of the women . . . No, I won't tell you what they did to me. He said he would—Oh, Gavin, I cannot say the things he said to me." She felt Gavin stiffen.

"I will go to him and—"

"No!" Alice said almost frantically, her hands clasping his muscular arms. "You cannot! I mean . . ." She lowered her arms and her lashes. "I mean, it's already done. The betrothal has been signed and witnessed. There is nothing anyone can do now. If my father withdrew me from the bargain, he would still have to pay my dowry to Chatworth."

"I will pay it," Gavin said stonily.

Alice gave him a look of surprise; then more tears gathered in her eyes. "It wouldn't matter. My father will not allow me to marry you. You know that. Oh, Gavin, what am I to do? I will be forced to marry a man I do not love." She looked up at him with such a look of desperation that Gavin pulled her close to him. "How could I bear to lose you, my love?" she whispered against his neck. "You are meat and drink to me, sun and night. I . . . I will die if I lose you."

"Don't say that! How can you lose me? You know I feel the same about you."

She pulled away to look at him, suddenly happier. "Then you do love me? Truly love me, so that if our love is tested, I will still be sure of you?"

Gavin frowned. "Tested?"

Alice smiled through her tears. "Even if I marry Edmund, you will still love me?"

"Marry!" He nearly shouted as he pushed her from him. "You plan to *marry* this man?"

"Have I a choice?" They stood in silence, Gavin glaring at her, Alice with eyes demurely lowered. "I will go then. I will go from your sight. You needn't look at me again."

She was almost to her horse before he reacted. He grabbed her roughly, pulling her mouth to his until he bruised her. There were no words then; none were needed. Their bodies understood each other even if they couldn't agree. Gone was the shy young lady. In her place was the Alice of passion that Gavin had come to know so well. Her hands tore frantically at his clothes until they quickly lay in a heap.

She laughed throatily when he stood nude before her. His body was hard-muscled from many years of training. He was a good head taller than Alice, who often towered over men. His shoulders were broad, his chest powerfully thick. Yet his hips were slim, his stomach flat, the muscles divided into ridges. His thighs and calves bulged muscle, strong from years of wearing heavy armor.

Alice stepped away from him and sucked her breath in through her teeth as she devoured the sight of him. Her hands reached for him as if they were claws.

Gavin pulled her to him, kissed the little mouth that opened widely under his as her tongue plunged into his mouth. He pulled her close, the feel of her gown exciting against his bare skin. His lips moved to her cheek, to her neck. They had all night, and he meant to spend his time making love to her.

"No!" Alice said impatiently as she drew away sharply. She flung her mantle from her shoulders, careless of the expensive fabric. She pushed Gavin's hands away from the buckle of her belt. "You are too slow," she stated flatly.

Gavin frowned for a moment, but as layer after layer of Alice's clothes were flung to the ground, his senses took over. She was eager for him as he was for her.

What if she did not want to take too long before their bodies were skin to skin?

Gavin would have liked to savor Alice's slender body for a while, but she pulled him quickly to the ground, her hand guiding him immediately inside her. He did not think then of leisurely loveplay or kisses. Alice was beneath him, urging him on. Her voice was harsh as she directed his body, her hands firm on his hips as she pushed him, harder and harder. Gavin at one time worried that he would hurt her, but she seemed to glory in the strength of him.

"Now! Now!" she demanded beneath him and gave a low, throaty sound of triumph when he obeyed her.

Immediately afterward she moved from beneath him, away from him. She had told him repeatedly this was because of her warring thoughts as she reconciled her unmarried state with her passion. Yet he would have liked to have held her longer, enjoyed her body more, even perhaps made love to her again. It would be a slow lovemaking this time, now that their first passion was spent. Gavin tried to ignore the hollow feeling he had, as if he had just tasted something but was still not sated.

"I must leave," she said as she sat up and began the intricate process of dressing.

He liked to watch her slim legs as she slipped on the light linen stockings. At least watching her helped some of the emptiness dissipate. Unexpectedly, he remembered that soon another man would have the right to touch her. Suddenly he wanted to hurt her as she was hurting him. "I too have an offer of marriage."

Alice stopped instantly, her hand on her stocking and watched him, waiting for more.

"Robert Revedoune's daughter."

"He has no daughter—only sons, both of them married," Alice said instantly. Revedoune was one of the king's earls, a man whose estates made Edmund's look like a serf's farm. It had taken Alice a while, those years while Gavin was in Scotland, but she'd found out the history of all of the earls—of all of the richest men in England—before deciding that Edmund was the most likely catch.

"Didn't you hear that both sons died two months ago of wasting sickness?"

She stared at him. "But I've never heard a daughter mentioned."

"A young girl named Judith, younger than her brothers. I heard she had been prepared by her mother for the church. The girl is kept cloistered in her father's house."

"And you have been offered this Judith to marry? But she would be her father's heiress, a wealthy woman. Why would he offer to—?" She stopped, remembering to conceal her thoughts from Gavin.

He turned his face from her, and she could see the muscles in his jaw working, the moonlight glinting on his bare chest, still lightly covered in sweat from their lovemaking.

"Why would he offer such a prize to a Montgomery?" Gavin finished for her, his voice cold. Once the Montgomery family had been wealthy enough to stir the envy of King Henry IV. Henry had declared the entire family traitorous and then set about breaking up the powerful family. He had done so well that only now, one hundred years later, was the family beginning to regain some of what it had lost. But the memories of the Montgomery family were long, and none of them cared to be reminded of what they had once been.

"For the right arms of my brothers and myself," Gavin said after a while. "The Revedoune lands border ours on the north, and he fears the Scots. He realizes that his lands will be protected if he allies himself to my family. One of the court singers heard him say that the Montgomeries, if they produced nothing else, made sons who lived. So it seems I am made an offer of his daughter if only I will give her sons."

Alice was nearly dressed now. She stared at him. "The title will pass through the daughter, won't it? Your eldest son would be an earl, and you when her father dies."

Gavin turned abruptly. He hadn't thought of that, nor did he care about it. It was strange that Alice, who cared so little for worldly goods, should think of it first.

"Then you will marry her?" Alice asked as she stood over him and watched as he hastily began to put on his clothes.

"I've not made a decision. The offer only came two days ago, and then I thought—"

"Have you seen her?" Alice interrupted.

"Seen her? You mean the heiress?"

Alice clamped her teeth together. Men could be so dense at times. She recovered herself. "She is beautiful, I know," Alice said tearfully. "And once you are wed to her, you will never remember me."

Gavin stood quickly. He didn't know whether to be angry or not. The woman talked of their marriages to other people as if they made no difference to their relationship. "I have not seen her," he said quietly.

Suddenly the night seemed to be closing in on him. He'd wanted to hear Alice deny the talk of her marriage, but instead he found himself talking of the possibility of his own marriage. He wanted to get away—away from the complexities of women and back to the soundness and logic of his brothers. "I don't know what will happen."

Alice frowned as he took her arm and led her to her horse. "I love you, Gavin," she said quickly. "Whatever happens, I will always love you, always want you."

He quickly lifted her into the saddle. "You must return before someone discovers you're gone. We wouldn't like such a story to get to the brave and noble Chatworth, would we?"

"You are cruel, Gavin," she said, but there was no sound of tears in her voice. "Am I to be punished for what is out of my hands, for what I cannot control?"

He had no answer for her.

Alice bent forward and kissed him, but she knew his mind was elsewhere and this frightened her. She pulled sharply on the reins and galloped away.

Chapter Two

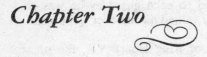

IT WAS VERY LATE WHEN GAVIN RODE INTO SIGHT OF THE Montgomery castle. For all that their property had been stolen from them by a greedy king, these walls remained theirs. A Montgomery had lived here for over four hundred years—since William conquered England and brought with him the already rich and powerful Norman family.

Over the centuries the castle had been added to, reinforced and remodeled until the fourteen-foot-thick walls enclosed over three acres. Inside, the land was divided into two parts; the outer and the inner bailey. The outer bailey housed the servants, the garrison knights and all the hundreds of people and animals it took to run the castle. The outer bailey also sheltered and protected the inner bailey, where the houses of the four Montgomery brothers and their private retainers stood. The entire complex set atop a hill, backed against a river. No trees were allowed to grow within half a mile of the castle: any ememy would have to approach in the open.

For four centuries the Montgomeries had held this fortress against an avaricious king and private wars. It was with pride that Gavin looked at the looming walls

that were his home. He walked his horse toward the
river then dismounted and led it through the narrow
river passage. Apart from the massive front gate, this
was the only entrance. The main gate was covered by a
portcullis: a spiked fence that could be lowered with
ropes. Now, at night, the guards would have had to
wake five men to raise it. So, Gavin went to the narrow
private entrance, a quarter mile of eight-foot-tall walls
that led to the back entrance, the top of the walls
guarded by men who walked back and forth on them all
night. Gavin nodded to each guard as he was challenged. No man who valued his life ever slept while on
duty.

During the reign of King Henry VII, the present
king, most castles had fallen into decline. When he had
taken the throne, sixteen years ago in 1485, he decided
to break the power of the great barons. He banned
private armies and he put gunpowder under the control
of the government. Since the barons could no longer
wage private wars for profit, their fortunes suffered.
The castles were expensive to maintain, and one after
another the thick walls were abandoned for the comfort
of a manor house.

But there were those who through good management
and hard work still retained the use of the powerful old
structures. The Montgomeries were such a family, and
they were respected throughout England. Gavin's
father had built a strong, comfortable manor house for
his five children, but he'd built it inside the castle walls.

Once inside the bailey, Gavin saw that there was
much activity. "What has happened?" he asked the
stableboy who took his horse.

"The masters have just returned from a fire in the
village."

"Bad?"

"No, sire, only some of the merchants' houses. The
masters needn't have gone." The boy shrugged, as if to
say that there was no understanding nobles.

Gavin left him and entered the manor house, built

against the ancient stone tower that was used now for little except storage. The brothers preferred the comfort of the big house. Several of the knights were settling down to sleep, and Gavin greeted a few of them as he hurried up the broad oak stairs to his own quarters on the third floor.

"Here is our wayward brother," Raine called to him cheerfully. "Miles, do you think he rides about the countryside at night and neglects his responsibilities? Half the village could have burned to the ground if we acted as he does."

Raine was the third Montgomery brother, the shortest and stockiest of the four. He was a powerful, thick man. He would have been formidable looking, and on a battlefield he was; but most of the time, as now, his blue eyes danced and deep, long dimples pierced his cheeks.

Gavin looked at his younger brothers, but he did not smile.

Miles, his clothes blackened with soot, poured a flagon of wine and offered it to Gavin. "You have had some bad news?" Miles was the youngest brother, a serious man with piercing gray eyes that missed nothing. His smile was rarely seen.

Raine was immediately contrite, "Is something wrong?"

Gavin took the wine and sank heavily onto a carved walnut chair, facing the fire. It was a large room with an oak floor, covered in places by carpets from the Orient. On the walls were heavy wool tapestries of hunting scenes and the Crusades. The ceiling was of heavy, arched timbers, both decorative and functional. White plaster filled the gap between the beams. It was a man's room and the large, dark furniture in it was carved intricately. At the southern end was a deep bay window with seats covered in red sendal. The glass in the mullioned windows was from France.

All three of the brothers were dressed in simple, dark clothes. Linen shirts, loosely gathered at the neck, fit close to their bodies. Over these were wool doublets, long vestlike garments that reached to the top of their thighs. A heavy, short, long-sleeved jacket went over the doublet. The men's legs, exposed from the top of the thigh, were encased in dark wool hose, tightly fitting the massive bulges of muscle. Gavin wore heavy boots to his knees. At his hip was slung a sword in a jeweled scabbard.

Gavin drank deeply of the wine, then watched silently as Miles refilled it. He could not share his unhappiness about Alice—even with his brothers.

When Gavin did not speak, Miles and Raine exchanged glances. They knew where Gavin had been and could guess what news had given him an air of doom. Raine had met Alice once, at Gavin's discreet urging, and found in her a coldness he did not like. But to the besotted Gavin, Alice was perfection in a woman. Whatever he thought of her, Raine had sympathy for Gavin.

Not so Miles. He was untouched by even the hint of love for a woman. To him, one woman was the same as another; one served the same purpose as well as any. "Robert Revedoune sent another messenger today," Miles interrupted the silence. "I think he is worried that if his daughter isn't delivered of a son soon, she might die and leave him no one to inherit."

"Is she sickly?" Raine asked. He was the humanitarian of the brothers, concerned for a hurt mare, a sick serf.

"I've not heard so," Miles answered. "The man is mad with grief that his sons are gone and that he has merely one puny daughter left. I've heard he beats his wife regularly to repay her for so few sons."

Raine frowned into his wine cup. He did not believe in beating women.

"Will you give him his answer?" Miles pressed as Gavin still did not answer.

"One of you take her," Gavin said. "Bring Stephen from Scotland or you, Raine, you need a wife."

"Revedoune wants only the eldest son for his daughter," Raine grinned. "Otherwise I would be more than willing."

"Why this haggling?" Miles said angrily. "You are twenty-seven years old, and you need a wife. This Judith Revedoune is rich—she brings an earldom with her. Perhaps through her the Montgomeries can begin to regain what we once had."

Alice was lost to him and the sooner he faced that the sooner he could begin to heal, Gavin decided. "All right. I agree to the marriage."

Immediately, Raine and Miles let out the breath they had not realized they'd been holding.

Miles set his wine down. "I asked the messenger to stay. I'd hoped to tell him your answer."

As Miles left the room, Raine's sense of humor took over. "I have heard she is only this tall," he held his hand near his waist, "and she has teeth the size of a horse's. Besides that . . ."

The old tower was drafty; the wind whistled through the cracks. The oiled paper over the windows did little to keep out the cold.

Alice slept comfortably, nude beneath a linen coverlet, filled with goose down.

"My lady," Ela whispered to her mistress. "He is here."

Drowsy, Alice rolled over. "How dare you wake me!" she said in a fierce whisper. "Who is here?"

"The man from the Revedoune household. He—"

"Revedoune!" Alice said as she sat up, fully awake now. "Bring me my robe and fetch the man to me."

"Here?" Ela was aghast. "No, my lady, you cannot. Someone could hear you."

"Yes," Alice said absently. "It is too great a risk. Let me dress. I'll meet him under that elm tree by the kitchen garden."

"At night? But—"

"Go now! Tell him I will be there soon." Alice

quickly threw her arms into her bedrobe, a gown of thick crimson velvet lined with gray squirrel fur. She wrapped a wide belt about her waist and slipped her feet into soft leather slippers dyed gold.

It had been nearly a month since she'd seen Gavin, and in all that time she'd had no word from him. But only days after their night in the forest, she had heard that he was to marry the Revedoune heiress. And now a tourney to celebrate the match was being cried from one end of England to the other. Every man of importance was being invited; every knight with any skill was asked to participate. At every word she heard, Alice grew more jealous. How she'd like to sit beside a husband such as Gavin and watch a tourney fought to celebrate *her* marriage. No such plans were being made for her wedding.

Yet, for all she heard of the plans, nowhere could she hear a word about Judith Revedoune herself. The girl was a name with no face or figure to it. Two weeks ago, Alice had come upon the idea of purchasing a spy to find out about this elusive Judith, to find what she looked like, what Alice must compete with. She gave Ela orders that she was to be told when the man arrived, no matter what time.

Alice's heart was beating quickly as she ran through the path of the weed-choked garden. This Judith was an absolute toad, Alice told herself. She *had* to be.

"Ah, my lady," the spy said when Alice was near. "Your beauty outshines the moon in radiance." He grabbed her hand and kissed it.

He disgusted her, yet he was the only man she could find who had access to the Revedoune family. The price she'd had to pay him was outrageous! He was a slimy, oily man, but at least his lovemaking had not been so. Was any man's, she wondered. "What news?" Alice asked impatiently as she hurriedly pulled her hand away. "Did you see her?"

"Not . . . closely—"

"Closely? Did you see her or not?" Alice demanded, looking straight into his eyes.

"Yes, I saw her," he answered firmly. "But she is heavily guarded." He wanted to please this blonde beauty, so he knew he must conceal the truth. He had seen Judith Revedoune, but only from a distance, as she was riding away from the manor with her women. He wasn't even sure which bundled figure was the heiress.

"Why is she kept guarded? Is her mind not sound that she cannot be trusted to be free?"

Suddenly he was afraid of this woman who questioned him so sharply. There was power in those cold blue eyes. "There are rumors, of course. She is seen by no one except her women and her mother. She has lived her life among them, and always she has prepared for the church."

"The church?" Alice began to feel some of the tension leave her. It was common knowledge that whenever a deformed or retarded daughter was born, if the family were rich enough, the creature would be pensioned and given to the nuns to care for. "Then you think she could have a weak mind or be malformed in some way?"

"Why else, my lady, would she be kept hidden all her life? Robert Revedoune is a hard man. His wife limps from a time when he threw her down the stairs. He wouldn't want the world to see that he has a monster for a daughter."

"But you aren't sure this is the reason she is hidden?"

He smiled, feeling safer. "What other reason could there be? If she were sane and whole, wouldn't he bring her out for the world to see? Wouldn't he have offered her in marriage before his sons' deaths forced him to do so? What man would allow his only daughter to enter the church? Only when a man has many daughters does he allow that."

Alice was staring quietly ahead into the night. Her silence made the man grow bolder. He leaned closer to her, put his hand over hers and whispered into her ear. "You have no reason to fear, my lady. There will be no beautiful bride to turn the Lord Gavin's head from you."

Only Alice's sharply drawn breath gave any indication she had heard. Did even the most common of men know about her and Gavin? With the skill of a great actress, she turned and smiled at the man. "You have done well and you shall be . . . suitably rewarded." She left no doubt as to the meaning of her words.

He bent and kissed her neck.

Alice moved away, hiding her revulsion. "No, not tonight," she whispered intimately. "Tomorrow. Arrangements must be made so we can spend more time together." She ran her hand under the loose tabard, along his upper thigh, and smiled seductively when his breath caught. "I must go," she said with seeming reluctance.

There was no hint of a smile on her face when her back was to him. She had one more stop to make before she returned to bed. The stableboy would be glad to help her. She would not allow any man to speak freely of Gavin and her . . . and this one would pay for his words.

"Good morning, Father," Alice said cheerfully as she bent to brush her lips against the cheek of the gnarled and filthy old man. They were on the second floor of the tower, a floor left open as one enormous room. This was the great hall: a room used for eating, sleeping for the castle retainers, and all the daily activities.

She looked into her father's empty cup. "Here, you!" she said sharply to a passing servant. "Bring my father more ale."

Nicolas Valence took his daughter's hand in both of

his and looked up at her in gratitude. "You are the only one who cares, my lovely Alice. All the others—your mother and sisters—try to keep me from my drink. But you understand how it comforts me."

She pulled away from him, hiding her feelings at his touch. "But of course, dear Father. That is because I alone love you." She smiled sweetly at him.

After all these years Nicolas still marveled that he and his ugly little wife could have created such a lovely girl. Alice's pale beauty was a sharp contrast to his own darkness. And when the others raged at him and hid his liquor, Alice sneaked bottles to him. It was true—she did love him. And he loved her, too. What little coin there was, didn't he give it to her for her clothes? His lovely Alice wore silk while her sisters wore homespun. He'd do anything for her. Hadn't he told that Gavin Montgomery that she couldn't marry him, just as Alice had told him to? Of course Nicolas didn't understand why a young girl wouldn't want to marry such a strong and rich man like Gavin. But Alice had been right. He picked up his refilled cup and drained it. She'd been right—now she was to marry an earl. Of course Edmund Chatworth was nothing like one of those handsome Montgomeries, but Alice aways knew what was best.

"Father," Alice said smiling, "I would like a favor from you."

He drank yet a third cup of ale. Sometimes Alice's favors were not easy to grant. He changed the subject. "Did you know that a man fell off the wall last night? A stranger. No one seems to know where he came from."

Alice's expression changed. Now the spy would tell no one of Gavin or that she asked about the Revedoune heiress. Quickly, she dismissed the thought. The man's death meant nothing to her. "I want to go to the wedding of the Revedoune woman to Gavin."

"You want an invitation to the wedding of an earl's daughter?" Nicolas was incredulous.

"Yes."

"But I cannot. How could I?"

This time, Alice waved the servant away and refilled her father's cup herself. "I have a plan," she said quickly and smiled her sweetest smile.

Chapter Three

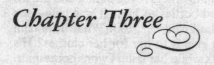

THE FIRE RAGED UP THE SIDE OF THE STONE AND HUNGRILY devoured the wooden second story of the merchant's shop. The air was thick with smoke and the men and women who formed a line to pass the buckets of water were blackened. Only their eyes and teeth remained white.

Gavin, his body bare from the waist up, used the long-handled ax viciously as he chopped away the building next to the blazing shop. The vigor with which he worked did not betray the fact that he had been working like this for a full two days.

The town where the building burned, where three others stood in ashes, was his. Twelve-foot walls enclosed the town, running down the hill from the great Montgomery castle. This town's taxes supported the Montgomery brothers; in return, the knights protected and defended the inhabitants.

"Gavin!" Raine bellowed over the roar of the flames. He too was filthy from smoke and sweat. "Come away from there! The fire is too close to you!"

Gavin ignored his brother's warning. He did not look up at the burning wall that threatened to fall on him.

His chopping became more vigorous as he fought to knock the seasoned timbers inside the lower stone walls, where the man on the ground could soak them with water.

Raine knew it was no use to yell at Gavin anymore. He tiredly signaled the exhausted men behind him to continue pulling the timbers off the wall. Raine was past exhaustion, yet he had had four hours of sleep—four more than Gavin. Raine knew from experience that if one square inch of what Gavin considered his was endangered, the man would neither sleep nor rest until it was safe.

Raine stood on the ground, his breath held as Gavin worked beside and under the burning wall. It would collapse at any moment and Raine could only hope that Gavin would soon finish hacking away the timbers and climb down the ladder to the safety of the ground. Raine murmured every oath he knew as Gavin flirted with death. The merchants and serfs gasped as the wall of fire teetered back and forth. Raine thought he would like to forcibly bring Gavin down the ladder, but Raine knew his strength was no greater than his older brother's.

Suddenly the timbers fell inside the stone walls, and Gavin was immediately on the ladder. He had no more than touched the ground when Raine made a flying leap and knocked his brother out of the path of the sheet of fire.

"Damn you, Raine!" Gavin bellowed in his brother's ear as Raine's heavy body lay on top of him. "You're crushing me. Get off!"

Raine was too used to Gavin to take offense. He stood up slowly, his muscles aching from the work of the last few days. "That's the thanks I get for saving your life! Why the hell did you stay up there so long? Another few seconds, and you would have been roasted."

Gavin stood up quickly, his soot-blackened face turned toward the building he had just left. The fire was contained inside the stone walls now and would not be leaping to the next building. When he was satisfied that the buildings were safe, he turned to his brother. "How could I have let the building burn?" he asked as he flexed his shoulder. It was scraped and bleeding where Raine had skidded him across the gravel and debris. "If the fire had not been stopped, I might not have had a town left."

Raine's eyes blazed. "I would rather have lost a hundred buildings than you."

Gavin grinned. His even white teeth shone against the blackness of his dirty face. "Thank you," he said quietly. "But I think I'd rather lose a little flesh than another building." He turned away and went to direct the men in the dousing of the structure that was next to the one he had hacked to pieces.

Raine shrugged and walked away. Gavin had been master of the Montgomery estate since he was sixteen years old, and he took his responsibility very seriously. What was his was his, and he would fight to the death to keep it. Yet the lowest serf, the worst thief, if they were residents of the Montgomery holdings, would get the fairest treatment from Gavin.

Late at night, Gavin returned to the manor house. He went to the winter parlor, a room off the great hall that served as a family dining room. The floors were covered with thick carpets from Antioch. The room was a recent addition and was paneled with the new linenfold paneling, the walnut carved to look like the draping of fabric. One end of the room was dominated by an enormous fireplace. The stone mantel above was sculpted with the Montgomery leopards.

Raine was already there, clean and dressed in black wool, an enormous silver tray in front of him heaped high with roast pork, chunks of warm bread, dried apples and peaches. He fully planned to eat every pound of the food. He grunted and pointed toward a large wooden tub filled with steaming hot water set before a roaring fire.

Gavin's fatigue was catching up with him. He slipped off his braies—a tight garment of hose and underpants—and his boots, then slipped into the water. It stung his recently blistered and cut body. A young servant girl appeared out of the shadows and began to wash Gavin's back.

"Where is Miles?" Raine said between mouthfuls.

"I sent him to Revedoune's. He reminded me that the engagement was to take place today. He went as my proxy." Gavin leaned forward, letting the girl wash him. He did not look at his brother.

Raine nearly choked on a piece of pork. "You what!"

Gavin looked up in surprise. "I said I sent Miles as my proxy for the engagement to the Revedoune heiress."

"Good God, haven't you any sense at all? You can't send someone else as if you were purchasing a prize mare. She's a woman!"

Gavin stared at his brother. The firelight showed the deep hollow in Gavin's cheek as his jaw muscles began to flex. "I am well aware that she is a woman. If she weren't, I wouldn't be forced to marry her."

"Forced!" Raine leaned back against the chair, incredulous. It was true that while Gavin's three younger brothers were traveling freely about the country, visiting castles and manors in France and even the Holy Land, Gavin had been chained to a ledger. He was twenty-seven and in eleven years, except for the recent uprising in Scotland, he had hardly left his own home. Gavin did not know that his brothers often made allowances for what they considered his ignorance of women other than the daughters of the lower classes.

"Gavin," Raine began patiently, "Judith Revedoune is a lady—an earl's daughter. She has been taught to expect certain things from you, such as courtesy and respect. You should have gone in person to tell her that you wish to marry her."

Gavin held out his arm as the servant girl ran a soapy cloth over it. The front of her coarse woolen dress was wet, and it clung to her full breasts. He looked into her eyes and smiled at her, beginning to feel the first risings of desire. He glanced back at Raine. "But I don't want to marry her. Certainly she cannot be so ignorant to think I'm marrying her for any reason besides her lands."

"You cannot tell her that! You must court her and—"

Gavin rose out of the tub and stood while the girl climbed on a stool and poured warm water over him to rinse him. "She will be *mine,*" he said flatly. "She will do as I tell her to. I have seen enough highborn ladies to know what they are like. They sit in their upstairs solars and sew and gossip while they eat honeyed fruit and grow fat. They are lazy and stupid; they have had everything they ever wanted. I know how to treat those women. I sent to London a week ago and ordered some new tapestries from Flanders—something silly like a nymphet cavorting about a woods so she won't be frightened by scenes of war. I'll hang them in the solar and give her access to all the silk threads and silver needles she can use, and she will be content."

Raine sat quietly and thought of the women he had met in his journeys about the country. Most of them were like Gavin's description, but then there were women of intelligence and fire who were more like companions to their husbands. "What if she wishes to have a hand in the estate affairs?"

Gavin stepped out of the tub and took the soft cotton towel the girl handed him. "She will not interfere in what is mine. She will tend to what I tell her, or she will repent it."

Chapter Four

Sunlight streamed through the open windows, slanting across the rush-covered floor, playing with little dust motes that glittered like specks of gold. It was a perfect spring day, the first of May, the sun shining, the air filled with the sweetness that only spring can bring.

It was a large, open room, half of the entire fourth floor of the half-timbered house. The windows facing south admitted enough light to warm the room. It was a plain room, for Robert Revedoune would not part with money for what he considered frivolous, such as carpets and tapestries.

This morning, though, the room did not look so sparse. Every chair was covered with a splash of color. There were garments everywhere; beautiful, lush, brilliant garments, all new, all part of the dowry of Judith Revedoune. There were silks from Italy, velvets from the Orient, cashmeres from Venice, cottons from Tripoli. Jewels winked everywhere: on shoes, belts, circlets. There were emeralds, pearls, rubies, enamels. And all of it was laid upon a background of fur: sable, ermine, beaver, squirrel, curly black lamb, lynx.

Judith sat alone amid this splendor, so quietly that someone entering the room might not have seen her except that Judith's person outshone any fabric or jewel. Her little feet were encased in soft green leather, lined and bordered with white ermine, spots of black dotting the fur. Her dress fitted her body tightly about the bodice, the long sleeves draping from wrist to past her waist. The waist was snug, revealing its tininess. The square neckline was low; above it, Judith's full breasts showed to advantage. The skirt was a soft bell that swayed gently when she walked. The cloth was of gold tissue, fragile and heavy, iridescent and shimmering in the sun. Her waist was encircled with a narrow belt of gold leather set with emeralds. On her brow was a thin cord of gold, a large emerald suspended in the middle. A mantle of emerald-green taffeta hugged her shoulders, fully lined with ermine.

On another woman the sheer brilliance of her green and gold gown might have been overwhelming. But Judith was more beautiful than any gown. She was a small woman with curves to make a man gasp. Her auburn hair hung down her back to her waist, ending in heavy curls. Her strong jaw was set and she held her chin high. Even now as she thought of the dreadful events to come, her lips were full and soft. But her eyes were what riveted attention. They were a rich, deep gold that grabbed the sunlight and reflected it off the gold of her gown.

She turned her head slightly and looked outside at the beautiful day. At any other time she would have been pleased by the weather, wanting to ride across the fields of fragrant flowers. But today she sat very still, careful not to move and crease the gown. It was not the dress that kept her so still, but the heaviness of her thoughts. For today was her wedding day—a day she had long dreaded. This day would end her freedom and all happiness as she knew it.

Suddenly the door burst open and her two maids entered the large room. Their faces were pink from just having raced back from the church where they had gone to get an early look at the groom.

"Oh, my lady," Maud said. "He is so handsome! He is tall with dark hair, dark eyes and shoulders . . . !"

She held her arms out to their fullest extent. She sighed dramatically. "I don't see how he managed the doorways. He must turn to the side." Her eyes danced as she watched her mistress. She did not like to see Judith so unhappy.

"And he walks like this," Joan said as she threw back her shoulders until the blades nearly touched and took several long, firm strides across the room.

"Yes," Maud said. "He is a proud one. As proud as all those Montgomery men. They act as if they own the world."

"I wish they did," Joan giggled, then rolled her eyes at Maud, who tried hard not to laugh with her.

But Maud was more interested in her mistress, and for all their teasing, Judith had not given even a hint of a smile. Maud held her hand, signaling Joan to be silent. "My lady," she said quietly, "is there anything you wish? There is time before you leave for the church. Perhaps—"

Judith shook her head. "I am past help now. Is my mother well?"

"Yes, she is resting before she must ride to the church. It is a long distance and her arm—" Maud stopped, sensitive to her mistress's look of pain. Judith blamed herself for Helen's broken arm. Her own conscience was enough without Maud's clumsy reminders. Maud could have kicked herself. "You are ready, then?" she asked gently.

"My body is ready. It's just my thoughts that need more time. Would you and Joan see to my mother?"

"But my lady—"

"No," Judith interrupted. "I would like to be alone. It may be my last moment of privacy for some time. Who knows what tomorrow will bring?" She looked back toward the window.

Joan started to reply to her melancholy mistress's words, but Maud stopped her. Joan could not understand Judith. She was rich, this was her wedding day and, best of all, her husband was a young and handsome knight. Why was she not happy? Joan shrugged her shoulders in dismissal as Maud pushed her through the doorway.

For weeks the preparations for Judith's wedding had been taking place. It was to be a sumptuous and elaborate affair, and would cost her father a year's rents. She had kept the books for every purchase, noting the thousands of ells of cloth to be used for the massive canopies to shelter the guests, totaling the food to be served; a thousand pigs, three hundred calves, a hundred oxen, four thousand venison pasties, three hundred tuns of ale. On and on the lists went.

And all for something she desperately did not want.

Most girls were reared to think of marriage as part of their future, but not Judith. From the day of her birth, Judith had been treated differently. Her mother had been worn out from miscarriages and years spent with a husband who beat her at every opportunity when finally her daughter was born. Helen looked at the tiny bit of red-haired life and lost her heart to it. Whereas she never fought her husband, for this child she would risk hell. She wanted two things for her little Judith: protection for her against a brutal and violent father, and guaranteed protection from all such men for all Judith's life.

For the first time in her many years of marriage, Helen stood up to the husband she feared so much. She demanded of him that her daughter be given to the church. Robert couldn't have cared less what was done with the girl or her mother. What did a daughter matter to him? He had his sons from his first wife, and all this groveling, mewling creature could produce were dead babies and one worthless daughter. He laughed and agreed to allow the girl to go to the nuns when she was of age. But to show that sniveling creature who was his wife what he thought of her demands, he tossed her down the stone stairs. Helen still limped from where her leg had been broken in two places from that fall, but it had all been worth it. She kept her daughter to her in complete privacy. There were times when Helen might not have remembered she was married. She liked to think of herself as a widow, living alone with her lovely daughter.

They were happy years. She trained her daughter for the demanding career of a nun.

And now it was all to be thrown away. Judith was to become a wife: a woman who had no power other than what was given to her by her husband and ruler. Judith knew nothing about being a wife. She sewed poorly and knit not at all. She did not know how to sit quietly for hours, allowing her servants to work for her. But worst of all, Judith did not even know the meaning of subservience. A wife must keep her eyes lowered to her husband, must take his advice in all things; but Judith had been taught that she would one day be a prioress, the only woman considered to be an equal by men. Judith had looked at her father and brothers with level eyes, never flinching even when her father raised his fist at her, and for some reason this seemed to amuse Robert. She had a pride that was uncommon in women—or even in most men, for that matter. She walked with her shoulders back, her spine straight.

No man would tolerate her quiet, even voice which discussed the relationship of the king to the French or talked of her own radical views as to the treatment of the serfs. Women were supposed to talk of jewels and adornments. Judith was often content to let her maids choose her clothing; but let two bushels of lentils be missing from the storehouses, and Judith's wrath was formidable.

Helen had gone to great pains to keep her daughter hidden from the outside world. She was afraid that some man might see her and want her and Robert would agree to the match. Then her daughter would be taken from her. Judith should have entered the convent when she was twelve, but Helen could not bear to part with her. Year after year she'd selfishly kept her daughter near her, only to have all the time and training come to nothing.

Judith had had months to prepare herself for marriage with a stranger. She had not seen him, nor did she care to. She knew she'd see enough of him in the future. She had known no men besides her father and brothers and therefore anticipated a life spent with a man who hated women, who beat them, who was uneducated and unable to learn anything except how to use his strength. Always she'd planned to escape such an existence, now she knew it was not to be. In ten years' time would she be like her mother: shaking, eyes shifting from side to side, always afraid?

Judith stood, the heavy gold gown falling to the floor, rustling prettily. She would not! Never would she show her fear to him; no matter what she felt, she would hold her head high and look him straight in the eye.

For a moment, she felt her shoulders droop. She was frightened of this stranger who was to be her lord and master. Her maids laughed and talked of their lovers with joy. Could the marriage of a nobleman be like that? Was a man capable of love and tenderness, just as a woman was? She would know in a short while. She straightened her shoulders again. She would give him a chance, Judith vowed silently. She would be a mirror of him. If he were kind, she would be kind. But if he were like her father, then she would give as good as she got. No man had ever ruled her and none ever would. Judith made that a vow also.

"My lady!" Joan called excitedly as she burst into the room. "Sir Raine and his brother Sir Miles are outside. They've come to see you." Joan gave her mistress a look of exasperation when Judith stared at her maid blankly. "They are your husband's brothers. Sir Raine wants to meet you before the wedding."

Judith nodded and stood to greet the visitors. The man she was to marry showed no interest in her; even the betrothal was done by proxy, and now it was not him but his brothers who came to greet her. She took a deep breath and forced herself to stop trembling. She was more scared than she realized.

Raine and Miles walked down the broad spiral stairs of the Revedoune house side by side. They had arrived only last night; Gavin had postponed facing his forth-coming marriage for as long as possible. Raine tried to get his older brother to meet his bride, but he refused. He said he would see her for years to come—why start the curse early?

When Miles had returned from his duty of proxy at the engagement, Raine had been the one to question him about the heiress. As usual, Miles said little, but Raine knew he was hiding something. Now that Raine had seen Judith, he knew what it was.

"Why didn't you tell Gavin?" Raine asked. "You know he's dreaded what he calls his ugly heiress."

Miles did not smile, but his eyes glowed in memory of the vision of his sister-in-law. "I thought perhaps it would do him some good to be wrong for once."

Raine smothered his laughter. Gavin sometimes treated his youngest brother as if he were a boy instead of a twenty-year-old man. Miles's silence in not telling Gavin of his fiancée's beauty was one small punishment for all the times Gavin had ordered his little brother about. Raine gave a short laugh. "To think Gavin offered her to me and I didn't even try! If I had seen her, I would have fought him for her. Do you think it's too late?"

If Miles answered, Raine didn't hear him. His thoughts were elsewhere as he remembered his first sight of his little sister-in-law, whose head hardly reached his shoulder. He saw that only before he was close enough to see her face. After one look at her eyes, as pure and rich a gold as any from the Holy Land, he saw nothing else. Judith Revedoune had looked up at him with intelligence, evenly, as if she were assessing him. Raine had merely stared, unable to speak as he felt himself being pulled under by the current of those eyes. She did not simper or giggle like most young maidens, she met him as an equal. He found the sensation heady. Miles had to nudge Raine to make him speak to her. Raine never heard a word anyone said, but merely stood and stared. He had a vision of carrying her away from this house and these people, of making her his. He knew he must leave before he had other such indecent thoughts of his brother's wife.

"Miles," he said now, his dimples cutting deeply into his cheeks, as they always did when he tried not to laugh aloud, "perhaps we can both repay our elder brother for demanding too many hours on the training field."

"What do you plan?" Miles's eyes burned with interest.

"If I remember correctly, I just saw a hideous dwarf of a woman with rotted teeth and an incredibly fat backside."

Miles began to smile. Truthfully, they had seen just such a hag on the staircase. "I see what you mean. We must not lie, but neither need we tell all the truth."

"My idea exactly."

It was still early morning when Judith followed her maids down the wooden stairs to the great hall on the second floor. There were fresh rushes on the floor, the tapestries had been taken from storage and hung, and running from the door to the far side of the room was a thick path of rose petals and lilies. These she would walk on when she returned from the church—a married woman.

Maud walked behind her mistress, holding aloft the long train of the fragile gold dress and the ermine-lined mantle. Judith paused just before she left the house, taking a deep breath to steel herself.

It took her eyes a moment to adjust to the bright

sunlight and see the long line of people who had come
to attend the celebration of the marriage of an earl's
daughter. She was unprepared for the cheer that
greeted her; a cheer of welcome and of pleasure at the
sight of the splendid young woman.

Judith smiled in return, nodding her head toward the
mounted guests and at the serfs and merchants who
also had come to the festivities.

The procession to the church would be like a parade,
meant to show the wealth and importance of the king's
earl, Robert Revedoune. Later he could claim so many
earls, so many barons, came to honor his daughter's
wedding. The jongleurs headed the procession, herald-
ing the way enthusiastically for the beautiful bride.
Judith was lifted onto a white horse by her father, who
nodded approval at her dress and bearing. She rode
sidesaddle for this auspicious occasion; the unaccus-
tomed position felt awkward, but she did not show it.
Her mother rode behind her, flanked by Miles and
Raine. The multitude of guests followed in order of
importance.

With a great clash of cymbals, the jongleurs began
singing and the procession started. They progressed
slowly, following the music makers and Robert Revedoune who walked, leading the reins of his daughter's horse.

In spite of all her vows and promises, Judith found
herself growing more nervous with each step. Now her
curiosity about her new husband began to eat at her.
She sat erect, but her eyes strained toward the church
door where two figures stood; the priest and the
stranger who was to be her husband.

Gavin was not so curious. His stomach was still
uneasy after the description that Raine had given him.
It seemed the girl was simpleminded as well as ugly. He
tried not to look at the rapidly approaching procession
but the noise of the jongleurs and the deafening cheers
of the thousands of serfs and merchants who lined the
way to watch, kept him from hearing his own thoughts.

In spite of himself, his eyes were drawn to the procession. He had not realized they were so close! When Gavin looked up and saw the auburn-haired girl on the white horse, he had no idea who she was. It was a full minute before he realized that she was his bride. The sun flashed off her as if she were a pagan goddess come to life. He stared, his mouth slightly open. Then he broke into a grin. Raine! Of course Raine would lie. Gavin was so relieved, so happy, that he did not notice that he was leaving the church portal, taking the steps two and three at a time. Custom dictated that the groom wait for the bride's father to lift her from her horse, escort her up the steps, then present her to her new master. But Gavin wanted to get a better look at her. He did not hear the laughter and cheers of the onlookers as he shouldered his father-in-law aside and put his hands on his bride's waist to swing her off her mount.

At close view, she was even more striking. His eyes feasted on her lips, soft, full and inviting. Her skin was creamy and pure, smoother than the finest satin. He nearly gasped when he finally gazed into her eyes.

Gavin smiled at her in pure pleasure, and she smiled back at him, exposing white, even teeth. The roar of the crowd brought him back to reality. Reluctantly, Gavin set her on the ground and offered his arm to her, clasping his hand over hers as if she might try to flee. He had every intention of keeping this new possession.

The onlookers were thoroughly pleased by Gavin Montgomery's impetuous behavior, and they gave voice to their approval. Robert scowled at being pushed aside then saw that each of the guests was laughing.

The marriage ceremony was performed outside the church so all could witness the joining, rather than the few who could squeeze inside the church. The priest asked Gavin if he would take Judith Revedoune for his wife. Gavin stared at the woman beside him, her hair unbound, flowing in thick, soft waves to her waist where it curled under perfectly. "I will," he replied.

Then the priest asked Judith as she stared just as openly at Gavin. He wore gray from head to foot. The doublet and the broad-shouldered jacket were of soft Italian velvet. The jacket was fully lined with a dark mink that formed a wide collar, the fur narrowly edging the front of the garment. His only ornament was the sword slung low about his hips, its hilt embedded with a large diamond that flashed in the sunlight.

Her maids had said Gavin was handsome, but Judith had no idea that she would see a man with such an air of strength about him. She had expected some blond and delicate young man. Instead, she looked at his thick black hair curling along his neck, saw the lips that smiled at her and then the eyes that suddenly made chills run along her spine.

To the joy of the crowd, the priest had to repeat his question. Judith felt her cheeks burning as she said, "Yes." Most definitely, she would take Gavin Montgomery.

They gave promises to love, honor and obey, and when the rings were exchanged, the temporarily silent crowd let out another roar that threatened the church roof. As Judith's dowry was read to the guests and onlookers, it could hardly be heard. Judith and Gavin, a beautiful young woman and handsome young man, were a great favorite with them. The bride and groom were handed baskets of silver coins which they tossed to the people at the foot of the steps. Then the couple followed the priest into a quiet and relatively dark cathedral.

Gavin and Judith were given places of honor in the choir, above the press of the guests below. The two were like children, stealing glances at one another throughout the long, solemn mass. The guests watched adoringly, enchanted by this marriage with its fairytale beginning. The jongleurs were already composing songs to be sung at the banquet later. The serfs and middle class were outside the church, comparing observations on the exquisite clothes of the guests and most of all on the beauty of the bride.

But there was one person who was not happy. Alice Valence sat beside the fat, dozing figure of her husband-to-be, Edmund Chatworth, and stared at the bride with all the hatred in her soul. Gavin had made a fool of himself! Even the serfs had laughed at him when he bounded down the stairs after that woman like a boy running toward his first horse.

How could anyone think that red-haired bitch was beautiful? Alice knew that freckles always accompanied red hair.

She looked away from Judith to Gavin. Gavin was the one who made her angry. Alice knew him better than he knew himself. For all that a pretty face could send him somersaulting like a clown, she knew that his emotions ran deep. When he said he loved her, he did And she would remind him of that as soon as possible She would not allow him to forget her when he was bedded with that red-haired devil.

Alice looked at her hands and smiled. There was a ring . . . Yes, she had it with her. She felt a little more secure as she looked back at the bride and groom, a plan forming in her mind.

She saw Gavin take Judith's hand and kiss it, ignoring Raine who reminded him that they were in church. Alice shook her head. The silly woman didn't even know how to react. She should have lowered her lashes and blushed; Alice's blush was quite becoming. But Judith Revedoune merely stared at her husband, watching his every move as he pressed his lips to the back of her hand. Most unfeminine, Alice thought.

At that moment Alice was not unobserved. Raine glanced down from the choir loft at Alice and saw the scowl that creased her perfect brow. He was sure she had no idea she was doing so; Alice was so careful to show only what she wanted to be seen.

Fire and ice, he thought. Judith's beauty was like fire to Alice's icy blondeness. He smiled as he thought how easily fire melted ice, but then remembered that it all depended on the heat of the fire and the greatness of the block of ice. His brother was a sane and sensible man, rational in every aspect except one—Alice Valence. Gavin adored her; he was insane when anyone even hinted at her flaws. His new wife held an attraction for him, but for how long? Could she overcome the fact that Alice held his heart? Raine hoped so. As he looked from one woman to the other, he realized that Alice might be a woman to worship, but Judith was a woman to *love*.

Chapter Five

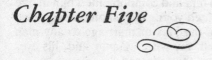

AT THE END OF THE LONG WEDDING MASS, GAVIN TOOK Judith's hand and led her down the steps to the altar where they knelt before the priest as he blessed them. The holy man gave Gavin the kiss of peace, which he then transmitted to his wife. It should have been a kiss of duty; but though it was over quickly, Gavin's lips were lingering, causing Judith to gaze at him, her golden eyes mirroring her pleasure as well as surprise.

Gavin grinned widely with pure joy, took her hand in his and led her at a half-run from the church. Once outside, the crowd threw a shower of grains that by sheer volume was almost lethal. He lifted Judith onto her horse, her waist tiny even when swathed in layers of fabric. He would have liked to put her onto his mount with him, but he'd committed enough of a *faux pas* when he'd first seen her. He started to take the reins of her horse, but Judith led her own animal and he was pleased; his wife would need to be a good horsewoman.

The bride and groom led the procession back to the Revedoune manor house, Gavin holding her hand tightly as they entered the freshly cleaned great hall. Judith looked at the rose petals and lilies spread on the floor. Only a few hours ago, these flowers had seemed an omen of the dreadful thing that was about to happen to her. Now, looking at Gavin, his gray eyes smiling into hers, the idea of being his wife did not seem so dreadful at all.

"I would give a great deal to know your thoughts," Gavin said, his lips close to her ear.

"I was thinking that this marriage does not seem nearly as bad as I once thought."

Gavin was stunned for a moment then he threw back his head and bellowed with laughter. Judith had no idea that she had insulted him and complimented him in one sentence. A well-trained young lady should never have admitted to disliking the idea of marriage to any man chosen for her. "Well, my wife," Gavin said, his eyes sparkling, "I am more than pleased."

Their first words to each other had been spoken— and then there was time for no more. The bride and groom must stand in line and greet the hundreds of guests who congratulated them.

Judith stood quietly beside her husband and smiled at one guest after another. She knew very few of them since her life had been so secluded. Robert Revedoune stood to one side, watching his daughter, making sure that she did nothing wrong. He would not be certain he had her off his hands until the marriage was consummated.

Judith had been concerned that her clothes would be overly rich but as she watched the guests, murmuring "thank yous," she knew her attire was conservative. The guests were dressed in peacock colors; several of them, all on one body. The women wore reds, purples and greens. There were checks, stripes, brocades, appliqués, and lush embroidery. Judith's gold and green stood out through its understatement.

Raine suddenly grabbed Judith's waist, lifted her high above his head, then planted a sound kiss on each cheek.

"Welcome to the Montgomery clan, little sister," he said sweetly, deep dimples in his cheeks.

Judith liked his honesty and openness. Miles came next. She had met him when he came as proxy for Gavin. He had stared at her like one of the hawks in the mews.

Miles still stared at her in that odd, piercing way, and she stole a glance at her husband, who seemed to be badgering Raine about some jest about an ugly woman. Raine, shorter than Gavin, wore a black velvet jacket trimmed with silver. He was a handsome man with his deep dimples and his laughing blue eyes. Miles was as tall as Gavin, but of slighter build. Of the three brothers, Miles's clothes were the brightest. He wore a dark green wool doublet and a brilliant green jacket, lined with dark sable. About his slim hips was a wide leather belt set with emeralds.

They were all strong, handsome men; but as she saw them together, Gavin seemed to outshine the others. At least, it seemed so to Judith. Gavin felt her eyes on him and turned toward her. He took her hand from her side and kissed her fingers. Judith felt her heart race as he put the tip of one finger in his mouth, touching it to his tongue.

"I think you should wait a while, brother, although I can see the reason for your impatience," Raine laughed. "Tell me again about fat, overbred heiresses."

Gavin released his wife's hand reluctantly. "You can laugh at me all you like—but it is I who has her, so I have the last laugh. Or maybe 'laugh' is not the right word."

Raine gave a throaty sound and nudged Miles.

"Come on, let's see if we can find any more golden-eyed goddesses in this place. Give your new sister-in-law a kiss of welcome and let's go."

Miles lifted Judith's hand and kissed it lingeringly, his eyes on hers all the while. "I think I shall save the kiss for a more private time," he said before following his brother.

Gavin put his arm around Judith's shoulders possessively. "Don't let them upset you. They're only teasing."

"I rather like their teasing."

Gavin smiled down at her, then abruptly released her. Touching her had nearly set him on fire. The bedding was many hours away. If he was to live through the day, he knew he must keep his hands off her.

Later, as Judith accepted a kiss from a withered woman, countess of someplace, wearing a shimmering gown of purple satin, she felt Gavin stiffen beside her. She followed his eyes down the line to a woman so exquisite that several men did little but gape at her. When she came to stand before the bride, Judith was taken aback at the hatred that smoldered in those blue eyes. She was almost tempted to cross herself in protection. Titters drew Judith's attention and she saw that several people were greatly enjoying the sight of the two women, both beautiful, but so different, face to face.

The blonde woman moved quickly past Gavin, refusing to meet his eyes and Judith noticed an expression of pain on her husband's face. It was a puzzling and disconcerting encounter which she did not understand.

Finally the reception was over. All the guests had spoken to the newly wedded couple, Judith's father had given each person a gift, according to his or her importance and at long last the trumpets sounded for the feasting to begin.

While the guests had greeted the bride and groom, the tables had been set about the great hall. Now they were being covered with food: chicken, duck, quail, crane, pheasant, partridge, as well as pork and beef. There were meat pies and twelve kinds of fish. Vegetables, seasoned with spices from the Orient, were abundant. The first strawberries of the season would be served, as well as a few of the rare and expensive pomegranates.

The estate's portable wealth was seen in the gold and silver dishes used by the most important guests who sat at the head table on a slightly elevated platform. Judith and Gavin had matching glasses—tall, slender, made of silver, the bases of finely worked gold.

In the center of the grouping of tables was an open area. Here jongleurs played and sang, Eastern dancers moved enticingly, acrobats cavorted and one traveling troupe put on a play. The noise was tremendous, filling the two-story-high room.

"You do not eat much," Gavin said, trying not to shout, but it was difficult to be heard over the din.

"No." She looked at him and smiled. The idea that this stranger was her husband kept running through her mind. She would like to touch the cleft in his chin.

"Come," he said and took her hand, helping her rise. There were catcalls and jeers, obscenities by the dozen when Gavin led his bride out of the great hall, but neither looked back. They strolled outside. The fields were full of spring flowers, which swept along the skirt of Judith's long gown. To their right were the tents of tomorrow's tourney participants. From each tent crown flew a pennant which identified its occupant, and everywhere was the Montgomery leopard. The banner held three leopards, placed vertically, worked in glittering gold thread, set on a ground of emerald-green.

"They are all your relatives?" Judith asked and Gavin looked over her head.

"Cousins and uncles. When Raine called us a clan, he meant it as such."

"And are you happy with them?"

"Happy?" He shrugged. "They are Montgomeries,"

he said, and that seemed to answer the question for him.

They stopped on a little hillside, from where they could see the tents below. He held her hand as she spread her skirts and sat down. He stretched out beside her, full length, his hands behind his head.

Judith sat with her back to his face. His legs stretched before her. She could see the way the muscle curved out above his knee then rounded toward his thighs. Judith knew without a doubt that each of his thighs were bigger than her waist. Unexpectedly, she shivered.

"Are you cold?" Gavin asked, at once sensitive. He raised himself on his elbows and watched as she shook her head. "I hope you didn't mind leaving for a while. You will think I have no manners—first at the church and now this. But it was too noisy, and I wanted to be alone with you."

"I too," she said honestly as she turned to face him.

He lifted one hand and took a curl of her hair, watching it wrap itself about his wrist. "I was surprised when I saw you. I had heard you were ugly." His eyes sparkled as he rubbed the curl between his fingers.

"Where did you hear that?"

"It was common talk that that was the reason Revedoune kept his daughter hidden."

"It was more that I was hidden from *him*." She would say no more, but Gavin understood. There was little he liked about the bully of a man who beat anything smaller than himself and groveled before anything larger.

Gavin grinned at her. "I am quite pleased with you. You are more than a man could hope for."

Suddenly Judith remembered the sweet kiss in church. What would it be like to kiss again, at leisure? She had so little experience with the ways of men and women.

Gavin's breath stopped as he saw her gazing at his

mouth. A quick glance at the sun told him it was still many hours before he could have her all to himself. He would not start what he could not finish. "We must return," he said abruptly. "Our behavior will set tongues wagging for years as it is." He helped her stand then, as she stood so close to him, he looked down at her hair, inhaling the spicy fragrance of it. He knew it was warm from the sun, and he meant only to place a chaste kiss on the part of it; but Judith lifted her face to smile at him. In moments, his arms were around her, his lips on hers.

Judith's small education about men and women had come from her maids, who giggled and compared the lovemaking of one man to another. So Judith reacted to Gavin's kiss, not with the reticence of a proper lady, but with all the enthusiasm she felt.

His hand went behind her neck, and her lips opened under his. She pressed her body close to his. How large he was! The muscles of his chest were hard against her softness, his thighs like iron. She liked the feel of him, the smell of him. Her arms tightened about him.

Suddenly Gavin drew back, his breath coming in short, shallow gasps. "You seem to know too much of kissing," he said angrily. "Have you had much?"

Her mind and body were too full of the newness of tingling sensations to be aware of his tone. "I have kissed no man before. My maids told me it was pleasant, but it is more than pleasant."

He stared, knowing an honest answer when he heard one. "Let's return now and pray for an early sunset."

Judith turned her reddened cheeks away from him and followed his lead.

They walked back toward the castle slowly, neither of them speaking. Gavin seemed to be absorbed in the erecting of yet another tent. If he had not held his wife's hand so tightly, she would have thought he'd forgotten her.

With his head turned away, he did not see Robert

Revedoune waiting for them. But Judith did. And she recognized the rage in his eyes and braced herself.

"You little slut!" Robert hissed. "You are panting after him like a bitch in heat. I'll not have all of England laughing at me!" He raised his hand and brought the back of it across Judith's face.

It took Gavin a moment to react. He would not have imagined a father striking his daughter. When he did react, he plunged his fist into his father-in-law's face until the older man sprawled on the ground in a complete daze.

Judith glanced at her husband. His eyes were black, his jaw flexed to granite.

"Don't you dare touch her again," Gavin ordered in a low, deadly voice. "What is mine I keep—and care for." He stepped toward Revedoune again.

"Please, no," Judith said and grabbed her husband's arm. "I am unhurt, and you have repaid him for what was only a little slap."

Gavin did not move. Robert Revedoune's eyes went from his daughter to his son-in-law. He knew better than to speak. Slowly he got up and walked away.

Judith pulled on her husband's sleeve. "Don't let him ruin the day. He knows nothing except his fists." Her mind was whirling. The few men she had known would have thought it a father's right to strike his daughter. Maybe Gavin thought only of her as property, but something in the way he had spoken made Judith feel protected, loved almost.

"Here, let me look at you," Gavin said, his voice showing that he was working hard at controlling his temper.

He ran his fingertips over her lips as he felt for any bruised places or broken skin. She studied the darkness of his jaw where his whiskers lay just below the cleanly shaven skin. His touch made her knees weak. She lifted her hand and placed one fingertip on the cleft in his chin. He stopped his exploration and looked into her eyes. They stared at each other silently for a long moment.

"We must return," he said very sadly. He took her arm and led her back to the castle.

They had been gone longer than they realized. The food had been cleared away, the trestle tables dismantled and stacked against the wall. The musicians were tuning their instruments as they got ready to play for the dancing.

"Gavin," someone called, "you'll have her all your life. You shouldn't hoard her now."

Judith clung to Gavin's arm, but she was quickly pulled away into a circle of energetic dancers. As she was pushed and pulled through the quick, vigorous steps, she tried to keep her eyes on her husband. She did not want to let him out of her sight.

A man's chuckle made her look up. "Little sister," Raine said, "you should give the rest of us a glance once in a while."

Judith smiled at him just before a strong arm whirled her about, feet off the floor. When she returned to Raine's side, she said, "How can I ignore such handsome men as my brothers-in-law?"

"Well said, but if your eyes don't lie, my brother is the only one to put the light of the stars in those bits of gold."

Again someone whirled Judith away, and as she was lifted in the man's arm, she saw Gavin as he grinned down at a pretty little woman in a purple and green taffeta gown. Judith watched as the woman touched the velvet across Gavin's chest.

"Where's your smile?" Raine asked when she came back to him. He turned and look at his brother.

"Do you think she's pretty?" Judith asked.

Raine controlled himself from laughing aloud. "Ugly! She is a little brown mouse of a woman, and Gavin would not have her." Since everyone else already has, he thought to himself. "Ah," he sighed.

"Let's leave here and get some cider." He grabbed her arm and led her to the opposite side of the room from Gavin.

Judith stood quietly in Raine's shadow and watched as Gavin led the brown-haired woman onto the dance floor. Each time he touched the woman, a swift feeling of pain shot through Judith's breast. Raine was absorbed in some talk with another man. She put her cup down and walked slowly through the shadows at the edges of the hall and made her way outside.

Behind the manor house lay a small walled garden. All her life, when she needed to be alone, Judith had gone to this garden. The image of Gavin holding the woman in his arms was branded in fire before her eyes. Yet why should she care? She had known him not even a full day. Why should it matter if he touched someone else?

She sat down on a stone bench, hidden from the rest of the garden. Could she be jealous? She had never experienced the emotion in her life but all she knew was that she did not want her husband either looking at or touching other women.

"I thought I would find you here."

Judith glanced up at her mother, then down again.

Helen quickly sat beside her daughter. "Is something wrong? Has he been unkind to you?"

"Gavin?" Judith asked slowly, liking the sound of the name. "No. He is more than kind."

Helen did not like what she saw on Judith's face. Her own had once been like that. She grabbed her daughter's shoulders although the movement hurt her half-healed arm. "You must listen to me! I have put off talking to you for too long. Each day I hoped something would happen to prevent this marriage, but nothing did. I will tell you something that you must hear. Never, *never* must you trust a man."

Judith wanted to defend her husband. "But Gavin is an honorable man," she said stubbornly.

Helen dropped her hands to her lap. "Ah yes, they are honorable to each other—to their men, to their horses, even; but to a man a woman means less than his horse. A woman is more easily replaced, less valuable. A man who would not lie to the lowliest serf would think nothing of creating the biggest tales to his wife. What does he lose? What is a woman?"

"No," Judith said. "I cannot believe all men are like that."

"Then you will have a long and unhappy life as I have had. If I had learned this at your age, my life would have been different. I believed myself to be in love with your father. I even told him so. He laughed at me. Do you know what it does to a woman to give her heart to a man and have him laugh at it?"

"But men do love women—" Judith began. She could not believe what her mother said.

"They love women, but only the one whose bed they occupy—and when they tire of her, they love another. There is only one time when a wife has any control over her husband, and that is when she is new to him and the bed magic is upon him. Then he will 'love' you and you can control him."

Judith stood, her back to her mother. "All men cannot be as you say. Gavin is . . ." She could not finish.

Helen, alarmed, went to her daughter and stood before her. "Don't tell me you think you are in love with him. Oh Judith, my sweet Judith, have you lived in this house for seventeen years and learned nothing, seen nothing? Your father was the same way once. Although you may not believe it, I was once beautiful and he was pleased with me. This is why I say these things to you. Do you think I want to tell my only child this? I prepared you for the church, to spare you. Please listen to my words. You must establish yourself with him from the first; then he will listen to you. Never show him your fear. When a woman reveals that, it makes the man feel strong. If you make demands from the first, he may listen to you—but soon it will be too late. There will be other women and—"

"No!" Judith shouted.

Helen gave her a look of great sadness. She could not save her daughter from the hurt that awaited her. "I must return to the guests. You will come?"

"No," Judith said softly. "I will follow in a moment. I must think for a while."

Helen shrugged and left by the side gate. There was no more she could do.

Judith sat quietly on the stone bench, her knees tucked under her chin. She defended her husband against what her mother said. Over and over she thought of hundreds of ways to show that Gavin was so very unlike her father, most of them created from her imagination.

Her thoughts were interrupted by the sound of the gate opening. A thin woman entered the garden. Judith recognized her immediately. She dressed to have people notice her. The left side of her bodice was green taffeta; the right was red. The colors were reversed on her skirt. She moved with an air of purpose. From her hidden bench behind the honeysuckle, Judith watched. Her first impression in the receiving line had been that Alice Valence was beautiful, but now she did not seem so. Her chin appeared weak, her little mouth stingy, as if it would give as little as possible. Her eyes glittered like ice. Judith heard a heavy, male footstep outside the wall, and she moved toward the smaller gate her mother had used. She wanted to give the woman and her lover privacy, but the first words stopped her. It was a voice she had come to recognize.

"Why did you ask me to meet you here?" Gavin asked stiffly.

"Oh, Gavin," Alice said, her hands going to his arms. "You are so cold to me. Can you have forgotten me? Is your love for this new wife so strong?"

Gavin frowned at her, not touching her, but not

moving away either. "You can talk to me of love? I begged you to marry me. I offered to take you without a dowry. I offered to repay your father what he gave to Chatworth, yet still you would not marry me."

"You hold this against me?" she demanded. "Didn't I show you the bruises from my father? Didn't I tell you of the times he locked me away without food or water? What was I to do? I met you when I could. I gave you all I had to give a man, yet this is how I am repaid. Already you love another. Tell me, Gavin, did you ever love me?"

"Why do you talk of my loving another? I haven't said I love her." His annoyance remained unabated. "I married because the offer was good. The woman brings riches, lands and a title also, as you yourself pointed out to me."

"But when you saw her—" Alice said quickly.

"I am a man and she is beautiful. Of course I was pleased."

Judith meant to leave the garden. Even when she saw her husband with the blonde woman, Judith meant to leave, but it was as if her body turned to stone and she could not move. Each word she heard Gavin speak thrust a knife through her heart. He had begged this woman to marry him and taken Judith, because of her wealth, as a second choice. She was a fool! She had been seeing their touches, their caresses as a spark of love, but it was not so.

"Then you don't love her?" Alice persisted.

"How could I? I have spent less than a day with her."

"But you *could* love her," Alice said flatly and turned her head to one side. When she looked back at him, there were tears in her eyes—great, lovely, shining tears. "Can you say you will never love her?"

Gavin was silent.

Alice sighed heavily, then smiled through her tears. "I had hoped we could meet here. I had some wine sent."

"I must return."

"It won't take long," she said sweetly as she led him to a bench against the stone wall.

Judith watched Alice, fascinated. She was watching a great actress. She'd seen the way Alice turned her head and deftly stuck her fingernail in the corner of her eye to produce the needed tears. Alice's words were melodramatic. Judith watched as Alice seated herself carefully on the bench, avoiding crushing the stiff taffeta of her dress, then poured two goblets of wine. In a slow, elaborate production, she slipped a large ring from her finger, opened the hinged lid and slowly poured a white powder into her drink.

As she began to sip the wine, Gavin knocked the goblet from her hand, sending it flying across the garden. "What are you doing?" he demanded.

Alice leaned languidly against the wall. "I would end it all, my love. I can withstand anything, if it is for us. I can bear my marriage to another, yours to another, but I must have your love. Without it I am nothing." Her lids dropped slowly and she had a look of such peace, as if she were already one of God's angels.

"Alice," Gavin said as he gathered her in his arms, "you cannot mean to take your own life."

"My sweet Gavin, you don't understand what love is to a woman. Without it I am already dead. Why prolong my agony?"

"How can you say you have no love?"

"You do love me, Gavin? Me and me alone?"

"Of course." He bent and kissed her mouth, the wine still on her lips. The setting sun deepened the applied color on her cheeks. Her dark eyelashes cast a mysterious shadow across her cheeks.

"Swear it!" she said firmly. "You must swear to me that you will love only me—no one else."

It seemed a small price to pay to keep her from killing herself. "I swear it."

Alice rose quickly. "I must return now, before I am missed." She seemed completely recovered. "You won't forget me? Even tonight?" she whispered against his lips, her hands searching inside his clothes. She didn't wait for his answer, but slipped from his grasp and through the gate.

The sound of clapping made Gavin turn. Judith stood there, her dress and eyes ablaze in a reflection of the setting sun.

"That was an excellent performance," she said as she lowered her hands. "I haven't been so entertained in years. That woman should try the stage in London. I hear there is need for good mummers."

Gavin advanced toward her, his face mirroring his rage. "You lying little sneak! You have no right to spy on me!"

"Spy!" she snarled. "I left the hall for some air after my *husband*"—she sneered the word—"left me to do for myself. And here in the garden I am a witness to that same husband groveling at the feet of a pasty-faced woman who twists him about her fingers like a bit of yarn."

Gavin drew back his arm and slapped her. An hour before he would have sworn that nothing could have made him harm a woman.

Judith slammed against the ground, landing in a mass of swirling hair and gold silk. The sun seemed to set a torch to her.

Gavin was instantly contrite. He was sick at himself and what he had done. He knelt to help her stand.

She retreated from him and her eyes glinted hatred. Her voice was so quiet, so flat, that he could hardly hear her. "You say you did not want to marry me, that you did so only for the wealth I bring you. Neither did I want to marry you. I refused until my father held my mother before me and snapped her arm like a splinter of wood. I have no love for that man—but for you I have even less. He is an honest man. He does not one hour stand before a priest and hundreds of witnesses and swear undying love—then in another hour pledge that same love to someone else. You are no man, Gavin Montgomery. You are lower than the serpent in the Garden of Eden, and always I will curse the day I was joined to you. You made that woman a vow and now I make you one. As God is my witness, you will rue this day. You may get the wealth you hunger for, but I will never give myself to you freely."

Gavin moved away from Judith as if she'd turned to poison. His experience with women was limited to whores and friendships with a few of the court ladies. They were demure, like Alice. What right did Judith have to make demands of him, to curse him, to make vows before God? A husband was a woman's god, and the sooner this one learned that the better.

Gavin grabbed a handful of Judith's hair and jerked her to him. "I will take whatever I want whenever I want, and if I take it from you, you will be grateful." He released her and pushed her back to the ground. "Now get up and prepare yourself to become my wife."

"I hate you," she said under her breath.

"What does that matter to me? I bear you no love either."

Their eyes locked—steel gray against gold. Neither moved until the women came to prepare Judith for her wedding night.

Chapter Six

A SPECIAL ROOM HAD BEEN READIED FOR THE BRIDE AND
groom. A large corner of the solar had been partitioned
off around one of the fireplaces. An enormous bed had
been set up in the room and sheets of the softest linen
were spread across it. A coverlet of gray squirrel, lined
with crimson silk fell across the sheets. Rose petals
littered the bed.

Judith's maids and several of the women guests
helped undress the bride. When she was nude, they
pulled the covers back, and Judith entered the bed. Her
mind was not on what was taking place around her. She
kept calling herself a fool. In just a few hours, she had
forgotten seventeen years of what she had learned was
true about men. For a few hours she had believed a
man could be kind and good, capable even of love. But
Gavin was the same—perhaps even worse than the
others.

The women laughed riotously at Judith's silence. But
Helen knew there was more than just nervousness
involved with her daughter's behavior. She whispered a
silent prayer, asking God to help her daughter.

"You are a fortunate woman," an older woman
murmured in Judith's ear. "My first marriage found me
wedded with a man five years older than my father. I
wonder now that no one helped him perform his
duties."

Maud giggled, "Lord Gavin will need no help—I'll wager that."

"Perhaps the Lady Judith will need help, and I would offer my . . . ah . . . services," laughed someone else.

Judith barely heard them. All she remembered hearing was her husband pledging his love to another woman, the way he held Alice and kissed her. The women drew the sheet just over Judith's breasts. Someone combed her hair so that it cascaded softly over her bare shoulders to rest in thick auburn curls around her hips.

Through the oak door the women heard the noise of the men arriving with Gavin carried aloft on their shoulders. He entered feet first, already half-undressed, the men yelling their offers of assistance, their wagers as to the competence of his performance of the task ahead. They were silent as they stood him on his feet and stared at the bride who waited in the bed. The sheet accented her creamy shoulders and the full swelling of her breasts. The candlelight deepened the shadow above the sheet. Her bare throat pulsed with life. Her face was set in a firm, serious expression that caused her eyes to darken, as if they smoked. Her lips were hard, as if carved of some warm vermilion marble.

"Get it done with!" someone shouted. "Do you torture him or me?"

The silence was broken. Gavin was quickly undressed and pushed to the bed. The men watched avidly as Maud drew the covers aside, giving them a glance of bare hips and thigh.

"Now out!" a tall woman ordered. "Leave them be."

Helen gave her daughter one last look, but Judith gazed down at her hands in her lap and saw no one.

When the heavy door slammed shut, the room suddenly seemed unnaturally quiet and Judith was achingly aware of the man beside her. Gavin sat looking at her. The only light in the room was from the flames in the fireplace across from the foot of the bed.

The light danced on her hair, played with the shadows of her delicate collarbones. At this moment, he remembered nothing of a quarrel. Nor had he any thoughts of love. He knew only that he was in bed with a desirable woman. He moved his hand to touch her shoulder to see if the skin was as smooth as it looked.

Judith drew sharply away from him. "Don't touch me!" she said through clenched teeth.

He looked at her in surprise. There was hatred in her golden eyes, her cheeks flushed red. If possible, her anger made her even more beautiful. Never had he felt such a raging desire. His hand went about her neck, his thumb digging into the soft flesh. "You are my wife," he said in a low voice. "You are mine!"

She resisted him with all her strength, but it was nothing compared to his. Easily, he pulled Judith's face to his. "Never will I belong to you!" she spat at him before his lips closed on hers.

Gavin meant to be gentle with her, but she enraged him. This woman made him want to curse her, to strike her again. But most of all he wanted to possess her. His mouth came down brutally hard on hers.

Judith tried to move away from him; he hurt her. This was no sweet kiss of the afternoon, but more of a punishment to discipline her. She tried to kick at him, but the sheet that separated them entangled her feet and she could hardly move.

"I will help you," Gavin said and tore the sheet away, pulling it from under the mattress. His hand still held Judith's neck, and when the sheet was gone and she lay nude before him, he relaxed his grip as he gazed upon her. He stared at her in wonder; her full breasts, small waist, round hips. Then he looked back at her face, her eyes blazing. Her lips were reddened from his kiss, and suddenly there was no power on earth that could have stopped him from taking her. He acted as a starving man—one desperate for food—who would kill or maim to get what he must have.

He pushed her to the mattress and Judith saw the

look in his eyes. She did not understand it, but she was afraid of it. He planned more than a cuff of his fist now. Of that she was sure.

"No!" she whispered and struggled against him.

Gavin was a seasoned knight. Judith had no more strength to him than a gnat to a piece of granite. And he paid her as much attention. He did not make love to her, but used her body. He was beyond thinking of her as anything but what he desired and so desperately needed. He moved on top of her, one thigh forcing hers apart. He kissed her again, hard.

When Gavin felt the tiny membrane that stopped him, for a moment he was bewildered. But he plunged on, oblivious to the pain he caused Judith. When she cried out, he stopped her lips with his and continued.

After he finished, he rolled from her, one heavy arm across her breasts. It had been a release for him, but for Judith there had been nothing resembling pleasure.

In minutes, she heard his slow breathing and she knew he was asleep. Silently, she slipped from under his arm and left the bed. The coverlet of squirrel pelts had been knocked to the floor. She picked it up and encircled her body with it. She stared at the fire, telling herself she would not cry. Why should she cry? Married against her will to a man who vowed, on her wedding day, that he would never love her, could never love her. A man who told her she was nothing to him. What reason had she to cry when the life before her appeared to be so pleasant? Could she look forward to years of doing little else but bearing his children, sitting at home while he roamed the countryside with his beautiful Alice?

She would not! She would find her own life and, if possible, her own love. Her husband would come to mean as little as possible to her.

She stood silently, controlling her tears, and all she could seem to remember was the sweetness of Gavin's kiss that afternoon, so different from his attack of tonight.

Gavin stirred in the bed and opened his eyes. At first he did not recall where he was. He turned his head, saw the emptiness beside him. She had gone! Every inch of his skin tightened until he noticed Judith in front of the fireplace. He did not think of his sudden fear, but was relieved that she was still with him. She seemed to be in another world and did not hear him turn onto his back. The sheets were liberally sprinkled with blood and Gavin frowned at them. He knew he'd hurt her, but he didn't understand why. Alice had been a virgin when he took her, but she had shown no pain.

He looked back at his wife, so small, so alone. It was true he had no love for her but he had used her harshly. A maiden did not deserve rape.

"Come back to bed," he said softly, smiling a bit. He would make love to her slowly, by way of apology.

Judith straightened her shoulders. "No, I will not," she said firmly. She must begin by not letting him control her.

Gavin stared at her back, aghast. The woman was impossible! She made every sentence a contest of wills. His jaw set, he rose from the bed to stand before her.

Judith had not really seen him nude before and his bare chest, covered with dark hair over sun-bronzed skin, drew her eyes. He looked formidable.

"Have you not learned that you will come to me when I call?"

She lifted her chin and met his eyes. "Have you not learned that I will give nothing to you freely?" she countered.

Gavin stretched out his hand and took a curl from her hip, winding it about his wrist, again and again, pulling Judith nearer as she shrank from the pain. The coverlet fell away and he pulled her bare skin against his.

"Now you use pain to take what you want," she whispered, "but in the end I will win because you will grow tired of fighting."

"And what will you have won?" he asked, lips close to her.

"Freedom from a man I hate, a brutal, lying, dishonorable—" She stopped when he kissed her. It was not the kiss of an hour before, but one of gentleness.

At first, Judith refused to react to him but her hands went to his arms. They were hard, the muscles prominent, and his skin was so very warm. She became aware of the hair on his chest against her breasts.

As his kiss deepened, he loosened his hand from her hair, his arms encircling her shoulders. He moved her so her head tucked into the curve of his shoulder.

Judith gave up thinking. She was a mass of sensation—every feeling new and undreamed of. She pressed closer, running her hands over his back, feeling the way the muscles moved, so different from the smoothness of her own back. He began to kiss her ears, little nibbles on the lobes. Gavin gave a low, throaty chuckle when Judith's knees turned to water and she collapsed against the strength of his arm behind her back. He bent, put his other arm beneath her knees, his mouth never leaving her neck, and carried her to the bed. He kissed her body from her forehead to her toes and Judith lay silent, only her senses alive.

Before long she could bear no more kissing. She ached all over, and she pulled his hair to better meet his mouth. She fastened on his lips hungrily, with greed.

Gavin's senses, too, were reeling. Never had he had the leisure to make love to a woman as he did tonight, and never had he imagined the pleasure of it. Judith's passion was as fierce as his own, yet neither rushed their lovemaking. When he moved atop her, her arms held him tightly, pulling him nearer. There was no pain for Judith this time; she was ready. She moved with him, slowly at first, until they exploded together joyously.

Eventually Judith fell into a deep, exhausted sleep,

her leg thrown over Gavin's, her hair twisted round and round his arm.

But Gavin did not fall asleep immediately. He knew that this was the first time for this soft woman he held, but in a way he felt as if he had just lost his virginity, too. And that was certainly an absurd idea. He could not possibly remember all the women he'd taken to his bed. But tonight was infinitely different. Never had he experienced such passion. With other women, when he felt his arousal at its height, they drew back. But not Judith. She had given as much as he gave.

He picked up a lock of her hair from across his neck and held it up, letting the firelight play though the strands. He held it to his nose, then to his lips. She moved against him and he snuggled closer. Even in sleep she wanted him nearby.

Gavin's eyes grew heavy. For the first time he could ever remember, he was sated and content. Ah, but there was the morning. He smiled before he drifted asleep.

Jocelin Laing returned his lute to its leather case and gave a barely perceptible nod to the blonde lady before she left the room. There had been several offers that night from women to share their beds. The excitement of the wedding and especially of seeing the handsome couple undressed and put to bed had sent many people off to find pleasure of their own.

The singer was an especially handsome young man; hot, dark eyes under long, thick lashes; dark hair that waved away from perfect skin that stretched over high cheekbones.

"Busy tonight?" one of the other singers called, laughing.

Jocelin smiled as he fastened his lute case but did not answer.

"I envy a man with a bride such as that." The other man nodded toward the stairs.

"Yes, she is beautiful," Jocelin agreed. "But there are others."

"Not like that one." The man moved closer to his friend. "There are some of us meeting with a few of the brides' women. You are welcome to come."

"No," Jocelin said quietly. "I cannot."

The singer gave Jocelin a sly look, gathered his psaltery and left the great hall.

When the enormous room was quiet, the floor spread with hundreds of straw mats for the sleeping retainers and guests of lesser importance, Jocelin made his way upstairs. He wondered how the woman he went to meet could have arranged a private room. Alice Valence was not rich, and though her beauty had won her an earl's ring, she was not one of the higher-born guests. On this night, when the castle was overflowing, only the bride and groom had a room alone. The other guests shared beds set out in the ladies' solar or in the master bedroom. The beds were large—often eight-foot squares—and with the heavy curtains surrounding them, they seemed like individual chambers.

Jocelin had no trouble entering the room set aside for the unmarried women; several men had slipped through the door already. It was easy to see the bed curtains slip aside and glimpse the blonde. He went to her quickly. The sight of her filled him with desire. Alice held out her arms, hungry for him, almost violent in her passion and any attempt Jocelin made to prolong their pleasures met with resistance. She was like a storm, full of lightning and thunder.

When it was over, she did not want Jocelin to touch her. Always alert to a woman's moods, he obeyed her unspoken wish. Never had he seen a woman who did not want to be held after lovemaking. He started to don his hastily discarded clothes.

"I will be married in a month," she said quietly. "You will come to my husband's castle then."

He did not comment. They both knew he would be

there; he just wondered how many other men she asked.

A single ray of sunshine came through the window, its heat tickling Judith's nose. Sleepily, she brushed at it then tried to turn away but something held her by the hair. She lazily opened her eyes and saw the strange bed canopy overhead. When she remembered where she was, she felt her face grow hot. Even her body seemed to blush.

She moved her head toward the other side of the bed and looked at her sleeping husband. His lashes were short, thick and dark, a new growth of beard starting on his cheeks. Asleep, his cheekbones were not as sharp. Even the deep cleft in his chin seemed relaxed.

Gavin lay on his side, facing her and Judith let her eyes roam over him. His broad chest was liberally covered with dark, curling hair. The muscles made large, shapely mounds. His arms was capped by a round, firm muscle. Her eyes drew down to his hard, flat stomach. It was only after a moment that her eyes went lower. What she saw did not seem so powerful but as she watched, his manhood began to grow.

She gasped and her eyes flew back to his. He was awake, watching her, his eyes growing darker by the moment. No longer was he the relaxed boy-man she had awakened to, but a man of passion. Judith tried to move away but Gavin still held her trapped by her hair. What was worse, she did not truly *want* to resist. She remembered that she hated him; but more than that, she remembered her pleasure when he made love to her.

"Judith," he whispered and the tone of his voice made chills run along her arms.

He kissed the corner of her mouth. Her hands pushed weakly against his shoulders but even at his slight touch, her eyes closed in surrender. He kissed her cheek, her earlobe. Then, as she gasped for breath, his mouth came down on hers. His tongue sweetly touched the tip of hers. She drew back, startled. He smiled at her as if he understood. Last night Judith thought she'd learned all there was to know about love between a man and a woman, but now she thought, perhaps she knew very, very little.

His eyes were smoky-gray as he pulled her to him again. He ran his tongue along her lips, touching the inner corners especially. She parted her teeth for him and tasted of him. He was better than the richest honey; hot and cold, soft and firm. She explored his mouth as he had explored hers. She had no idea of shyness. In truth, she had no ideas at all.

She ran her hands over him as he lowered his head to her neck, running his tongue along the pulse beat there. Instinctively she leaned her head back, her breathing deeper, quicker.

When his lips and tongue touched her breasts, she nearly cried out. She thought perhaps she might die under such torture. She tried to pull his head back to her mouth but he gave a deep, guttural laugh that made her shiver. Maybe he did own her.

When she thought that she would lose her mind, he moved on top of her, his hand caressing the inside of her thighs until she was shaking with desire. When he entered her, she cried out; there was no relief to her torment. She clutched at him, her legs about his waist as she rose to meet each thrust. Finally, when she was sure she would explode, she felt the pulsing throbs that released her. Gavin collapsed on top of her, holding her so close that she could hardly breathe. But at the moment she didn't really care if she ever did breathe again.

An hour later the maids came to dress Judith, waking the bridal couple. Suddenly she was very aware of her hair and her body wrapped around Gavin's. Maud and Joan had several things to say about Judith's abandonment. The sheets were stained, and there were more linens on the floor than on the bed. The squirrel coverlet was on the other side of the room by the fireplace.

The maids pulled Judith up and helped her to wash. Gavin lazily lolled on the bed and watched every movement.

Judith would not look at him; she could not. She was embarrassed to the very depths of her soul. She detested the man. He was everything she hated; dishonorable, a liar, greedy, yet she had acted with no pride when he touched her. She'd made a vow to him—and to God—that he would get nothing from her, but he took more from her than she'd wanted to give.

She hardly noticed as her maids slipped a thin linen chemise over her head, then a gown of deep green velvet. The dress had been embroidered with intricate gold designs. The front of the skirt was divided, revealing a wide stripe of the silk underskirt. The sleeves were full and gathered at the wrists. They were cut in places, and the lighter green silk underdress was pulled through the slashes.

"And now, my lady," Maud said as she handed Judith a large, flat ivory box.

Judith stared at her maid in surprise as she held the box open. On a black velvet bed lay a wide collar of gold filagree, the tiny wire in places as thin as hair. Along the bottom of the necklace was a row of emeralds, many of them perfectly matched in size, none of them bigger than a raindrop. "It is . . . beautiful," Judith whispered. "How did my mother—"

"It is your bride's gift from your husband," Maud said, her eyes sparkling.

Judith could feel Gavin's eyes on her back. She whirled and faced him. The sight of him in bed, his skin so dark against the whiteness of the sheets, made her knees weak. It took great will, but she bent one knee and curtsied. "Thank you, my lord."

Gavin's jaw clenched at her coldness. He would have liked the gift to thaw her somewhat. How could she be so hot in bed, so cold and haughty out of it?

Judith turned back to her maids and Maud finished fastening the buttons of the gown. Joan plaited the top layer of her mistress's hair, and intertwined the braids with gold ribbons. Before they finished, Gavin commanded them to leave the room. Judith did not look at him as he hurriedly shaved and dressed in a dark brown doublet and hose, a tawny wool jacket over it, the lining of golden lynx.

When he stepped toward her, she had to forcibly calm her hammering heart. He held his arm out for her and led her to the waiting guests below.

They attended mass together, but for this mass there was no hand kissing or staring at each other. They were solemn and sober throughout the service.

Chapter Seven

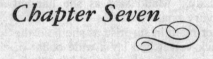

THE GROUNDS OUTSIDE THE REVEDOUNE MANOR RANG with noise, the air charged with excitement. Brilliantly colored pennants were everywhere, fluttering from the stands and from the tents that covered the field. The clothing flashed in the sunlight like jewels. Children dashed in and out of knots of people. Vendors, with large boxes hanging about their necks, hawked their wares, selling anything from fruit and pies to holy relics.

The lists itself was a sand-covered field a hundred yards long with two rows of wooden fences along both sides. The inner fence was short—only three feet high—but the outer one was eight feet. The space inside was for the squires and horses of the participating knights. Outside the tall fence, the merchant class and the serfs pressed for a view of the games and jousts.

The ladies and the knights who did not participate sat on terraced benches high enough above the lists to see everything. The benches were canopied and marked with sendal banners displaying the colors of each family. Several areas bore the Montgomery leopards.

Before the joust began, the knights walked about in their armor. Depending on the wealth of the knight, the quality and modernity of the armor varied greatly. There could be seen the old-fashioned chain mail or the newer plates sewn onto leather. The richest knights wore the new Maxmilian armor from Germany. It covered a man from head to foot in fine steel. There was not an inch that went unprotected. It was a heavy protection, weighing well over a hundred pounds. On top of the helmets were plumes showing the colors of the knight.

As Judith and Gavin walked toward the tourney grounds, Judith was bewildered by all the noise and smells surrounding them. It was new and exciting to her, but Gavin had his own contradictory thoughts. The night had been a revelation. Never had he come near enjoying a woman as much as he had Judith. Too often his couplings had been hurried or secret meetings with Alice. Gavin did not love the woman who was his wife—in fact, he found talking to her infuriating—but never had he known such uninhibited passion.

Judith saw Raine coming toward them. He was dressed in full armor for the joust. The steel was etched with tiny gold fleurs-de-lis. He carried his helmet under his arm, and he walked as if he were used to the enormous weight of the armor. And he was.

Judith did not realize she dropped her hand from Gavin's arm when she recognized her brother-in-law. Raine came toward her quickly, a dimpled smile on his face, a smile that had turned many feminine knees to water.

"Hello, my little sister," he grinned down at her. "This morning I thought I had dreamed such beauty, but I see you are more than I remembered."

She was delighted. "And you make the day brighter. Will you enter the events?" She nodded toward the sand-covered field.

"Both Miles and I will take part in the joust."

Neither of them seemed to be aware of Gavin as he scowled at them.

"And these ribbons I see the men wearing," Judith said. "What do they mean?"

"A lady may choose a knight of her favor and give him a token."

"Then I may give you a ribbon?" She smiled at him.

Raine was immediately on one knee before her, the hinges of the armor creaking, steel against steel clanging. "I would be honored."

Judith lifted the transparent veil that covered her hair and took one of the gold ribbons from a braid. It was obvious that her maids had known about the giving of favors to a knight.

Raine smiled at her as he put his hand on his hip and she tied the ribbon around his upper arm. Before she finished, Miles walked to the other side of her and knelt also. "You would not favor one brother over the other, would you?"

Today, when she looked at Miles, she understood what other women had understood about him since he had his first beard. Yesterday she had been a virgin and had not known the meaning of his intense gaze. She blushed prettily and bent her head to slip another ribbon around her other brother's arm.

Raine saw the blush and began to laugh. "Don't start on her, Miles," he laughed, for Miles's women were a common joke about the Montgomery castle. Stephen, the second brother, once complained that Miles had impregnated half the serf girls by the time he was seventeen, the other half by eighteen. "Don't you see Gavin glaring at us?"

"I see both of you making fools of yourselves," Gavin said with a snarl. "There are other women here. Go find one of them to parade yourselves before like braying jackasses."

Judith had barely finished tying the knot of the ribbon on Miles before Gavin's fingers bit into her arm and he forced her away. "You're hurting me!" she said, trying to pry his fingers loose but making no progress.

"I will more than hurt you if you flaunt yourself before other men again."

"Flaunt!" she jerked her arm but only succeeded in tightening Gavin's grip. All around her were knights kneeling to ladies, receiving ribbons, belts, sleeves of gowns, even jewels, and yet he accused her of flaunting herself. "A dishonest person always believes dishonesty of others. Maybe you seek to accuse me of your own faults."

He stopped and stared at her, his eyes dark. "I accuse you only of what I know to be true. You're hot for a man, and I will not have you playing the whore for my brothers. Now sit here and cause no more strife among us." He turned on his heel and stalked away, leaving Judith alone in the stands garlanded with the Montgomery crest.

For a moment, Judith's senses did not function; she could neither see nor hear. What Gavin said was unjust and she could have dismissed it as such, except that he'd thrown in her face what they did in private—that she could not forgive. Had she done wrong in responding to his touch? If so, how did one stop? She could barely remember the events of the night. It was all one delicious red-velvet blur to her. His hands on her body had sent waves of delight through her; after that, she recalled little. Yet he threw it at her as if she were unclean. She blinked back tears of frustration. She was right to hate him.

She mounted the steps to enter the Montgomery seats. Her husband had left her alone to meet his relatives. Judith held her head high and refused to let anyone see that tears were beginning to well.

"Lady Judith."

A soft voice finally penetrated her senses, and she turned to see an older woman dressed in the somber habit of a nun.

"I would like to introduce myself. I met you yesterday, but I am not sure you will remember. I am Gavin's sister, Mary." Mary was staring at her brother's back. It was not like Gavin to walk away and leave a woman unattended. All four of her brothers—Gavin, Stephen, Raine and Miles—were extremely courteous. Yet Gavin had not smiled once at his bride, and although he did not participate in the games, he went to the tents. Mary could not understand him at all.

Gavin walked through the crowds to the tents at the end of the lists. Many people slapped him on the back and gave him knowing winks. The closer he got to the tents, the louder came the familiar clang of iron and steel. He hoped that the sanity of mock war would calm him.

He held his shoulders back, kept his eyes straight ahead. No one would have guessed the blind rage that filled him. She was a bitch! A conniving, masterful bitch! All he could think was that he wanted to beat her and make love to her at the same time. He had stood there and watched as she smiled so sweetly at his brothers; yet when she looked at him, it was as if he were something detestable.

And all he could think of was the way she'd been with him during the night. She had kissed him greedily, held him to her hungrily, but only after he had forced her to come to him. He'd raped her once, used the pain of her hair twisted around his arm to command her to him the second time. Even the third time, he had had to act against her initial protest. Yet she laughed and gave his brothers gold ribbons—gold like her eyes. If she gave such passion to him whom she freely admitted she hated, what would she be like with a man she liked? He had watched her with Raine and Miles, imagined them touching her, kissing her. Suddenly it was all Gavin could do to keep from knocking her to the ground. He wanted to hurt her, and he had. At least there was some satisfaction in that, except that he got no pleasure from it. In truth, the expression on her face only made him more furious. The damn woman had no right to look at him so coldly.

Angrily, he threw back the flap of Miles's tent. Since Miles was on the field, it should have been empty, but it wasn't. Alice stood there, her eyes sedately lowered, her little mouth submissive. She was a welcome relief to Gavin, who'd had too much in the last day of a woman who snarled at him then drove him insane with her body. Alice was what a woman should be—calm, a subordinate to a man. Without thought, he grabbed her, kissing her violently. He enjoyed it when she melted in his arms. She offered no resistance, and he was glad of that.

Alice had never seen Gavin in such a mood, and she silently thanked whoever was responsible. Yet, for all her desire, she was no fool. A tournament was too public, especially when so many of Gavin's relatives camped nearby. "Gavin," she whispered against his lips, "this is neither the place nor the time."

He pulled away from her immediately, feeling that at that moment he could not stand another reluctant female. "Go then!" he stormed as he left the tent.

Alice looked after him, a frown creasing her smooth brow. Obviously, the pleasure of bedding his new wife had not turned him from herself, as she feared it might. But still he was not the Gavin she knew.

Walter Demari could not take his eyes off Judith. She sat quietly in the Montgomery pavilion, listening attentively to her new relatives as they welcomed her to the family. Every minute since he'd first seen her, when she left the castle to ride to the church, he had watched her. He'd seen Judith slip away to the walled garden behind the tower, seen the look on her face when she returned. He felt as if he knew her, and more than that . . . he loved her. He loved the way she walked, with her head up, her chin firm, as if she were ready to face the world no matter what lay ahead. He loved her eyes, her little nose.

He'd spent the night alone, thinking of her, imagining her as his.

Now, after a sleepless night, he began to wonder why she was not his. His family was as rich as that of the Montgomeries and more. He'd been a frequent visitor to the Revedoune manor, a friend to Judith's brothers.

Robert Revedoune had just purchased a lapful of fried wafers from one of the vendors and was holding a mug of verjuice.

Walter did not hesitate or take time to explain what had become a burning issue to him. "Why didn't you offer the girl to me?" he demanded, towering over the seated man.

Robert looked up in surprise. "What ails you, boy? You should be on the field with the other men."

Walter sat down and ran his hand through his hair. He was not an unattractive man, but neither was he handsome. He had eyes of a nondescript blue and a too-prominent nose. His lips were thin, shapeless, and could easily be cruel. His sandy hair was carefully curled into a tight little roll about his neck. "The girl, your daughter," he repeated. "Why didn't you offer her to me? I spent enough time with your sons. I'm not rich, but my estates rival those of Gavin Montgomery."

Robert shrugged, eating a wafer, the jelly oozing out between the crisp layers, and drinking deeply of the sour verjuice. "There are other rich women for you," he observed noncommittally.

"But not like her!" Walter responded vehemently.

Robert looked at him in surprise.

"Can't you see she is beautiful?" Walter asked.

Robert looked across the pavilions that separated

him from his daughter. "Yes, I see she is beautiful," he said with disgust. "But what is beauty? It fades in no time. Her mother once looked like that, and you see her now."

Walter did not have to look back at the nervous, emaciated woman who sat on the edge of her seat, ready to spring should her husband decide to cuff her. He ignored Robert's remark. "Why did you keep her hidden? What need was there to keep her from the world?"

"It was her mother's idea." Robert smiled slightly. "She paid for the keeping of the girl, and it made no difference to me. Why do you ask me these things now? Can't you see the joust is about to begin?"

Walter grabbed Robert by the arm. He knew the man well, knew him for the cowardice of his actions. "Because I want her. Never have I seen a woman more desirable. She should have been mine! My lands ajoin yours. I am a fit match for her, yet you did not even show her to me."

Robert pulled his arm away from the young man. "You! A fit match?" he sneered. "Look at the Montgomeries that surround the girl. There is Thomas, nearly sixty years old. He has six sons, all living, and all producing more sons. Next to him sits Ralph, his cousin, with five sons. Then Hugh with—"

"What has this to do with your daughter?" Walter interrupted angrily.

"Sons!" Robert bellowed in the man's ear. "The Montgomeries produce more sons that any other family in England. And what sons! Look at the family the girl married into. The youngest, Miles, won his spurs on the field of battle before he was eighteen, and already he has fathered three sons of the serf girls. Raine spent three years touring the country from one tournament to the next. He was undefeated and won a fortune of his own. Stephen serves now in Scotland with the king, and already he leads armies though he is only twenty-five. And last comes the eldest. At sixteen he was left alone with estates to run, brothers to care for. He had no guardian to help him learn the work of a man. What other sixteen-year-olds could do as he did? Most of them whine when they are not given their way."

He looked back at Walter. "And now you ask why I give Judith to such a man? If I cannot produce sons that are strong enough to live, perhaps I can get grandsons from her."

Walter was furious. He'd lost Judith merely because the old man dreamed of grandsons. "I could give her sons!" Walter said through clenched teeth.

"You!" Robert began to laugh. "How many sisters do you have? Five? Six? I lose count of them. And what have you done? Your father runs your estates. You do little, except hunt and tickle the serf girls. Now leave me and don't cry to me again. If I have a mare I want bred, I give her to the best stallion. It will be left at that." He turned back to look at the joust, dismissing Walter from his mind.

But Demari was not a man to be dismissed so easily. Everything Robert said was true. Walter had done little of merit in his short life, but that was only because he had not been forced to as the Montgomery men had been. Walter had no doubt that had he been forced, by the early death of his father, into a position of responsibility, he would have done as well or better than any other man.

He left the stands a changed man. A seed had been planted in his mind and that seed began to grow. He watched the games begin, the gold Montgomery leopard everywhere, and as he saw it glitter in the sun, he began to think of it as an enemy. He wanted to prove to Robert and to the Montgomeries, but mostly to himself, that he was everything they were. The longer he stared at the green and gold pennants, the more he was sure he hated the Montgomeries. What had they done to deserve the rich Revedoune lands? Why should they have what should have been his? For years he'd suffered the company of Judith's brothers, yet had never taken anything in return. Now, when there was something he wanted and should have had, he was denied it because of the Montgomeries.

Walter left the fence and started walking toward the Montgomery pavilion. The growing anger at the injustice he felt gave him courage. He would talk to this Judith, spend time with her. After all, by rights, she was his, wasn't she?

Chapter Eight

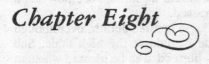

JUDITH SLAMMED SHUT HER CHAMBER DOOR SO HARD THAT even the stone walls seemed to shake. It was the end of the first day of her marriage, and it could easily qualify as the most horrible day of her life. It should have been happy, a day full of love and laughter—but not with the husband she had! There had not been an opportunity missed by Gavin to humiliate her.

In the morning he accused her of being a whore for his brothers. When he stalked away and left her to herself, she talked to other people. One man, Walter Demari, was kind enough to sit by her and explain the workings of the tourney. For the first time that day, she began to enjoy herself. Walter had a knack for seeking the ridiculous, and she greatly enjoyed his humor.

Gavin suddenly reappeared and commanded her to follow him. Judith didn't want to cause a scene in public, but in the privacy of Raine's tent, she told Gavin what she thought of his behavior. He left her alone to take care of herself, but when she showed any enjoyment, he took it away from her. He was like a small boy with a toy he didn't want but made sure no one else could have it. He'd sneered at Judith then, but she saw with satisfaction that he had no answer for her.

When Raine and Miles came in she and Gavin stopped their quarrel. Later, she walked with Miles back to the tourney. It was then that Gavin truly demeaned her. As soon as Alice Valence appeared, he practically ran forward. Gavin looked as if he could eat her, devour her, yet at the same time he looked at her with reverence, as if she were saintly. Judith had not missed the sidelong look of triumph Alice gave her. Judith pulled her eyes away, straightened her back and took Miles' arm. She would let no one see how she'd been publicly embarrassed.

Later, at dinner, Gavin ignored Judith, even though they were seated side by side at the high table. She laughed at the jester, pretended to be pleased when an extremely handsome jongleur composed and sang a song to her beauty. Truthfully, she hardly heard him. Gavin's nearness had an unsettling effect on her, and she could enjoy nothing.

After the meal, the trestle tables were dismantled and pushed against the wall to make room for dancing. After one dance together, for the sake of propriety, Gavin had proceeded to whirl one woman after another in his arms. Judith had more invitations to dance than she could accept, but soon she pleaded fatigue and ran up the stairs to the privacy of her room.

"A bath," she demanded of Joan, whom she'd dragged from a corner of the stairwell where she was intertwined with a young man. "Bring a tub and hot water. Maybe I can wash away some of today's stench."

Contrary to what Judith believed, Gavin had been very aware of his wife's presence. There had not been a moment when he had not known where she was or whom she was with. It seemed she had talked for hours to some man at the tourney. She laughed at his every word, smiling up at him until the man was obviously besotted.

Gavin had pulled her away for her own good. He knew Judith had no idea how she affected a man. She was like a child. Everything was new to her. She looked up at the man with nothing hidden, nothing held in reserve. She laughed openly at what he said, and Gavin could see the man took her friendliness for more than she meant it to be.

Gavin meant to explain this to her, but when she attacked him, accusing him of all manner of insulting things, he would have died rather than explain his actions. He'd feared that he might wrap his hands about her lovely throat. At least Alice's brief appearance had calmed him. Alice was like a cool drink for a man just stepped from the rages of hell.

Now as he held his hands on the fat hips of an unattractive young woman, he watched Judith mount the steps. He did not dance with her, afraid he might apologize. For what? he wondered. He'd been kind to Judith until that time in the garden when she'd started acting insane, making vows she had no right to make. He was right in taking her away from the man who obviously thought her smiles meant more than they did, but she made Gavin feel as if he were wrong.

He waited a while, danced with two more women, but Judith did not return to the great hall. Impatiently, he climbed the stairs. In those brief seconds, he imagined all sorts of things she could be doing.

When he opened the door to the chamber Judith lay up to her neck in a tub of steamy water. Her auburn hair was piled atop her head in a soft mass of curls. Her eyes were closed, her head resting on the rim of the tub. The water must have been very hot because her face was lightly dampened with sweat. All his muscles froze at the sight of her. She had frowned at him, raged at him and even then she was magnificent, but now she was innocence personified. Suddenly he knew that this was what he wanted from her, this was all he needed. What did it matter that she despised him? She was his and his alone. His heart was pounding as he closed the door behind him.

"Joan?" Judith said languidly. Receiving no answer, her eyes flew open. She saw the look on Gavin's face and knew his thoughts. In spite of herself, her heart began beating quickly. "Leave me to my privacy," she managed to whisper.

He ignored her as he advanced, his dark eyes grown darker. He bent over her, took her chin in his hand. She tried to pull away but he held her fast. He kissed her, roughly at first but then his grip and kiss became gentle, deep.

Judith felt herself drifting. The pleasure of the hot water, his hand on her cheek, his kiss, weakened her. He pulled away from her and looked into her eyes, the gold warm and glowing. All thoughts of hatred were gone from them. There was only the nearness of their bodies. Their hunger for each other overcame any hostility or even thoughts of who loved whom.

Gavin knelt by the tub, his hand moving to the back of Judith's neck. He kissed her again, ran his mouth along the curve of her neck. She was moist and warm and the rising steam was like his growing passion. He was ready, but he wanted to prolong his pleasure, drag it out to the height of near-pain. Her ears were sweet and smelled of the rose-scented soap she used.

Suddenly he wanted to see her—all of her. Gavin put his hands under Judith's arms and lifted her. She gasped at the unexpected movement, at the coolness of the air after the heat of the water. A soft, warm towel hung within arm's reach, which Gavin wrapped her in. Judith did not speak. Somewhere, buried in her mind, was the knowledge that words would break the spell. He touched her tenderly—no harsh demands, no bruising. He sat on a bench before the fire and stood her between his legs as if she were a child.

Had someone spoken of such a scene, Judith would have denied that it could happen, that Gavin was an insensitive brute. She felt no embarrassment by her nudity while he remained fully clothed, only wonder at the magic of the moment. Gavid dried her carefully. He was a bit clumsy, too rough at times, too gentle at others.

"Turn," he commanded and she obeyed as he dried her back. He tossed the towel to the floor and Judith held her breath. But he did not speak. Then he ran his fingers down the deep indentation of her spine. She could feel the chills his touch brought. His one finger said more than a hundred caresses.

"You are beautiful," he whispered throatily as he placed his palms on the curve of her hips. "So very beautiful."

She did not breathe, even when she felt his lips on the side of her neck. His hands moved so torturously slow to her stomach, across her ribs and up to her breasts, which waited for him, begged for him. She released her pent-up breath and leaned back against him, her head resting against his shoulder, his mouth still on her neck. He ran his hands over her, touching her skin, exploring her body.

When Judith was nearly insane with desire, he carried her to the bed. In seconds, his clothes were on the floor and he was beside her. She pulled him to her, sought his mouth. He laughed at her grasping hands, teasing her, but there was no ridicule in his gray eyes. There was only the wish for prolonging their pleasure. A sparkle came to her eyes, and she knew she would have the last laugh. Her hands moved downward. When she found what she sought, there was no more laughter in his eyes. They were black with passion as he pushed her down beside him.

It was only moments before they cried out together, both released from their sweet torment. Judith felt drained, her bones weak as Gavin moved partially away, though his leg was still across hers, his arm across her breasts. She sighed deeply just before falling asleep.

Judith woke the next morning, stretching like a cat after a nap. Her arm slid across the sheet only to meet emptiness. Her eyes flew open. Gavin was gone and by the sun streaming through the window, it was late morning. Her first thought was to hurry outside, but the warm bed and the memory of last night kept her where she was. Judith turned to her side, ran her hand over the indented place beside her, buried her face in his pillow. It still smelled of Gavin. How quickly she'd come to know his scent.

She smiled dreamily. Last night had been heaven. She remembered Gavin's eyes, his mouth—he filled her every vision.

A soft knock on the door sent her heart beating, then calmed abruptly when Joan opened it.

"You were awake?" Joan asked, a knowing smile on her face.

Judith felt too good to take offense.

"Lord Gavin rose early. He arms himself."

"Arms himself!" Judith sat bolt upright in the bed.

"He only wishes to join the games. I don't understand why; as the bridegroom, he doesn't have to."

Judith lay back against the pillow. She understood. This morning she could have soared from the top of the keep and come only lightly to earth. She knew Gavin must feel the same. The joust was a way to expend his energy.

She threw back the covers and jumped from the bed. "I must dress. It is late. You don't think we could have missed him?"

"No," Joan laughed. "We won't miss him."

Judith dressed quickly in a gown of indigo blue velvet with an underskirt of light blue silk. About her waist was a thin belt of soft blue leather studded with pearls.

Joan merely combed her mistress's hair and put a

transparent blue gauze veil edged in seed pearls on it. It was held in place by a braided circlet of pearls.

"I'm ready," Judith said impatiently.

Judith walked rapidly to the tourney grounds and took her place in the Montgomery pavilion. Judith's thoughts were at war with each other. Had she imagined last night? Had it been a dream? Gavin had made love to her. There was no other word for it. Of course she was very inexperienced, but could a man touch a woman as he touched her and not feel something for her? The day seemed brighter suddenly. Maybe she was a fool, but she was willing to try to make something of this marriage.

Judith craned her neck to see the end of the tourney field, to catch a glimpse of her husband, but there were too many people and horses in the way.

Quietly, Judith left the stands and walked toward the tents. She stopped along the outer fence, oblivious to the serfs and merchants who crowded about her. It was some minutes before she saw him. Gavin in normal attire was a powerful man, but Gavin in full armor was formidable. He mounted an enormous war-horse of dark gray, its trappings of green serge, green leather stamped and painted with golden leopards. He swung easily into the saddle, as if the hundred pounds of armor weighed nothing. She watched as his squire handed him his helmet, his shield, and finally his lance.

Judith's heart leaped to her throat and nearly choked her. There was danger in this game. She watched breathlessly as Gavin charged forward on his great horse, his head lowered, his arm braced against the lance. His lance struck the opponent's shield squarely just as his own shield was hit. The lances broke and the men rode to opposite ends of the field to obtain new ones. Fortunately, the lances used in battle were stronger than the wooden ones used in games. The object was to break three lances without losing the stirrups. If a man was unseated before three runs were made, he had to pay the worth of his horse and armor to his adversary—no trifling sum. Thus had Raine made a fortune on the tournament circuit.

But men did get hurt. Accidents happened constantly. Judith knew this and she watched fearfully as Gavin rode again, and again neither man lost his stirrups.

A woman near Judith giggled, but she paid no attention until words reached her. "Her husband is the only man who carries no favor—yet she gives gold ribbons to his brothers. What do think of such a hoyden?"

The words were malicious and meant for Judith's ears; yet, when she turned, no one showed any interest in her. She looked back at the knights who walked among the horses or stood at the end of the field near her. What the woman said was true. All the knights had ribbons or sleeves waving from their lances or helmets. Raine and Miles had several, and on one arm they each wore a frayed gold ribbon.

Judith only meant to run across the edge of the field and catch Gavin before he charged his opponent for the third time. She was new to the joust and had no idea that what she did was dangerous. The war-horses, bred for strength, size and endurance, were trained to help a man in times of war. They could use their great hooves to kill as easily as a man used a sword.

She did not hear the gasps as man after man pulled his horse back from her racing figure. Neither was she aware that several of the people in the stands had seen her and now stood, their breaths held.

Gavin looked up from his squire as he was handed a new lance. He could feel the gradual hush come over the crowd. He saw Judith immediately and realized there was nothing he could do. By the time he dismounted, she would have reached him. He stared, every muscle rigid.

Judith had no ribbon to give him but she knew he must have a favor from her. He was *hers!* She pulled off her gossamer veil as she ran across the sand, slipping the braid of pearls back over her hair.

When she reached Gavin she held up the veil for him. "A favor," she smiled tentatively.

He did not move for a moment then lifted his lance and held it down beside her. Quickly, Judith knotted a corner of the veil securely above the shaft. When she looked up at him and smiled, he leaned forward, put his hand behind her head and nearly lifted her from the ground as he kissed her. The nosepiece of the helmet was cold against her cheek and his kiss was hard. When he released her to sink back on her heels in the sand, she was dazed.

Judith was unaware of the suddenly quiet crowd, but not so Gavin. His bride had risked her life to give him a favor, and now he held his lance high—in triumph. His grin seemed to reach from one side of the helmet to the other.

The crowd's roar of approval was deafening.

Judith whirled, saw that every eye was upon her. Her cheeks flamed and her hands covered her face. Miles and Raine ran from the sidelines, threw their arms protectively around her and half-carried her to safety.

"If you hadn't pleased Gavin so much, I would turn you over my knee for that," Raine said.

Another cheer went up as Gavin unhorsed his opponent. Judith did not enjoy being the center of so much laughing. She picked up her skirts and made her way as quickly as possible back to the castle. Perhaps a few minutes alone in the garden would help her cheeks return to their normal color.

Alice slammed into the tent of the Earl of Bayham, a rich place of silk walls and Byzantine carpets erected for the comfort of Edmund Chatworth.

"Something is wrong?" a deep voice behind her asked.

Alice whirled to glare at Roger, Edmund's younger brother. He sat on a low bench, his shirt removed as he carefully ran the edge of his sword along a whetstone he turned with his foot. He was a handsome man, blond hair streaked by the sun, a straight aquiline nose, a firm mouth. There was a curved scar by his left eye that in no way detracted from his good looks.

Many times Alice wished Roger were the earl instead of Edmund. She started to answer his question, then stopped. She could not tell him of her anger as she saw Gavin's wife making a spectacle of herself in front of several hundred people. Alice had offered him a favor, but he would not take it. Gavin said there was too much talk of them already, and he would not cause more.

"You play with fire, you know," Roger said as he ran his thumb along the edge of the sword. When Alice made no comment, he continued. "The Montgomery men do not see things as we do. To them right is right and wrong is wrong. There is nothing in between."

"I have no idea what you mean," Alice responded haughtily.

"Gavin will not be pleased when he finds you have lied to him."

"I have not lied!"

Roger raised one eyebrow. "And what reason did you give him for marrying my brother the earl?"

Alice sat down heavily on a bench opposite Roger.

"You didn't think the heiress would be so beautiful, did you?"

Alice's eyes blazed as she looked up at him. "She is not beautiful! Her hair is red and she is sure to be covered with freckles." She smiled snidely. "I must ask what cream she uses to cover them on her face. Gavin will not think her so desirable when he sees—"

Roger cut her off. "I was at the bedding ceremony and saw a great deal of her body. There were no freckles. Don't delude yourself. Do you think you can hold him when he is alone with her?"

Alice stood and walked to the tent flap. She would not let Roger see how the words upset her. She *must* keep Gavin. At all costs, she must keep him. He loved her, deeply and sincerely, as no one had ever loved her.

She needed that as much as she needed Edmund's wealth. She did not let people see inside her; she hid her hurt well. As a child she'd been a beautiful daughter born among a gaggle of ugly, sickly sisters. Her mother gave all her love to the others, feeling Alice had enough attention from her nurses and the castle visitors. Scorned by her mother, Alice turned to her father for love. But the only thing Nicolas Valence cared for came from a bottle. So Alice learned to take what was not given to her. She manipulated her father into buying rich clothes for her, and her enhanced beauty made her sisters' hate for her stronger. Besides her elderly maid, Ela, no one loved her, until Gavin. Yet all the years of struggling, trying to obtain even a few pennies, made her desire financial security as much as love. Gavin was not wealthy enough to give her that security, but Edmund was.

Now, one-half of what she needed was being taken from her by a red-haired witch. Alice was not one to sit back and let the future take care of itself. She would fight for what she wanted . . .

"Where is Edmund?" she asked Roger.

He nodded his head to the linen partition across the back of the tent. "Asleep. Too much wine and too much food," he said in disgust. "Go to him. He will need someone to hold his sick head."

"Easy, brother!" Raine commanded Miles. "His head is sore enough without banging it against a tent pole."

They carried Gavin on his shield, his legs hanging off the edge, his feet dragging in the dirt. He had just finished unhorsing his second opponent when the man's lance slipped upward, just before he fell. The blow caught Gavin just above his ear. It was a hard blow which dented his helmet. Gavin saw only blackness and heard a ringing in his head that drowned all other noise. He managed to stay in his saddle, more from training than strength, as his horse turned and went back to the end of the field. Gavin looked down at his brothers and his squire, gave a sickly smile, then slowly fell into their uplifted arms.

Now Raine and Miles transferred their brother to a cot inside their tent. They removed the damaged helmet and put a pillow beneath his head.

"I will fetch a leech," Raine said to his brother. "And you find his wife. There is nothing a woman likes more than a helpless man."

Several minutes later, Gavin began to regain consciousness. Cool water was being pressed on his hot face. Cool hands touched his cheek. He was dazed when he opened his eyes. His head roared. At first he couldn't remember whom he saw.

"It is I, Alice," she whispered. He was glad there were no loud noises. "I have come to care for you."

He smiled a bit and closed his eyes again. There was something he should remember, but couldn't.

Alice saw that in his right hand he still clutched the veil Judith had given him. Even as he fell from his horse, he'd managed to loosen it from his lance. She didn't like what that seemed to signify.

"Is he badly hurt?" a woman asked anxiously outside the tent.

Alice leaned forward and pressed her lips to Gavin's unresponsive ones, guiding his arm till it went about her waist.

The light from the opened tent on his face and the pressure on his lips made Gavin open his eyes. His senses came back to him then. He saw his wife, flanked by the scowling figures of his brothers, staring at him as he embraced Alice. He pushed her away and tried to sit up. "Judith," he whispered.

All the color drained from her face. Her eyes were dark and enormous. And the look she gave him was again of hatred. Then, suddenly, it changed to one of coldness.

The quick change of pressure in his injured skull as he tried to sit up was too much for Gavin. The pain was unbearable. Gratefully, everything went black. He fell heavily back onto the pillow.

Judith turned quickly on her heel and left the tent, Miles close beside her, as if she needed protection from some evilness.

Raine's face was dark when he looked back at his brother. "You bastard—" he began, then stopped when he saw Gavin was again unconscious. Raine turned to Alice, who looked up at him triumphantly. He grabbed her upper arm and pulled her to her feet. "You planned this!" he sneered. "God! How can I have such a fool for a brother? You're not worth one of Judith's tears, yet I think you have already caused her many."

Raine was further enraged when he saw a slight smile at the corner of her mouth. Without thought, he drew back his arm and slapped Alice with the back of his hand. He did not release her arm. When she looked back at him, Raine drew his breath in sharply at what he saw. Alice was not angry. Instead, she stared at his mouth. There was the unmistakable fire of passion in her eyes.

He was shocked and disgusted as he'd never been in his life. He threw her against a tent pole so hard she could scarcely draw her breath. "Get away from me!" he said quietly. "And fear for your life if our paths ever cross again."

When she was gone, Raine turned back to his brother, who was beginning to move again. A leech who came to attend to Gavin's sore head, stood shaking in the corner of the tent. The anger of one of the Montgomeries was no pretty sight.

Raine spoke to the man over his shoulder. "See to him—and if you have any treatment that will cause him more pain, use it." He turned and left the tent.

It was night when Gavin woke from a deep, drugged sleep, induced by something the leech made him drink.

The tent was dark and he was alone. Gingerly, he swung his legs over the edge of the cot and sat up. His head felt as if someone had made a deep cut from one corner of his eye, across the back of his head to the other eye, and now the two halves were being pulled apart. He propped his head in his hands, closing his eyes against the awful ache.

Gradually, Gavin was able to open them. His first thought was that it was odd that he was alone. He would have thought either his squire or his brothers would be with him. He straightened his back and was aware of a new pain. He had slept several hours in his armor, and every hinge, every ridge had imprinted itself, through leather and felt, into his skin. Why had his squire not undressed him? Usually the boy was very conscientious.

Something on the floor caught his eye and he bent and lifted Judith's blue veil. He smiled as he touched it, remembering clearly how she'd run toward him, smiling, her hair flowing behind her. He'd never been so proud in his life as when she handed him the favor, although he'd held his breath when she came so near the war-horses. He ran his fingers across the border of seed pearls, held the gauze against his cheek. He could almost smell the scent of her hair, but of course that was impossible after the veil had been next to his sweaty horse. He thought of her face when he looked down at her. Now, that was a face worth fighting for!

Then Gavin seemed to remember it changing. He dropped his head back in his hands. There were pieces of the puzzle missing. His head hurt so much that it was difficult to remember. He could see a different Judith— not smiling, not snarling as she had the first night of their marriage, but a Judith who looked at him as if he no longer existed. It was a struggle to fit all the pieces together. Gradually, he remembered the lance hitting his head, then someone speaking to him.

Suddenly it was all clear. Judith had seen him holding

Alice. It was strange that he could not remember wanting Alice's comforting.

It took all Gavin's effort to stand. He had to remove his armor. He was too tired and weak to walk while weighed down so heavily. No matter how much his head hurt, he had to find Judith and talk to her.

Two hours later, Gavin stood inside the great hall. He'd looked everywhere for his wife but could not find her. Every step caused him more pain until now he was nearly blind with the constant ache and the weariness of fighting it.

Through a haze, he saw Helen as she carried a tray of drinks to some guests. When she returned, he pulled her to a darkened corner of the hall. "Where is she?" he asked in a hoarse whisper.

Helen's eyes blazed at him. "You ask me now where she is?" she sneered at him. "You have hurt her, as all men hurt women. I tried to save her from this. I told her all men were vile, evil creatures not to be trusted—but she wouldn't listen. No, she defended you and what did it earn her? I saw her lip on her wedding night. You beat her before you even bedded her. And this morning many people saw your brother throw that Valence whore—your whore—from your tent. I would die before I told you! Better I had killed us both before I gave Judith to such as you."

If his mother-in-law said any more, Gavin did not hear her. He was already walking away.

He found Judith, minutes later, sitting beside Miles on a bench in the garden. Gavin ignored his younger brother's malevolent scowl. He didn't want to argue. All he wanted was to be alone with Judith, to hold her as he had last night. Perhaps then his head would stop throbbing.

"Come inside," he said quietly, each word difficult.

She rose immediately. "Yes, my lord."

He frowned slightly and held his arm out for her but she did not seem to see it. He slowed for her to walk beside him but she still walked a bit behind him and to one side. He led them into the manor and up to their room.

After the noise of the great hall, the chamber was a haven, and he sank onto a cushioned bench to take off his boots. He looked up to see Judith standing at the foot of the bed, unmoving. "Why do you stare at me so?"

"I am waiting for your command, my lord."

"My command?" he frowned, for all the movement hurt his pounding head. "Then undress yourself for bed." He was puzzled by her. Why didn't she rage at him? He could have handled her anger.

"Yes, my lord," Judith answered. Her voice was a monotone.

When he was undressed, Gavin went slowly to the bed. Judith was already there, the covers to her neck, her eyes staring up at the canopy. He climbed under the covers and moved close to her. Her skin against his was soothing. He ran his hand down her arm but Judith did not react. He leaned over, began to kiss her but her eyes did not close and her lips were unresponsive.

"What ails you?" Gavin demanded.

"Ails me, my lord?" she said evenly, looking steadily into his eyes. "I don't know what you mean. I am yours to command, as you have told me often enough. Tell me your wish and I will obey. Do you wish to mate with me? Then I will obey." She moved her thigh against his and it took Gavin a few minutes to realize that she had spread her legs for him.

He stared at her, aghast. He knew crudity was not natural to her. "Judith," he began, "I wanted to explain about this morning. I—"

"Explain, my lord? What must you explain to me? Do you explain your actions to the serfs? I am yours no less than they are. Just tell me how I may obey you and I will."

Gavin began to move away from her. He did not like the way Judith looked at him. At least, when she hated

him, there had been life in her eyes. Now there was
none. He left the bed. Before he knew what he did, he
pulled on doublet and boots, his other clothes thrown
over his arm, and left the cold chamber.

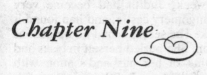

Chapter Nine

THE MONTGOMERY CASTLE WAS SILENT AS JUDITH LEFT
the big, empty bed and slipped her arms into a
mink-lined, emerald-green velvet bedrobe. It was very
early morning, and the castlefolk were not awake yet.
Since Gavin had dumped her on the doorstep of his
family estate, Judith had hardly been able to sleep. The
bed seemed too large and too empty to give her much
peace.

The morning after Judith refused to respond to his
lovemaking, Gavin had demanded they depart for his
home. Judith had obeyed, speaking to him only when
necessary. They traveled for two days before reaching
the Montgomery gates.

Upon entering the castle, she had been impressed.
The guards on top of the two massive towers that
flanked the gate had challenged them even though they
could see the Montgomery leopards flying. The drawbridge was lowered over the wide, deep moat and the
heavy spiked portcullis was raised. The outer bailey
was lined with modest, neat houses, stables, the
armorer, the mews, and storage sheds. Another gate
had to be unlocked before they entered the inner bailey
where Gavin and his brothers lived. The house was four

stories with mullioned glass windows in the top floor. A bricked courtyard was in the center, and Judith could see a garden with fruit trees just blooming behind a low wall.

She wanted to tell Gavin what she thought of his stewardship, but he had not given her a chance. He had done little more than give a few orders then abandoned her amid the baggage. It was up to Judith to introduce herself to the retainers.

During the past week, Judith had become very familiar with the Montgomery castle, and had found it a joyful place to work. The servants had no objections to a woman's direction. She buried herself in tasks and tried hard not to think of her husband's affair with Alice Valence. Most of the time Judith was successful. Only at night did her loneliness haunt her.

A noise in the courtyard made her run to the window. It was too early for the servants to be about, and only a Montgomery would be allowed through the smaller back gate. The light was too dim to tell who was dismounting the horses below.

She flew down the stairs to the great hall.

"Be careful, man," Raine bellowed. "Do you think I am made of iron that I can stand so much banging about?"

Judith stopped at the foot of the stairs. Her brother-in-law was being carried into the room, feet first, one leg heavily bandaged. "Raine, whatever has happened to you?"

"Cursed horse!" he said through clenched teeth. "It can't see where it is going even on the brightest of days."

She went to him as his men set him down in a chair by the empty fireplace. "Am I to understand that your horse caused this?" she smiled.

Raine stopped frowning, his cheeks beginning to dimple. "Well, maybe it was partly my own fault. He stepped into a hole and threw me. I came down on my leg and it snapped under me."

Judith immediately knelt and began to unwrap his foot which was propped on a stool.

"What are you doing?" he asked sharply. "The leech has already set it."

"I don't trust him and will see for myself. If it isn't set straight, it could leave you lame."

Raine stared at the top of her head then called to his man. "Fetch me a glass of wine. I'm sure she won't be satisfied until she causes me more agony. And fetch my brother. Why should he sleep when we are awake?"

"He isn't here," Judith said quietly.

"Who isn't here?"

"Your brother. My husband," Judith said flatly.

"Where did he go? What business called him away?"

"I am afraid I don't know. He set me on the doorstep and left. He didn't speak to me of any matter that needed his attention."

Raine took the cup of wine his vassal held for him and watched his sister-in-law as she probed the bone of his leg. At least the pain kept him from giving full vent to the anger he felt for his brother. He had no doubt that Gavin had left his beautiful bride to go to that whore, Alice. His teeth clamped down on the rim of the cup as Judith touched the break.

"It is only a little out of line," she observed. "You hold his shoulders," she said to one of the men behind Raine, "and I will pull the leg."

The heavy sendal of the tent was coated with water. Fat droplets collected on the ceiling and as the rain outside jarred the tent, the water dripped down.

Gavin swore loudly as more water hit his face. Since he'd left Judith, it had done little but rain. There was nothing that was not wet. And worse than the water was the tempers of his men—blacker even than the sky. They had been roaming the countryside for well over a week, camping in a different place each night. Their food was hastily prepared in between cloudbursts and consequently was usually half raw. When John Bassett,

Gavin's chief vassal, had asked his master the reason for the meandering journey, Gavin had exploded. John's level look of sarcasm made Gavin avoid his men.

He knew his men were miserable; he was himself. But at least he knew the reason for the seemingly pointless trip. Or did he? That night at Judith's father's house, when she'd been so cold to him, he decided to teach her a lesson. She felt secure in a place where she'd spent her life, surrounded by friends and family. But would she dare to act so disagreeably when she was alone in a strange household?

It worked out well when his brothers decided to leave the newly wedded couple alone. In spite of the rain dripping through the sendal of the tent, he began to smile at an imagined scene. He could see her facing some crisis—perhaps something cataclysmic, such as the cook burning a pot of beans. She would be frantic with worry, would send a messenger for him, to beg him to return and save her from disaster. The messenger would not be able to find his master since Gavin was not at any of his estates. More calamities would occur. When Gavin returned, he would find a tearful, repentant Judith who would fall into his arms, grateful to see him again, relieved that he'd come to save her from a fate worse than death.

"Oh yes," he said, smiling. All the rain and discomfort would be worth it. He would talk sternly to her and when she was completely contrite, he would kiss away her tears and carry her to their bed.

"My lord?"

"What is it?" Gavin snapped as the delicious vision was interrupted, just when he was about to imagine what he'd allow Judith to do in the bedroom, in order to obtain his forgiveness.

"We were wondering, sir, when we were to go home and get out of this cursed rain."

Gavin started to growl that it was not the man's business, then closed his mouth. He began to smile.

"We will return tomorrow." Judith had been alone for eight days. That was time enough for her to learn some gratitude . . . and humility.

"Please, Judith," Raine pleaded as he grabbed her forearm. "I have been here two days, yet you have not given me a moment of your time."

"That isn't true," she laughed. "Only last evening I spent an hour with you at the chessboard, and you showed me some chords on the lute."

"I know," he said, still pleading, but dimples appearing on his cheeks, although he didn't smile. "It's just so awful here alone. I can't move for this cursed leg, and there is no one to keep me company."

"No one! There are over three hundred people here. Surely one of them—" She broke off as Raine looked at her with such sad eyes that she laughed. "All right, but only one game. I have work to do."

Raine gave her a dazzling smile as she went to the other side of the chessboard. "You are the best at the game. None of my men can beat me as you did last night. Besides, you need a rest. What do you do all day?"

"Put the castle to rights," Judith responded simply.

"It always seemed to me to be in order," he said as he moved a pawn forward. "The stewards—"

"The stewards!" she said sharply as she maneuvered her bishop to attack. "They don't care as does one who owns an estate. They must be watched, their figures checked, their journals read and—"

"Read? Do you read, Judith?"

She looked up in surprise, her hand on her queen. "But of course. Don't you?"

Raine shrugged. "I never learned. My brothers did, but it didn't interest me. I have never known a woman who could read. My father said women couldn't learn to read."

Judith looked at him in disgust as her queen put his

king in mortal danger. "I think you should learn that a woman can often best a man, even a king. I believe I have won the game." She stood.

Raine stared at the board in wonder. "You can't have won so soon! I didn't even see it. You kept me talking so that I couldn't concentrate." He gave her a look from the corner of his eye. "And my leg pains me so that it's hard for me to think."

Judith looked at him with concern for a moment, then began to laugh. "Raine, you are a liar of the first water. Now I must go."

"No, Judith," he said as he lunged and grabbed her hand and began to kiss it. "Judith, don't leave me," he begged. "In truth, I am so bored I may go mad. Please stay with me. Just one more game."

Judith was laughing very hard at him. She placed her other hand on his hair as he began making outrageous promises of undying love and gratitude if she would only stay with him an hour longer.

And that was how Gavin found them. He had forgotten his wife's beauty by half. She was not dressed in the velvets and sables she had worn at their marriage, but in a simple, clinging gown of soft blue wool. Her hair was pulled back into one long, thick auburn braid. If anything, the plain garment made her even more lovely than before. She was innocence, yet the lush curves of her body showed her to be all woman.

Judith became aware of her husband's presence first. The smile on her face died immediately and her entire body stiffened.

Raine felt the tension in her hand and looked up at her questioningly. He followed the direction of her eyes and saw his scowling brother. There was no doubt as to what Gavin thought of the scene. Judith started to pull her hand away from Raine's grasp, but he held it firmly. He would not give the impression of a guilty man to his angry brother. "I have been trying to persuade Judith to spend the morning with me," Raine said lightly. "I have been confined to this room for two days with nothing to do, but I can't persuade her to give me more of her time."

"And no doubt you have tried every persuasion," Gavin sneered, his look directed at his wife who stared at him coldly.

Judith jerked her hand away from Raine. "I must return to my work," she said stiffly, as she left the room.

Raine attacked first before Gavin had a chance to do so. "Where have you been?" he demanded. "Only three days married, and you drop her on the doorstep like so much baggage."

"She seems to have handled the situation well," Gavin said as he sank heavily into a chair.

"If you hint at something dishonorable—"

"No, I don't," Gavin said honestly. He knew his brothers well, and Raine would not dishonor his sister-in-law. It was just a shock after what he had expected . . . and hoped . . . to find awaiting him. "What happened to your leg?"

Raine was embarrassed to confess falling from his horse, but Gavin didn't laugh as he usually would have. Wearily, Gavin lifted himself from the chair. "I must see to my castle. I have been away a long time and I'm sure it's close to falling down about my ears."

"I wouldn't count on that," Raine said as he studied the chessboard, going over each of Judith's moves in his head. "I've never seen a woman work as Judith does."

"Bah!" Gavin said condescendingly. "How much woman's work can one do in a week? Embroider five ells of cloth?"

Raine looked up at his brother in surprise. "I didn't say she did woman's work, I said I haven't seen a woman work as she does."

Gavin didn't understand, but neither did he press Raine for an explanation. As the lord, Gavin had too much to do. The castle always seemed to flounder mightily after he'd been away for a while.

Raine knew his brother's thoughts and called after him. "I hope you find something that needs doing," he laughed.

Gavin had no idea what his brother was talking about and dismissed the words as he left the manor house. He was still angry that the scene he'd dreamed had been destroyed. But at least, there was hope. Judith would be glad he had returned to solve all the problems that had developed in his absence.

When Gavin rode through the baileys that morning, he had been so anxious to get to his weeping wife that he hadn't noticed any changes. Now he observed subtle alterations. The half-timbered buildings in the outer bailey looked cleaner—almost new, in fact, as if they'd been recently chinked and whitewashed. The gutters that ran along the back of the buildings looked as if they'd been emptied recently.

He stopped in front of the mews. Here the falcons were kept—merlins, peregrines, sparrow hawks, tiercels. His falconer stood in front of the building, a hawk tied by the leg to a post, while the man slowly swung a lure about the bird.

"Is that a new lure, Simon?" Gavin asked.

"Yes, my lord. It's a bit smaller and can be swung faster. The bird is forced to fly faster, and its aim must be truer."

"Good idea," Gavin agreed.

"It's not mine, sir, but the Lady Judith's. She made the suggestion."

Gavin stared. "The Lady Judith told you, a master falconer, of a better lure?"

"Yes, my lord," Simon grinned, revealing two missing teeth. "I'm not so old as I don't know a good idea when I hear one. The lady's as smart as she is lovely. Came down here first morning she was here and watched me for a long time. Then, just sweet as can be,

she made a few suggestions. Come inside, my lord, and
see the new perches I made. Lady Judith said the old
ones was the cause of the birds' sore feet. She said tiny
mites get in them and hurt the birds."

Simon started to lead the way into the building, but
Gavin didn't follow. "Don't you want to see?" Simon
asked sadly.

Gavin hadn't recovered from the fact that his grizzled
falconer had taken advice from a woman. Gavin had
tried to make hundreds of recommendations to Simon,
as his father had, but to their knowledge, Simon had
never done what either man wanted. "No," Gavin said,
"I'll see later what changes my wife has made." He
could not keep the sarcasm from his voice as he turned
on his heel. What right did the woman have to interfere
with his mews? Certainly women liked hawking as well
as men, and certainly Judith would have her own
hawk—but the care of the mews was a man's work.

"My lord!" a serf girl called, then blushed when
Gavin looked at her so fiercely.

She curtsied and held out a mug to him. "I thought
perhaps you'd like some refreshment."

Gavin smiled at the girl. Here at least was a woman
who knew how to act properly. He looked into her eyes
as he sipped; then his attention was drawn to the drink.
It was delicious! "What is this?"

"It's the spring's strawberries and the juice of last
year's apples after they are boiled, then a bit of
cinnamon."

"Cinnamon?"

"Yes, my lord. The Lady Judith brought it with her
from her home."

Gavin abruptly thrust the empty mug back at the girl
and turned away. Now he was truly starting to get
annoyed. Had everyone gone mad? Quickly, he made
his way to the far end of the bailey, to his armorer's. At
least in that hot place of forged iron he would be safe
from a woman's interference.

The sight that greeted him was shocking. His armorer, an enormous man, naked from the waist up, muscles bulging from his arms, sat quietly by a window—sewing. "What is this?" Gavin demanded angrily, suspicious already.

The man smiled and held up two small pieces of leather. It was a design for a new hinge that could be used on a knight's armor. "See, the way this is made, the hinge is much more flexible. Clever, isn't it?"

Gavin clenched his jaw tightly. "And where did you get this new idea?"

"Why, from the Lady Judith," the armorer answered, then shrugged when Gavin stormed from the shed.

How dare she! he thought. Who was she to interfere in what was his, to make change after change without so much as asking his approval? These estates were *his!* If any changes were to be made, they were to be made by him.

He found Judith in the pantry, a vast room attached to the kitchen, kept separate from the house for fear of fire. She was buried, head and shoulders, inside an enormous bin of flour. Her auburn hair was unmistakable. He stood close to her, taking full advantage of his height.

"What have you done to my home?" he bellowed.

Instantly, Judith came out of the bin, narrowly missing banging her head on the cover. In spite of Gavin's height and his loud voice, she was not afraid of him. Until her wedding less than two weeks ago, she had never been near a man who wasn't angry. "Your home?" she answered in a deadly voice. "And pray, what am I? The kitchen maid?" she asked as she held out her arms, covered in flour to her elbows.

They were surrounded by castle servants who backed against the walls in fear, but who would not have missed such a fascinating scene for anything.

"You know damn well who you are, but I will not

have you interfering in my business. You have altered too many things—my falconer, even my armorer. You are to tend to your own business and not to *mine!*"

Judith glared up at him. "Then pray tell me what I'm to do if I'm not to speak to the falconer or whoever else needs advisement."

Gavin was puzzled for a moment. "Why, women's things. You are to see to women's things. Sew. See that the maids cook and clean and . . . make face creams." He felt the last suggestion was inspired.

Judith's cheeks blazed, her eyes glittering with little splinters of golden glass. "Face creams!" she snarled. "So now I am ugly and need face creams! Perhaps I should also make lash darkeners and rouges for my pale cheeks."

Gavin was bewildered. "I didn't say you were ugly, just that you are not to set my armorer to sewing."

Judith's jaw was set firmly. "Then I will not do so again. I will let your armor stay stiff and cumbersome before I talk to the man again. What else may I do to please you?"

Gavin stared at her. The argument was not going his way at all. "The mews," he said weakly.

"Then I will let your birds die of soft feet. Is there anything else?"

He stood there dumbly with no answer for her.

"Now I assume we understand each other, my lord," Judith continued. "I am not to protect your hands, I am to let your birds die, and I am to spend my days concocting face creams to cover my ugliness."

Gavin grabbed her by the upper arm and lifted her from the floor so that they faced each other. "Damn you, Judith, you are not ugly! You are the most beautiful woman I have ever seen." He stared at her mouth, so close to his.

Her eyes softened and her voice was sweeter than honey. "Then I may set my poor brain to something besides beauty enhancers?"

"Yes," he whispered, weakened by the nearness of her.

"Good," she said firmly. "Then there is a new arrowhead I should like to talk with the armorer about."

Gavin blinked in astonishment, then set her on the floor so hard her teeth jarred together. "You will not—" He broke off as he stared at her defiant eyes.

"Yes, my lord?"

He stormed from the kitchen.

Raine sat in the shade of the castle wall, his bandaged leg thrust before him, sipping Judith's new cinnamon drink and eating rolls still warm from the oven. Every now and then he tried to suppress a chuckle as he watched his brother. Gavin's wrath was apparent in his every move. He rode his horse as if a demon chased him and thrust his lance viciously through the stuffed quintain that represented his foe.

Already the fight in the pantry was being told and retold. In another day it would reach the king in London. In spite of his mirth, Raine felt sorry for his brother. He'd been bested publicly by a bit of a girl.

"Gavin," he called. "Give the animal a rest and come sit awhile."

Reluctantly, Gavin did as his brother bid when he realized that his horse was covered with foam. He threw the reins to his waiting squire and walked tiredly to sit beside his brother.

"Have a drink," Raine offered.

Gavin started to take the mug then stopped. "Her new drink?"

Raine shook his head at his brother's tone. "Yes, Judith made it."

Gavin turned to his squire. "Fetch me some beer from the cellar," he commanded.

Raine started to speak then saw his brother's eyes strain across the courtyard. Judith walked from the manor house, across the sand-covered training field toward the line of war-horses tethered at the edge. Gavin's eyes watched her hotly; then, as she stopped by the horses, he started to rise.

Raine grabbed his brother's arm and pulled him down to the seat again. "Let her alone. You'll only start another quarrel which you will no doubt lose again."

Gavin started to speak, then stopped when his squire handed him a mug of beer.

When the boy was gone, Raine spoke again. "Don't you do anything except bellow at the woman?"

"I don't—" Gavin began, then stopped and gulped more beer.

"Look at her and tell me one thing that is wrong with her. She is beautiful enough to rival the sun. She works all day to set your home to rights. She has every man, woman and child, including Simon, eating from her hand. Even the war-horses dantily take apples from her palm. She is a woman of humor, and she plays the best damn game of chess in England. What more could you want?"

Gavin had not taken his eyes from her. "What do I know of her humor?" he said bleakly. "She has never even called me by my name."

"And why should she?" Raine demanded. "When have you ever so much as said a kind word to her? I don't understand you. I have seen you woo serf girls with more ardor. Doesn't a beauty like Judith deserve sweet words?"

Gavin turned on him. "I am not a simpleton to be told by a younger brother how to pleasure a woman. I was in women's beds when you were with your wet nurse."

Raine did not reply but his eyes were dancing. He refrained from mentioning that there were only four years' difference in their ages.

Gavin left his brother and went to the manor house where he called for a bath to be prepared. As he sat in the hot water, he had time to think. As much as he hated to admit it, Raine was right. Perhaps Judith did have a reason to be cool to him. Their marriage had started on the wrong foot. It was too bad he had had to strike her on their first night, too bad she had entered his tent at the wrong time.

But that was over now. Gavin remembered how she said he would get nothing from her but what he took. He smiled as he lathered his arms. He'd spent two nights with her and knew she was a woman of great passion. How long could she keep from his bed? Raine was right, too, when he mentioned his brother's ability to woo a woman. Two years ago, he'd made a wager with Raine about a certain icy countess. In a surprisingly short time Gavin had climbed into her bed. Was there a woman he could not win when he set his mind to it? It would be a pleasure to bring his haughty wife to heel. He would be sweet to her, court her until she begged him to come to her bed.

Then, he thought, nearly laughing aloud, she would be his. He would own her and she would never again interfere in his life. He would have everything he wanted—Alice to love and Judith to warm his bed.

Clean and dressed in fresh clothes, Gavin felt as if he were a new man. He was elated at the idea of trying to seduce his lovely wife. He found her in the stables, precariously suspended from a high rail of a stall gate, talking soothingly to one of the war-horses as the farrier cleaned and trimmed an overgrown hoof. Gavin's first thought was to tell her to go away from the beast before she was hurt. Then he relaxed. She was very good with horses.

"He's not an animal that is easily tamed," he said quietly as he went to stand beside her. "You have a way with horses, Judith."

She turned to him with a suspicious look.

The horse felt her tension and jumped, the farrier

barely able to move before the hoof struck him. "Hold him still, my lady," the man ordered without looking back. "I have more to do and I can't get it done if he prances about."

Gavin started to open his mouth to ask the man what right he had to speak to his mistress in such a tone, but Judith didn't seem to take offense at the man's words.

"I will, William," she said as she held the horse's bridle firmly and stroked the soft nose. "You weren't hurt were you?"

"No," the farrier answered gruffly. "There! It's done now." He turned to Gavin. "My lord! Were you about to say something?"

"Yes. Do you always order your mistress about as you did just now?"

William turned red.

"Only when I need to be ordered about," Judith snapped. "Please go, William, and see to the other animals."

He obeyed instantly. Judith looked defiantly at Gavin. Instead of the anger she expected, he smiled.

"No, Judith," he said. "I didn't come to quarrel with you."

"I didn't know there was anything else between us."

He winced, then reached out and caught her hand, pulling her reluctantly after him. "I came to ask if I could present you with a gift. See the stallion in the far stall?" he asked and pointed as he dropped her hand.

"The dark one? I know him well."

"When you came from your father's house, you brought no horse of your own."

"My father would rather part with all the gold he owned than one of his horses," she said, referring to the wagonloads of portable wealth that had accompanied her to the Montgomery estate.

Gavin leaned against the gate of an empty stall. "That stallion has produced some beautiful mares. They are kept on a demesne farm some distance away. I thought perhaps tomorrow you would go with me and choose one for your own."

Judith didn't understand his sudden kindness, nor did she like it. "There are palfreys here that are sufficient for my needs," she said evenly.

Gavin was quiet for a moment, watching her. "Do you hate me so much, or do you fear me?"

"I do not fear you!" Judith said, her back as straight as an iron rod.

"Then you will go with me?"

She stared into his eyes then nodded curtly.

He smiled at her—a genuine smile—and Judith unexpectedly remembered what seemed a long time ago; their wedding day, when he had smiled at her often.

"Then I will look forward to tomorrow," he said before leaving the stables.

Judith stared after him, frowning. What did he want from her now? What reason did he have for giving her a gift? She did not puzzle over the matter for long, for there was too much work to be done. The fishpond was a place she had neglected, and it desperately needed cleaning.

Chapter Ten

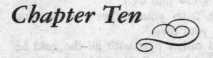

THE GREAT HALL OF THE MANOR HOUSE WAS ALIVE WITH the flickering light from the fireplaces. Some of the more favored of the Montgomery men were playing cards, dice, chess, cleaning weapons or simply lounging. Judith and Raine sat alone at the opposite end of the room.

"Please play the song, Raine," Judith begged. "You know I am no good at music. Didn't I say so this morning, and that I would play a game of chess with you?"

"And would you like for me to play a song the length of your game?" He strummed two chords on the fat-bellied lute. "There, I'm sure I've played as long as you did," he teased.

"It's not my fault you were beaten so quickly. You use your men only to attack and don't protect yourself from the attack of others."

Raine stared, his mouth open, then began to laugh. "Is this a bit of wisdom I hear, or an unadorned insult?"

"Raine," Judith began, "you know exactly what I mean. I would like for you to play for me."

Raine smiled down at her, the firelight gleaming on her auburn hair, the wool dress showing off her tantalizing body. But her beauty wasn't what threatened to drive him insane. Beauty was sometimes found even in the serfs. No, it was Judith herself. He had never met a woman with her honesty, her logic, her intelligence. If she were a man . . . He smiled. If she were a man, he wouldn't be in such danger of falling hopelessly in love with her. He knew he had to get away from Judith soon even though his leg was only half-healed.

Raine glanced over her head and saw Gavin leaning against the door frame, watching his wife's profile illuminated by the flames. "Here, Gavin," he called. "Come and play for your wife. I find this leg pains me too much to enjoy anything. I have been giving Judith lessons, but she is no good at all." His eyes twinkled as he looked down at his sister-in-law, but she merely stared at her hands which were clasped in her lap.

Gavin strode forward. "I'm glad to hear there is something that my wife doesn't do to perfection," he

laughed. "Do you know that today she had the
fishpond cleaned? I hear the men found a Norman
castle at the bottom of it." He stopped when Judith
stood.

"You must pardon me," she said quietly. "I find I am
more tired than I knew, and I wish to retire." Without
another word, she left the hall.

Gavin, the smile gone from his face, sank into a
cushioned chair.

Raine looked at his brother with sympathy. "Tomorrow I must return to my own estates."

If Gavin heard, he made no acknowledgment.

Raine signaled to one of the servants to help him to
his chamber.

Judith glanced about the bedchamber with new eyes.
No longer was it hers alone. Now her husband had
come home, and he had the right to share it with her.
Share the room, share the bed, share her body. She
undressed hastily and climbed beneath the sheets.
She'd dismissed her maids earlier, wanting some solitude. Although Judith was tired after the day's activities, she stared at the linen canopy with open eyes.
After a long while, she heard footsteps outside the
door. She held her breath for a long moment then
hesitantly the footsteps retreated. She was glad, of
course, Judith told herself, but that didn't warm the
cold bed. Why should Gavin want her, she thought as
quick tears came to her eyes. No doubt he'd spent the
last week with his beloved Alice. No doubt his passion
was completely spent and he wanted no more from his
wife.

In spite of her thoughts, her fatigue from the long
day eventually conspired to make her sleep.

She awoke very early. It was still dark in the room;
only the faintest light came through the shutters. The
entire castle was still asleep, and Judith found the
silence pleasant. She knew she could not sleep longer,

nor did she want to. This still-dark time of the morning was her favorite.

She quickly dressed in a simple gown of finely woven dark blue wool called perse. Her soft leather slippers made no sound on the wooden steps or as she walked through the sleeping men in the great hall. Outside, the light was dark gray but her eyes quickly adjusted. Beside the manor house was a little walled garden. It had been one of the first things Judith had seen at her new home and one of the last she felt she could give her attention to. There were rows of roses, a great variety of color, their blooms almost hidden beneath dead stems on the long-neglected bushes.

The fragrance in the cool early morning air was heady. Judith smiled as she bent over one of the bushes. The other work had been necessary, but the pruning of the roses was a labor of love.

"They belonged to my mother."

Judith gasped at the voice so near her. She had heard no one approach.

"Everywhere she went, she collected slips of other people's roses," Gavin continued as he knelt beside Judith, touching one of the blooms.

The time and the place seemed otherworldly. She could almost forget that she hated him. She turned back to her pruning. "Your mother died when you were small?" she asked quietly.

"Yes. Too small. Miles hardly knew her."

"And your father didn't remarry?"

"He spent the rest of his life mourning her, what little time was left to him. He died only three years after her. I was only sixteen."

Judith had never heard him sound so sad before. Truthfully, she had heard little in Gavin's voice except anger. "You were very young to have been left with the running of your father's estates."

"A year younger than you, yet you seem to run this property well. Far better than I did, or have done since." There was admiration in his voice, yet a bit of hurt also.

"But I was trained for this work," she said quickly.

"You were trained only as a knight. It would have been harder for you to learn what to do."

"I was told you were trained for the church." He was surprised.

"Yes," Judith said as she moved to another bush. "My mother wished for me to escape a life such as she has known. She spent her girlhood in a nunnery and was very happy there. It was only when she married that—" Judith stopped, not wanting to finish the sentence.

"I don't understand how life in a nunnery could prepare you for what you've done here. I would have thought you spent your days in prayer."

She smiled down at him as he sat in the gravel path beside her. It was getting lighter now, the sky beginning to turn a rosy pink. She could hear the clatter of the servants in the distance. "Most men feel that the worst thing that could happen to a woman would be to deprive them of a man's company. I assure you that a nun's life is far from empty. Look at St. Anne's. Who do you think runs those estates?"

"I never thought about it."

"The prioress manages estates that make the king's look poor. Yours and mine together could fit into a corner of St. Anne's. My mother took me to meet the prioress last year. I spent a week at her side. She is a constantly busy woman ordering the work of thousands of men and acres of land. She does not"—Judith's eyes sparkled—"have time for woman's work."

Gavin was startled for a moment then he began to laugh. "A thrust well delivered." What had Raine said about her sense of humor? "I stand corrected."

"I'd think you'd know more about a nunnery since your sister lives there."

A special glow came over Gavin's face when his sister was mentioned. He smiled. "I cannot imagine Mary running anyone's estates. Even as a child, she was so sweet and shy that she seemed of another world."

"And so you let her enter a convent."

"It was her wish, and when I inherited from my father, she left us. I wanted her to remain here and not marry if she didn't want to, but she wanted to be near the sisters."

Gavin stared at his wife, thinking that she had come very close to spending her life in a convent. The sunlight caught fire in her auburn hair; the way she looked at him, without anger or hatred, made his breath catch.

"Ow!" Judith broke the spell as she looked down at her finger, nicked on a rose thorn.

"Let me see," Gavin said as he took her small hand in his larger one. He brushed away a drop of blood from her fingertip then raised it to his lips, as he looked into her eyes.

"Good morning!"

Both of them looked up at the window above the garden.

"I hate to disturb your lovemaking," Raine called down from the manor house, "but my men seem to have forgotten me. And with this damned leg, I am little more than a prisoner."

Judith pulled her hand from Gavin's and looked away, her cheeks, for some reason, flushing.

"I will go and help him," Gavin said as he stood. "Raine says he is leaving today. Maybe I can hurry him along. Will you ride with me this morning to choose a mare?"

She nodded her head but didn't look at him before he left the garden.

"I see you're making some progress with your wife," Raine said as Gavin roughly helped him down the stairs.

"It would have been more if someone hadn't started bellowing out the window," Gavin remarked bitterly.

Raine snorted with laughter. His leg hurt and he

didn't look forward to the long journey to another estate, so he was in a bad mood. "You didn't even spend the night with her."

"Of what concern is that to you? Since when do you notice where I sleep?"

"Since I met Judith."

"Raine, if you—"

"Don't even say it. Why do you think I am going when my leg hasn't even begun to heal?"

Gavin smiled. "She is lovely, isn't she? In a few days I will have her eating out of my hand; then you'll see where I sleep. A woman is like a hawk. You must starve it until it is eager for food; then it will be easily tamed."

Raine stopped on the stairs, his arm about Gavin's shoulder. "You are a fool, brother. You may be the biggest fool ever created. Don't you know that the master is often the servant of his hawk? How many times have you seen men carry their favorite hawk about on their wrists, even in church?"

"You talk nonsense," Gavin said, "and I don't like being called a fool."

Raine set his teeth together as Gavin jerked his leg. "Judith is worth two of you and a hundred of that icy bitch you think you love."

Gavin stopped at the foot of the steps, gave his brother a malevolent look and moved away so quickly Raine had to grab the wall to keep from falling. "Don't you speak of Alice again!" Gavin said in a deadly voice.

"I damned well will speak of her! Someone needs to. She is ruining your life and Judith's happiness. And Alice isn't worth a strand of Judith's hair."

Gavin raised his fist then dropped it. "It's good that you're leaving today. I won't listen to anymore about my women from you." He turned on his heel and stalked away.

"Your women!" Raine called after him. "One owns your soul and the other you treat with contempt. How can you call them *yours?*"

Chapter Eleven

THERE WERE TEN HORSES INSIDE THE FENCED AREA. EACH one was sleek and strong with long legs that inspired visions of the animals running across flowery fields.

"I am to choose one, my lord?" Judith asked as she leaned across the fence rail. She looked up at Gavin beside her, watching him suspiciously. All morning he had been exceptionally pleasant; first in the garden, and now as he gave her a gift. He'd helped her on the mount, taken her arm when she, in an unladylike gesture, climbed atop the rails. She could understand his irritation, his scowls, but she was quite leery of this new kindness.

"Any one that you want," Gavin answered, smiling at her. "They have all been gentled and are ready for a bridle and saddle. Do you see one you like?"

She looked back at the horses. "There isn't one I don't like. It's not easy to choose. I think that one, the black one."

Gavin smiled at her choice, a mare with a high-stepping, dainty gait. "She is yours," he said. Then, before he could help her down, Judith was on the ground and through the gate. Within minutes, Gavin's man had the mare saddled and Judith swung onto her animal's back.

It felt wonderful to ride a good horse again. To Judith's right lay the road to the castle; to her left, the dense forest, a hunting ground for the Montgomeries. Without thought, she took the road to the forest. For too long she had been confined inside walls and jammed between people. The great oaks and beeches looked inviting, their branches connecting overhead to form a private shelter. Judith did not look back to see if she was being followed, but only plunged ahead toward the waiting freedom.

She rode hard, testing the mare and herself. They were compatible, as she knew they would be. The horse enjoyed the run as much as Judith.

"Quiet now, sweet one," Judith whispered when they were well inside the forest. The mare obeyed, daintily picking her way between the trees and bushes. The ground was covered by ferns and hundreds of years of accumulated foliage. It was a soft carpet and a silent one. Judith breathed deeply of the clean, cool air and let her mount decide the way.

The sound of running water caught Judith's attention, as well as her mare's. A stream, deep and cool, ran swiftly between the trees, sunlight playing through the overhanging branches. She dismounted and led her horse to the water. As the mare quietly drank, Judith pulled handfuls of sweet grass and began to rub the sides of the horse. They had galloped hard for several minutes before reaching the forest, and the mare was sweaty.

Judith was engrossed in her pleasant task, glorying in her horse, the day, the roaring water. The mare perked up her ears and listened, then backed away nervously.

"Quiet, girl," Judith said, stroking the soft neck. The horse took another, sharper step backward, threw her head back and neighed. Judith whirled, grabbing at the reins of the frightened animal and missed.

A wild boar approached, sniffing the air. It was wounded, its tiny eyes glassy with pain. Judith tried again to get the reins of her horse but the boar began its charge and the mare, wild with fear, took off. She grabbed her skirts and began to run. But the charging pig was faster than she. Judith made a running leap at a low-hanging tree branch, caught it and began to pull herself up. Strong from a lifetime of work and exercise, she swung her legs to another branch just as the boar reached her. It was no easy task to keep herself on the tree as the crazed boar charged and recharged the trunk at her feet.

Finally, Judith was able to stand on the lowest branch while holding onto another one above her head. As she looked down at the boar, she realized she was very high off the ground. She stared with sightless fear, her knuckles turning white as she grasped the overhead branch with all her strength.

"We must spread out," Gavin ordered his man, John Bassett. "There's not enough of us to go in pairs, and she couldn't have gone far." Gavin tried to keep his voice level. He was angry at his wife for galloping away on a strange horse into a forest unknown to her. He'd stood with the horses and his men, watching her ride away. He expected that as soon as she reached the edge of the woods, she would return. It took him a moment to realize that Judith was going into the forest.

Now he could not find her. It was as if she'd vanished, swallowed by the trees. "John, you go north, around the edge of the trees. Odo, take the south. I'll try the center."

Inside, the forest was quiet. Gavin listened carefully for any sign of her. He'd spent a great deal of his life here and knew every inch of the woods. He knew the mare would probably head for the stream that ran through its center. He called Judith several times, but there was no answer.

Then his stallion pricked up his ears. "What is it, boy?" Gavin questioned, listening hard. The horse took a step backward, his nostrils flaring. The animal was trained in hunting, and Gavin recognized the signals. "Not now," he said. "Later we'll look for game."

The horse didn't seem to understand, but pulled his head down against the reins. Gavin frowned then let him have his head. He heard the sound of the boar rooting at the base of the tree before he saw it. He would have led his mount around the beast had his eye not caught sight of a bit of blue in the tree above.

"God's teeth!" he whispered as he realized Judith was pinned in the tree. "Judith!" he called but got no answer. "You'll be safe in a moment."

His horse put its head down in anticipation of the charge, while Gavin drew his longsword from the scabbard on the side of the saddle. The stallion, well trained, ran very close to the boar and Gavin leaned half out of the saddle, his powerful thighs gripping hard as he bent and sent the sword through the animal's spine. It squealed once and kicked before it died.

Gavin jumped quickly from the saddle and retrieved the weapon. He looked up at Judith and was astonished at the sheer terror on her face. "Judith, it's all right now. The boar is dead. He can't hurt you." Her terror seemed out of reason with the danger. She had been safe enough in the tree.

She didn't answer but kept staring at the ground, her body as rigid as his iron lance.

"Judith!" he said sharply. "Are you hurt?"

Still she neither answered nor acknowledged his presence.

"It's only a short jump," he said as he held his arms up for her. "Let go of the branch above and I'll catch you."

She didn't move.

Gavin was puzzled as he looked again at the dead boar, then up at his terrified wife. Something besides the pig frightened her. "Judith," he said quietly and moved so he was in the line of her vacant stare. "Is it the high place that frightens you?" He wasn't sure, but she seemed to move her head in a tiny nod. Gavin grabbed the lowest branch near her feet and easily swung himself up beside her. He put his arm about her waist, but she gave no hint that she was aware of him.

"Judith, listen to me," he said calmly and quietly. "I'm going to take your hands and lower you to the ground. You must trust me. Don't be *afraid.*" He had to pry her hands loose and she grabbed onto both of his hands in panic. Gavin braced himself against a branch, and lowered Judith to the ground.

Her feet had no sooner touched the earth than he jumped down beside her. She was trembling as he pulled her into his arms. She clutched at him fiercely, desperately. "Hush, now," he whispered as he stroked her head. "You're safe now." Judith's trembling didn't stop, and Gavin felt her knees give way. He lifted her into his arms, and carried her to a tree stump, where he sat and held her as if she were a child. He'd had little experience with women outside of bed and none with children, but he knew her fear was extraordinary.

He held Judith tightly, as tightly as he could without crushing her. He smoothed her hair away from her cheek where she'd begun to perspire, her face hot. He rocked her and held her even closer. Had someone told him that being only a few feet off the ground could cause such terror, he would have laughed, but now he didn't find it amusing. Judith's fear was very real and his heart went out to her, that she should suffer so. Her small body was shaking, her heart beating as wildly as a bird's and he knew he must make her feel safe again. Gavin began to sing, quietly at first, not really paying attention to the words. His voice was rich and soothing. He sang a love song, of a man returning from the Crusades to find his true love waiting for him.

Gradually, he felt Judith begin to relax against him, the awful trembling subsiding. Her hold on him loosened, but Gavin didn't release her. He smiled and kissed her temple as he hummed the tune. Her breathing became more even until she lifted her head from his shoulder. She pushed away, but he held her firmly, not wanting to release her. Judith's need of him was oddly reassuring, although Gavin would have said he didn't like clinging women.

"You will think that I'm a fool," she said softly.

He didn't answer.

"I don't like high places," Judith continued.

He smiled and hugged her to him. "I guessed that," he laughed. "Though I would say that 'like' was a mild word. Why are you so afraid of high places?" He was laughing now, glad that she had recovered. Gavin was startled when she stiffened. "What have I said? Don't be angry."

"I'm not," she said sadly, relaxing again, comfortable in his arms. "I don't like to think of my father— that's all."

Gavin pushed her head back to his shoulder. "Tell me about it," he said seriously.

Judith was quiet for a moment, then when she did speak, he could hardly hear her. "Actually, I remember little of it—only the fear remains with me. My maids told me of it many years later. I was three years old and something disturbed my sleep. I left the room and went to the great hall, which was alive with light and music. My father was there with his friends and all of them were drunk." Her voice was cold, as if she told a story about someone else.

"When my father saw me, he seemed to think it a great joke. He called for a ladder and carried me, under his arm, to the top of it and set me on a high windowsill, well above the hall. As I said, I remember none of this. My father and his friends fell asleep, and in the morning the maids searched for me. It was a long time before they found me, though I must have heard them call. It seems I was too frightened to speak."

Gavin stroked her hair and began to rock her again.

The thought of a man setting a three-year-old child twenty feet above the floor, then leaving her all night, made his stomach turn over. He grabbed her shoulders and held Judith away from him. "But you are safe now. See, the ground is quite' near."

She gave him a tentative smile. "You have been good to me. Thank you."

Her thanks did not please him. It saddened Gavin that she had been so harshly used in her short life that she felt her husband's comforting was a gift. "You have not seen my woods. What do you say we stay here awhile?"

"But there is work—"

"You are a demon for work. Don't you ever play?"

"I'm not sure I know how," she responded honestly.

"Well, today you will learn. Today shall be for picking wildflowers and watching the birds mate." He wiggled his eyebrows at her and Judith gave a very un-Judith-like giggle. Gavin was enchanted. Her eyes were warm, her lips sweetly curved, and her beauty was an intoxicating sight. "Then come," he said as he lifted her to set her on her feet. "There is a hillside nearby that is covered with flowers and some rather extraordinary birds."

When Judith's feet touched the ground, her left ankle buckled beneath her. She grabbed Gavin's arm for support.

"You're hurt," he said as he knelt to look at her ankle. He turned and saw Judith bite her lip. "We'll put it in the cold stream water. That should keep it from swelling." He swept her into his arms.

"I can walk if you'll help me a bit."

"And have my knighthood taken from me? We are taught, you know, in the ways of courtly love. The rules are quite firm about beautiful ladies in distress. They must be carried whenever possible."

"Then I am only a means to further your knightly status?" Judith asked seriously.

"Of course, since you are a great burden to tote about. You must weigh as much as my horse."

"I do not!" she protested vehemently then saw his eyes were sparkling. "You're teasing me!"

"Didn't I say the day was for merriment?"

She smiled and leaned against his shoulder. It was pleasant to be held so close.

Gavin set her at the edge of the stream, then carefully removed her shoe. "The hose must go," he smirked. He watched with delight as Judith raised the skirt of her long gown to reveal the top of her hose, tied with a garter just above the knee. "If you need assistance . . ." he leered as she rolled the silk tube off her leg.

Judith watched Gavin as he gently bathed her foot in the cold water. Who was this man who touched her so gently? He could not be the man who had slapped her, who had flaunted his mistress before her, who had raped her on their marriage night.

"It doesn't seem to be hurt badly," he said as he looked back at her.

"No, it doesn't," she said quietly.

A sudden breeze blew a lock of hair across her eyes. Gently, Gavin brushed it away. "What do you say I build a fire and we roast that hideous pig?"

She smiled at him. "That would be pleasant."

He scooped her from the bank, then tossed her playfully in the air. She grabbed his neck in fright. "I could grow to like this fear of yours," he laughed, as he pressed her to him. He carried her across the stream to a hill which was indeed covered with wildflowers, and built a fire under an overhanging rock ledge. In minutes he returned with a dressed haunch of the boar and set it to roasting over the fire. He wouldn't let Judith move or help in any way. When the meat was cooking and there was a plentiful supply of firewood, Gavin left her again and returned in moments with his tabard raised about his hips, as if he carried something.

"Close your eyes," he said, and when she obeyed, he showered her with flowers. "You can't go to them, so they must come to you."

She looked at him, her lap and the ground around her covered in a riot of sweet-smelling blossoms. "Thank you, my lord," she said, smiling brilliantly.

He sat down beside her, one hand behind his back, leaning close to her. "I have another gift," he said as he held out three fragile columbines to her.

They were beautiful, delicate things of light violet and white. She reached to take them but he moved them from her grasp. She looked at him in surprise.

"They're not free." He was teasing her again, but the expression on her face showed him she didn't know it. He felt a pang of remorse that he had hurt her so badly that she should look at him so. Suddenly Gavin wondered if he were any better than her father. He ran a finger lightly down her cheek. "It's a small price to pay," he said gently. "I would like to hear you call me by my name."

Her eyes cleared and were warm again. "Gavin," she said quietly as he handed her the flowers. "Thank you, my . . . Gavin for the flowers."

He sighed lazily and leaned back on the grass, his hands behind his head. "My Gavin!" he repeated. "It has a nice sound to it." He moved one hand and idly twisted a curl of her hair about his palm. Her back was to him as she gathered the flowers around and put them into a bouquet. Ever orderly, he thought.

Unexpectedly, it occurred to him that it had been years since he'd had a peaceful day on his own lands. Always the responsibility of the castle had nagged at him, but in a few days his wife had so ordered matters that he could lie about in the grass and think of little but the sound of honeybees and the silky texture of a beautiful woman's hair.

"Were you really angry about Simon?" Judith asked.

Gavin could barely remember who Simon was.

"No," he smiled. "I just didn't like a woman to accomplish what I couldn't. And I'm not so sure that this new lure is better."

She whirled to face him. "It is! Simon agreed instantly. I'm sure the hawks will catch more game now and—" She stopped when she saw him laughing at her. "You are a vain man."

"I?" Gavin asked, bracing himself upon his elbows. "I am the least vain of men."

"Haven't you just said you were angry because a woman did what you couldn't?"

"Oh," Gavin said as he relaxed back on the grass, his eyes shut. "That's not the same. A man is always surprised when a woman does anything but sew and manage children."

"You!" Judith said in disgust then grabbed a handful of grass with a clod of dirt attached to it and threw it in his face.

He opened his eyes in surprise then pulled the grime from his mouth. His eyes narrowed. "You will pay for that," he said as he stealthily moved toward her.

Judith backed away, fearful of the pain she knew he would cause her. She started to rise but he grabbed her bare ankle and held it fast. "No," she began before he descended on her . . . and began to tickle her. Judith was surprised as much as anything, then she began to giggle. She drew her knees to her chest to try to keep his hands from her sides, but he was merciless.

"Do you take it back?"

"No," she gasped. "You are vain—a thousand times more vain than a woman."

His fingers ran up and down her ribs until she thrashed about under him.

"Please stop," she cried, "I can't stand any more!"

Gavin's hands stilled and he leaned close to her face "Are you beaten?"

"No," she said, but added quickly, "though you may not be as vain as I thought."

"That is a sorry apology."

"It was made under torture."

He smiled down at her, the setting sun making her skin golden, her hair spread about her like a fiery sunset. "Who are you, my wife?" he whispered, devouring her with his eyes. "You curse me one moment, enchant me the next. You defy me until I could take the life from you; then you smile at me, and I am dazed at your loveliness. You are like no other woman I have ever known. I have yet to see you put needle to thread, but I have seen you up to your knees in the muck of the fishpond. You ride a horse as well as a man, yet I find you in a tree shivering like a child in a mortal fear. Are you ever the same from one moment to the next? Do two days ever find you the same?"

"I am Judith. I am no one else, nor do I know how to be anyone else."

His hand caressed her temple; then he bent and touched his lips to hers. They were sunwarmed and sweet. He had barely tasted of her when the heavens suddenly opened with an enormous blast of thunder and began to empty a heavy torrent of rain on them.

Gavin uttered a very foul word Judith had never heard before. "To the overhang!" he said, then remembered her ankle. He picked her up and raced with her to the deep shelter, where the fire sputtered and crackled, the meat fat dripping into it. Gavin's temper was not helped by the abrupt shower. Angrily, he went to the fire. One side of the meat was burned black, the other raw. Neither of them had thought to turn it.

"You're a poor cook," he said. He was annoyed at having a perfect moment destroyed.

She gave him a blank look. "I sew better than I cook."

He stared at her, then began to laugh. "Well met." He looked out at the rain. "I must see to my stallion. He won't like standing in this with his saddle on."

Always concerned for the welfare of animals, Judith turned on him. "You've left your poor horse unattended all this time?"

He did not like her tone of command. "And where, pray tell, is your mare? Do you care so lightly for her that you don't care what has become of her?"

"I—" she began. She had been so enthralled with Gavin that she had given her horse no thought at all.

"Then set yourself to rights before you order me about."

"I wasn't ordering you."

"And pray, what else then?"

Judith turned away from him. "Go then. Your horse waits in the rain."

Gavin started to speak then changed his mind as he went into the rain.

Judith sat rubbing her ankle, scolding herself. She seemed to make him angry at every turn. Then she stopped. What did it matter if she made him angry? She hated him, didn't she? He was a vile, dishonorable man and one day of kindness wouldn't change her feelings of hatred for him. Or could it?

"My lord."

She heard the voice as if from far away.

"My Lord Gavin. Lady Judith." The voices came closer.

Gavin swore under his breath as he tightened the cinch he had just loosened. He'd forgotten all about his men. What spell had that little witch cast on him that he forgot his horse and even worse, forgot his men who diligently searched for them? Now they rode about in the rain, wet, cold and no doubt hungry. For all he would have liked to go back to Judith, perhaps spend the night with her, his men must come first.

He walked his horse across the stream and up the hill. They would have seen the fire by now.

"You are unharmed, my lord?" John Bassett asked when they met, water dripping off his nose.

"Yes," Gavin said flatly, not looking at his wife who

leaned against the rock ledge. "We were caught in the storm and Judith hurt her ankle," he began, then stopped when John looked pointedly at the sky. A spring cloudburst was hardly a storm, and both Gavin and his wife could have ridden the one horse.

John was an older man, a knight of Gavin's father, and he was experienced in dealing with young men. "I see, my lord. We have brought the lady's mare."

"Damn, damn, damn!" Gavin muttered. Now she'd made him lie to his men. He went to her mare and savagely tightened the cinch.

For all the pain in her injured ankle, Judith hobbled quickly toward him. "Don't be so rough with my horse," she said possessively.

He turned on her. "Don't be so rough with *me*, Judith!"

Judith silently stared through the half-open shutter at the starlit night. She wore a bedrobe of indigo blue damask lined with light blue silk, trimmed around the neck, down the front and around the hem with white ermine. The rain had cleared and the night air was fresh. Reluctantly, she turned away from the window to her empty bed. Judith knew what was wrong with her, though she hated to admit it. What sort of woman was she that she pined for the caresses of a man she despised? She closed her eyes and could almost feel his hands and his lips on her body. Had she no pride that her body betrayed her mind? She slipped off the robe and slid, nude, into the chilly bed.

Her heart nearly stopped when she heard heavy footsteps pause outside the room. She waited, breathlessly, for a long while before the steps receded down the hall. She banged her fist into the feather pillow and it was a long, long time before she slept.

Gavin stood outside her door for several minutes before going to the room he now used. What was wrong with him? he demanded of himself. Where did this new

timidity with women come from? She was ready for
him; he'd seen it in her eyes. Today, for the first time in
many weeks, she'd smiled at him and for the first time
ever, she'd called him by his first name. Could he risk
losing that little gain by forcing his way into her
chamber and again risk causing new hate?

What did it matter if he raped Judith again? Hadn't
he enjoyed it the first night? He undressed quickly and
slid into the empty bed. He didn't want to rape her
again. No, he wanted her to smile at him, to call his
name and hold her arms out to him. Gone from his
mind were all thoughts of triumph. He fell asleep
remembering the way she'd clung to him when she'd
been frightened.

Chapter Twelve

GAVIN WOKE VERY EARLY AFTER A FRETFUL NIGHT'S SLEEP.
The castlefolk were beginning to stir, but the sound was
still subdued. His first thought was of Judith. He
wanted to see her. Had she really smiled at him
yesterday?

He dressed quickly in a linen shirt and a coarse
woolen doublet, secured with a wide leather belt. He
pulled linen hose over his muscular calves and thighs,
tieing them to the linen braies that he wore as a
loincloth. Afterward, he hurried down the stairs to the
garden and there cut a fragrant red rose, its petals
kissed by pearly drops of dew.

The door to Judith's chamber was closed. Silently, Gavin opened it. She was asleep, one hand tangled in her hair which was spread across her bare shoulders and the pillow beside her. He placed the rose on the pillow and gently removed a curl from her cheek.

Judith opened her eyes slowly. It seemed a part of her dreams to see Gavin so near. She touched his face gently, her thumb on his chin, feeling the unshaved bristles, her fingers on his cheeks. He looked younger than usual, the lines of care and worry gone from his eyes. "I didn't think you were real," she whispered, watching his eyes as they softened.

He moved his head slightly and bit the tip of her finger. "I am very real. It's you who seem to be a dream."

She smiled wickedly at him. "Then we are well pleased with our dreams, aren't we?"

He laughed as he put his arms around her roughly and rubbed his cheek on the tender flesh of her neck, delighting in her squeals of protest as his whiskers threatened to remove her skin. "Judith, sweet Judith," he whispered as he nibbled her earlobe. "You are always a wonder to me. I don't know if I please you or not."

"And would it matter so much if you did not?"

He drew back from her and touched her temple. "Yes, I think it would matter."

"My lady!"

They both looked up as Joan burst into the room.

"A thousand pardons, my lady," Joan said, sniggering. "I didn't know you were so well occupied, but the hour grows late and there are many who call for you."

"Tell them to wait," Gavin said heatedly as he held Judith tightly as she tried to push him away.

"No!" Judith said. "Joan, who summons me?"

"The priest asks if you wish to begin the day without mass. Lord Gavin's man, John Bassett, says some horses from Chestershire have arrived. And there are three cloth merchants who want to have their wares inspected."

Gavin stiffened and released his wife. "Tell the priest we will be there and I will see the horses after mass. And tell the merchants—" he stopped, disgusted. Am I master of this house or not? he demanded of himself.

Judith put her hand on his arm. "Tell the merchants to store their wares and attend mass with us. I will see them after mass."

"Well?" Gavin asked the skinny maid. "You've been told what to do. Now go."

Joan hugged the door to her back. "I must help my lady dress."

Gavin began to smile. "I will do that. Perhaps I'll find some pleasure in this day besides duty."

Joan smirked at her mistress before she slinked around the door and closed it.

"Now, my lady," Gavin said as he turned back to his wife. "I am yours to command."

Judith's eyes sparkled. "Even if it concerns the matter of your horses?"

He groaned in mock agony. "It was a silly quarrel, wasn't it? I was angry at the rain more than at you."

"And why should the rain have made you angry?" she teased.

He leaned back over her. "It kept me from a sport I much desired."

She put her hand on his chest, felt his heart hammering. "Do you forget the priest waits?"

He leaned back. "Come, then, up with you and let's see to your dressing. If I can't taste, I may at least look my fill."

Judith gazed into his eyes for a moment. It had been nearly two weeks since he'd made love to her. Maybe he had left her right after their marriage to go to his mistress. But Judith realized that Gavin was hers right now, and she would make the most of that possession. Many people told her she was beautiful, but she usually dismissed them as flatterers. She knew her curved body was quite different from the thin one of Alice Valence. But once Gavin had desired her body. She wondered if she could make those eyes darken from gray to black.

She slowly pulled an edge of the coverlet back and stuck out one bare foot, then drew the coverlet to mid-thigh. She flexed both feet. "I think my ankle has quite recovered, don't you?" She smiled up at him innocently, but he wasn't looking at her face.

Very slowly, she moved the coverlet away from her firm, round hip, then exposed her navel, her flat stomach. She slipped slowly out of the bed and stood before him in the early morning light.

Gavin stared at her. He hadn't seen her nude in weeks. She had long, slim legs, round hips, a tiny waist and full rosy-tipped breasts.

"Damn the priest!" Gavin muttered as he held out a hand to touch the curve of her hip.

"Do not blaspheme, my lord," Judith said seriously. Gavin looked up at her in surprise.

"It's always a wonder to me that you wished to hide all that under the guise of a nun." Gavin sighed heavily as he looked at her, his palms aching with the desire to touch her. "Be a good girl and fetch your clothes. I cannot bear this sweet torture any longer. Another moment, and I would rape you before the priest's very eyes."

Judith turned to her clothes chest and hid her smile. Would it be rape, she wondered.

She took her time dressing, enjoying his eyes upon her and his strained silence. She slipped on a thin cotton chemise embroidered with tiny blue unicorns. It barely reached to mid-thigh. Matching drawers came next. Then she put her leg up on the edge of the bench where Gavin sat stonily, and carefully pulled the silk stockings over her legs, held in place by garters.

She reached across him for her dress of rich, brown cashmere from Venice. Silver lions were embroidered down the front and along the hem. Gavin's ·hands trembled as he fastened the buttons down the back. A silver filigree belt completed the costume, but Judith could not seem to manage the simple buckle by herself.

"Done," she said after a long time of struggling with the uncooperative garments.

Gavin let out his long-held breath.

"You make an excellent maid," she laughed, whirling about in a sea of brown and silver.

"No," Gavin said honestly. "I would die in less than a week. Now come below with me and don't tease me anymore."

"Yes, my lord," Judith said obediently, her eyes twinkling.

Within the inner bailey was a long field with a heavy carpet of sand. Here the Montgomery men and their chief vassals trained. A straw dummy swung from a gibbet which the men made sword passes at as they rode their war horses. A ring attached between two poles was the object of more passes with both sword and lance. There was also a man who was slashing at a four-inch post buried deeply in the ground by using a two-handed grip on his sword.

Gavin sat down heavily on a bench at the edge of the training ground. He took off his helmet and ran his hand through his sweat-dampened hair. His eyes were sunken into dark pits, his cheeks drawn, his shoulders aching with weariness. It had been four days since that morning he'd helped Judith dress. During that time he'd slept very little, ate even less, so that now his senses were taut.

He leaned his head back against the stone wall and thought that there was little more that could have happened. Several serfs' cottages had caught fire, and the wind had sent sparks into the dairy. He and his men had fought the fire for two days, sleeping on the ground where they fell. One night he'd spent in the stables with a mare that delivered a colt by breech birth. Judith stayed with him throughout the night, holding the horse's head, handing Gavin cloths and ointments before he knew he needed them. Never had he felt so close to anyone as he had then. At dawn, with a feeling of triumph, they stood together and watched the little colt take its first shaky steps.

Yet for all their closeness in spirit, their bodies were as far apart as ever. Gavin felt that at any moment he might go insane with wanting her. He wiped the sweat from his eyes as he stared across the yard and saw Judith walking toward him. Or did he imagine it? She seemed to be everywhere before his eyes, even when she was not.

"I brought you something cool to drink," she said, holding out a mug to him.

He stared at her intently.

She put the mug beside him on the bench. "Gavin, are you well?" she asked as she put a cool hand on his brow.

He grabbed her violently and pulled her down. His lips sought hers hungrily, forcing them open. He didn't think that she might deny him; he was past caring.

Her arms went about his neck and her response to his kiss was as eager as his. Neither cared that half the castlefolk watched. There was no one but the two of them. Gavin moved his lips to her neck. He wasn't gentle. He acted as if he would devour her if at all possible.

"My lord!" someone said impatiently.

Judith opened her eyes to see a boy standing nearby, a rolled paper in his hand. She suddenly remembered who and where she was. "Gavin, there is a message for you."

He didn't move his lips from her neck, and Judith had to concentrate very hard to keep her mind on the waiting boy.

"My lord," the boy said. "It's an urgent message."

He was very young—before his first beard—and he looked on Gavin's kissing of a woman as a waste of time.

"Here!" Gavin said as he snatched the parchment from the boy. "Now go and don't bother me anymore."

He threw the paper on the ground before turning once again to his wife's lips.

But Judith was now very aware of their public place. "Gavin," she said sternly, struggling to get off his lap. "You must read it."

He looked up at her as she stood over him, his breath coming hard and fast. "You read it," he said as he grabbed the mug of liquid Judith had brought. Maybe it would cool his hot blood.

Judith unrolled the paper with a worried frown, her face draining of color as she read.

Instantly Gavin was concerned. "Is it bad news?" When she looked up, his breath stopped, for there again he saw the coldness in her eyes. Her beautiful, warm, passionate eyes flashed daggers of hate at him.

"I am three times a fool!" she said through clenched teeth as she threw the parchment in his face. She turned on her heel and stalked toward the manor house.

Gavin took the parchment from his lap.

My dearest, I send this in private so I may tell you of my love freely. Tomorrow I wed Edmund Chatworth. Pray for me, think of me, as I will think of you. Remember always that my life is yours. Without your love I am nothing. I count the moments until I am yours again.

All my love,
Alice

"Trouble, my lord?" John Bassett asked.

Gavin put the missive down. "More than I have ever known. Tell me, John, you are an older man. Perhaps you know something about women."

John chuckled. "No man does, my lord."

"Is it possible to give your love to one woman, yet desire another until you are nearly mad?"

John shook his head as he watched his master staring after his wife's retreating form. "Does this man also desire the woman he loves?"

"Surely!" Gavin answered. "But perhaps not . . . not in the same manner."

"Ah, I see. A holy love, as for the Virgin. I am a simple man. If it were me, I'd take the earthly one. I think love would come if the woman were a joy in bed."

Gavin propped his elbows on his knees, his head in his hands. "Women were created to tempt men. They are the devil's own."

John smiled. "I think that if I were to meet old Scratch, I might thank him for that bit of evil work."

For Gavin, the next three days were hell. Judith would neither look at him nor speak to him. If at all possible, she would not be anywhere near him. And the more haughtily she treated him the more furious he became.

"Stay!" he ordered her on one night as she started to leave the room when he entered.

"Of course, my lord," she said as she curtsied. Judith kept her head bowed, her eyes never meeting his.

Once Gavin thought her eyes were red, as if she'd been crying. But that was nonsense, of course. What reason did she have to cry? *He* was the one being punished, not her. He'd shown he wanted to be kind, yet she chose to despise him. Well, she'd gotten over it once, and she would get over it again. Yet the days passed, and still Judith was cold to him. He heard her laughter, but when he appeared, the smile died on her face. He felt he should slap her, force her to respond to him; even anger was better than the way she looked through him. But Gavin couldn't hurt her. He wanted to hold her and even apologize. For what? He spent his days riding hard, training hard, yet at night he didn't sleep. He found himself making excuses to be near her, just to see if he could touch her.

Judith had cried until she was nearly ill. How could she have forgotten so soon that he was such a vile man? Yet for all the anguish the letter caused, she had to steel herself from running to his arms. Judith hated Gavin yet her body burned for him every moment of every hour of every day.

"My lady," Joan said quietly. Many of the servants had learned to tiptoe about their master and mistress lately. "Lord Gavin asks you to come to him in the great hall."

"I will not!" Judith replied without hesitation.

"He said it was urgent, to do with your parents."

"My mother?" she asked, immediately concerned.

"I don't know. He said only that he must speak with you at once."

As soon as Judith saw her husband, she knew something was very wrong. His eyes were like black coals, his lips so tightly drawn that they appeared to be only a slash across his face.

He turned his wrath on her. "Why didn't you tell me you were pledged to somone else before me?"

Judith was bewildered. "I told you I was pledged to the church."

"You know I don't mean the church. What about that man you laughed and flirted with at the tournament? I should have known then."

Judith could feel the blood beginning to pound through her veins. "You should have known what? That any man would be a more suitable husband than you?"

Gavin took a step forward, his manner threatening, but Judith did not retreat. "Walter Demari has lain claim to you and your lands. To prove his claim, he has killed your father and taken your mother captive."

Immediately, all the anger left Judith. She felt

deflated and weak. She grabbed a chair back to steady herself. "Killed? Captive?" she managed to whisper.

Gavin calmed somewhat and put a hand on her arm. "I didn't mean to tell you like that. It's just that the man lays claim to what is *mine!*"

"Yours?" Judith stared at him. "My father killed, my mother captured, my lands seized—and you dare talk to me of what you have lost?"

He drew away from her. "Let's talk reasonably. Were you pledged to Walter Demari?"

"I was not."

"Are you sure?"

She only glared at him in answer.

"He says that he will return your mother to safety if you will go to him."

She turned instantly. "Then I will go."

"No!" Gavin said and pulled her back to the seat. "You cannot! You are mine!"

She stared up at him, her mind concentrating on business. "If I am yours and my lands are yours, how does this man plan to get them? Even if he fights you, he cannot fight all your kin."

"Demari doesn't plan to do so." Gavin's eyes bored into hers. "He has been told we don't sleep together. He asks for an annulment, that you declare before the king your distaste for me and your desire for him."

"And if I do this, he will release my mother, unharmed?"

"That is what he says."

"And what if I don't make this declaration before the king? What will happen to my mother?"

Gavin paused before answering. "I don't know. I cannot say what will become of her."

Judith was silent for a moment. "Then I am to choose between my husband and my mother? I am to choose whether I give in to the greedy demands of a man I hardly know?"

Gavin's voice was different from anything she'd ever

heard before. It was cold as hardened steel. "No, you do not choose."

Her head came up sharply.

"We may quarrel often within our own estates, even within our own chambers, and I may concede to you often. You may change the falconer's lures and I may be angry at you, but now you will not interfere. I don't care if you were pledged to him before we married, or even if you spent your childhood in bed with him. This is a matter of war now, and I will not argue with you."

"But my mother—"

"I will try to get her out safely, but I don't know whether I can."

"Then let me go to him. Let *me* try to persuade him."

Gavin was unyielding. "I cannot allow that. Now I must go and gather my men. We will leave early tomorrow morning." He turned and left the room.

Judith stood at the window of her bedchamber for a very long time. Her maid came and undressed her, putting her mistress' arms into a green velvet mink-lined robe. Judith was hardly aware of anyone else's presence. Her mother, who had sheltered her and protected her all her life, was threatened because of a man Judith hardly knew. She remembered Walter Demari only vaguely as a pleasant young man who talked to her of the tournament rules. She remembered clearly the way Gavin had said she had enticed the man.

Gavin. Gavin. Gavin. Always back to him. All roads led to her husband. He demanded, he commanded what she was to do. She was given no choice. Her mother was to be sacrificed to Gavin's fierce possessiveness.

But what would she do if she had a choice?

Suddenly her eyes glinted gold. What right did that odious little man have to interfere in her life? He played God when he made others choose between what was not his to own. Fight! her mind cried out. Her mother had taught her pride. Would Helen want her only child to stand meek and quiet before the king and give in to some strutting popinjay merely because the man said she must?

No, she would not! And Helen would not want it so. Judith turned toward the door, not sure of her destination, but an idea, sparked by her new anger gave her courage. "So! Demari's spies say we don't sleep together, that our marriage could be annulled," she murmured as she walked down the deserted hall.

Her convictions were firm until she came to the open doorway of the room Gavin used. He stood before the window, lost in thought, one leg propped on the window seat. It was one thing to make noble boasts of pride, but another to confront a man who every night found reasons for avoiding his wife's bed. Alice Valence's icily beautiful face floated before her. Judith bit her tongue, the pain keeping the tears from her eyes. She had made her decision and now she must live with it; tomorrow her husband would go to war. Her bare feet were soundless on the rush-covered floor as she went to stand just a few feet behind him.

Gavin felt, more than saw, her presence. He turned slowly, his breath held. Her hair looked darker in the candlelight, its rich color gleaming against the green velvet. The dark mink emphasized the rich creaminess of her skin. He could not speak. The nearness of her, the quiet room, the candlelight were even more than his dreams. She stared at him then slowly untied the belt of her robe and it glided languidly over her smooth skin, falling to her feet.

His gaze roamed over her as though he were unable to fully comprehend her beauty. Only when he looked back at her eyes did he see she was troubled. Was that expression fear? As if . . . he would reject her? The possibility struck him as so humorous he nearly laughed aloud.

"Gavin," she whispered.

She had barely finished the syllable when she was in his arms, being carried to his bed, his lips already fastened to hers.

Judith was afraid of herself as well as of him. He could sense it as he kissed her. He'd waited a long time for her to come to him. He'd stayed away from her for weeks, hoping she could learn to trust him. Yet now, as he held her, he felt no great sense of triumph.

"What is it, sweet? What troubles you?"

His concern for her made her want to cry. How could she tell him of her pain?

When he carried her to the bed and the candlelight danced over her body, her breasts rising with each breath, he forgot all thoughts of anything but the nearness of her. His clothes were hastily thrown aside and he gently eased himself down beside her. He wanted to savor his skin touching hers, inch by slow inch.

When the torture was more than he could bear, he grabbed her to him fiercely. "Judith, I have missed you."

She lifted her face to his to be kissed.

They had been apart too long to proceed slowly. Their need of each other was urgent. Judith grabbed a handful of flesh and muscle on Gavin's back. He gasped and laughed throatily. When her hands clawed at him again, he grasped both hands in one of his and held them over her head. She struggled to free herself, but he was too strong. When he entered her, she gasped, then thrust her hips up to meet his. He released her hands and she pulled him closer and closer to her. They made love quickly, almost harshly, before they obtained the release they sought. Then Gavin collapsed on her, their bodies still joined.

They must have dozed, but sometime later Judith was wakened by Gavin's slow rhythmic movement. Half-sleep, only half-aroused, she began to answer him with lazy sensual movements of her own. Minute by minute, her mind became more deeply lost to the feelings of her body. She didn't know what she wanted, but she was not content with her position. She was not aware of Gavin's consternation as she pushed him to the side, her hips never leaving his. Once he was on his back, she was astride him.

Gavin lost no time in wonder. His hands slid up her stomach to her breasts. Judith's head arched back and her throat, so smooth and white in the darkness, further inflamed him. He clutched at her hips, both of them lost to their rising passion. They exploded together in a flash of blue and white stars.

Judith collapsed above Gavin and he held her close to him, her hair wrapping itself around their sweat soaked bodies, encasing them in a silk cocoon. Neither one mentioned what ran through their minds: Tomorrow Gavin would leave to do battle.

Chapter Thirteen

THE CHATWORTH MANOR WAS A TWO-STORY BRICK HOUSE with carved stone windows set with imported glass. It was long and narrow, and on either end was a stained-glass bay window. Behind the house was a lovely walled courtyard. Stretching for two acres before the house was lush lawn, at the end of which was the earl's private hunting forest.

Three people were emerging from these woods, walking across the lawn toward the manor. Jocelin Laing, his lute slung across his shoulder had an arm around two kitchen maids, Gladys and Blanche. Jocelin's hot, dark eyes were made even smokier by the afternoon he'd spent satisfying the greedy women. But Jocelin did not think of them as greedy. To him, all women were jewels, each one to be enjoyed for its own special brilliance. There was no jealousy or possessiveness in him.

Unfortunately, that was not the case with the women. At the moment, both were dreading leaving Jocelin.

"You were brought here for *her?*" Gladys demanded.

Jocelin turned his head and looked at her until she looked away and blushed. Blanche was not so easily awed. "It's a wonder Lord Edmund allowed you to come. He keeps Lady Alice like a prisoner. He doesn't even allow her to go riding unless he is with her."

"And Lord Edmund does not care for a horse hitting his soft backside," Gladys chimed in.

Jocelin looked puzzled. "I thought this was a love match—a poor woman marrying an earl."

"Love! Bah!" Blanche laughed. "That woman loves no one but herself. She thought Lord Edmund was a simpleton she could use as she wished, but he is far from simple. We know—don't we, Gladys—since we've lived here for years?"

"Oh yes," Gladys agreed. "She thought she could run the castle. I know her kind. But Lord Edmund would rather burn the place to the ground than give her free rein."

Jocelin frowned. "Then why did he marry her? He could have had his choice of women. Lady Alice had no lands to offer."

"She is beautiful," Blanche answered shrugging. "He loves beautiful women."

Jocelin smiled. "I am beginning to like this man. I agree with him most heartily." He gave Blanche and Gladys lascivious looks which made their cheeks flush and their eyes lower.

"Jocelin," Blanche continued, "he's not like you."

"No, he's not," Gladys said as she ran her hand along Jocelin's thigh.

Blanche gave her a strong look of reprimand. "Lord Edmund likes only her beauty. He cares nothing for the woman herself."

"Such as poor Constance," Gladys added.

"Constance?" Jocelin asked. "I don't know her."

Blanche laughed. "Look at him, Gladys. He has two women with him now—yet he worries that he doesn't know a third."

"Or is it that he worries whenever there is any woman he doesn't know?" Gladys asked.

Jocelin put his hand to his forehead in mock despair. "I am found out! I am undone!"

"That you are," Blanche laughed as she began to kiss his neck. "Tell me, sweet, are you ever faithful to any woman?"

He began to nibble her ear. "I am faithful to all women . . . for a time."

They arrived at the manor house, giggling.

"Where have you been?" Alice hissed at him as soon as he entered the great hall.

Blanche and Gladys hurried off to their duties in far parts of the house.

Jocelin was unperturbed. "You missed me, my lady?" he smiled, taking her hand and kissing it after making sure no one was about.

"No, I did not," Alice said honestly. "Not as you mean. Were you out with those hussies this afternoon while I sat here alone?"

Jocelin was immediately concerned. "You have been lonely?"

"Oh, yes, I have been lonely!" Alice said as she sank into a cushioned window seat. She was as gently lovely as when he'd first seen her at the Montgomery wedding; but now she had a finer-drawn look to her, as if she'd lost weight, and her eyes moved nervously from one point to another. "Yes," she said quietly. "I am lonely. I have no one here who is my friend."

"How can that be? Surely your husband must love one as beautiful as you."

"Love!" she laughed. "Edmund loves nobody. He keeps me as if I were a bird in a cage. I see no one, talk to no one." She turned to look at a shadow in the room, her beautiful face twisted with hatred. "Except her!" she snarled.

Jocelin looked toward the shadow, unaware anyone was near them.

"Come out, you little slut," Alice sneered. "Let him see you. Don't hide away like some eater of carrion. Be proud of what you do."

Jocelin strained his eyes until he saw a young woman step forward, her figure slight, her shoulders bowed forward, her head lowered.

"Look up, you whore!" Alice commanded.

Jocelin's breath stopped when he looked into the young woman's eyes. She was pretty—not of the beauty of Alice or the woman he'd seen as a bride, Judith Revedoune, but lovely nonetheless. It was her eyes that made him stare. They were violet pools filled with all the troubles of the world. He had never seen such agony and despair.

"He sets her on me like a dog," Alice said, regaining Jocelin's attention. "I cannot move without her following me. I tried to kill her once, but Edmund revived her. If I hurt her again, he threatened to lock me away for a month. I—" Just then Alice noticed her husband coming toward her.

He was a short, fat man with large jowls and a sleepy heavy-eyed look. No one would guess that any mind except the simplest existed behind that face. But Alice had learned too well of his cunning intelligence.

"Come to me," she whispered to Jocelin before he nodded briefly to Edmund and left the hall.

"Your taste has changed," Edmund observed. "That one doesn't look at all like Gavin Montgomery."

Alice only stared at him. She knew there was no use

talking to him. She'd been married only a month, and every time she looked at her husband, she remembered the morning after her wedding. She had spent her wedding night alone.

In the morning, Edmund had called her to him. He was a changed man from the one Alice had first met.

"I trust you slept well," Edmund had said quietly, his little eyes in his too-fleshy face watching her.

Alice lowered her lashes prettily. "I was . . . lonely, my lord."

"You can stop your acting now!" Edmund ordered as he rose from his chair. "So! You think you can rule me and my estates, do you?"

"I . . . I have no idea what you mean," Alice stammered, her blue eyes meeting his.

"You—all of you, all of England—think I am a fool. Those muscled knights you thrash about with call me a coward because I refuse to risk my life fighting the king's battles. What do I care for anyone's battles except my own?"

Alice was stunned speechless.

"Ah, my dear, where is that simpering little look you wear for the men, those who drool over your beauty?"

"I don't understand."

Edmund walked across the room to a tall cabinet and poured himself some wine. It was a large, airy room set on the top floor of the lovely manor house of the Chatworth estate. All the furniture was of oak or walnut, finely carved, with wolf and squirrel pelts flung over the backs of the chairs. The glass he now drank from was made of rock crystal with little gold feet.

He held the crystal up to the sunlight. There were Latin words at the base of the vessel promising good fortune to the owner. "Do you have any idea why I married you?" He didn't give Alice a chance to answer. "I'm sure you must be the most vain woman in England. You probably thought I was as blind as that love-sick Gavin Montgomery. I know at least that you never even asked yourself why an earl would want to marry a penniless chit who slept with any man who had the equipment to please her."

Alice stood up. "I won't listen to this!"

Roughly, Edmund shoved her back into the chair. "Who do you think you are that you can tell me what you will do? I want you to understand one thing. I did not marry you for any love of you or because I was in awe of your so-called beauty."

He turned away from her and poured himself another glass of wine. "Your beauty!" he sneered. "I can't see what that Montgomery would want with a boy like you when he has that Revedoune woman. Now, there's a woman to stir a man's blood."

Alice tried to attack Edmund with her hands made into claws, but he easily knocked her aside.

"I'm tired of these games. Your father owns two hundred acres in the middle of my estates. The filthy old man was about to sell it to the Earl of Weston, who has been my enemy and my father's enemy for years. Do you know what would have happened to my estates if Weston owned land in the middle of them? A stream runs through there. If he dammed it, I'd lose hundreds of acres of crops as well as my serfs dying of thirst. Your father was too stupid to realize I only wanted you to get the land."

Alice could only stare. Why hadn't he spoken to her about the land Weston wanted? "But, Edmund. . . ." she said in her softest voice.

"Don't speak to me! For the last months I have had you watched. I know every man you've taken to your bed. And that Montgomery! Even at his wedding you threw yourself at him. I know about the time in the garden with him. Suicide! You? Ha! Did you know his wife saw your little play? No, I thought not. I drank myself into a stupor so that I wouldn't hear the laughter aimed at me."

"But, Edmund—"

"I told you not to speak to me. I went ahead with the

marriage because I couldn't bear the land going to Weston. Your father has promised the deed to me when you produce a grandchild for him."

Alice leaned back against the chair. A grandchild! She almost smiled. When she'd been fourteen, she'd found herself pregnant and had gone to a filthy old woman in the village. The hag had removed the fetus. Alice had nearly died from the bleeding, but she'd been glad to get rid of the brat. She'd never destroy her slim figure for some man's bastard. In the years since, through all the men, she had never gotten pregnant again. She had always been glad that the operation had damaged her so she couldn't have children. Now, Alice knew her life had become hell.

It was an hour later, after Jocelin had finished playing for a group of kitchen wenches, that he walked along the wall of the great hall. The tension in the Chatworth castle was nearly unbearable. The servants were disorderly and dishonest. They seemed to be terrified of both the master and the mistress and did not waste time in telling Jocelin of the horrors of life in the castle. The first weeks after their marriage, Edmund and Alice had fought violently. Until, one of the servants laughed, the master discovered the Lady Alice liked a hand taken to her. Then Lord Edmund locked her away from everyone, kept her from all amusements and, most of all, kept her from enjoying any of his wealth.

Whenever Jocelin asked the reason for Edmund's punishments, the servants shrugged. It had something to do with the wedding of the Revedoune heiress and Gavin Montgomery. It started then, and they often heard Lord Edmund screaming that he would not be made a fool of. Already Edmund had had three men killed who were supposedly Alice's lovers.

Everyone laughed when Jocelin's face turned parchment-white. Now, as he walked away from the servants, he vowed to leave the Chatworth castle tomorrow. It was too dangerous here.

The very slightest of sounds, coming from a dark corner of the hall made him jump. He calmed his racing heart, then laughed at his nervousness. His senses told him there was a woman in the shadows and she was crying. As he moved toward her, she drew back, like a cornered wild animal.

It was Constance, the woman Alice hated so much. "Be still," he said quietly, his rich voice purring. "I won't harm you." Cautiously, he moved his hand to touch her hair. She looked up at him in fear, and he felt his heart go out to her. Who could have treated a woman so to make her so frightened?

She cradled her arm against her side as if in pain. "Let me see," he said gently and touched her wrist. It was some moments before she released her arm enough so he could touch it. The skin was not broken nor were any bones, as he at first suspected. In the dim light he could see it was reddened, as if someone had viciously twisted the skin.

He wanted to hold her, to comfort her, but her terror of him was almost tangible. She was shaking with fear. He knew it would be kinder to let her go than to force himself on her any longer. He stepped back and she fled quickly. Jocelin stood looking after her for a long while.

It was very late at night when he slipped into Alice's bedchamber. She was waiting for him, her arms open and eager. For all his experience, Jocelin was surprised at the violence of her actions. She grabbed him, her nails clawing into the skin of his back, her mouth seeking his, biting his lips. He drew away with a frown and she growled with keen irritation.

"You plan to leave me?" she demanded, her eyes narrow. "There were others who tried to leave me." Alice smiled when she saw his face. "I see you've heard about them," she laughed. "If you please me, you will find no cause to join them."

Jocelin did not like her threats. His first impulse was to leave. Then the candle by the bed flickered and he became acutely aware of how lovely she was, like cool marble. He smiled, his dark eyes glowing. "I would be a fool to go," he said as he ran his teeth along the cord of her neck.

Alice leaned her head back and smiled, her nails again digging into his skin. She wanted him quickly and with as much force as possible. Jocelin knew he hurt her and he also knew she enjoyed it. He did not receive any pleasure from their lovemaking; it was a selfish demonstration of Alice's demands. Yet he obeyed her, his mind never far from the idea of leaving her and her household on the morrow.

Finally she groaned and pushed him from her. "Go now," she commanded and moved away.

Jocelin felt sorry for her. What was life without love? Alice would never have love, for she never gave any.

"You did please me," she said quietly as he started to open the door. He could see the marks his hand had made on her neck, and he could feel the rawness of his back. "I will see you tomorrow," she said before he left.

Not if there is any chance of escape, Jocelin said to himself as he walked down the dark corridor.

"Here you, boy!" Edmund Chatworth said as he threw open his chamber door, flooding the corridor with candlelight. "What are you doing here, skulking about the hall at night?"

Jocelin shrugged idly and refastened his hose, as if he'd just answered a call of nature.

Edmund stared at Jocelin, then at the closed door of his wife's chamber. He started to speak, then shrugged his shoulders as if to say that it wouldn't be worth pursuing the matter. "Can you hold your tongue, boy?"

"Yes, my lord," Jocelin answered warily.

"I don't mean about a small matter—but one larger, more important. There is a sack of gold in it for you if you don't speak." He narrowed his eyes. "And death to you if you do."

"Over there," Edmund said as he stepped aside and poured himself a flagon of wine. "Who would have thought a few taps would have killed her?"

Immediately, Jocelin went to the far side of the bed. Constance lay there, her face battered almost beyond recognition, her clothes torn off her body, hanging by a seam about her waist. Her skin was covered by scratches and small cuts; great lumps formed on her arms and shoulders. "So young," Jocelin whispered as he sank heavily to his knees. Her eyes were closed, her hair a mass of tangles and dried blood. As he bent and pulled her body gently into his arms, he felt her cold skin. Tenderly, he smoothed the hair away from her lifeless face.

"The damned bitch defied me," Edmund said as he stood behind Jocelin and looked at the woman who'd been his mistress. "Said she'd rather die than bed with me again." He snorted in derision. "In a sense, I only gave her what she wanted." He drained the last of the wine and turned to get more.

Jocelin did not dare to look up at him again. His hands were fists beneath the girl's body.

"Here!" Edmund said as he tossed a leather bag next to Jocelin. "I want you to get rid of her. Tie some stones to her and throw her in the river. Only don't let it be known what happened here this night. The news might cause problems. I will say she went back to her family." He drank more wine. "Damned little slut. She wasn't worth the money it took to clothe her. Only way I could get any movement from her was to hit her. Otherwise she lay like a log under me."

"Why did you keep her then?" Jocelin asked quietly as he removed his mantle to wrap the dead girl in it.

"Those damned eyes of hers. Prettiest things I ever saw. I could see them in my sleep. I set her on that wife of mine to report what went on, but the girl was a poor spy. Would never tell me a thing." He chuckled. "I think Alice hit her to make sure she said nothing. Well," Edmund noted as he turned away from Jocelin and the girl, "you have been paid. Take her away and do what you want with the body."

"A priest—"

"That old bag of wind?" Edmund laughed. "The Angel Gabriel couldn't waken the man after he has had his usual nightly flask of wine. Say some words over her yourself if you like, but no one else! You understand?" He had to content himself with Jocelin's nod. "Now get out of here. I'm tired of looking at her ugly face."

Jocelin neither spoke nor looked at Edmund as he swung Constance into his arms.

"Here, boy," Edmund said, surprised. "You left the gold." He dropped the bag onto the stomach of the corpse.

Jocelin used every bit of strength he had to keep his eyes lowered. If the earl saw the hate that burned there, Jocelin would not live to escape in the morning. Silently, he carried the body from the chamber, down the stairs and out into the starry night.

The stableman's wife, a fat, toothless old crone whom Jocelin had treated with respect and even affection, had given him a room atop the stables to use as his own. It was a warm place set in the midst of bales of hay. It was quiet and private; few people even knew of its existence. He would take the girl there, wash her and prepare her body for burial. Tomorrow he would take her outside the castle walls and give her a proper burial. Perhaps not in hallowed ground, blessed by the church, but at least in someplace free and clean of the stench of the Chatworth castle.

The only way to reach his room was by climbing a ladder set against the outside of the stables. Carefully, he settled Constance across his shoulders and carried her aloft. Once inside, he placed her tenderly on a soft bed of hay then lit a candle beside her. The sight of her in Edmund's room had been a shock, now it was a horror. Jocelin dipped a cloth in a bucket of water and began to wash the caked blood from her face. He did not realize there were tears in his eyes as he touched the

battered form. Taking a knife from his hip, he cut away
what was left of her dress and continued bathing her
bruises.

"So young," he whispered. "And so beautiful." She
was pretty—or had been—and even now, in death, her
body was so lovely, slim and firm, though a little too
much of her ribs showed.

"Please."

The word was whispered, so low that Jocelin almost
did not hear her. He turned his head and saw her eyes
were open, or one of them since the other was swollen
shut.

"Water," she gasped through a parched and burning
mouth.

At first he could only stare in disbelief then he
grinned in sheer joy. "Alive," he whispered. "Alive!"
He quickly got some watered wine, then carefully
cradled her head in the crook of his arm while he held a
cup to her swollen lips.

"Slowly," he said, still smiling. "Very slowly."

Constance leaned back against him, frowning as she
tried to swallow, revealing deep bruises about her
throat.

He ran his hand over her shoulder, and realized it
was still cold to touch. What a fool he was to take
Edmund's word of her death! She was freezing. That's
what made her seem so cold. She lay on his one
blanket, and since Jocelin knew of no other way to
warm a woman, he lay beside her, holding her close to
the warmth of him as he drew the blanket across both
of them with great concern. Never had he lain with a
woman and felt this way.

It was late when Jocelin woke, the girl cradled close
to him. She stirred in his arms, grimacing because of
her aching body. He moved from her side and placed a
cool cloth on her brow, which had grown too warm with
the beginnings of a fever.

Now, in the light of day, Jocelin began to see the
situation realistically. What was he to do with the girl?

He couldn't very well announce that she was alive. Edmund would take Constance as his again as soon as she was well. There was little likelihood that she could survive a second beating. If Edmund did not kill her, Jocelin was sure Alice would. With new eyes, Jocelin looked about the little room. It was private, well sealed against outside noises and difficult to reach. With luck and a great deal of care, he might be able to keep her hidden there until she was well. If he kept her alive and safe, then he would worry about what came next.

He lifted her and gave her more of the watered wine, but her swollen throat could take little of it.

"Joss!" a woman called from the foot of the ladder.

"Damn!" he said under his breath, cursing for the first time in his life his lack of freedom from women.

"Joss, we know you're there. If you don't come down, we'll come up."

He walked through a maze of baled hay to the open doorway and smiled down at Blanche and Gladys. "A beautiful morning, isn't it? And what might you two charming ladies want of me?"

Gladys giggled. "Are we to shout it for all the castle to hear?"

He grinned again and after one last glance over his shoulder, descended the ladder. He put an arm around each woman's shoulders. "Perhaps we could talk to the cook this morning. I find I'm famished."

The following four days were hell for Jocelin. Never in his life had he had to keep a secret, and his constant acts of subterfuge were exhausting. Had it not been for the stableman's wife, he would not have been successful.

"I don't know what you have hidden up there," the old woman said, "but I've lived long enough not to be surprised by anything." She cocked her head at Jocelin, admiring his looks. "It would be my guess it's a woman." She laughed at the expression on his face. "Oh, yes, it's a woman, all right. Now I must set my mind to figuring out why she must be kept hidden."

Jocelin started to speak but she held up her hand. "No need to explain. No one loves a mystery more than I do. Let me have my puzzle and I'll help you keep the other women from your room, though that won't be easy with the numbers that plague you. Someone ought to put you in a jar and pickle you, boy. You ought to be preserved—that's for certain. No other three men alive could pleasure as many girls as you do."

Jocelin turned away in exasperation. He was worried about Constance, and almost everyone had begun to notice his distraction. All except Alice. She demanded more and more of Jocelin, calling him constantly to play for her and every night to her bed, where the violence she desired drained him more each night. And constantly he had to listen to Alice's hatred of Judith Revedoune, and of how Alice was going to visit King Henry VII and get Gavin Montgomery back.

He looked to see if anyone watched him as he climbed the ladder to the little loft room. For the first time, Constance was awake to greet him. She sat up, clutching the blanket about her nude body. For days, while she'd been dazed with fever, Jocelin had cared for her, becoming as familiar with her body as his own. It did not occur to him that he was a stranger to her.

"Constance!" he said joyfully, not completely aware of her fear. He knelt beside her. "How good it is to see your eyes again." He took her face in his hands to examine the bruises which were healing quickly, thanks to her youth and Jocelin's care. He started to move the mantle from her bare shoulders to attend to her other wounds.

"No," she whispered, closing the mantle.

He looked down at her in surprise.

"Who are you?"

"Ah, sweet, don't be afraid of me. I'm Jocelin Laing. You met me before with the Lady Alice. Don't you remember?"

At the mention of Alice's name, Constance's eyes darted from one side of the room to the other. Jocelin pulled her into his arms—a place where she'd spent much time though did not know it. She tried to pull away from him, but she was too weak.

"It's all over now. You're safe. You are here with me and I won't let anyone harm you."

"Lord Edmund—" she whispered against his shoulder.

"No, he doesn't know you're here. No one does, only me. I've kept them all from knowing about you. He thinks you're dead."

"Dead? But—"

"Quiet." He smoothed her hair. "There will be time for talk later. First you must heal. I have brought you a soup of carrots and lentils. Can you chew?"

She nodded against him, not relaxed but not stiff either. He moved her to arm's length. "You can sit?" She nodded again, and he smiled as if she had accomplished a great feat of strength.

Jocelin had become adept at sneaking warm pots of food into the loft. No one seemed to think it odd that he carried his lute over his shoulder and the lute case in his arms. But each night he filled the case with food he hoped would nourish the feverish Constance.

He held the bowl and began to feed her as if she were a child. She moved her hand to take the spoon from him, but she shook too much to hold it. When she could eat no more, her eyes dropped in exhaustion. She would have fallen if Jocelin hadn't caught her. Too weak to protest, he cradled her in his lap and she drifted off to sleep easily, indeed feeling protected.

When Constance woke, she was alone. It took a few moments to remember where she was. The young man with thick black lashes who hummed in her ear couldn't have been real. What was real was Edmund Chatworth's hands about her throat, Alice's twisting of her arms, pulling her hair, any method to give pain that would not show.

Hours later, Jocelin returned and he held Constance in his arms, both snuggled deep under his mantle. He was not aware of time passing. For the first time in his life, the desires of women did not rule him. Constance's complete dependency on him brought an emotion he'd never known before—the beginning of love. All the love he'd ever felt for all the women was being concentrated into one fierce and burning passion.

But Jocelin was not a free man. There were others who watched him.

Chapter Fourteen

THE LONG, THIN BLACK LEATHER OF THE WHIP SNAKED angrily across the man's back. His back was already crisscrossed with many oozing stripes. He screamed loudly each time the whip struck him and twisted his hands frantically away from the braided rawhide thongs that held him to the post.

John Bassett looked toward Gavin, who nodded curtly. Gavin had no stomach for the punishment, and he had even less respect for the man's womanly screams.

John Bassett cut the bindings and the man fell into the grass. No one made any move to help him. "Shall I leave him?" John asked.

Gavin looked toward the castle across the narrow valley. It had taken two weeks to find Walter Demari. The wily little man seemed more interested in a cat-and-mouse chase than in getting what he wanted. For the last week, Gavin had camped outside the walls and worked on his attack. He had gone to the walls and called up challenges to the guards at the gate, but his words were ignored. Yet, even while the challenges were made, four of Gavin's men quietly dug beneath the ancient walls. But the walls were deep, the foundations broad. It was going to take much too long to break through. He feared that Demari would grow tired of waiting for Gavin's surrender and kill Helen.

As if he didn't have enough problems, one of his men, this mewling creature at his feet, had decided that since he was a knight of one of the Montgomeries, he was close to God. During the night, Humphrey Bohun had ridden into the nearest town and raped a merchant's fourteen-year-old daughter, then ridden back to camp triumphant. He was bewildered by Lord Gavin's rage when the girl's father told of his daughter.

"I don't care what you do with him. Just make sure he's out of my sight within the next hour." Gavin pulled his heavy leather gloves from where they hung over his belt. "Call Odo to me."

"Odo?" John's face took on a hard look. "My lord, you can't be thinking again of traveling to Scotland."

"I must. We've discussed this before. I don't have enough men to declare a full attack on the castle. Look at it! It looks as if a good wind would crumble the rest of the stones away but I swear the Normans knew how to build a fortress. I think it's made of poured rock. If we're to get inside before the end of the year, I'll need Stephen's help."

"Then let me go for him."

"And when were you last in Scotland? I have an idea where Stephen is, and tomorrow morning I'll take four men and find him."

"You'll need more protection than just four men."

"I can ride faster with fewer," Gavin said. "I can't afford to split up my men. Half of them are with Judith. Now, if I ride away with half again, it will leave you too unprotected. Let's just hope Demari doesn't realize I've gone."

John knew Lord Gavin was right, but he didn't like

his master riding away without a good guard. But he'd learned long ago that it was no use trying to argue with a man as stubborn as Gavin.

The man at their feet groaned, recalling their attention to him. "Get him out of here!" Gavin said and stalked toward where his men were building a catapult.

Without thinking, John put a strong arm under the knight's shoulder and lifted him.

"All this because of a little slut!" the man hissed, spittle forming at the corners of his mouth.

"Shut up!" John ordered. "You had no right to treat the girl like a heathen. If it'd been me, I would have had you hanged." He half-dragged the bleeding man to the edge of the camp, where John gave him a shove that sent him sprawling. "Now get out of here and don't come back."

Humphrey Bohun pulled the grass out of his mouth and looked after John's retreating form. "Oh, I'll be back. And it'll be me who's holding the whip next time."

The four men were very quiet as they made their way to waiting horses. Gavin had not told anyone except John Bassett of his journey to find Stephen. The three men who rode with him had all fought with Gavin in Scotland and they knew the rough, wild countryside. The group would travel as lightly as possible, without a herald carrying the Montgomery banner before them. All the men wore brown and green in an attempt to draw as little attention to themselves as possible.

They slipped silently into their saddles and walked their horses away from the sleeping camp.

They were barely ten miles from the camp when they were surrounded by twenty-five men wearing Demari's colors.

Gavin drew his sword and leaned over to Odo. "I will attack and cut a path through. You escape and get to Stephen."

"But my lord! You will be killed!"

"Do as I say," Gavin commanded.

Demari's men encircled the little group very slowly. Gavin looked about to find their weakest spot. They looked at him smugly, as if they knew the battle was already won. Then Gavin saw Humphrey Bohun. The rapist grinned in delight to see his former master so cornered.

Immediately, Gavin knew where he'd made his mistake. He'd spoken to John about his journey in front of this piece of filth. Gavin nodded to Odo, lifted his long steel broad sword with both hands on the hilt and charged. Demari's men were stunned. They had orders to take Lord Gavin prisoner. They'd assumed that when he was outnumbered more than six to one, he would surrender docilely.

That moment of hesitation cost Humphrey Bohun his life and allowed Odo to escape. Gavin hacked at the traitor, and he died before he could even grab his sword. Another and another fell under Gavin's sword as it flashed brilliantly against the rays of the rising sun. Odo's well-trained animal leaped over the dead bodies and the screaming horses, and galloped for the safety of the woods. He had no time to see if anyone followed him. He kept his head low and molded himself to his horse.

Gavin had chosen his men well. The two who were now beside him backed their horses together, the animals trained to follow the commands given by their masters' knees. The three men fought valiantly and when one of them fell, Gavin felt part of himself fall. They were his men and he was close to them.

"Cease!" a voice commanded over the clash of steel against steel, the cries of anguish.

The men drew back quickly and when their eyes cleared, they began to access the damage. At least fifteen of Demari's men lay dead or wounded, unable to stay on their mounts.

The horses of the men in the middle still stood their ground, rump to rump in pinwheel fashion. The man on Gavin's left had a deep slash across the top of his arm. Gavin, heaving with exertion, was covered with blood, but very little of it was his own.

The remaining of Demari's men looked on in silent tribute to the unarmored fighters.

"Take them!" said the man who seemed to be the leader of the attackers. "But see that Montgomery comes to no harm. He is needed alive."

Gavin lifted his sword again but suddenly there was a sharp sting and his hands were immobilized. A thin whip had been thrown, and his arms were pinned to his sides.

"Tie him."

Even as Gavin was dragged from his horse, his foot caught one man in the throat.

"Are you afraid of him?" the leader demanded. "You'll die anyway if you don't obey me. Tie him to that tree. I'd like him to watch how we treat captives."

Chapter Fifteen

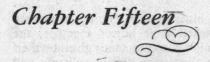

JUDITH WAS KNEELING IN THE ROSE GARDEN, HER LAP full of blossoms. Gavin had been gone a month now, with no word for the last ten days. There wasn't a moment that she didn't glance out a window or through a doorway to see if a messenger had arrived. She swayed between wanting to see him and dreading his return. He had too much hold over her, as he'd proven when she'd gone to his room the night before he left to fight for her lands. Yet she knew well enough that he had no such ambiguous feelings toward her. For him only the blonde Alice existed; his wife was only a toy to be used when he needed amusement.

She heard the clatter of arms as the men rode through the double gate that separated the inner bailey from the outer. She stood quickly, the roses falling to her feet as she picked up her skirts and began to run. None of them was Gavin. Judith released her pent-up breath, lowered her skirts and walked more sedately.

John Bassett sat atop his war-horse looking many years older than he had when he left some weeks before. His hair, graying at the temples, was even whiter now. His eyes were sunken, dark circles under them. The side of his chain mail had been torn and the edges of the cut were rusted from blood. The other men were no better; their faces haggard, their clothes torn and filthy.

Judith stood silently while John dismounted. "Take the horses," she said to a stableboy. "See that they are cared for."

John looked down at her a moment; then, with resignation, started to kneel to kiss her hand.

"No!" Judith said quickly. She was too practical to allow him to waste more energy in what, to her, was a useless gesture. She put her arm about his waist, guided his arm about her shoulders.

John stiffened, taken aback by the familiarity of his little mistress. Then he smiled fondly at the top of her head.

"Come and sit by the fountain," she said as she led him to the tiled pool just inside the garden wall. "Joan!" she commanded, "bring some of the other maids and send someone from the kitchen with food and wine."

"Yes, my lady."

She turned back to John. "I'll help you remove your armor," she said before he could protest.

Women came from inside the castle and soon the four men were bared from the waist up, their armor sent for repair. Each man ate ravenously of hot bowls of thick stew.

"You don't ask me the news," John said between bites, his elbow raised so Judith could clean and bandage the wound in his side.

"You will tell me," she said. "If it were good, my husband would have returned also. I can wait a long time for bad news."

John set the bowl down and looked at her.

"Is he dead?" she asked, not looking up at him.

"I don't know," he said quietly. "We were betrayed."

"Betrayed!" she cried, apologizing when she realized she'd hurt John's wound.

"One of the garrison knights, a new man named Bohun, slipped through the night to tell Demari that Lord Gavin planned to ride to his brother for help at dawn. Lord Gavin hadn't gone far when he was overtaken."

"But he was not killed?" Judith whispered.

"I don't believe so. We found no body," John said harshly, returning to his food. "Two of the men who rode with my lord were killed . . . killed in such a way that it lies heavy on me. This is no ordinary man we deal with, but a devil!"

"Was there no ransom message or any word that they held him prisoner?"

"No. Nothing. The four of us must have gotten there moments after the battle. There were some of Demari's men still there. We fought them."

She tied the last knot on the bandage then looked up at him. "Where are the other men? There couldn't be only four left."

"They still camp outside Demari's walls. We go to fetch Lord Miles and his men. Lord Raine's leg wouldn't have had time to heal."

"And do you think Miles will be able to free Gavin?"

John didn't answer but concentrated on the stew.

"Come, you can tell me the truth."

He looked at her. "It's a strong castle. It can be taken without reinforcements only if we lay siege."

"But that would take months!"

"Yes, my lady."

"And what of Gavin and my mother who are held prisoner there? Wouldn't they be the first to starve if the food were gone?"

John stared at his bowl.

Judith stood, her fists clenched, her nails digging into her palms. "There is another way," she said evenly. "I will go to Walter Demari."

John's head shot up, one eyebrow raised. "And what can you do that men cannot?" he asked cynically.

"Anything that is required of me," Judith answered quietly.

John nearly threw his bowl. Instead, he grabbed her arm, his strong hand hurting her. "No! You don't know what you're saying. Do you think we deal with a sane man? Do you think he will free Lord Gavin and your mother if you were to give him what he wants? If you saw the men—what were once men," he added, "who rode with Lord Gavin, you wouldn't consider giving yourself to this Demari. There was no need for such torture, yet he seemed to do it for joy alone. If he were a man, I would consider your idea, but he isn't."

She shook her arm until John released it. "What else is there to do? A siege would most certainly cause their deaths, but you say a siege is the only way to attack. If I were to get inside the castle, perhaps I could find Gavin and my mother and arrange an escape for them."

"An escape!" he snorted. John had forgotten that she was the Lady Judith and had the authority to order him about; she was just a young and inexperienced girl now. "And how would you get out? There are only two entrances; both guarded well."

Judith squared her shoulders, her chin held high. "What choice do you have? If Miles were to lead an attack, Demari would surely put Gavin to death, as well as my mother. Do you love Gavin so little that you don't care whether he dies or not?"

Suddenly John knew she was right. And he knew that he would be the one to turn her over to Walter Demari's bloody hands. She had struck John's heart when she mentioned love for Lord Gavin. John couldn't love the young man more if he were his own son. She was right that there was a chance to save Lord Gavin if she surrendered herself. Lord Gavin might have him hanged for endangering Judith, but he knew he was going to obey her. "You are trying for martyrdom," John said quietly. "What is to keep Demari from killing you also?"

Judith smiled at him, put her hands on his shoulder, for she also knew she'd won. "If he killed me, he would lose the Revedoune lands. If I have learned nothing else, I know how much men will do for my property." Her eyes glinted for a moment. "Now, come inside where we may talk more freely. You and I have a great deal of planning to do."

He followed her dumbly. She acted as if they prepared the menu for a woodland picnic rather than gave herself, as a lamb to slaughter, to a butcher.

Judith wanted to leave immediately, but John persuaded her to wait and give him and his men some rest. Truthfully, he hoped to talk her out of her madness and to find an alternate plan, but her logic bewildered him.

For every reason he gave that she should not go, Judith gave ten more sensible ones why she should. And he agreed with her; he could see no other way of any chance of saving the prisoners . . . if they were prisoners.

But oh, how he dreaded Lord Gavin's wrath! He said as much to Lady Judith. She laughed. "If he is safe enough to indulge his anger, I will kiss his hand in thanksgiving."

John shook his head in wonder. The woman was too

clever by half again. He didn't envy Lord Gavin the taming of her.

They couldn't take many men as a guard—they could not leave the estate unprotected—and already many of Gavin's knights waited for him. They were thankful it was only two days' travel to Demari's property.

Judith worked hard while John rested and ate. She ordered the loading of several wagons of grain and preserved meats to be prepared at the campsite. Another cart was given over to her clothes; the most beautiful of silks, velvets, brocades, cashmeres, along with a large ironbound chest filled with jewels.

When John mumbled something about women being ostentatious, Judith took him to task.

"Walter Demari hungers for some woman he believes to be beautiful. Would you like me to appear before him in homespun? He would say he'd changed his mind and have me thrown to the bottom of a well. He must be a vain man, or he wouldn't demand that a woman he hardly knows repudiate her husband and claim him as her true love. Therefore, I will play to his vanity and wear my most exquisite clothes for him."

John stared at her a moment, then turned away. He didn't know whether to praise her or be angry at himself for not thinking of what she said first.

For all the facade she showed to the world, Judith was scared. But for the life of her, she couldn't think of any alternative plan.

She lay awake all night thinking. Demari had sent no message of exchange. Perhaps he had already killed Gavin and Helen, and Judith was turning herself over to him for no reason.

She ran her hands over her stomach, knew it was still hard and flat. She was sure now that she carried Gavin's child. Was the baby part of the reason she worked to save her husband?

When the sun rose, Judith dressed slowly in a practical wool gown. She was strangely sedate, almost as if she walked to certain death. She went below to the little chapel for mass. She would pray for all of them—her husband, her mother and her unborn child.

Walter Demari sat before a wooden table in the great hall of his father's estate. Once the table had been a finely carved piece, but over time most of the heads of the beasts had been broken away, the necks rubbed smooth. Absently, Walter kicked at a chicken that pecked at the hose on his short, thin legs. He studied the parchment in front of him and refused to look at his surroundings. His father refused to give him anything but this run-down, neglected old tower. Walter buried his resentment deeply and concentrated on the task before him. When he was wed to the heiress to the Revedoune lands, then his father wouldn't dismiss him as if he didn't exist.

Behind Walter stood Arthur Smiton, a man Walter considered his friend. Arthur had helped Walter at every turn, agreeing that Walter should have had the lovely heiress instead of Gavin Montgomery. To repay Arthur for his loyalty, Walter had made the man his chief vassal. It was Arthur who had succeeded in capturing Lord Gavin.

"Arthur," Demari complained, "I don't know how to word the message. What if she won't come? If she does hate her husband, why should she risk so much for him?"

Arthur didn't let his emotions show. "Do you forget the old woman we hold? Isn't she the girl's mother?"

"Yes," Walter said and returned his attention to the parchment before him. It wasn't easy asking what he did. He wanted marriage to the Lady Judith in exchange for the freedom of her husband and mother.

Arthur stood behind Walter for a moment, then moved away to pour himself a cup of wine. He needed a firm stomach to be able to withstand Walter's mewling. The love-sick young man made Arthur ill. Walter had come back from the Montgomery-

Revedoune wedding so enthralled with the bride that he'd hardly been able to do anything except talk of her. Arthur looked on him with disgust. Walter had everything—lands, wealth, a family, hope for the future. He was not like Arthur, who had pulled himself up from the muck that had been his family. Anything he had he'd acquired through intelligence, physical strength and, quite often, treachery and lying. There was nothing that he wouldn't do to get what he wanted. When he'd seen the spineless Walter mooning about a bit of a girl, Arthur developed a plan.

It hadn't taken long to learn of the quarrels the new bride had with her husband. Arthur, only a knight in Walter's garrison, had found a ready ear when he spoke of an annulment and a second marriage to Walter. Arthur couldn't have cared less about the girl, but the Revedoune lands were worth any amount of fighting. Walter hadn't wanted to attack Robert Revedoune, but Arthur knew Revedoune would stop at nothing to keep his daughter wed to the Montgomery family. It had been easy to kill the old man once he allowed them, as friends, inside his castle walls. His wife Helen had followed docilely and Arthur laughed, recognizing a well-trained woman when he saw one. He admired Revedoune for that.

"My lord," a nervous servant announced, "there are visitors outside."

"Visitors?" Walter asked, his eyes hazy.

"Yes, my lord. It is the Lady Judith Montgomery, surrounded by her men-at-arms."

Walter jumped up, the writing table upset, as he started after the servant.

Arthur grabbed his arm. "I pray you, my lord, take care. Perhaps it's a trap."

Walter's eyes burned. "What trap could there be? The men won't fight and endanger their lady."

"Perhaps the lady herself . . ."

Walter jerked away from him. "You go too far. Be careful you don't find yourself in the cellar with Lord

Gavin." Stormily, he left the old tower, kicking sawdust-dry rushes out of his way. Arthur's word of caution had penetrated his brain, and now he ran up the narrow stone stairs to the top of the wall in order to be sure it was indeed the Lady Judith who waited below.

There was no mistaking her. The auburn hair that flowed down her back was not to be confused with anyone else's. "It is she," he whispered excitedly, then seemingly flew down the stairs, across the bailey to the front gate.

"Open it, man!" he bellowed to the gatekeeper. "And be quick about it!" The heavy iron-tipped portcullis was drawn upward slowly, Walter waiting impatiently.

"My lord," Arthur said at his side. "You can't let her bring her men inside. There are over a hundred of them. We could be attacked from within."

Walter turned his eyes away from the gate that creaked in protest as it rose. He knew Arthur was right, yet he wasn't sure what else to do.

Arthur fixed the weak blue eyes with his own dark ones. "I will ride out to meet her. You can't be risked. I will ride no farther than the range of the crossbowmen. When I'm sure it is the Lady Judith, my men and I will escort her through the gate."

"Alone?" Walter asked eagerly.

"She may have a personal guard if she so insists, but none other. We cannot allow her whole garrison to enter," he repeated.

The portcullis was up, the drawbridge down as Arthur mounted his horse and rode out, followed by five other knights.

Judith sat very still on her mount as she watched the raising of the gate. It took every ounce of her courage not to turn away. The old castle might be crumbling in places, but it looked very formidable when she was so close to it. She felt as if it was about to swallow her.

"There is time yet to leave, my lady," John Bassett observed as he leaned forward.

Six men were riding toward her, and she very much wanted to turn away. Then her stomach turned over and she had to swallow a sudden attack of nausea. Her child was reminding her of its presence. The baby's father and grandmother were inside those old walls and, if she could, she was going to get them out.

"No," she said to John with more strength than she actually felt. "I must attempt the task."

When the leader of the approaching men was close to Judith, she knew at once that he was the instigator of the whole plot. She remembered Walter as mild and meek but this man's mocking dark eyes showed no weakness. His clothes flashed with jewels; every color, every variety and size. His dark hair was covered by a small velvet cap, whose wide band on it held at least a hundred jewels. It looked almost like a crown.

"My lady," he said, bowing as he sat atop his horse. His smile was mocking, almost insulting.

Judith stared at him, her heart beating quickly. There was a coldness in his eyes that frightened her. He would not be one to easily overrule.

"I am Sir Arthur Smiton, chief vassal to Lord Walter Demari. He bids you welcome."

Welcome! Judith thought, controlling herself not to spit the word at him, thinking of her father butchered, her husband and mother held captive, several lives already lost. She inclined her head toward him. "You hold my mother captive?"

He looked at her speculatively, as if he tried to take her measure. She'd been sent no message, yet she knew what was needed.

"Yes, my lady."

"Then I will go to her." Judith urged her horse forward, but Arthur grabbed the bridle.

To a man, the one hundred knights who surrounded Judith drew their swords.

Arthur didn't lose his smile. "You can't think to enter our gates with so many men."

"You would have me go alone?" she asked, aghast. It was what she'd expected, but perhaps she could persuade Smiton to allow some of her men to accompany her. "You would perhaps have me leave my maid behind? Or my personal guard?"

He watched her intently. "One man. One woman. No more."

She nodded, knowing it was no use to argue. At least John Bassett would be with her. "Joan," she called as she turned and saw the girl eyeing Arthur speculatively. "Prepare the cart with my goods and follow me. John—" She turned and saw that he was already giving orders for the establishment of a camp outside the castle walls.

Judith rode across the drawbridge, under the arched stone gate, with her back straight. She wondered if she would ever leave the walls alive. Walter Demari stood waiting to help her dismount. She remembered him as a gentle young man, neither handsome nor ugly; but now his blue eyes showed weakness, his nose was too big, and his thin lips looked cruel.

He stared at her. "You are even more beautiful than I remembered."

She had dressed carefully that morning. A band of pearls encircled her head. Close to her body she wore a red silk petticoat with a wide border of white fur. Her gown was of maroon velvet, the hem embroidered with gold scrollwork. The sleeves were tight except at the shoulder, where the velvet was slit and the red silk pulled through. The neck was cut deep, her breasts swelling above the fabric. When she walked, she lifted the velvet overskirt and exposed the fur-trimmed silk beneath.

Judith managed to smile at this man of treachery, even as she twisted away from the hands about her waist. "You flatter me, my lord," she said, while looking at him through her lashes.

Walter was enchanted. "You must be tired and in need of refreshment. We would have had food prepared, but you weren't expected."

Judith didn't want him to think about why she came without a request. As she watched Walter's adoring look, she knew she would do well in establishing herself to be a shy young woman, the bashful bride. "Please," she said, her head bowed, "I would like to see my mother."

Walter didn't answer, but continued staring at her, her thick lashes touching her soft cheek, the pearls on her forehead echoing the creaminess of her skin.

John Bassett stepped forward, his jaw rigid. He was a big man, as tall as Gavin, but heavier with age. The steel-gray of his hair only emphasized the hardness of his body. "The lady wishes to see her mother," he said sternly. His voice was even, but it radiated power.

Walter hardly noticed John, he was too enraptured with Judith. But Arthur was very aware of him and recognized danger. John Bassett would need to be disposed immediately. Given the freedom of the castle, such a man could cause much trouble.

"Of course, my lady," Walter said, holding his arm out to her. One would have thought her visit was one of pleasure.

They made their way to the second-floor entrance of the tower; for in time of battle, the wooden steps were cut away to make the entrance several feet from the ground. Judith studied the interior as they walked across the great hall toward the stone steps. It was a filthy place, littered with bits of bone among the dry rushes on the floor. Dogs lazily nosed about the refuse. The deeply recessed windows had no wooden shutters, and in places the stones had fallen away, because the chinking was crumbling. She wondered if such a poor structure was indicative of the guardianship of the place. She meant to find out.

Helen sat in a chair in a little room cut into the thick stone walls on the third floor. Charcoal burned in a brass brazier; the tower had been built before fireplaces were known.

"Mother!" Judith whispered and ran forward to place her head against her mother's knees.

"My daughter," Helen gasped, then pulled Judith into her arms. It was a while before their tears quieted enough so they could speak. "You are well?"

Judith nodded, then looked past her mother to the men who stood there. "Are we to have no privacy?"

"Of course," Walter said then turned toward the door. "You will leave also," he said to John Bassett.

"No. I will not leave my lady alone."

Walter frowned, but he didn't want to upset Judith in any way.

"You should have left with them," Judith said sternly when Walter and Arthur were gone.

John sat heavily in a chair by the charcoal brazier. "I will not leave you alone."

"But I wish for some privacy with my mother!"

John neither spoke nor looked at her.

"He is a stubborn man," Judith said disgustedly to Helen.

"Is it stubborn when I don't let you have your way at all times?" he asked. "You are stubborn enough to rival a bull."

Judith opened her mouth to speak, but Helen's laugh stopped her.

"You are indeed well, my daughter." She turned to John. "Judith is all I have ever wanted her to be, and more," she said fondly, stroking her daughter's hair. "Now tell me why you are here."

"I . . . Oh, Mother," she began, tears starting in her eyes again.

"What is it? You can speak freely."

"No, I cannot!" she said passionately as she looked over at John so close by.

John gave her a look of such blackness that she was almost afraid of him. "Do not doubt my honesty. Talk to your mother. No word of what I hear will be repeated."

Knowing she could trust him, Judith relaxed as she sat on a cushion at her mother's feet. She wanted to talk, desperately needed to talk. "I have broken a vow to God," she said softly.

Helen's hand paused for a moment on her daughter's head. "Tell me of it," she whispered.

The words tumbled over themselves trying to escape. Judith told how she had tried again and again for some degree of love in her marriage, yet she had been thwarted at every effort. Nothing she did could loosen the hold Alice Chatworth had over Gavin.

"And your vow?" Helen asked.

"I vowed I would give nothing to him that he did not take. But I freely went to him the night before he came here." She blushed, thinking of that night of love, Gavin's hands and lips on her body.

"Judith, do you love him?"

"I don't know. I hate him, I love him, I despise him, I adore him. I don't know. He is so big—there is so much of him—that he devours me. I am always aware of him. When he enters a room, he fills it. Even when I hate him the most, when I see him holding another woman or reading a letter from her, I cannot rid myself of him. Is this love?" she asked as she gazed beseechingly up at her mother. "Is it love or merely possession by the devil? He is not kind to me. I'm sure he has no love for me. He has even told me so. The only place he is good to me is—"

"In bed?" Helen smiled.

"Yes," Judith said and looked away, her cheeks red.

It was several moments before Helen replied. "You ask me of love. Who knows less of it than I? Your father also had such a hold on me. Did you know that one time I saved his life? The night before he had beaten me, and the next morning, as I rode out with him, my eye was black and swollen. We rode alone, away from the escort, and Robert's horse bolted and threw him. He fell into the swamp along the north edge of one of the estates. The more he moved, the deeper he sank. My whole body ached from his beating, and my first thought was to ride away and let him die. But I couldn't. Do you know, he laughed at me, called me a fool when I'd saved him?"

She paused a moment. "I tell you this to show you that I understand the way he has a hold on you. So did my husband. I know the power Gavin has over you, for my own marriage was the same. I can't say it was love, and I can't say yours is."

They sat quietly for a moment, both staring at the glowing charcoal.

"And now I rescue my husband as you rescued yours," Judith said. "Even though yours lived to beat you again, and mine will return to another woman."

"Yes," Helen said sadly.

"Did having a child matter?"

Helen considered. "Perhaps if the first ones had lived, but there were three dead, all boys. Then when you came, and you were a girl. . . ." She didn't finish the sentence.

"Do you think it would have mattered had the first one lived and been a son?" Judith persisted.

"I don't know. I don't believe he beat his first wife, who gave him sons. But he was younger then." She stopped abruptly. "Judith! Are you with child?"

"Yes. Two months gone."

John jumped to his feet in a clatter of armor and steel sword against stone. "You have ridden all this way and you are with child!" he demanded. He had been so quiet the two women had forgotten his presence. He put his hand to his forehead. "Hanging will be too good for me. Lord Gavin will torture me, as well I deserve, when he hears of this."

Judith was on her feet instantly, gold eyes blazing. "And who will tell him? You are sworn to secrecy!"

"How do you plan to keep this a secret?" he asked with heavy sarcasm.

"When it must be known, I plan to be far away from this place." Her eyes softened. "You wouldn't tell, would you, John?"

His expression didn't change. "Don't try such cajolery on me. Save it for that fish of a man, Walter Demari."

Helen's laugh interrupted them. It was good to hear her laugh, a sound too seldom heard in her unhappy life. "It does me good to see you like this, my daughter. I was afraid marriage might tame you and break your spirit."

Judith wasn't listening. John had heard too much. She had said too many intimate things in his hearing; now her cheeks were beginning to stain red.

"No," John said, with a sigh. "It would take more than a mere man to tame this one. Don't plead more, child. I will say nothing of what I have heard unless you ask me to."

"Not even to Gavin?"

He gave her a worried look. "I haven't seen him yet. I would give a great deal to know where he is being held, if he is well."

"Judith," Helen said, bringing their attention back to her. "You have yet to tell me why you are here. Did Walter Demari send for you?"

John sat down heavily in the chair. "We are here because the Lady Judith said we must come. She does not listen to reason."

"There was no other way," Judith said as she too sat down again. "What have they told you?" she asked her mother.

"Nothing. I was . . . brought here after Robert's death. I have spoken to no one for a week. Even the maid who empties the chamber pot doesn't speak to me."

"Then you don't know where Gavin is kept?"

"No, I gathered from your words only just now that he too was held. What does Lord Demari hope to gain?"

"Me," Judith said simply, then lowered her eyes before briefly explaining Walter's plan of annulment.

"But there can be no annulment if you carry Gavin's child."

"Yes," Judith said as she looked across her mother to John. "That is one reason it must be kept secret."

"Judith, what will you do? How do you expect to save yourself, Gavin, Joan and your husband's man from this place? You are no foil for stone walls."

John grunted in agreement.

"I don't know," Judith answered exasperatedly. "I could see no alternative. At least now I have a chance of getting you out. But first I must find Gavin. Only then—"

"Did you bring Joan?" Helen interrupted.

"Yes," Judith said, knowing her mother had some idea.

"Tell Joan to find Gavin. If there is a man to find, she can do it. She is little more than a bitch in heat."

Judith nodded.

"And now, what of Walter Demari?" Helen continued.

"I have seen him only a few times."

"Is he to be trusted?"

"No!" John said. "Neither he nor that henchman of his can be trusted."

Judith ignored him. "Demari thinks I am beautiful, and I plan to be beautiful as long as it takes to find Gavin and make an escape."

Helen looked down at her daughter, so lovely in the glow of the coals. "You know so little of men," she observed. "Men are not like account books, where you add the figures and they give you a manageable sum. They are all different . . . and much more powerful than you or I."

Suddenly John rose and looked toward the door. "They return."

"Judith, listen to me," Helen said quickly, "Ask Joan how to deal with Walter. She knows a great deal about men. Promise me you will follow her advice, and don't let your own thoughts sway you."

"I—"

"Promise me!" Helen demanded, her hands holding her daughter's head.

"I will do my best. It is all I can promise."

"Then that must do."

The door burst open and no more words were spoken. Joan and one of the castle maids came to fetch Judith so that she might prepare for supper with his lordship. She hastily bid her mother good-bye, then followed the women, John close behind them.

The fourth floor contained the ladies' solar, a large, airy room, freshly cleaned with new rushes on the floor, new whitewash on the stones, almost as if a guest had been expected. Judith was left alone with her maid, John outside, guarding the door. At least Walter trusted her enough not to assign a spy to her. Joan brought a basin of heated water to her mistress.

As Judith washed her face and hands, she looked at Joan. "Do you know where Lord Gavin is kept?"

"No, my lady," Joan said suspiciously. She was not used to being asked questions by her mistress.

"Could you find out where he is?"

Joan smiled. "I am sure I could. This is a place full of gossipmongers."

"Will you need silver to get this information?"

Joan was shocked. "No, my lady. I will but ask the men."

"And they will tell you just because you asked?"

Joan was gaining confidence. Her lovely mistress knew little beyond running estates and keeping accounts. "It matters much *how* a man is asked."

Judith wore a dress of silver tissue. The skirt parted

in front to reveal a wide expanse of deep green satin. The sleeves were large and bell-shaped, draping gracefully from wrist to halfway down the skirt. The sleeves were lined with more green satin. Her hair was covered with a matching French hood embroidered with silver fleurs-de-lis.

Judith sat down on a stool while Joan arranged the hood. "What if a woman wanted to ask something of Lord Walter?"

"Him!" Joan said heatedly. "I would not trust him, though that Sir Arthur who dogs him is not ill-favored."

Judith whirled to face her maid. "How can you say that? Arthur has such hard eyes. Anyone can see he is a greedy man."

"Lord Walter is not the same?" Joan pushed her mistress's head back around. She was feeling rather superior at the moment. "He is just as greedy, treacherous, brutal, and selfish. He is all of those and more."

"Then why—?"

"Because he is always the same. A woman would know what to expect from him, and that would be whatever suited his needs best. You could deal with that."

"Then Lord Walter is not the same?"

"No, my lady. Lord Walter is a child, yet a man. He changes with the wind. He will want a thing—then, when he has it, he won't want it anymore."

"And this would pertain to women also?"

Joan dropped to her knees before her mistress. "You must hear me and listen well. I know men as I know nothing else in this world. Lord Walter burns for you now. He is mad with desire, and as long as he keeps that rage inside him, you will be safe."

"Safe? I don't understand."

"He has killed your father and taken your mother and your husband as prisoners only because of this passion of his. What do you think would become of all of you were this fire to be doused?"

Judith still didn't understand. When she and Gavin made love, no fires were quenched for longer than a few moments. In truth, the more time she spent in his bed, the more she wanted him.

Joan began to talk with exaggerated patience. "All men are not as Lord Gavin," she said, reading Judith's mind. "If you were to give yourself to Lord Walter, you would have no more hold over him. To men such as him, the game is everything."

Judith was beginning to understand. "How can I keep him from me?" She was fully prepared to give herself to a hundred men if it would save the lives of those she cared for.

"He will not force you. He must believe that he has wooed you and won. You may ask a lot of him and he will give it gladly, but you must be clever about it. He will be jealous. Do not hint that you care for Lord Gavin. Let him think you despise the man. Hold the carrot before his nose, but don't allow him to nibble."

Joan rose from her knees and gave a final critical look to her mistress's gown.

"And what of Sir Arthur?" Judith asked.

"Lord Walter will rule him—and if worse comes to worst, he can be bought."

Judith rose and stared at her maid. "Do you think I will ever learn so much about men?"

"Only when I learn to read," Joan said, then laughed at the impossibility of such a statement. "Why do you need to know of many men when you have Lord Gavin? He is worth all my men together."

As they left the chamber to descend the stairs to the great hall, Judith thought, Do I have Gavin? Do I want him?

Chapter Sixteen

"MY LADY," WALTER SAID AS HE TOOK JUDITH'S HAND and kissed it. She kept her eyes lowered, as if in shyness. "It has been a long time since I saw you last, and you seem to have grown more lovely. Come and sit at the high table with me. We have prepared a late supper for you."

He led her to the long table set on a platform. The tablecloth was old and spotted, and the dishes were of battered pewter. When they were seated, he turned to her. "Your chamber is comfortable?"

"Yes," she answered quietly.

He smiled, puffing his chest out a little. "Come, my lady, you need not fear me."

Fear you! she thought furiously, her eyes meeting his. Then she recovered herself. "It is not fear I feel, but wonder. I am unused to the company of men, and those I have known . . . they have not been kind to me."

He took her hand in his. "I would amend that if I could. I know a lot about you, though you know little of me. Did you know I was a friend of your brothers?"

"No," she said in astonishment, "I didn't. Was it then my father pledged me in marriage to you?" she asked in wide-eyed innocence.

"Yes—no—" Walter stuttered.

"Ah, I understand, my lord. It was after my dear brothers' untimely death."

"Yes! It was then," Walter grinned.

"My poor brothers had so few friends. It was good they had you for a while. And my father! I would not speak ill of the man, but he was forever misplacing things. Perhaps he misplaced the betrothal agreement between us."

"There was no—" Walter began, then took a drink of wine to stop his words. He couldn't admit there had been no such document.

Judith put a tremulous hand on his forearm. "I have said something wrong? You will beat me?"

He quickly turned back to her and saw there were tears in her eyes. "Sweet Judith," he said as he kissed her hand passionately. "What is wrong with the world that a lovely innocent such as you is so terrified of men?"

Ostentatiously, Judith wiped a tear from her eye. "Forgive me. I have known so few and . . ." She lowered her eyes.

"Come, give me a smile. Ask some task or gift from me, and I will give it."

Judith looked up immediately. "I would like to have better quarters for my mother," she said firmly. "Perhaps on the floor with me."

"My lord!" Sir Arthur interrupted from Judith's other side. He had been listening to every word of their conversation. "There is too much freedom on the fourth floor."

Walter frowned. He wanted very much to please his sweet, shy captive, and being reprimanded before her by his man was not a means to that end.

Instantly, Arthur saw his mistake. "I meant, my lord, only that she should have a trustworthy guard near her, for her own sake." He looked at Judith. "Tell me, my lady, if you had only one man to guard you, whom would you choose?"

"Why, John Bassett," she said quickly. She could have bitten her tongue as soon as the words were out.

Arthur gave her a smug look before returning his

gaze to Walter. "There. From the lady's own mouth. She has chosen the guard for Lady Helen."

And leave me without help should I try to escape, Judith thought. Sir Arthur looked at her as if he could read her thoughts.

"An excellent idea!" Walter said. "That pleases you, my lady?"

She could think of no reason to give for keeping John to herself, and perhaps his absence would give her more freedom. "That would please me greatly, my lord," she said sweetly. "I know John will care for my mother well."

"And now we may turn to more pleasant matters. What do you say we ride out and hunt tomorrow?"

"Hunt, my lord? I . . ."

"Yes? You may speak freely to me."

"It is a silly wish."

"Come, tell me," Walter smiled tolerantly.

"I have only recently left my home, and I was always confined to one part of the estates. I have never seen one of these older castles. You will laugh at me!"

"No, I will not," Walter laughed.

"I'd like to see all of it; the mews, the stables, even the buttery."

"Then I shall take you on a full tour tomorrow," he smiled. "It's a simple request, and I would do anything to give you pleasure, my lady." His eyes burned into hers and Judith lowered her lashes, mostly to keep him from seeing the anger that glinted in hers.

"My lord," she said softly, "I find I am very tired. May I be excused?"

"Of course. Your wish is my command." He stood and held her hand as she rose from her chair.

John stood close behind her, his arms folded across his chest. "I would like to speak to my man for a moment," she said, going to him before Walter could answer. "Sir Arthur has made you a guard to my mother," she said without preamble.

"I will not. Lord Gavin—"

"Hush!" she said as she put her hand on his arm. "I don't wish to be heard. What reason would you give that you cannot leave my side? That silly man thinks I am his already."

"He makes advances to you?"

"No, not yet, but he will. You must stay with my mother. I don't believe Sir Arthur will let her out of that damp place if you refuse. She won't be able to stand that much longer."

"You think too much of your mother and too little of yourself."

"No, you are wrong. I am safe, but she could get a bone chill. If I were in the damp, I would demand equal treatment."

"You lie," John said flatly. "You could be safe at home now if you were not so stubborn."

"Do you lecture me *now?*" Judith asked, exasperated.

"It won't do any good. I will go to Lady Helen only if you promise you will do nothing that is foolish."

"Of course. I will even swear it if you wish."

"You are too glib, but there is no time to argue. They come. I will expect messages often. Perhaps it will keep my mind from the tortures Lord Gavin will apply to me."

When Judith and her maid were alone, Joan burst out laughing. "I have never seen such mummery to equal yours tonight!" she laughed. "You would do well in London. Where did you learn the trick of touching your nail to your eye to produce tears?"

Judith drew in her breath sharply. Joan's words brought back a vivid picture of Alice in Gavin's arms. "I learned the trick from a woman who lives by false words," she said grimly.

"Whoever she was, she must have been the best. I was half-convinced by you myself. I hope you got what you wanted."

"You were sure I wanted something?"

"Why else would a woman show tears to a man?"

Judith thought of Alice again. "Why else?" she muttered.

"And did you get what you wanted?" Joan persisted.

"Mostly. But that Arthur tricked me. John has been sent to guard my mother. Guard! Bah! How can two prisoners, locked away, guard each other? My man-at-arms has changed to a lady's maid, put under lock and key, and I am again alone with one more person to try to take from this place."

Joan undid the lacings at Judith's side. "I am sure it was to his best interests to take John from you."

"You are right. But Lord Walter is a fool. The man's tongue runs away with him. I must be more careful that I talk to him only away from Sir Arthur."

"That, my lady, may be the most difficult of all tasks." Joan pulled aside the down-filled covers for her mistress.

"What are you going to do, Joan?" Judith asked as she watched her maid run a comb through her brown hair.

"I will find Lord Gavin," she smiled. Maid and mistress were taking on a more equal role. "I will see you tomorrow, and I'll have news of him then."

Judith hardly heard the door close behind her maid. She thought she was too worried to sleep, but it was not so. She fell asleep almost instantly.

Walter and Arthur stood at one side of the great hall. The tables had been cleared and the men-at-arms spread straw-filled mattresses on the floor for the night.

"I don't trust her," Sir Arthur said under his breath.

"Trust her!" Walter exploded. "How can you say such a thing after you've seen her? She is a delicate flower of a girl. She has been beaten and so mistreated that she fears the slightest frown."

"She didn't seem so frightened when she demanded better quarters for her mother."

"Demanded! She could never demand anything. It isn't in her nature to do so. She was merely concerned for Lady Helen. And that is another example of her sweet nature."

"Such sweet nature obtained a great deal from you tonight. Look at how she had you nearly admit there was no written agreement of marriage from her father."

"What does that matter?" Walter demanded. "She doesn't want her marriage to Gavin Montgomery."

"And what makes you so sure of that?"

"I have heard—"

"Heard! Bah! Then why did she come here? She cannot be so simple that she believes there is no danger for her."

"Do you imply that I would harm her?" Walter demanded.

Arthur stared at him. "Not while she is new to you." He knew Walter well. "You must wed her before you bed her. Only then will you truly own her. If you take her now without the church, she may hate you as you say she hates her husband."

"I don't need advice about women from you! I am the master here. Have you no duties?"

"Yes, my lord," Arthur smirked. "Tomorrow I must help my master show our defenses to our prisoner." He walked away just as Walter threw a wine goblet at his head.

Judith woke very early, while the room was still dark. Immediately she remembered Joan saying that the morning would bring word of Gavin. She threw back the cover hastily, and put her arms through the sleeves of a bedgown of cinnamon brocade from Byzantium. The brocade was woven with lighter flowers in the fabric and was lined with cream cashmere. The straw pallet where Joan was to sleep was empty. Judith clamped her teeth together in anger and suddenly began to worry. Had Joan left her, too? Had Arthur discovered Joan in some act of spying?

The door opened almost silently, and a heavy-lidded

Joan tiptoed through the shadows. "Where have you been!" Judith demanded in a tight whisper.

Joan's hand flew to cover her mouth to still the shriek gathering there. "My lady! You gave me a fright. Why aren't you in bed?"

"You dare to ask *me* why I'm not in bed?" Judith hissed before recovering herself. "Come, tell me of your news. Have you learned anything of Gavin?" Judith took her maid's arm and pulled her to the bed. They both sat cross-legged on the thick feather mattress.

But Joan's eyes didn't look directly into her mistress's intense golden stare. "Yes, my lady, I found him."

"Is he well?" Judith pressed.

Joan took a deep breath and rushed into her description. "It was hard to find him. He is well guarded at all times and the entryway is . . . difficult. But," she smiled, "as luck would have it, one of the guards seemed to like me quite well, and we spent a lot of time together. He is such a man! All night he—"

"Joan!" Judith said sharply. "You are hiding something from me, aren't you? What about my husband? How is he?"

Joan looked at her mistress, started to speak, then dropped her face into her hands. "It is too horrible, my lady. That they could do such a thing to him is beyond belief. He is a nobleman! Even the worst serfs are not treated as he is."

"Tell me," Judith said in a deadly voice. "Tell me everything."

Joan lifted her head, fighting tears and the turning of her stomach. "Few of the castlefolk know he is here. He was brought alone, during the night and . . . thrown below."

"Below?"

"Yes, my lady. There is a space below the cellar— little more than a hole dug out amid the foundations of the tower. The moat water seeps across the floor and things . . . slimy things . . . breed there."

"And this is where Gavin is kept?"

"Yes, my lady," Joan said quietly. "The ceiling of that hole is the cellar floor, and it is high above the hole's floor. The only descent is down a ladder."

"You have seen this place?"

"Yes, my lady." She bowed her head again. "And I have seen Lord Gavin."

Judith grabbed the girl's arms fiercely. "You have seen him and you waited this long to tell me?"

"I didn't believe that . . . that man was Lord Gavin." She looked up, agony etching her face. "He has always been so handsome, so strong, but now there is little more than skin on his bones. His eyes are black circles that burn through you. The guard, the man I spent the night with, opened the trapdoor and held a candle. The stench! I could barely look into the blackness. Lord Gavin—I wasn't at first sure it was he—covered his face from the brightness of just one candle. The floor, my lady—it crawled! There was no dry place on it. How does he sleep? There could be no place to lie down."

"You are sure this man was Lord Gavin?"

"Yes. The guard's whip licked at him, and he drew his hand away and stared up at us in hatred."

"Did he know you?"

"I don't think so. I feared that at first, but now I believe him to be beyond recognizing anyone."

Judith looked away in thought.

Joan touched her arm. "My lady, it is too late. He's not long for this world. He can't last for more than a few days, at most. Forget him. He is worse than dead."

Judith gave her a hard look. "Didn't you just say he is alive?"

"Only barely. Even if he were taken out today, the sunlight would kill him in moments."

Judith left the bed. "I must dress."

Joan looked at her mistress's straight back. She was glad she'd given up any idea of rescue. The shrunken, emaciated face still haunted her. Still, Joan was suspicious. She'd lived with Judith too long, and she knew her little mistress rarely let a problem go unsolved. There were times when Joan had been completely exhausted from arranging and rearranging some matter so that Judith could see it from all angles. Yet Judith never gave up. If she set her mind to the harvesting of a field before a certain date, it was harvested by then, even if Judith herself had to help in the threshing.

"Joan, I will need a garment of russet, very dark, like the serfs wear. And some boots—tall ones. It won't matter if they're too large—for I can lace them tight. And a bench. Make sure it is a long one, but narrow enough to fit through the trapdoor. Also, I will need an ironbound box. Not too big, but one I can strap to my stomach."

"Stomach?" Joan managed to get out. "You can't think— Haven't I explained to you that he is nearly dead, that he can't be rescued? You can't take a bench to him and think no one will notice. Food, perhaps, but—" Judith's look stopped her. She was a small woman, but when those gold eyes turned as hard as that, there was no disobeying her. "Yes, my lady," Joan said meekly. "A bench, boots, a servant's garments and . . . an iron box to fit your stomach," she said sarcastically.

"Yes, to fit my stomach," Judith said without humor. "Now help me dress." She lifted a yellow silk underdress from the large chest by the bed. There were twenty pearl buttons running from wrist to elbow. Over it she slipped a gown of tawny gold velvet with wide, hanging sleeves. A belt of brown silk cords threaded with pearls hung from her waist to the ground.

Joan took an ivory comb and began to arrange her mistress's hair. "Don't let him know you care anything for Lord Gavin."

"I don't need to be told that. Go now and find the things I want. And don't let anyone see you with them."

"I can't carry a bench about in secrecy."

"Joan!"

"Yes, my lady, I will do as I am told."

Hours later after he'd spend the morning escorting her through stables and dairies Walter said, "My lady, you must be tired; surely all this must have little interest for you."

"Oh, but it does!" Judith smiled. "The walls are so thick," she said with wide-eyed innocence. The castle was of the simplest form. It contained one large four-story stone tower set inside a single twelve-foot-thick wall. There were a few men atop the walls, but they looked sleepy and not very alert.

"Perhaps my lady would like to inspect the armor of the knights and look for flaws," Arthur said as he watched her.

Judith managed to keep her face blank. "I don't understand what you mean, sir," she said in confusion.

"Nor do I, Arthur!" Walter added.

Arthur didn't answer, but merely stared at Judith. She knew she had an enemy. He had easily seen through her interest in the fortifications. She turned to Walter, "I believe I'm more tired than I thought. It was indeed a long journey here. Perhaps I should rest."

"Of course, my lady."

Judith wanted to get away from him, be rid of his hand, so often on her arm or her waist. Gratefully, she left him at her chamber door. She fell upon the bed fully dressed. All morning her mind had been full of what Joan had told her of Gavin. She could imagine him half-dead from the filth of the hideous place where he was kept.

The door opened, but she paid it no attention. A noblewoman was rarely allowed privacy. Maids always slipped in and out of her room. She gasped when a male hand touched her neck.

"My lord Walter!" she cried, looking quickly about the room.

"Have no fear," he said quietly. "We are alone. I've seen to that. The servants know my punishments are harsh if I'm disobeyed."

Judith was flustered.

"Do you fear me?" he asked, his eyes dancing. "You have no need to. Don't you know I love you? I have loved you since I first saw you. I waited in the procession that followed you to church. Shall I tell you how you looked to me?" He picked up a curl of her hair and wound it around his arm. "You stepped into the sunlight, and it was as if that light darkened when presented with your greater radiance. Your gold dress, your gold eyes."

He held up the strand of hair, rubbing it with the fingers of his other hand against his palm. "How I wanted to touch this fine stuff then. It was then that I knew you were meant to be mine. Yet you married another!" he accused.

Judith was frightened, not of him or what he could do to her, but of what she'd lose if he took her now. She buried her face in her hands as if she were weeping.

"My lady! My sweet Judith. Forgive me. What have I done?" Walter asked in bewilderment.

She made an effort to recover herself. "I am the one to ask forgiveness. It is just that men . . ."

"Men what? You can tell me. I am your friend."

"Are you?" she asked, her eyes pleading and excessively innocent.

"Yes," Walter whispered, devouring her as best he could.

"I have never had a man friend before. First my father and my brother's—No! I won't speak ill of them."

"There is no need," Walter said as he touched the back of her hand with his fingertips. "I knew them well."

"And then my husband!" Judith said fiercely.

Walter blinked at her. "Do you dislike him then? Is it true?"

Her eyes flashed as she looked at him with such hatred he was taken aback. It was almost as if it were meant for him instead of her husband.

"All men are the same!" she said angrily. "They want only one thing from a woman, and if she doesn't give it, she is forced. Do you know how vile rape is to a woman?"

"No, I—" Walter was confused.

"Men know little of the finer things of life—music and art. I wish I could believe there was a man somewhere on earth who didn't paw at me and make demands."

Walter gave her a shrewd look. "And if you found such a man how would you reward him?"

She smiled sweetly. "I would love him with all my heart," she said simply.

He raised her hand to his lips and kissed it tenderly. Judith lowered her eyes. "Then I will hold you to that," he said quietly. "For I would do a lot to have your heart."

"It has belonged to no one else," Judith whispered.

He released her hand and stood. "Then I will leave you to your rest. Remember, I'm your friend and I will be near if you need me."

As he left the room, Joan slipped inside. "Lady Judith! He hasn't . . . ?"

"No, nothing happened," she said as she leaned back against the headboard. "I talked him out of what he wanted."

"Talked! You must tell me—. No, do not. I would never need to know how to talk a man from making love to me. Whatever you did was good. Can you keep him from you, though?"

"I don't know. He thinks I'm a cowering simpleton, and I don't know how long I can keep up the deception. I hate myself when I lie like that!" Judith turned to her maid. "Is everything prepared for tonight?"

"Yes, though it wasn't easy."

"You will be well rewarded when we leave here, if we

do. Now find some other women and prepare me a bath. I must scrub wherever that man has touched me."

John Bassett paced the floor of the room, his footsteps heavy. The toe of his soft slippers caught at something buried in the rushes, and he kicked at it in wrath. A beef bone, old and dry, went flying against the far wall. "A lady's maid." he cursed. Locked inside a room, allowed no freedom, his only company a woman who cowered from him.

Truthfully, it wasn't her fault that he was there. He turned and looked at her, huddled under a coverlet before the brazier. He knew her long skirts hid a badly sprained ankle which she had not allowed her daughter to see.

Suddenly his anger left him. It did him no good to let it eat at him. "I am poor company," he said as he moved a stool to the far side of the brazier and sat down. Helen looked at him with frightened eyes. He knew of her husband, and he was ashamed that he also had scared her. "It's not you who angers me, but that daughter of yours. How could a quiet and sensible woman such as yourself breed such a stubborn wench? She sought to rescue two prisoners, but now she has three to save—and with no more help than that hot-blooded maid of hers."

He turned and saw Helen was smiling, a smile of pure pride. "You take pride in such a daughter?" he asked, astonished.

"Yes, I do. She is afraid of nothing. And she always thinks of others first."

"She should have been taught to fear," John said fiercely. "Fear is good at times."

"If she were yours, how would you have taught her?"

"I would have—" John began. Obviously, beating was not the answer; he was sure Robert Revedoune had caused her a great deal of pain. He turned to Helen and smiled. "I don't believe she could have been taught. But if she were mine . . ." He smiled more broadly. "I would be proud of her, if she were mine. Though I doubt such beauty could have come from something as ugly as me."

"Oh, but you are not the least ugly," Helen said, her cheeks turning pink.

John stared at her, not having really looked at her before. The first time he'd seen her, at the wedding, he'd dismissed her as being haggard and plain, but now he could see she was neither. A month away from Robert Revedoune had done her much good. She didn't seem so nervous as before, and her hollow cheeks were filling out. Except for the widow's peak, her hair was covered, but he could see it was auburn, darker than her daughter's. And her eyes seemed to have tiny gold flecks in them.

"You stare at me, sir?"

With his usual bluntness, John said what he thought. "You are not old."

"I will be thirty-three years old this year," she answered. "That is an old woman."

"Bah! I remember a forty-year-old woman who—" He stopped and smiled. "Perhaps I shouldn't tell a lady that story. But thirty-three years is far from being old." He had an idea. "Do you know you are a rich woman now? You are a widow with great estates. Soon you will have men pounding at your door."

"No," she laughed, her cheeks flaming. "You jest."

"A rich as well as a beautiful widow," he teased. "Lord Gavin will have to cut through them to find you a husband."

"Husband?" Helen suddenly sobered.

"Here!" John commanded. "Don't look like that. Few are like that villain you married."

She blinked at what she should have considered rudeness; but coming from John, it was a statement of fact.

"Lord Gavin will find a good man for you."

She stared at him as if in speculation. "Were you ever married, John?"

He waited a moment before answering. "Yes, once when I was very young. She died of the plague."

"No children?"

"No. None."

"Did you . . . love her?" Helen asked timidly.

"No," he responded honestly. "She was a simple-minded child. It has long been a fault of mine that I cannot bear stupidity—in a man or a horse or a woman." He chuckled at some private thought. "Once I made a boast that I would lay my heart before a woman who could play a good game of chess. Do you know, I even once played a game with Queen Elizabeth?"

"And did she win?"

"No," he said in disgust. "She couldn't keep her mind on the game. I tried to teach Gavin and his brothers the game, but they are worse than some women. Only their father gave me a challenge."

Helen looked at him seriously. "I know the game. At least I know the moves."

"You?"

"Yes. I taught Judith to play, though she could never beat me. She was as the queen, always worrying about another problem. She couldn't give the proper concentration the game deserved."

John hesitated.

"If we are to spend some time here, perhaps you can give me lessons. I would appreciate any help."

John sighed. Maybe it was a good idea at that. At least it would help pass the time.

Chapter Seventeen

JUDITH'S CHAMBER WAS AS QUIET AS THE REST OF THE
Demari castle when she began her preparations to go to
Gavin in the pit.

"Give the guard this," Judith said as she handed Joan
a skin of wine, "and he will sleep through the night. We
could set barrels of oil on fire next to him, and he won't
wake."

"Which is what will happen when Lord Gavin sees
you," Joan muttered.

"I thought you believed him to be nearly dead. Now
don't talk any more, but do as I say. Is everything
ready?"

"It is. Are you feeling better?" Joan asked concerned.

Judith nodded, swallowing hard in memory of her
recent nausea.

"If you have kept anything down, you will lose it
when you step into that vile pit."

Judith ignored her comment. "Go now and give the
man his wine. I will wait a short time, then follow you."

Joan slipped silently from the room, an art she'd
learned through long years of practice. Judith waited
nervously for nearly an hour. She strapped the iron box
about her stomach, then slipped the rough wool
garment over her head. Had anyone noticed the serf
walking quietly amid the sleeping knights, they would

have seen a heavily pregnant woman, her hands at her lower back, supporting the burdensome weight of her belly. Judith had some difficulty managing the railless stone stairs that led to the cellar.

"My lady?" Joan called in a loud whisper.

"Yes." Judith made her way toward the single candle flame that Joan held. "Is he asleep?"

"Yes. Can't you hear him snoring?"

"I can hear nothing over my pounding heart. Set the candle down and help me unstrap this box."

Joan sank to her knees as Judith lifted her skirts to her waist. "Why did you need the box?" Joan asked.

"To store the food. To keep the . . . rats from it."

Joan shivered as her cold hands worked at the knots of rawhide. "There are more than rats down there. My lady, please—it isn't too late to change your mind."

"Are you saying you will go in my place?"

Joan's gasp of horror was her answer.

"Quiet, then. Think of Gavin who has to live there."

As the two women pulled the trapdoor back from the pit, the foul air made them turn their heads away. "Gavin!" Judith called. "Are you there?"

No answer came.

"Give me the candle."

Joan handed her mistress the taper and looked away. She didn't wish to look in the pit again.

Judith searched the black hole with the light. She had steeled herself for the worst, and she wasn't disappointed. Yet Joan had been wrong about the floor. It was not totally devoid of dry area—or at least comparatively dry. The dirt floor sloped away from the stone walls so that one corner was mere mud rather than the slime-infested water. In this corner Judith saw a hunched figure. Only the eyes that glared at her told her the heap was alive.

"Give me the ladder, Joan. When I'm on the bottom, send the bench down, then the food and wine. You understand?"

"I don't like this place."

"Neither do I." It wasn't easy for Judith to descend that ladder into hell. She dared not look down. There was no need to see what was on the floor; she could smell and hear the slithering movements. She set the candle on a jutting stone of the wall but didn't look at Gavin. She knew he worked to push himself upward.

"The bench now," Judith called up. It wasn't easy to maneuver the heavy piece down the ladder, and she knew Joan's arms were nearly pulled from their sockets. It was easier to lift it and set it against the wall next to Gavin. The box of food came next, followed by a large skin of wine.

"There," she said as she set the items on the edge of the bench then took a step toward her husband. She knew why Joan said he was near death. He was emaciated, his high cheekbones razor-sharp.

"Gavin," she said quietly and held her hand out to him, palm up.

He moved his thin and filthy hand slowly to touch her, as if he expected her to disappear. When he felt her warm flesh against his, he looked back at her in surprise. "Judith." The word was harsh, his voice hoarse from long disuse and a parched throat.

She took his hand firmly to hers than pulled him to sit on the bench. She held the skin of wine to his lips. It was a while before he understood he was to drink. "Slowly," Judith said as he began to gulp the heavy, sweet liquid. She put the wineskin down, then took a stoppered jar from the box and began to feed him rich, filling stew. The meat and vegetables had been cooked to a pulp easy for him to chew.

He ate little before he leaned back against the wall, his eyes closed in weariness. "It has been a long time since I have had food. A man doesn't appreciate what he has until it is taken from him." He rested a moment, then sat up again and stared at his wife. "Why are you here?"

"To bring you food."

"No, I don't mean that. Why are you in Demari's holdings?"

"Gavin, you should eat and not talk. I'll tell you everything if you will only eat more." She gave him a chunk of dark bread dipped in the stew.

Once again he turned his attention to eating. "Are my men above?" he asked, his mouth full. "I think I may have forgotten how to walk, but when I have eaten more, I will be stronger. They shouldn't have sent you down here."

Judith hadn't realized that her presence would make Gavin believe he was free. "No," she said as she blinked back tears. "I can't take you from here . . . yet."

"Yet?" He looked up at her. "What are you saying?"

"I am alone, Gavin. There are no men above. You are still a captive of Walter Demari, as is my mother, and now John Bassett."

He stopped eating, his hand paused above the jar. Abruptly, as if she had said nothing, he resumed. "Tell me all," he said flatly.

"John Bassett told me Demari had captured you and my mother. John saw no way to win you back except through siege." She stopped, as if finished with the story.

"So you came here and thought to save me?" He looked at her, his sunken eyes hot.

"Gavin, I—"

"And, pray, what good did you hope to do? To draw a sword and run them through and order my release?"

She clamped her jaw shut.

"I will have John's head for this."

"That is what he said," she muttered.

"What?"

"I said John knew you would be angry."

"Angry?" Gavin said. "My estates are left unguarded, my men are left leaderless, my wife is held prisoner by an insane man, and you say I am angry? No, wife, I am far more than angry."

Judith straightened her back, clenched her jaw. "There was no other way. A siege would have killed you."

"A siege, yes," he said fiercely, "but there are other ways to take this place than by siege."

"But John said—"

"John! He is a knight, not a leader. His father followed mine, as he follows me. He should have gone for Miles or even Raine, with his broken leg. I will kill John the next time I see him!"

"No, Gavin. He is not at fault. I told him I would go alone if he didn't bring me."

The candle made her eyes glow. The woolen hood had fallen away from her hair.

"I had forgotten how beautiful you are," he said quietly. "Let's not quarrel anymore. We can't change what has been done. Tell me what is happening above."

She told him of how she'd gotten better quarters for her mother, yet had also succeeded in getting John made prisoner. "But it is as well," she continued. "He wouldn't have allowed me down here."

"I wish he hadn't. Judith, you shouldn't have set foot in this place."

"But I had to bring you food!" she protested.

He stared at her, then sighed. He began to smile at her. "I pity John's having to deal with you."

She looked at him in surprise. "He said the same of you. Have I done so very wrong?"

"Yes," Gavin answered honestly. "You have put more people in danger, and any rescue now will be much more difficult."

She looked down at her hands.

"Come, look at me. It has been a long time since I saw anything that is even clean." He handed her the empty jar.

"I brought more food and a metal box to keep it in."

"And a bench," he said as he shook his head. "Judith, do you realize Demari's men will know who has sent these things when they see them? You must take them back."

"No! You need them."

He stared at her. All he'd done was complain about her. "Judith," he whispered, "thank you." He put his hand up, as if to touch her cheek, but stopped.

"You are annoyed with me," she said flatly, thinking that was why he wouldn't touch her.

"I don't want to soil you. I am more than filthy. I feel things crawl on my skin even now as you sit so close to me."

She took his hand and guided it to her cheek. "Joan said you were little more than alive, but she also said you looked up at the guard with defiance. If you still hated, you couldn't be so near death." She leaned toward him and he touched his mouth to hers. She had to content herself with that; he would not contaminate her further with his touch.

"Listen to me, Judith. You must obey me. I will brook no disobedience, do you understand? I'm not John Bassett you can twist about your fingers. And if you disobey me, it will no doubt cost many lives. Do you understand?"

"Yes," she nodded. She wanted guidance.

"Before I was taken, Odo was able to reach Stephen in Scotland."

"Your brother?"

"Yes, you don't know him. He will be told all of what Demari has done. Stephen will come soon. He is an experienced fighter, and these old walls won't stand long before him. But it will take days for him to travel from Scotland—even if the messenger can find him quickly."

"So what am I to do?"

"You should have stayed at home and waited with your embroidery frame," he said in disgust. "Then we would have had time. Now you must buy us time.

Agree to nothing Demari says. Talk to him of women's things, but don't talk to him of annulment or your estates."

"He thinks I'm a simpleton."

"Deliver all men from such simple women! Now you must go."

She stood. "I will bring more food tomorrow."

"No! Send Joan. No one will notice that cat slipping from one bed to the next."

"But I will come in disguise."

"Judith, who else has hair the color of yours? If one strand were to escape, you would be recognized. And if you were found out, there would be no reason to keep the rest of us alive. Demari must think you will comply with his plans. Now go and obey me for once."

She stood and nodded as she turned toward the ladder.

"Judith," he whispered. "Would you kiss me again?"

She smiled happily and before he could stop her, her arms were about his waist, holding him close to her. She could feel the change in his body, the weight he'd lost. "I have been frightened, Gavin," she confessed.

He lifted her chin in his hand. "You are braver than ten men." He kissed her longingly. "Now go and don't come again."

She nearly ran up the ladder and out of the dark cellar.

Chapter Eighteen

THE CASTLE WAS QUIET WHEN ARTHUR FINALLY ALLOWED his anger to explode. He knew he should have kept his temper under control, but he'd seen too much in one day.

"You are a fool!" Arthur said with a sneer. "Don't you see how the woman plays you like a master harper plays a psaltery?"

"You overstep yourself," Walter warned.

"Someone must! You're so besotted by her that she could slip a knife between your ribs and you would murmur, 'Thank you.'"

Walter suddenly looked into his cup of ale. "She is a sweet and lovely woman," he murmured.

"Sweet! Bah! She is as sweet as verjuice. She has been here three days, and look at how far you have gotten with negotiations for an annulment. What does she say when you ask her?" He didn't give Walter time to reply. "That woman has a convenient hearing loss. At times she just looks at you and smiles when you ask her a question. You would think she is both deaf and dumb. You never press her, but only return her smile with a mindless one of your own."

"She is a beautiful woman," Walter said in defense.

"Yes, she is enticing," Arthur acknowledged and smiled to himself. Judith Montgomery was beginning to stir his blood also, though not in the holy way she affected Walter. "But what has her beauty accomplished? You are no nearer your goal than when she arrived."

Walter slammed down his goblet. "She is a woman, damn you, not a man you can reason with! She must be wooed and won. Women must be loved. And there is her father and that vile husband of hers. They have frightened her."

"Frightened!" Arthur snorted. "I have never seen a woman less frightened in my life. A frightened woman would have stayed home in her bed behind her castle walls. This one comes riding to our gate and—"

"And asks for nothing!" Walter said triumphantly. "She has asked for nothing but better quarters for her mother, a simple request. She spends her days with me and is pleasant company. Judith has not so much as asked about the fate of her husband. Surely that shows she doesn't care about him."

"I'm not so sure," Arthur said thoughtfully. "It seems unnatural for her to care so little about him."

"She hates him, I tell you! I don't see why you don't kill him and be done with it. I would wed her atop the dead man's corpse if the priest would allow it."

"Then you would have the king upon your head! She is a rich woman. Her father had the right to give her to a man, but now he is dead. No one else has the right except the king. The moment her husband is dead, she becomes the king's ward, the revenues from her estates his. Do you think King Henry would give a rich widow to the man who tortured and killed her husband? And if you took her without his permission, he would be even more angry. I've told you time and again: the only way is if she stands before the king and asks publicly for a release from her marriage and declares for you. King Henry loves the queen and is greatly moved by such sentimentality."

"Then I am proceeding properly," Walter said. "I'm making the woman love me. I can see it in her eyes when she looks at me."

"I say again, you are a fool. You see what you wish. I am not so certain that she doesn't scheme something. A plan of escape, perhaps."

"Escape from me? I don't hold her captive. She is free to go when she wants."

Arthur looked at the man with revulsion. He was not only a fool, but stupid as well. If Arthur were not cautious, all his carefully laid plans would be destroyed by a golden-eyed goddess. "You say she hates her husband?"

"Yes. I know she does."

"Do you have proof other than servants' gossip?"

"She never speaks of him."

"Perhaps the love she bears him hurts her too much to speak of him," Arthur said snidely. "Perhaps we should put her hatred to a test."

Walter hesitated.

"You're not so sure of her now?"

"I am! What do you plan?"

"We will bring her husband up from the pit, bring him before her and see her reaction. Will she cry in horror to see him as he must be now? Or will she be glad to see him so tortured?"

"She will be glad," Walter said firmly.

"Let us hope you are right. But I believe you are not."

The new quarters Judith had gotten for Lady Helen were large, airy and cleaner. A stout wooden partition had been nailed into the walls of the fourth-floor solar, creating the room. It was secluded from the rest of the castle, protected by a door of four-inch-thick seasoned oak.

There was little furniture. A large bed draped with heavy linen occupied one corner. A straw pallet was on the other side of the chamber. Two people sat across from the glowing brazier, their heads nearly touching over a chessboard set on a low table.

"You have won again!" John Bassett said in astonishment.

Helen smiled at him. "You seem pleased."

"Yes, I am. At least these days haven't been dull." During the time they had been together he'd seen many changes in her. She had gained weight; her cheeks were losing their hollows. And she had begun to relax in his presence. Her eyes no longer darted from side to side. In truth, they rarely left John.

"Do you think my daughter is well?" Helen asked as she set the chess pieces back in their original positions.

"I can only guess. If she had been harmed, I think we would know. I don't think Demari will lose much time in seeing that we suffer the same fate."

Helen nodded. She found John's harsh truthfulness refreshing after having lived with lies for so long. She hadn't seen Judith since that first night, and had it not been for John's steadiness, she would have worried herself into illness. "Another game?"

"No. I must have a rest from your attacks."

"It is late. Perhaps . . ." she began, not wanting to go to bed and leave his company.

"Will you sit by me a moment?" he asked as he rose and stirred the coals in the brazier.

"Yes," she smiled. This was the part of the day she loved the best—being carried from one place to another in John's strong arms. She was quite sure her ankle was well, but he didn't ask after it, and she did not mention it.

He looked down at her head cradled against his shoulder. "You look more like your daughter each day," he said as he carried her to a chair closer to the fire. "It's easy to see where she gets her beauty."

Helen didn't speak, but smiled against his shoulder, delighting in the strength of him. He had no more than deposited her in the chair when the door burst open.

"Mother!" Judith said as she rushed to Helen's open arms.

"I have been worried about you," Helen said anxiously. "Where have they kept you? They haven't harmed you?"

"What news?" John's deep voice interrupted.

Judith pulled away from her mother. "No, I am unharmed. I couldn't come because I've had no time. Walter Demari keeps me at something every moment. If I mention a visit to you, he finds someplace I must go." She sat down on a stool John placed behind her. "As for the news, I have seen Gavin."

Neither John nor Helen spoke.

"They keep him in a hole below the cellar. It is a slimy place, and he cannot live much longer in it. I went to him and—"

"You went into the pit?" Helen asked, astonished. "Not while you carry a child! You endangered the baby!"

"Quiet!" John commanded. "Let her tell of Lord Gavin."

Judith looked at her mother, who usually cowered away from a man's sharp tones, but Helen only obeyed and showed no fear. "He was very angry at me for being here and said that he had already arranged for our rescue. His brother Stephen has been sent for."

"Lord Stephen?" John asked, then smiled. "Ah yes. If we can hold out until he comes, we will be saved. He is a good fighter."

"That is what Gavin said. I am to keep Demari from me as long as I can, to give Stephen time to bring his men."

"What else did Lord Gavin say?"

"Very little. He spent most of the time listing all that is wrong with me," Judith said in disgust.

"And are you able to keep Demari from you?" Helen wondered.

Judith sighed. "It's not easy. If he touches my wrist, his hand slides to my elbow. A hand on my waist rides up my ribs. I don't respect the man. If he were to sit down and talk reasonably to me, I would sign half the

Revedoune lands over to him for a copper if he would only free us all. Instead he offers me daisy chains and love poems. There are times when I want to scream in frustration."

"What of Sir Arthur?" John asked. "I cannot see that man making daisy chains."

"No, he just watches me. I am never away from his eyes staring at me. I feel there is something he plans, but I don't know what."

"It will be the worst, I'm sure," John said. "I wish I could help you!"

"No, there is nothing I need help with now. I can only wait for Lord Stephen to arrive and negotiate or fight—whichever must be done. I will talk with him then."

"Talk?" John raised one eyebrow. "Stephen is little given to talking over his battle plans with women."

A knock sounded on the door. "I must go. Joan waits for me. I'm not sure I want Demari to know I'm here."

"Judith." Helen grabbed her daughter's arm. "You are caring for yourself?"

"As well as I can. I am tired—that's all." She kissed her mother's cheek. "I must go."

When they were alone, John turned to Helen. "Here, don't cry," he said sternly. "It will help nothing."

"I know," Helen agreed. "She is just so alone. She has always been alone."

"And what of you—have you not also always been alone?"

"I don't matter. I am an old woman."

He grabbed her harshly under her arms and pulled her to him. "You are not old!" John said fiercely before his mouth came down on hers.

Helen had been kissed by no man except her husband—and him only at the beginning of their marriage. She was startled by the chill that ran up her spine. She returned his kiss, her arms going about his neck, drawing him closer to her.

He kissed her cheek, her neck, his heart pounding in his ears. "It is late," he whispered, then swung her into his arms and carried her toward the bed. Each night he helped her unbutton her simple gown since she had no other maid. He was always respectful and kept his eyes turned away when she climbed into bed. Now he set her on her feet by the bed, then turned to walk away.

"John," she called, "you will not help me with the buttons?"

He looked back at her, his eyes dark with passion. "Not tonight. If I were to help you undress, you wouldn't climb into that bed alone."

Helen stared at him, the blood pounding through her body. Her experiences with a man in bed had been brutal times. But now she gazed at John and knew he would be different. What would it be like to lie happily in a man's arms? She could hardly hear her own voice when she spoke. "I will still need help."

He walked to stand before her. "Are you sure? You are a lady. I am only your son-in-law's vassal."

"You have come to mean a lot to me, John Bassett, and now I would have you be all."

He touched the hood at her forehead, then pushed it away completely. "Come, then," he smiled. "Let me see those fastenings."

In spite of Helen's brave words, she was afraid of John. She had grown to love him over the last few days, and she wanted to give him something. She had nothing except her body. She gave herself as a martyr. She knew men received great pleasure from the joining in bed, but for her it had only been a quick, rather messy affair. She had no idea it could be any different.

She was surprised when he took his time undressing her. She thought a man would have thrown her skirts over her face and been done with it. John seemed to enjoy touching her. His fingers along her ribs sent little shivers through her skin. He lifted her dress over her head, then her underdress. He stepped away from her and looked at her as she stood wearing only the thin cotton chemise and her hose. He smiled warmly at her as if her body pleased him. He put his hands on her waist, then lifted the chemise away. His hands were on her breasts instantly, and Helen gasped in pleasure at his touch. He brought his lips to hers. She kept her eyes open as she stared in wonder. His gentleness sent waves of delight through her body. Her breasts ached against the rough wool of his doublet. She closed her eyes and leaned against him, her arms tightening. Never had she experienced this feeling before.

John pulled away from her and began to remove his clothing. Helen's heart was pounding. "Let me," she heard herself say, then drew back at her own boldness. John smiled at her with just the expression she was feeling—rising passion.

She'd never undressed a man before, except to help a visitor who she was helping to bathe. John's body was stout and muscular, and she touched his skin as each garment fell to the floor. Her breasts touched his arm, sending little sparks through her body.

When John was nude, he lifted Helen in his arms and carefully placed her in bed. She had a moment's regret that now the pain would begin and the pleasure end. John lifted her foot and set it in his lap. As Helen watched breathlessly, he untied her garter and rolled the cotton stockings off, kissing her leg every inch of the way. By the time he reached her toes, Helen could no longer hold herself up. Her body was strangely weak, her heart was now hammering in her throat. She reached her arms out for him to come to her, but he would not.

He reached for her other leg. Helen knew she could bear no more. Her body was beginning to ache for him. John laughed throatily and pushed away her clutching hands. It was an eternity before he'd kissed the other stocking off.

Helen lay back against the pillows, weakly. John came to her, kissed her, and her hands buried themselves into his shoulders. He ran his hand firmly down her side and pulled away her underpants. She pressed against him, could feel that he was ready for her. But John was not through with his torture of her. His head bent to her breasts, his tongue and teeth making little nibbles on the hard pink crests. Helen moaned, her head moving from side to side on the pillow.

John slowly moved a leg on top of her, then his whole weight. How good he felt! He was so strong and heavy. When he entered her, she cried out. She felt that she may as well be a virgin for all the experience she'd had in pleasure. Her husband had used her body, but John made love to her.

Her passion was as fierce as John's, and they came together in a fiery explosion. He pulled her close to him, his arm and one leg thrown across her as if he thought she'd try to escape. Helen burrowed herself even closer to him. If possible, she would have liked to slip inside his skin. Her body began to relax in the delicious pleasure of the aftermath of a night of love. She fell asleep with John's soft breath in her ear and on her neck.

Judith sat at the high table between Walter and Arthur. She picked at her food, unable to choke down the poorly cooked meal. But had it been the best food, it would not have mattered. She wore a cream silk undertunic and over it a gown of royal blue velvet. The large, hanging sleeves of the gown were lined with blue satin which was embroidered with tiny gold half-moons. A gold filigree belt with a buckle set with a single large cabochon sapphire was about her waist.

Walter's hands constantly touched her. They were on her wrists, her arm, her neck. He didn't seem to realize they were in a public place. But Judith was very aware of the twenty-five knights who unabashedly stared at her. She could feel the speculation in their eyes. As she jabbed her fork into a piece of beef, she wished it were Walter's heart. It was a difficult thing to swallow one's pride.

"Judith," Walter whispered hoarsely into her ear. "I could devour you." He pressed his lips to her neck, and she could feel shudders of revulsion shaking her. "Why do we wait? Can't you feel my love for you? Don't you know of my desire for you?"

Judith kept herself stiff, refusing to allow herself to pull her body away. He nibbled at her neck, nuzzled her shoulder and she couldn't show how she felt. "My lord," she managed to say after several hard swallows, "don't you remember your own words? You said we must wait."

"I cannot," he choked. "I cannot wait for you."

"But you must!" Judith said with more anger than she had intended and jerked her hand from his violently. "Listen to me. What if I give in to my passions for you and go to your bed? Don't you think a child would be made? What will the king say when we appear before him with my belly swollen? Do you think anyone would believe the child is not my husband's? No annulment can be had if I carry his child. And you know a divorce must come from the pope. I have heard that one takes years."

"Judith—" Walter began, then stopped. Her words made sense. They also appealed to his vanity. How well he remembered Robert Revedoune saying that he gave his daughter to the Montgomery men to get sons. He knew he—Walter—could give her sons! She was right. If they were to come together, they would create a son in the first mating. He took a deep drink of wine, his mind mixed with pride and frustration.

"When do we go to the king, my lord?" Judith asked bluntly. Perhaps she could arrange an escape on their journey.

They sat at the dinner table, but Walter paid little attention to his audience. Now Arthur spoke. "Are you anxious to declare your desire for an annulment to the king?"

She didn't answer him.

"Come, my lady, we are your friends. You can speak

freely. Is your passion for Lord Walter so deep that you cannot wait to declare it to the world?"

"I don't like your tone," Walter interjected. "She has nothing to prove. She is a guest, not a prisoner. She was not forced to come here."

Arthur smiled, his eyes narrowed. "Yes, she came freely," he said in a loud voice. Then, as he reached past Judith for a cut of meat, he lowered his voice. "But why did my lady come? I have yet to have an answer."

The meal seemed horribly long to Judith and she couldn't wait to leave. When Walter turned his back to her to speak to his steward, Judith seized the opportunity to get up from the table. She ran up the stairs, her heart pounding wildly. How much longer could she hold out against Walter Demari? Each minute his advances became more forward. She stopped running and leaned against the cold stone wall, trying to recover herself. Why did she always believe she could handle everything by herself?

"There you are!"

Judith looked up to see Arthur standing near her. They were alone in a deep recess of the thick walls.

"Are you looking for an escape route?" he smirked. "There is none. We are quite alone." His strong arm reached out and encircled her waist, pulling her close to him. "Where is that ready tongue of yours? Are you going to try to talk me out of touching you?" His hand ran over her arm, caressing it. "You are lovely enough to cause a man to lose his mind. I almost understand Walter's reluctance to bed you." He looked back at her face. "I see no fear in those gold eyes, but I would like to see them blaze with the heat of passion. Do you think I could make them do so?"

His hard lips swooped down on hers, but Judith felt nothing. She remained rigid against him.

He broke away from her. "You are an icy bitch," he growled, then crushed her closer to him. She gasped as the air was forced from her lungs. He took advantage of her open mouth and seized it again, thrusting his tongue inside until Judith gagged. His embrace hurt her; his mouth disgusted her.

Arthur pulled away from her again, loosening his hold, but he didn't release her. His eyes showed anger at first, then changed to mockery. "No, you are not cold. No woman with such hair and eyes could be. But who is it that melts that ice? Is it Walter with his hand-kissing, or perhaps it is that husband of yours?"

"No!" Judith said then closed her lips.

Arthur smiled. "For all Walter thinks otherwise, you are a poor actress." Arthur's face turned hard. "Walter is a stupid man, but I'm not. He thinks you came to this place out of love for him, but I don't believe it. If I were a woman, I would hope to use my beauty to free those I loved. Is it your plan to bargain yourself in exchange for your mother's and husband's release?"

"Let me go!" Judith demanded, twisting in his arms.

He held her more firmly. "You cannot escape me. Don't even try."

"What of Walter?" she challenged.

He laughed. "You play the game well, but beware that you play with fire and will get burned. Do you think I fear a bit of slime like Demari? I can handle him. Who do you think thought of this idea of annulment?"

Judith stopped struggling.

"Ah! So I have your attention. Listen to me. Walter will have you first, but you will be mine later. When he has grown tired of you and begins to take other women, you will be mine."

"I would sooner bed a viper," she hissed as his hand bit into her arm.

"Even to save that mother of yours?" he said in a deadly voice. "You have done a lot for her already. What more would you do?"

"You shall never know!"

He pulled her against him again. "Won't I? You

think yourself a lady of some power while you hold that fool Demari in your hands, but I will show you who has the power here."

"What . . . what do you mean?"

He smiled. "You will know soon enough."

She tried to recover from the awful feeling his words gave her. "What are you going to do? You wouldn't hurt my mother?"

"No, I'm not so unsubtle as that. Only a bit of fun. It will do me good to see you squirm. When you have had enough, come to my bed some night and we will talk."

"Never!"

"Don't be so hasty." Suddenly Arthur released her. "I must go. You have my words to think about."

When she was alone, Judith stood very still, breathing deeply to calm herself. She turned toward her room, but was startled to see a man standing quietly in the shadows. He leaned lazily against the opposite wall of the hall. A lute was slung across his broad shoulders, and he idly used a knife to trim his nails. Judith did not know what made her look at him, except that he could have heard some of Arthur's threats. Yet her eyes were drawn to him though he did not raise his head to look at her. As she stared at him, he lifted his face to look at her. His dark blue eyes looked at her with such hate that she gasped. Her hand flew to her mouth, and she bit the back of it.

She turned and ran down the hall to her room where she threw herself onto her bed. The tears came slowly, fighting their way up from the pit of her stomach before they found release.

"My lady," Joan whispered as she stroked Judith's hair. They had grown closer in the last few days as the difference in their stations was lessened. "Has he hurt you?"

"No, I have hurt myself. Gavin said I should have stayed home with my sewing. I'm afraid he was right."

"Sewing," the maid questioned, smiling. "You would

have snarled the threads worse than you snarl things here."

Judith looked up, aghast. Then, through her tears, she said, "You are good for me. I felt sorry for myself for a moment. You took Gavin food last night?"

"Yes."

"And how did he look?"

Joan frowned. "Weaker."

"How can I help them?" Judith demanded of herself. "Gavin said I was to wait for his brother Stephen, but how long? I must get Gavin out of that hole!"

"Yes, my lady, you must."

"But how?"

Joan was serious. "Only God can answer that."

That night, Arthur answered Judith's question. They sat at supper, a meal of soup and stews. Walter was quiet, not touching Judith as he usually did, but looking at her from the corner of his eye, as if he were judging her.

"Do you like the food, Lady Judith?" Arthur asked. She nodded.

"Let us hope the entertainment pleases you also."

She started to ask what he meant, but did not. She wouldn't give the man such satisfaction.

Arthur leaned forward to look at Walter. "Don't you think it's time?"

Walter started to protest, but then seemed to think better of it. It was obviously something he and Arthur had discussed thoroughly. Walter waved his hand to two men-at-arms waiting by the doorway, and the men left.

Judith could not even swallow the food in her mouth and had to wash it down with wine. She knew Arthur planned some trick, and she wanted to be ready for it. She glanced about the hall nervously. Again she saw the man she'd seen in the hallway that afternoon. He was tall and slim with dark blond hair with a few lighter streaks. His jaw was strong and set in a firm line above a cleft chin. But his eyes were what held her. They were a deep, dark blue that blazed with the fire of hatred—hatred that was directed toward her. He mesmerized her.

The sudden, abnormal silence of the hall and the sound of dragging chains drew her eyes away. In the bright light of the great hall, Judith didn't at first recognize the form being dragged between the two knights as human. It was more an odorous pile of rags than a man. It was these few seconds of nonrecognition that saved her. She became aware of Arthur and Walter staring at her, watching her. She looked in puzzlement to them, and as soon as she turned away, she realized that the figure being carried into the hall was Gavin. She didn't look at him again, but kept her eyes fastened on Walter. That would give her time to think. Why did they present him to her like this? Didn't they know she wanted to run to him and help him?

The answer came to her instantly as she realized that was just what Arthur wanted her to do. He wanted to show Walter that she did not hate her husband.

"You don't know him?" Walter asked.

Judith looked up, as if in surprise, at the filthy man being led into the hall. Then she began to smile, very slowly. "It is as I have always wanted to see him."

Walter gave a shout of triumph. "Bring him here! My lovely lady sees him as she hoped he would be," he declared to everyone in the hall. "Let her enjoy this moment—she has earned it."

The two guards brought Gavin to the table. Her heart was beating wildly. Judith could risk making no errors now. If she showed how her heart went out to her husband, that display would no doubt cause many deaths. She stood, her hand trembling, and raised her wine goblet. She threw the contents in his face.

The liquid seemed to revive Gavin, and he looked up at her. His face, lean and sharp, showed surprise. Then wonder. Slowly he looked at Walter and Arthur, who stood beside his wife.

Demari put his arm possessively about Judith's shoulders. "Look now at who holds her," he boasted.

Before anyone could react, Gavin threw himself across the table at Walter. The guards who held his chains were pulled forward, stumbling, falling into the dishes of food. Walter could not get away fast enough, and Gavin's filthy hands closed around the smaller, gaudily-dressed man across the table.

"Seize him!" Walter gasped weakly, using his fingernails to claw at Gavin's hands around his throat.

Judith was stunned as were the retainers. Gavin must be half-dead by now, but his strength was still enough to pull two men off balance and nearly kill his captor.

The guards recovered themselves and yanked on the chains around Gavin's wrists. It took three mighty tugs before they succeeded in freeing Walter. The end of a chain was laid heavily across Gavin's ribs. He grunted and crumpled on one leg for a moment before righting himself. "I will kill you for this," he said, his eyes boring into Walter's before another chain was put to his ribs.

"Take him away!" Walter ordered as he rubbed his nearly crushed throat. He shivered as he still stared at Gavin.

When Gavin had been removed, Walter collapsed into his chair.

Judith knew he would be most vulnerable now. "That was pleasant," she smiled, then turned quickly to the trembling Walter. "Not, of course what he did to you—I don't mean that. But it was good to know he saw me with someone I could . . . care for."

Walter gazed back at her, his spine straightening a bit.

"But of course I should be angry with you." She lowered her eyes seductively.

"Why? What have I done?"

"You really should not have brought such dirt into the presence of a lady. He looked so starved, I wonder he did not really want the food. How can he see what I now have when all he thinks of is nourishment and the things crawling on his skin?"

Walter considered this. "You are right." He turned to some men by the door. "Tell the guards to clean and feed him." He was ecstatic. Arthur had said Judith would cry when she saw her husband in such a state, but she had smiled!

Only Joan knew what that smile cost her mistress.

Judith turned away from Walter, wanting to leave the room and especially to leave his presence. She held her head high as she walked through the retainers.

"The woman deserves what she gets!" Said some men close to her.

"True. No wife has a right to treat a husband like that."

Each and every one of them despised her. And she too was beginning to hate herself. Judith walked slowly up the stairs to the fourth floor, wanting only privacy. At the top of the steps, an arm flew about her waist, and she was slammed against a man's chest that felt like iron. A knife went to her throat, the sharp edge nearly piercing her delicate skin. Her hands flew to his forearm, but they had no effect.

Chapter Nineteen

"SAY ONE WORD, AND I'LL TAKE THAT VIPEROUS HEAD OF yours off your body," said the deep voice, one she had never heard before. "Where is John Bassett?"

Judith could hardly speak but this was not a man to be disobeyed.

"Answer me!" he said as his arm tightened and the knife pressed harder against her throat.

"With my mother," she whispered.

"Mother!" he spat into her ear. "May that woman curse the day she gave birth to such as you!"

Judith couldn't see him, and she could hardly breathe from his arm cutting into her ribs and lungs. "Who are you?" she gasped.

"Yes, you should ask that. I am your enemy, and I would delight in ending your vile existence here if I didn't need you. How is John guarded?"

"I . . . cannot breathe."

He hesitated then loosened his grip, the knife easing away from her throat. "Answer me!"

"There are two men outside the door of the room he shares with my mother."

"Which floor? Come, answer me," he commanded as he tightened his hold once again. "Don't think some-one will come to save you."

Suddenly it was all too much for Judith and she

began to laugh. Quietly at first, but growing more hysterical with each word. "Save me? And pray, who would save me? My mother is held prisoner. My only guard is also held. My husband is kept in a sewer. A man I detest has the right to paw me before my husband while another whispers threats into my ear. Now I am attacked by a stranger in the dark of the hall!"

Her hands on his forearm pulled the knife closer to her throat. "I pray you, sir, whoever you are—finish what you have started. End my life, I beg you. For what use is it to me? Must I stand and watch my every friend and relative slaughtered before me? I do not wish to live to see that end."

The man's arm relaxed. Then he pulled away from her hands that tugged at the knife. He resheathed the blade, then grabbed her shoulders. Judith was not surprised to recognize the jongleur from the great hall.

"I want to hear more," he said, his voice less harsh.

"Why?" she asked as she stared up into his deadly blue eyes. "Are you a spy set upon me by Walter or Arthur? I have said too much already."

"Yes, you have," he agreed bluntly. "If I were a spy, I would have a lot to report to my master."

"Tell him then! Get it over!"

"I'm not a spy. I am Stephen, Gavin's brother."

Judith stared, her eyes wide. She knew it was true. That was why she had been drawn to him. There was something in Stephen's manner, if not his looks, that reminded her of Gavin. She was not aware that tears were running down her cheeks. "Gavin said you would come. He said I had made a mess of everything, but that you would set it all to right again."

Stephen blinked at her. "When did you see him that he said this?"

"On the second night here. I went to him in the pit."

"In the—?" He'd heard tales of the way Gavin was kept—that much he'd been able to learn—but he could not get near his brother. "Come and sit here," he said, leading Judith to a window seat. "We have much to discuss. Tell me everything, from the start."

Stephen listened quietly while she told of Walter's murdering her father and claiming her lands, of how Gavin went to counter Walter's attack.

"And Gavin and your mother were taken?"

"Yes."

"Then why are you here? Didn't Demari ask for some ransom? You should be raising it from the serfs."

"I didn't wait for him to ask. I came with John Bassett, and we were welcomed into the castle."

"Yes, I imagine you were," Stephen said sarcastically. "Now Walter Demari has everyone—you, Gavin, your mother, Gavin's head man."

"I didn't know what else to do."

"You could have sent for one of us!" Stephen said angrily. "Raine, with his broken leg, would have done better than you, a woman, could have. John Bassett should have known—"

Judith put her hand on Stephen's arm. "Don't blame him. I threatened to go alone if he didn't lead me."

Stephen looked down at her small hand, then back at her eyes. "What of that I saw below? The castlefolk say you hate Gavin and would do anything to be free of him. Perhaps you want your marriage ended."

Judith quickly drew her hand away. He was beginning to remind her very much of Gavin. Her temper flared. "What I feel for Gavin is between him and me, and not for others to know."

Stephen's eyes blazed. He grabbed her wrist until she clenched her teeth in pain. "Then it is true. You care for this Walter Demari?"

"No, I don't!"

He tightened his grip. "Don't lie to me!"

Men's violence had always made Judith furious. "You are just like Gavin!" she spat. "You see only what you wish to see. No, I am not as dishonest as your brother. It is he who grovels at an evil woman's feet. But I will not so lower myself."

Stephen looked puzzled and loosened his hold. "What evil woman? What is this talk of dishonesty?"

Judith jerked her wrist away and rubbed it. "I came to save my husband because he was given to me before God and because I now carry his child. I have an obligation to try to help him, but I don't do so for love for him. No!" she said passionately. "He gives his love to that blonde!" She stopped and looked at her wrist.

Stephen's laughter made her look up. "Alice," he smiled. "Then that is what this is about? It's not a serious war for estates, but a lover's quarrel, some woman's problem."

"*Woman's—*"

"Quiet! We will be heard."

"It is more than a woman's problem, I assure you!" she hissed.

Stephen sobered. "You may deal with Alice later, but I must be sure you won't go to the king and ask for an annulment. We cannot afford to lose the Revedoune estates."

So that was why he cared whether she wanted Walter or not. It didn't matter that Gavin betrayed her with another woman, but heaven help her if she should feel anything for another man. "I cannot have the marriage annulled while I carry his child."

"Who else knows of this child? Surely not Demari?"

"Only my mother and John Bassett . . . and my maid."

"Not Gavin?"

"No. I had no time to tell him."

"Good. He will have enough on his mind. Who knows this castle best?"

"The steward. He has been here twelve years."

"You have a ready answer," Stephen said suspiciously.

"For all that you and your brother think otherwise, I have a brain to think with and eyes to see."

He studied her in the dim light. "You were brave to come here, though misguided."

"Should I take that as a compliment?"

"As you wish."

Judith narrowed her eyes. "Your mother must have been glad her second sons were not as her first two."

Stephen stared at her, then began to smile. "You must lead my brother a merry chase. Now stop baiting me and let me see a way out of this mess you have made."

"I—!" she began then stopped. He was right, of course.

He ignored her outburst. "You succeeded in getting Gavin cleaned and fed, though your methods were disagreeable to my belly."

"Should I have run and embraced him?" she asked sarcastically.

"No, you did right. I don't believe he is well enough to travel yet, and he would be a hindrance to us as he is. But he is strong. In two days, with care, he will recover enough that we can escape. I must leave the castle and get help."

"My men are outside."

"Yes, I know. But my men are not here. I came nearly alone when I heard Gavin needed me. My men follow, but it will take at least two more days for them to reach us. I must go and lead them here."

She touched his arm again. "I will be alone again."

He smiled at her and traced the line of her jaw. "Yes, you will. But you will manage. See that Gavin is cared for and regains his strength. When I return, I will get all of you out of here."

She nodded, then looked down at her hands.

He lifted her chin and looked into her eyes. "Don't be angry with me. I thought you wanted Gavin dead. Now I see it isn't so."

She smiled tentatively. "I'm not angry. Only I am sick of this place, that man pawing me, the other—"

He put his finger to her lips. "Keep him from you a little longer. Can you do that?"

"I will try. I was beginning to give up hope."

He bent and kissed her forehead. "Gavin is fortunate," he whispered. Then he rose and left her.

Chapter Twenty

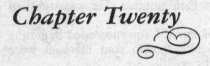

"HAVE YOU SEEN HIM?" JUDITH ASKED AS SHE ROSE FROM her bed. It was the morning after she'd seen Stephen, and now she asked Joan what she'd discovered about Gavin.

"Yes," Joan answered. "And he is handsome once again. I feared the filth of that place had taken his looks from him."

"You think too much of looks."

"And perhaps you think too little of them!" Joan retorted.

"But Gavin is well? He hasn't been harmed by that foul place?"

"I am sure the food you sent kept him alive."

Judith paused. And what of his mind? How had he reacted to her throwing wine in his face? "Fetch me the serf's garment I wore. It has been washed?"

"You cannot go to him," Joan stated flatly. "If you were caught—"

"Bring me the dress and give me no more orders."

Gavin was being kept inside a room carved out of the base of the tower. It was a dreary place; no light reached it. Its only entrance was an ironbound oak door.

Joan seemed to be well acquainted with the guards who stood on either side of the door. The discipline was lax in the Demari estate, and Joan used this to her advantage. She winked suggestively at one of the men.

"Open up!" Joan bellowed outside the door. "We bring foodstuffs and medicines sent from Lord Walter."

Cautiously, an old and dirty woman opened the massive door. "How do I know you come from Lord Walter?"

"Because I tell you I am," Joan answered and pushed past the crone. Judith kept her head lowered, the rough woolen hood drawn carefully over her hair.

"You can see him," the woman said angrily. "He sleeps now and has done little else since he came here. He's in my care and I do a good job."

"Surely!" Joan said sarcastically. "The bed looks filthy!"

"Cleaner than where he's been."

Judith gave her maid a slight nudge to stop her from baiting the old woman.

"Leave us then and we will tend to him," Joan said.

The woman, her hair gray and greasy, her mouth full of rotted teeth, appeared to be stupid, but she was not. She saw the small, hidden woman nudge the other, and she was aware that the nasty-tempered one quieted instantly.

"Well, what are you waiting for?" Joan demanded.

The old woman wanted to see the face beneath the hood. "I must get some medicines," she said. "There are others who are sick and need me, even if this one doesn't." When she had a jar in her hand, she walked past the woman who intrigued her. When she was near the candle, she dropped the jar. The woman, startled, looked up, giving the crone a brief glimpse of her eyes. The candlelight danced in the lovely golden orbs. The old woman worked hard at not smiling outright. She'd seen those eyes on only one person.

"You are clumsy as well as stupid," Joan hissed. "Get out before I set those rags you wear to flame."

The woman gave Joan a malevolent look before she noisily left the room.

"Joan!" Judith said as soon as they were alone. "It is I who will set you alight if you ever treat anyone like that again."

Joan was shocked. "What does she mean to anyone?"

"She is one of God's children, the same as you or I." Judith would have gone on, but she knew it was useless. Joan was an incurable snob. She belittled anyone she didn't think better than she was. Judith went to her husband, preferring to use her time tending to him rather than lecturing her maid.

"Gavin," she said quietly as she sat on the edge of the bed. The candlelight flickered over him, playing with the shadows of his cheekbones and his jaw line. She touched his cheek. It was good to see him clean again.

He opened his eyes, the deep gray of them made even darker by the candlelight. "Judith," he whispered.

"Yes, it is I," she smiled as she pushed the hood of the mantle back and revealed her hair. "You look better now that you are washed."

His expression was cold and hard. "I don't have you to thank for that. Or perhaps you think the wine in my face cleansed me."

"Gavin! You accuse me wrongly. Had I gone to you with any greeting, Walter would have put an end to your life."

"Wouldn't that have suited you well?"

She drew back. "I won't quarrel with you. We may pursue the matter at leisure once we are free. I have seen Stephen."

"Here?" Gavin said as he started to sit up, the covers falling off his bare chest.

It had been a long time since the night Judith had

been held against that chest. His sun-bronzed skin held her attention completely.

"Judith!" Gavin demanded. "Stephen is here?"

"He *was* here." She brought her eyes back to his. "He has returned to get his men."

"And what of my men? What are they doing? Or do they loll about outside the walls?"

"I don't know. I didn't ask."

"No, you wouldn't," he said with irritation. "When does he return?"

"Hopefully, tomorrow."

"Less than one day's time. Why are you here now? You have only one day to wait. If you were found here, you could cause great trouble."

Judith gritted her teeth. "Do you ever do anything except curse me? I came to this hell because you were held prisoner. I have risked much to see that you are cared for. Yet you curse me at every opportunity. Tell me, sir, what *would* please you?"

He stared at her. "You have much freedom here, don't you? You seem to go wherever you wish with no hindrance. How do I know that Demari isn't waiting outside for you?" Gavin grabbed her wrist. "Are you lying to me?"

She twisted loose. "I am amazed at your vileness. What reason do you have to call me a liar? You are the one who has lied to me from the first. You may believe whatever you want. I should not have helped you. Perhaps then I would have gotten some peace. Or even more, I should have gone to Walter Demari when he first offered marriage. That surely would have been preferable to life with you."

"It is as I thought," Gavin said viciously.

"Yes! It is just as you thought!" Judith answered in kind. Her rage at his insinuations and accusations made her just as blind as he.

"My lady!" Joan interrupted the argument. "We must go. We've spent too much time here already."

"Yes," Judith agreed. "I must go."

"Who waits to escort my wife back to her room?"

Judith just looked at him, too angry to speak.

"Lady Judith," Joan said urgently. Judith turned away from her husband.

When they were beside the door, Joan whispered to her mistress. "It does no good to try to talk to a man when he is eaten with jealousy."

"Jealous!" Judith said. "One must care for another to be jealous. Obviously he doesn't care for me." She straightened the concealing hood over her hair.

Joan started to reply as they opened the door and left the cell. She stopped abruptly, her body rigid. Judith, behind her, looked up to see what caused her maid's concern.

Arthur stood there, his hands on his hips, his legs spread wide, his face a hideous scowl. Judith ducked her head and turned away, hoping he hadn't seen her.

Arthur walked toward her, his arm extended. "Lady Judith, I would like to speak to you."

Judith knew that the walk up the three flights of stairs to Arthur's room was the longest she'd ever taken. Her knees shook with fear and what was worse, the sickness she often felt in the morning was rising in her throat. Her impetuousness had probably ruined Stephen's plans and . . . and . . . She couldn't let herself think of what the result would be if Stephen did not get to them in time.

"You are a fool," Arthur commented when they were alone in his chamber.

"I have been called that before," Judith said, her heart pounding.

"In daylight, you go to him! You couldn't even wait until night."

Judith kept her head lowered, concentrating on her hands.

"Tell me, what plans did you concoct?" He stopped suddenly. "I was a fool to think this could have worked. I am more stupid than that man I serve. Tell me, how did you plan to extricate yourself from this web of lies?"

Her chin came up. "I will tell you nothing."

Arthur narrowed his eyes. "He will suffer. And do you forget that mother of yours? I was right not to trust you. I knew it well but I was half-blinded by you also. Now I find I am in this as deeply as you. Do you know who Lord Walter will blame when his plans are destroyed? When he sees he is not to have the hand of the Revedoune beauty? Not you, my lady, but me. He is a child who has been given power."

"Am I to feel compassion for you? It was you who tore my life apart so that now my family and I live on the brink of death."

"We understand each other then. We care nothing for the other. I wanted your lands and Walter your person." He stopped and looked steadily at her. "Though your person has intrigued me much of late."

"And how do you expect to remove yourself from this tangle you have created?" Judith asked, changing the subject and turning the tables on him.

"Well you should ask. There is only one way open to me. I must see this annulment through to its finish. You won't appear before the king, but you will sign a paper saying that you wish an annulment. It will be worded so that he cannot refuse the request."

Judith came half out of her chair, another, stronger attack of nausea invading her. She ran to the corner of the room to the earthenware chamber pot and relieved her stomach of its meager contents. When she'd recovered herself, she turned back to Arthur. "Forgive me. The fish last night must have been tainted."

Arthur poured a goblet of watered wine. She took it with trembling hands. "You carry his child," he stated flatly.

"No! I do not!" Judith lied.

Arthur's face hardened. "Shall I call a midwife to examine you?"

Judith looked into her goblet and shook her head.

"You cannot ask for an annulment," he continued. "I'd not thought of a child being conceived so soon. It seems we sink deeper and deeper into the muck pile."

"Are you going to tell Walter?"

Arthur snorted. "That idiot thinks you to be pure and virginal. He talks of love and life with you. He doesn't know you are twice as clever as he is."

"You talk too much," Judith said, her stomach once again settling. "What do you want?"

Arthur looked at her with admiration. "You are a woman of intelligence as well as beauty. I would like to own you." He smiled, then turned serious. "Walter will find out about your loyalties and the child. It's only a matter of time. Would you give a fourth of the Revedoune lands if I were to take you out of here?"

Judith thought quickly. The estates meant little to her. Was Arthur a surer chance than waiting for Stephen? If she refused Arthur, he could tell Walter and all their lives would be forfeit—after Walter finished his use of Judith. "Yes, you have my word. There are five of us. If you see all of us safe, one quarter of the lands are yours."

"I cannot guarantee all—"

"All of us or no bargain."

"Yes," he said. "I know you mean it. I must have time to arrange matters. And you must go to the dinner table. Lord Walter will be angry if you're not there to simper by his side."

Judith wouldn't take his arm as they left the room. He knew she liked him even less for turning against his master, and this made him laugh. The idea of loyalty to anyone other than oneself amused him.

When the door to Arthur's room closed behind them, the chamber appeared to be empty. For several moments it was shrouded in silence. Then the slightest of slithering noises could be heard from under the bed. The old woman inched from her hiding place with great caution. She grinned as she looked again at the coin clasped tightly in her hand.

"Silver!" she whispered. But what would the master give to hear what she had just heard? Gold! She didn't understand all of it, but she'd heard Sir Arthur call Lord Walter stupid, and she knew he meant to betray his lord for some land the Montgomery woman owned. There was also something about a baby that the lady would have. That seemed very important.

Judith sat quietly by a window in the great hall, wearing a light gray undertunic and a dress of dark rose Flemish wool. The sleeves were lined with gray squirrel fur. The sun was setting, making the hall darker with each moment. She was beginning to lose some of the fear that had invaded her that morning after her talk with Arthur. She glanced at the sun with gratitude. Only one more day, and Stephen would return and everything would be all right.

She had not seen Walter since dinner. He had invited her to go riding with him, but hadn't appeared to take her with him. Judith assumed that some castle business kept him away.

She began to worry when the sun set and the tables were laid for supper. Neither Arthur nor Walter appeared. She sent Joan to find out what she could, but that was little enough.

"Lord Walter's door is sealed and guarded. The men would answer no questions, though I tried every persuasion."

Something was wrong! Judith knew it when she and Joan retired to their chamber that night and heard a bolt thrown across the door from the outside. Neither woman slept much.

In the morning, Judith stood dressed in a severe gown of dark brown wool. She wore no ornament or jewels. She waited silently. The bolt was released and a man, dressed in chain mail for battle, boldly entered her room.

"Follow me," he said.

When Joan tried to come with her mistress, she was pushed back and the door rebolted. The guard led Judith to Walter's chamber.

The first sight she saw when the door was opened was what was left of Arthur chained to the wall. She turned her face away, her stomach heaving.

"Not a pretty sight is it, my lady?"

She looked up to see Walter lounging on a cushioned chair. His red eyes and his manner showed he was very drunk. His words were slightly slurred.

"But then, I have found you are no lady." He rose, stood still a moment as he tried to focus, then went to a table and poured himself more wine. "Ladies are true and good—but you, sweet beauty, are a whore." He walked toward her and Judith stood very still. There was nowhere to run. He grabbed her hair, pulling her head back. "I know everything now." He turned Judith's head so she had to look at the bloody figure. "Take a long look at him. He told me a lot before he died. I know you think I'm stupid, but I'm not so stupid that I can't control a woman." He pulled her back to look at him. "You did all this for your husband, didn't you? You came here to find him. Tell me: How much would you have done to save him?"

"I would have done anything," she said calmly.

He looked at her then smiled, pushing her away from him. "Do you love him so much?"

"It's not a question of love. He is my husband."

"But I offered you more love than he could ever have," Walter said, tears in his eyes. "All England knows that Gavin Montgomery hungers for that Alice Chatworth."

Judith had no answer to give him.

Walter's thin lips turned to a snarl. "I will not try to reason with you anymore. It's far past that time now."

He went to the door and opened it. "Take that thing away and throw it to the pigs. When you have finished with him, bring Lord Gavin and chain him in the same way."

"No!" Judith screamed as she ran to Walter and put both hands on his forearm. "Please don't harm him anymore. I will do what you say."

He slammed the door. "Yes, you will do as I say, and you will do it before that husband you prostitute yourself for."

"No!" Judith whispered.

Walter smiled at her whitened face. He turned and opened the door again and watched as the guards dragged Arthur's body away. "Come here!" Walter commanded when they were again alone. "Come and kiss me as you do that husband of yours."

She shook her head numbly. "You will kill us anyway. Why must I obey you? Perhaps I will bring our torture to a quicker end if I disobey you."

"You are indeed shrewd," Walter smiled. "But I would have it the opposite way. For every act you refuse me, I will slice a bit from Lord Gavin's flesh."

She looked at him in horror.

"Yes, you understand me."

Judith could hardly think. Stephen, she pleaded silently, don't take longer than you said. Perhaps she could prolong Walter's hurting of Gavin until Stephen and his men began their attack. The door opened again. Four burly guards entered, Gavin chained between them. This time Walter was taking no chances.

Gavin looked from Walter to his wife. "She is mine," he said under his breath and took a step forward. One of the guards brought the flat of a sword across Gavin's head and he slumped forward, unconscious.

"Chain him!" Walter commanded.

Tears came quickly to Judith's eyes. Tears at Gavin's bravery. Even though he was chained, he still attempted to fight. Gavin's body was bruised and battered, weak from near starvation yet he still fought. Could she do any less? Her only chance was to stall for time until Stephen arrived. She would do whatever Walter asked.

He saw the resignation in her eyes. "A wise decision," Walter laughed when Gavin's arms were spread out, the iron rings about his wrists. Walter dismissed the guards. Laughingly he threw a cup of wine in Gavin's face. "Come now, my friend, you must not sleep through this. You have occupied my cellar a long time, and I know you couldn't have enjoyed your wife much there. Look at her. Isn't she lovely? I was ready to fight a battle for her. Now I find I don't have to." He held out his hand. "Come here, my lady. Come to your master."

Gavin's booted foot lashed out at Walter. The little man barely had time to step back.

A small whip hung over a side table. The leather was still bloody from use on Arthur's body. Walter flicked it, cutting Gavin across the face. A long gash appeared immediately, but Gavin didn't seem to notice. He lifted his foot again, but Walter was far out of range.

As Walter lifted the whip a second time, Judith ran in front of her husband, throwing her arms out to protect him.

"Get away!" Gavin growled at her. "I will fight my own battles."

Judith could only hiss at the absurdity of his words. Both of his arms were chained to a wall that was already covered with another man's blood, yet he thought he could fight a madman. She stepped away. "What do you want?" she asked Walter in a dead voice. She could feel Gavin's eyes boring into her back.

"Come here," he said slowly, careful not to get within reach of Gavin's feet.

Judith hesitated, but she knew she must obey. She took his hand, although his clammy flesh made her skin crawl.

"Such a lovely hand," Walter said as he held it up before Gavin's eyes. "Come, have you nothing to say?"

Gavin turned his eyes to Judith's, and a chill ran up her spine.

"My dear, I believe we wish to see more of your exquisite body." Walter turned to Gavin. "I have seen it often, have enjoyed it often. She was made for a man. Or should I say for many men?" Walter looked at Judith, his eyes hard. "I said you were to let us see what lies beneath those clothes. Do you think so little of your husband as to refuse him one last look?"

With trembling hands, Judith worked at the ties of the brown wool. She wanted to take as much time as possible.

"Here! You are too slow!" Walter slurred as he threw his goblet aside and drew his sword. He slashed the tunic and surcoat away, then dug his fingers into the neck of the bodice of her chemise. His nails slashed at the soft skin of her neck. Her underclothing was torn from her in a like manner.

She bent as if to cover herself, but the point of Walter's sword on her belly made her stand straight.

Her creamy shoulders gave way to her full breasts which, in spite of misery, stood high and proud. Her waist was still small, not yet distended by the child. Her legs were long and slim.

Walter stared at her in wonder. She was more than he had imagined her to be.

"Beautiful enough to kill for," Walter whispered.

"As I will kill you for this!" Gavin shouted. He strained violently against the chain.

"You!" Walter laughed. "What can you do?" He grabbed Judith, his arm about her waist. He turned her so she faced her husband, fondling her breast. "Do you think to rip the chains out of the wall? Look at her well, for it will be the last thing you see."

His hand slid to Judith's belly. "And look at this. It is flat now, but soon it will grow with my child."

"No!" Judith cried.

He tightened his grip about her waist until she

couldn't breathe. "I have planted my seed there and it grows. Think of that while you rot in hell!"

"I would think of no woman you had touched," Gavin said, his eyes on his wife. "I would sooner mate with an animal."

Walter pushed Judith away. "You will regret those words."

"No! Do not!" Judith said as Walter advanced on Gavin with a drawn sword.

Walter was very drunk and the blade fell far wide of Gavin's ribs—especially as Gavin agilely sidestepped it. "You will hold still!" Walter shouted and aimed again, this time at his prisoner's head. The weapon, so inaccurately handled, did not slash but more slapped. The wide blade caught Gavin's ear and his head fell forward.

"Do you fall asleep?" Walter screamed as he tossed the sword aside and went for Gavin's throat with his bare hands.

Judith didn't waste a moment. She ran for the sword. Before she could think what she was doing, she took the handle in two hands and brought it down with all her might between Walter's shoulder blades. He stood suspended for a moment. Then, very slowly, Walter turned and looked at Judith before he fell. She swallowed hard as she began to realize she had killed a man.

Without warning, an enormous crash rocked the tower to its very foundations. She had no time to waste. The key to the rings about Gavin's wrists hung on the wall. Just as she unlocked the rings he began to stir.

Gavin caught himself as he started to collapse. He opened his eyes to see his wife standing near him, her nude body flecked with blood. Walter, a sword protruding from his back, lay at his feet. "Cover yourself!" he said angrily.

Judith had forgotten her unclothed state during the turmoil. Her garments lay in a heap, cut beyond repair. She opened a chest at the foot of the bed. It was filled with Walter's clothing. She hesitated. She didn't want to touch anything of his.

"Here!" Gavin said and flung a woolen tunic at her. "It's fitting you should wear his attire." He went to the window, giving her no time to speak.

Truthfully, she couldn't. The enormity of having slain a man was weighing on her.

"Stephen is here," Gavin announced. "He has tunneled under the wall and the stones have collapsed." He went to Walter, put his foot on the dead man's back and withdrew the sword. "You severed his spine," Gavin noted calmly. "I will know to watch my back. You are skillful."

"Gavin!" a familiar voice called from outside the door.

"Raine!" Judith whispered, tears beginning to form in her eyes. Gavin threw back the bolt.

"You are well?" Raine asked as he grabbed his brother's shoulders.

"Yes, as well as can be expected. Where is Stephen?"

"Below, with the others. The castle was easily captured once the wall was down. The maid and your mother-in-law wait below with John Bassett, but we cannot find Judith."

"She is there," Gavin said coldly. "See to her while I find Stephen." He pushed past Raine and left the room.

Raine stepped inside. At first he didn't see Judith. She sat on a chest at the foot of the bed wearing a man's tunic. Her bare legs hung below the hem. She looked up at him with tearful eyes. She was a forlorn-looking creature, and his heart went out to her. Raine clumped across the room to her, his leg still heavily bandaged. "Judith," he whispered and held out his arms to her.

Judith didn't hesitate to seek the comfort of his strength. Sobs tore through her. "I killed him," she cried.

"Who?"

"Walter."

Raine held her tighter, her feet nowhere near the floor. "Did he deserve killing?"

Judith buried her face in his shoulder. "I had no right! God—"

"Quiet!" Raine commanded. "You did what must be done. Tell me, whose blood is on the wall?"

"Arthur's. He was Walter's vassal."

"Come now, don't cry so much. All will be well. Come below, and your maid will help you dress." He didn't want to know why her own clothes lay slashed on the floor.

"My mother is well?"

"Yes, more than well. She looks at John Bassett as if he were the Messiah come again."

She drew away from him. "You blaspheme!"

"Not I, but your mother. What will you say when she lights candles at his feet?"

She started to reprimand Raine, then smiled, the tears drying on her cheeks. She hugged him fiercely. "It is so good to see you again."

"Always, you give more to my brother than to me," came a solemn voice from the doorway.

She looked up to see Miles, his eyes as much on her bare legs as anything. She had been through too much to blush. Raine let her down and she ran to hug Miles.

"Has it been bad?" he asked as he held her close.

"More than bad."

"Well, I have news to cheer you," Raine offered. "The king summons you to court. It seems he has heard so many reports of you from your wedding that he wishes to see our little golden-eyed sister."

"To court?" Judith asked.

"Let her down!" Raine said to Miles with false annoyance. "You hold her too long for brotherly affection."

"It's just this new fashion she wears. I hope it will set a trend," Miles said as he set her on the floor.

Judith looked up at them and smiled. Then her tears

began again. "It's good to see you both. I will go and dress," she said as she turned.

Raine swept his mantle from his shoulders and enveloped her in it. "Go then. We will wait downstairs for you. We leave today. I don't want to see this place again."

"Nor do I," Judith whispered, not looking back but carrying a vivid image of the room in her mind.

Chapter Twenty-One

"YOU KNOW OF THE CHILD?" STEPHEN ASKED GAVIN as they walked side by side in the Demari castleyard.

"I have been told," he said coldly. "Here, let's sit in the shade. I'm not used to the sunlight yet."

"They kept you in a pit?"

"Yes, for nearly a week."

"You don't look too starved. Did they feed you then?"

"No, Jud—my wife had her maid send food."

Stephen glanced up at what remained of the old tower. "She risked a great deal to come here."

"She risked nothing. She wanted Demari as much as he wanted her."

"That didn't seem to be true when I talked to her."

"Then you are wrong!" Gavin said with force.

Stephen shrugged. "She is your concern. Raine says you are summoned to court. We may travel together. I am also to appear before the king."

Gavin was tired and wanted nothing more than to sleep. "What does the king want with us?"

"He wants to see *your* wife and he wants to present me with one."

"You are to marry?"

"Yes, a rich Scottish heiress who hates all Englishmen."

"I know what it is to be hated by your wife."

Stephen grinned. "But the difference is that you care. I do not. If she doesn't behave, I will lock her up and never see her again. I'll say she is barren and adopt a son who will inherit her lands. Why don't you do the same with this wife of yours if she displeases you?"

"Never see her again!" Gavin said, then caught himself when Stephen began to laugh.

"She stirs your blood? You don't need to tell me. I've seen her. Did you know I threatened her life after I saw her throw the wine in your face? She grabbed my blade and begged me to end it for her."

"You were fooled," Gavin said disgustedly, "as Raine and Miles are. They sit at her feet and gaze at her with cow eyes."

"Speaking of cow eyes, what do you plan to do about John Bassett?"

"I should marry him to her. If Lady Helen is anything like her daughter, his life will be hell. It is little enough punishment for his stupidity."

Stephen bellowed with laughter. "You are changing, brother. Judith obsesses you."

"Yes, as a boil on my backside. Come, let's hurry these people and leave this place."

Outside the Demari estate was the camp Gavin had left. John Bassett had not known about Gavin's tunneling under the walls, for Gavin never told any of his men all his plans. When Gavin had been taken captive and John had returned to the Montgomery estate, the men Gavin had chosen kept on with their digging. It had taken days, with no man getting more than a few hours' sleep at a time. As the men dug, they braced the earth over their heads with timbers. When they were nearly through to the other side, they built a hot fire inside the tunnel. Once the timber burned away, a section of the wall collapsed with a deafening crash.

In the ensuing confusion of setting up camp, Judith was able to escape for a few moments alone. A river ran through the trees beyond the open ground of the camp. She walked through the woods and found a secluded spot where she was hidden, yet able to enjoy the sound and sight of the water.

She had not realized how tense she'd been during the last week. The incessant conniving, the lying she'd done while Walter's captive had taken a toll on her. It was good to feel peaceful and free again. Now, in just a few brief moments, she wouldn't think of her husband or of any other of her many problems.

"You too seek solace," came a quiet voice.

She had heard no one approach. She looked up to see Raine smiling at her.

"I will go if you wish. I don't want to intrude."

"You aren't. Come and sit with me. I only wanted to put myself far away from noise and people for a while."

He sat beside her, his long legs stretched before him, his back against a rock. "I'd hoped to find things better between you and my brother, but they don't look as though they are," he said without preamble. "Why did you kill Demari?"

"Because there was no other way," Judith said, her head bowed. She looked up, her eyes full of tears. "It is an awful thing to have taken someone's life."

Raine shrugged. "It is necessary at times. What of Gavin? Didn't he explain such to you? Didn't he offer you comfort for what you did?"

"He has said very little to me," she said bluntly. "Let's talk of other things. Your leg is better?"

Raine started to speak, then they both looked toward the river when they heard a woman laugh. Helen and John Bassett walked along the edge of the water. Judith started to call to her mother, but Raine stopped her. He didn't think the lovers should be disturbed.

"John," Helen said, gazing at him with love. "I don't think I can bear it."

John tenderly pushed a bit of hair from her cheek. She looked like a radiant young girl. "We must. It will be no easier for me to have you taken from me, to see you wed to another."

"Please," she whispered, "I cannot bear the thought. Is there not some way—?"

John put his fingertips on her lips. "No, don't say it again. We cannot be wed. We have these few hours now—that's all."

Helen flung her arms about his chest, holding him as tightly as she could. John embraced her until he nearly crushed her. "I would leave everything for you," she whispered.

"And I would give anything if I could have you." He buried his cheek against the top of her head. "Come, let's go. Someone may see us here."

She nodded and the two of them walked away, slowly, their arms locked about each other.

"I didn't know," Judith said at last.

Raine smiled at her. "It happens at times. They will get over the pain. Gavin will find a new husband for your mother, and he will fill her bed."

Judith turned to him, her eyes a blaze of gold. "A new husband!" she hissed. "One who will fill her bed! Do men ever think of anything else?"

Raine looked at her in fascination. She'd never turned her wrath toward him. It was not just her beauty that fascinated him, but her spirit. He again felt the stirrings of love for her. He smiled. "There is little else to think of about women," he teased, only half-serious.

Judith started to speak until she saw the laughter in Raine's eyes, the dimples in his cheeks. "Is there no way for them?"

"No, none. John's parents are not even of noble birth, and your mother was married to an earl." He put his hand on her forearm. "Gavin will find a good man for her, one who will manage her property well and who will be kind to her."

Judith didn't answer him.

"I must go," Raine said abruptly as he awkwardly rose. "Curse this thing!" he said vehemently. "I had an ax blade in my leg that didn't cause me as much pain as this break."

She looked up at him. "At least it's set properly," she said, her eyes twinkling.

Raine winced at the memory of the pain when Judith had reset his leg. "I will remember not to come to you should anything else need doctoring. I'm not man enough to take any more of your healing. Will you return now to the tents?"

"No, I will sit alone awhile."

He looked about the place. It seemed safe enough, but he couldn't be sure. "Don't stay past sundown. If I don't see you before then, I will come for you."

She nodded and looked back at the water as he walked away. Raine's concern had always made her feel warm and protected. She remembered how glad she'd been when she saw him at the castle. His arms about her made her feel safe and secure. Then why didn't she look at him with passion? It was odd that she felt only the most sisterly affection for a man who treated her so kindly, while her husband—

She wouldn't think of Gavin while in this quiet spot. Any thoughts of him made her too angry. He'd believed Walter's words that she was carrying that man's child. Her hands went to her stomach protectively. Her child! Whatever happened, the baby would always be hers.

"What do you plan for her?" Raine asked as he made a great show of easing himself into a chair in Gavin's tent. Stephen sat to one side, running a knife along a whetstone.

Gavin was on the other side, eating, as he had been

doing ever since he left the castle. "I assume you mean my wife," Gavin said as he speared a piece of roast pork. "You seem overconcerned with her," he challenged.

"And you seem to ignore her!" Raine spat. "She killed a man for you. That's not easy for a woman—yet you don't even speak to her of it."

"What comfort could I give her after my brothers have given her so much?"

"She gets little enough elsewhere."

"Shall I have my squire fetch swords?" Stephen asked sarcastically. "Or perhaps you would like full armor?"

Raine relaxed immediately. "You are right, brother. I just wish that this other brother of mine were as sensible."

Gavin glared at Raine, before looking back at his food.

Stephen watched Gavin's eating for a moment. "Raine, are you trying to interfere between Gavin and his wife?"

Raine shrugged and adjusted his leg. "He doesn't treat her well."

Stephen smiled in understanding. Raine had always been a fighter for the underdog. He would champion any cause that he felt needed him. The silence between the brothers grew heavy until Raine rose and left the tent.

Gavin looked after him then pushed the food away, full at last. He stood and walked toward his cot.

"She carries the man's child," Gavin said after a time.

"Demari's?" Stephen asked then gave a low whistle at Gavin's nod. "What will you do with her?"

Gavin sank onto a chair. "I don't know," he said quietly. "Raine says I didn't comfort her, but how could I? She killed her lover."

"Was she forced?"

Gavin hung his head. "I don't believe so. No, she couldn't have been. She had the freedom of the castle. She came to me in the pit and again when I was brought from there and taken to a tower cell. Had she been forced, she wouldn't have had such freedom."

"That's true, but doesn't her visiting you mean that she desired to help you?"

Gavin's eyes blazed. "I don't know what she desires. She seems to be on the side of whoever holds her. When she came to me, she said she did everything for me; yet when she was near Demari, she was wholly his. She is a clever woman."

Stephen ran his thumb along the edge of his knife, testing it. "Raine seems to think a great deal of her, and Miles also."

Gavin snorted. "Miles is too young to know yet that women have anything besides a body. And Raine . . . he has championed her cause for long."

"You could declare the child to be another's and set her aside."

"No!" Gavin said almost violently, then looked away.

Stephen laughed. "You are still hot for her? She is beautiful but there are other beautiful women. What of Alice, whom you declared you loved?"

Stephen was the only person Gavin had ever confided in about Alice. "She was married not long ago to Edmund Chatworth."

"Edmund! That bit of slime! Didn't you offer her marriage?"

Gavin's silence was his answer.

Stephen put his knife back in the case at his side. "Women aren't worth the worry you spend on them. Take that wife of yours and bed her, and don't give her another thought." He dismissed the subject and rose. "I think I'll go to sleep. It's been a long day. I'll see you tomorrow."

Gavin sat alone in his tent, the darkness rapidly

gathering. Set her aside, he thought. He could do that since she carried another man's child. But he couldn't imagine not seeing her.

"Gavin," Raine interrupted his thoughts. "Has Judith returned? I told her she mustn't stay out past sunset."

Gavin rose, his jaw clenched. "You think too much of my wife. Where was she? I'll find her."

Raine smiled at his brother. "By the stream, through there," he pointed.

Judith knelt by the side of the river, her hand playing in the cool, clear water.

"It's late. You must return to the camp."

She looked up, startled. Gavin towered over her, his gray eyes dark in the fading daylight. His expression was closed.

"I don't know these woods," he continued. "There may be danger."

She stood, her shoulders back. "That would suit you, wouldn't it? A dead wife is surely better than a dishonored one." She lifted her skirts and strode past him.

He grabbed her forearm. "We must talk, seriously and without anger."

"Has there been anything else between us except anger? Say what you must—I grow weary."

His face softened. "Does the burden of the child tire you?"

Her hands flew to her stomach. Then she straightened, her chin up. "This baby will never be a burden to me."

Gavin looked across the water, as if he struggled with some great problem. "For all that has happened since, I believe you meant well when you gave yourself into Demari's hands. I know you have no love for me, but your mother was held also. For her alone, you would have risked what you did."

Judith nodded, frowning slightly.

"I don't know what happened after you came to the castle. Perhaps Demari was kind to you and you needed kindness. Perhaps even at the wedding, he . . . offered you kindness."

Judith couldn't speak as her bile rose.

"As for the child, you may keep it and I won't set you aside, as perhaps I should. For if the truth were known, maybe some of the blame is mine. I will care for the child as if he were my own, and he shall be given some of your lands to inherit." Gavin paused and stared at her. "Do you say nothing? I have tried to be honest . . . and fair. I don't believe you could ask for more."

It took Judith a moment to recover herself. Her teeth were clamped together when she spoke. "Fair! Honest! You don't know the meaning of those words! Just look at what you're saying. You are willing to concede that I came to the castle for honorable purposes, but after that, you insult me horribly."

"Insult you?" Gavin asked, bewildered.

"Yes! Insult me! Do you believe me to be so baseborn, that I would give myself freely to a man who threatened my mother and my husband—for before God, you are that! You say I needed kindness! Yes, I do, as I have never had kindness from you. But I'm not so shallow as to break my vows to God for a little thoughtfulness. Once I broke such a vow, but I won't do so again." She looked away, her face warm with memory.

"I have no idea what you mean," Gavin began, his own temper flaring. "You talk in riddles."

"You hint that I am an adulteress. Is that a riddle?"

"You bear the man's child. How else can I say it? I have offered to care for the baby. You should be grateful that I don't cast you aside."

Judith stared at him. He didn't ask if the child was his. He assumed that Walter's words were the true ones. At her wedding, Judith's mother had said that a man would believe the lowest-born serf before he believed a woman. It was true. And if Judith denied sleeping with Walter? Would he believe her? There would be no way to prove her words.

"You have no more to say?" Gavin demanded, tight-lipped.

Judith glared at him, speechless.

"Then you agree to my terms?"

Well, she would play the game his way. "You say you give my child my lands. You sacrifice little."

"I keep you! I could set you aside."

She laughed. "You could always have done so. Men have that right. You keep me while you desire me. I'm no fool. I would have something more than just an inheritance for my child."

"You ask payment?"

"Yes, for coming to you at the castle." The words hurt. She was crying inside, but refused to show it.

"What do you want?"

"I would have my mother given in marriage to John Bassett."

Gavin's eyes opened wide.

"You are her nearest male relative now," Judith pointed out. "You have the right."

"John Bassett is—"

"Don't tell me. I know too well. But can't you see how she loves him?"

"What has love to do with it? There are estates to be considered, properties to be joined."

Judith put her hands on his arms, her eyes pleading. "You don't know what it is to live without love. You have given yours, and I have no chance for it. But my mother has never loved a man as she loves John. It's in your power to give her what she most needs. I beg you, don't let your animosity toward me keep you from letting her have some happiness."

He stared down at her. She was so beautiful but he saw also a lonely young woman. Had he really been so harsh to her that she needed Walter Demari, if even for a few moments? She said he'd given his love, yet at that moment he couldn't remember Alice's face.

He pulled Judith into his arms. He remembered how frightened she was when she'd been treed by the boar. So little courage—yet she'd confronted an enemy, as if she alone could slay dragons.

"I don't hate you," he whispered, holding her close, his face buried in her hair. Raine once asked what was wrong with her, and now Gavin asked himself that question. If she did carry another man's infant, wasn't it his fault for leaving her unprotected? In all their marriage, Gavin could remember being kind to her only once. The day they had spent together in the woods. Now his conscience hurt him. He'd planned that day only to woo her back to his bed. He thought only of himself and not of her. He bent and put his hand under her knees. He sat down on the sweet-smelling grass, his back against a tree and held her curled in his arms. "Tell me what happened at the castle," he said gently.

She didn't trust him. Always, when she trusted him, he flung her words back in her face. But his body felt good to her. This feeling is all we share, Judith thought. Only lust exists between us. Not love or understanding—or, least of all, trust.

Judith shrugged, refusing to reveal anything to him. Her lips were so close to his neck. "It's over now. It is better forgotten."

Gavin frowned, wanting to press her to talk to him but her nearness was more than he could bear. "Judith," he whispered as his mouth came down on hers.

Her arms went about his neck and drew him closer, her mind going blank at the touch of him. Forgotten were any ideas of understanding and trust.

"I have missed you," Gavin whispered against her neck. "Do you know that when I first saw you at Demari's, I thought I was dead?"

She leaned her head away, giving Gavin the arch of her slender throat.

"You were like an angel bringing light and air and

your beauty into that . . . place. I was afraid to touch you for fear that you weren't real—or that you were real, and I would be destroyed if I dared touch you." He fumbled with the laces at her side.

"I am most real," Judith smiled.

He was so enchanted by her look that he pulled her to face him and kissed her deeply. "Your smiles are rarer and more precious than diamonds. I have seen so few of them." His face blackened suddenly with memory. "I could have killed you both when I saw Demari touch you."

She stared at Gavin in horror, then tried to push away.

"No!" he said and held her close. "Do you give him more than me, your husband?"

Judith was in an awkward position, but she managed to draw her hand back and slap him across the cheek.

His eyes blazed as he caught her hand in his, crushing her small fingers together. Then suddenly he pulled her hand to his mouth and kissed it. "You are right. I am a fool. It's done. It's behind us. Let's look to the future and to tonight only." His mouth captured hers and Judith fought any rage. In truth, she thought of nothing at all as his hands roamed beneath her clothes.

They were hungry for each other, more than hungry. The starvation Gavin had experienced in the tent was nothing compared to what he felt at having to do without his wife.

The indigo-blue wool dress was torn away, as was the linen undertunic. The tearing fabric added to the passion, and Judith's hands struggled with Gavin's clothes. But his hands were faster than hers. Instantly, his clothes lay in a heap on top of hers.

Frantically, Judith pulled him to her and Gavin more than met her ardor. Within moments they came together in a fiery starburst that left them both exhausted.

Chapter Twenty-Two

"HE THINKS HE'S BETTER THAN US," BLANCHE SAID spitefully. She and Gladys were in the Chatworth buttery, filling jugs with wine for the eleven o'clock meal.

"Yes," Gladys said but with less venom. She missed Jocelin very much, but she was not angry about it as Blanche was.

"What business do you think keeps him away from us?" Blanche asked. "He spends little enough time with her," she jerked her head upward to indicate Alice Chatworth's room. "And he is seldom in the hall."

Gladys sighed. "He seems to spend most of his time alone in the hayloft."

Blanche suddenly stopped her task. "Alone! Is he alone, though? We haven't thought of that. Could he keep a woman up there?"

Gladys laughed. "Why would Jocelin want just one woman when he can have many? And what woman is missing? Unless he has one of the serfs, I know of no one who could have been missing so long."

"Then what else could hold a man like Jocelin? Here, you!" Blanche called to a passing serf girl. "Finish filling these mugs."

"But I—," the girl began but Blanche gave her arm a vicious pinch. "I will," she said sullenly.

255

"Come, Gladys," Blanche called. "While Jocelin is busy somewhere else, let's put an end to this mystery."

The two women left the little buttery and walked the short distance to the stables.

"See, he removes the ladder each time he leaves," Blanche observed. She walked quietly into the stables, Gladys close behind her. Blanche put a finger to her lips and pointed to the fat stableman's wife. "The old dragon keeps watch over him," she whispered.

The girls took the ladder, being careful not to make any noise. They placed it against the outside wall, the end braced against the opening to Jocelin's room. Blanche lifted her skirts and climbed up. When they were once inside, their view of the little room blocked by the stacks of hay, a woman's voice reached them.

"Jocelin? Is that you?"

Blanche smiled in malicious triumph at Gladys and led the way into the open area. "Constance!"

The woman's lovely face was still battered, but it was beginning to heal. Constance retreated, her back against a pile of hay.

"So! You are the reason Jocelin neglects us. I thought you left the castle," Gladys said.

Constance could only shake her head.

"No! She didn't," Blanche spat. "She saw Jocelin and decided he was to be hers. She couldn't bear to share him."

"That isn't so," Constance said, her lower lip trembling. "I nearly died. He cared for me."

"Yes, and you care for him, don't you? What sorcery did you use to charm him?"

"Please . . . I meant no harm."

Blanche was not listening to the woman's pleas. She knew Jocelin had not put the marks Constance now bore on her face and body. Only Edmund Chatworth could have done that. "Tell me, does Lord Edmund know where you are?"

Constance's eyes widened in horror.

Blanche laughed. "See, Gladys, she is the lord's mistress—yet she betrays him with another. What do you say we return her to her master?"

Gladys looked at the terrified young woman with sympathy.

Blanche grabbed her friend's upper arms, her fingers digging into the soft flesh. "She has betrayed us, yet you hesitate before giving some of her own in return? This conniving little bitch has taken Joss from us. She had Lord Edmund, but she wanted more. She wasn't content with one man, but she must have all of them at her feet."

Gladys turned to Constance with a look of hate.

"If you do not go with us, we will tell Lord Edmund that Jocelin has been hiding you," Blanche smiled.

Constance silently followed them down the ladder. She would not allow herself to think, only to know that she protected Jocelin. In all her life, no one had offered her tenderness. Her world was filled with people like Edmund and Blanche and Alice. Yet, for nearly two weeks, she had lived in a dream in Jocelin's arms. He had talked to her, sung to her, held her close and made love to her. He whispered that he loved her and she believed him.

Now, following Blanche and Gladys was like waking from a dream. Unlike Jocelin, Constance did not make plans for when they would leave the Chatworth castle, when she was fully healed. She knew that the time they had in that loft was all the time they would ever know. Docilely, she followed the women, accepting her fate; the idea of escape or struggling never entered her mind. She knew where they led and when she entered Edmund's chamber, her chest tightened as if iron bands were drawn about it.

"Stay here and I will fetch Lord Edmund," Blanche ordered.

"Will he come?" Gladys asked.

"Oh, aye, when he hears what I will say to him. Do not let her leave the room."

Blanche was back in moments, a furious Edmund on her heels. He did not like having his dinner interrupted, but the mention of Constance had made him follow the presumptuous servant girl. Once in the room, he slammed and bolted the door behind him, his eyes on Constance, ignoring the nervous looks of the two maids.

"So, my sweet Constance, you did not die after all." Edmund put his hand under her chin and lifted her face to meet his. He saw only resignation there. Her bruises marred her beauty, but she would heal. "Those eyes," he whispered. "They have haunted me for a long time."

He heard a noise behind him and turned to see the two maids trying to sneak the bolt from the door. "Here!" he commanded and grabbed the arm of the nearest one, Gladys. "Where do you think you're going?"

"To our duties, my lord," Blanche said, her voice unsteady. "We are your most loyal servants."

Gladys had tears in her eyes as Edmund's fingers bit into her skin. She tried to pry his fingers loose.

Edmund flung the girl to the floor. "Did you think you could bring her here and leave her like so much baggage? Where has she been?"

Blanche and Gladys exchanged glances. They hadn't thought of this. All they wanted to do was get Constance away from Jocelin. They wanted things the way they once were, with Jocelin teasing them, making love to them.

"I—I don't know, my lord," Blanche stuttered.

"You think I'm a fool?" Edmund said and advanced on her. "The girl has been well hidden, or I would have known of her. Her presence has not been part of the castle gossip."

"No, my lord, she . . ." Blanche could not think fast enough to create a story. Her tongue tripped her.

Edmund stopped, then looked at Gladys cringing on the floor. "There is something to this story that you hide. Whom do you protect?" He grabbed Blanche's arm and twisted it painfully behind her back.

"My lord! You hurt me!"

"I will do more than that if you lie to me."

"It was Baines of the kitchen," Gladys said loudly, wanting to protect her friend.

Edmund released Blanche's arm as he considered this. Baines was a thoroughly disliked man, foul, evil-tempered, he knew that. But Edmund also knew Baines slept in the kitchen. He had no privacy, certainly not enough to hide a battered girl until she was healed. It would have caused talk throughout the castle.

"You lie," Edmund said in a deadly voice, then advanced slowly on her.

Gladys cringed away from him, half-crawling across the rushes. "My lord," she said, every fiber of her body trembling.

"It is your last lie," he said as he grabbed her about the waist. She started struggling when he saw him carrying her toward the open window.

Blanche stared in horror as Edmund carried the fighting Gladys. When they reached the window, Gladys held her arms out against the framework but she was no match for Edmund's strength. He gave one push at the small of her back and she fell forward, clutching at the air. Her scream, as she fell three stories to the courtyard below, seemed to make the walls tremble.

Blanche could only stare, her knees turning to water, her stomach heaving.

"Now," Edmund said as he turned back to Blanche. "I wish to know the truth. Who kept her?" he nodded toward Constance who stood silently against the wall. Edmund's murder of Gladys had not shocked Constance; it was what she had expected.

"Jocelin," Blanche whispered.

At the name, Constance's head came up. "No!" She could not bear for Jocelin to be betrayed.

Edmund smiled. "That pretty singer?" He was the one who took her that night—a fact Edmund had forgotten. "Where does he sleep that he could keep her unnoticed?"

"Above the stables in the loft." Blanche could hardly speak. She kept looking at the window. Only a moment before, Gladys had been alive. Now her body lay broken and crushed on the pavement.

Edmund nodded at Blanche's answer; he knew the truth when he heard it. He took a step toward her and she cringed away from him, her back to the door.

"No, my lord, I told you what you wanted to know." He kept coming toward her, a slight smile on his face. "And I brought you Constance. I am a true servant to you."

Edmund liked her terror; it proved that he was strong. He stood close to her, reached a fat hand to caress the line of her jaw. There were tears in her eyes, tears of fear. Even as he struck her, he smiled.

Blanche fell to the floor, her hand on the side of her face, her eye already turning purple.

"Go," he said, half-laughing as he threw open the door. "You have learned your lesson well."

Blanche was out of the room before the door closed. She ran down the stairs and out the manor house. She kept running through the castle yard, through the open gate. She did not answer the calls of the men from atop the walls. She only knew that she wanted to be away from anything to do with the Chatworth estate. Only when the pains in her side forced her, did she stop. Then she walked, never once looking back.

Jocelin slipped four plums inside his doublet; he knew how much Constance loved fresh fruit. In the last weeks, his life had begun to revolve around what Constance did and did not like. Watching her unfold, petal by soft petal, had been the most delightful thing that had ever happened to him. Her gratitude for every pleasure, no matter how small, was warming, though his heart ached at the thought of her life before—that a bouquet of flowers could make her cry.

And in bed, he smiled wickedly. He was not such a martyr as to forgo all selfish pleasures. Constance wanted to repay him for his kindness and wanted to show him her love. At first her anticipation of pain had made her rigid, but the feel of Jocelin's hands on her body, knowing they would not hurt her, made her wild with passion. It was as if she wanted to crowd all the love she would ever know into a few short weeks.

Jocelin smiled as he thought of their future together. He would stop traveling and settle down, would make a home for Constance and himself. Then they would have several violet-eyed children. Never in his life had he wanted more than freedom and a comfortable bed and a warm woman. But never had he been in love before. Constance had changed his whole life. Just a few more days—as soon as Constance was well enough to stand the long journey, they would leave.

Jocelin was whistling as he left the manor house and walked past the kitchen toward the stables. He froze when he saw the ladder leaning against the wall. Of late he had been careful to remove the ladder. The stable-man's wife kept a sharp eye on it for him, and Jocelin rewarded her with numerous smiles and a few genuinely affectionate hugs. He did not think of any danger to himself, but only to Constance.

He ran the last few feet and sped up the ladder. His heart was beating wildly as he searched the tiny room, as if he'd find her beneath the hay. He knew without a doubt that Constance would not leave on her own. No, she was like a fawn, timid and fearful.

Tears blurred his eyes as he made his way down the ladder. Where would he find her? Perhaps some of the women played a joke on him and he would find her safe in some corner, munching on a raisin bun. Jocelin did not believe it, even as he pictured the dream.

He was not surprised when he saw Chatworth at the
foot of the ladder, flanked by two armored guards.
"What have you done with her?" Jocelin demanded as
he jumped from the second rung of the ladder, his
hands going for Edmund's throat.

Edmund's face was beginning to turn blue before his
men could disengage Jocelin. They held him securely
by the arms.

Edmund pulled himself from the dust and looked
with disgust at his ruined clothing. The velvet would
never be the same again. He rubbed his bruised throat.
"You will pay for this with your life."

"What have you done with her, you piece of pig's
offal?" Jocelin sneered.

Edmund gasped. No one had ever dared talk to him
like that before. He drew back his hand and slapped
Jocelin across the face, cutting the corner of his mouth.
"Indeed, you will pay for this."

He stepped out of range of Jocelin's feet, more wary
of the jongleur than he had been. Behind that face
lurked a man he had not guessed existed, thinking
Jocelin only to be another pretty boy. "I will enjoy
this," he sneered. "Tonight you will spend in the
oubliette, and tomorrow you will see your last sunrise.
All day you will suffer. But tonight perhaps you will
suffer more. While you sweat in that jar, I will take the
woman."

"No!" Jocelin yelled. "She has done nothing. Let her
go. I will pay for taking her."

"Yes, you will. As for your noble gesture, it is
hollow. You have nothing to bargain with. I have you
both. Her for my bed, and you for any other pleasures I
choose. Take him and let him think on what it means to
defy an earl."

Constance sat at the window of Edmund's room.
Spirit was gone from her. No more would she see
Jocelin again, no more would he hold her in his arms

and tell her he loved her more than the moon loved the stars. The only hope was that he had managed to escape. She had seen the way that Blanche ran from the room. Constance prayed that the woman had gone to warn Jocelin. She knew that Blanche cared for him, had heard her call for him. Surely, Blanche had warned Jocelin, and together they were safe.

Constance felt no jealousy. In truth, she wanted only Jocelin's happiness. If he'd asked her to die for him, she would gladly have done so. What did her poor life matter?

A commotion and the sunlight on a familiar head drew her attention. Two burly guards half-dragged a struggling Jocelin across the yard. As she watched, one of the men cuffed Jocelin hard on the collarbone, causing Joss to slump to one side. With difficulty, he kept on his feet. Constance held her breath, wanting to call to him, but she knew it would endanger him more. As if he sensed her, he twisted and looked up at the window. Constance lifted her hand. Through her tears, she could see the blood on his chin.

As the guards jerked Jocelin around, Constance suddenly realized where they were taking him, and her heart stopped. The oubliette was a horrible device; a jug-shaped chamber cut into the bowels of solid rock. A prisoner must be lowered through its narrow neck by a pulley. Once inside, he could neither sit nor stand, but must half-squat, his back and neck continually bent. There was little air and quite often no food or water. Nobody could last more than a few days, and only the strongest that long.

Constance watched the guards strap Jocelin to the pulley and lower him into that hellhole. She stared for a few moments longer as the cover was fastened, then looked away. There was no hope now. Tomorrow Jocelin would be dead, if he lived through the night, for Edmund would surely devise some additional torture.

On a table a large wine beaker and three glasses were

set. These glasses were for Edmund's private use, as he saved all the most beautiful objects for himself. She did not think of what she did, for her life was over and only one last act was needed to complete the deed. Smashing a glass against the table, she took the jagged base in her hand and went to the cushioned window.

It was a lovely day, summer in full bloom. Constance hardly felt the sharp edge as she slashed it across one wrist. She looked at the blood flowing from her body with a sense of relief. "Soon," she whispered. "Soon I will be with you, my Jocelin."

Constance cut her other wrist and leaned back against the wall, one wrist in her lap, the other on the windowsill, her blood seeping into the mortar of the stones. A soft summer breeze blew at her hair and she smiled. One evening she and Jocelin had gone to the river, spending the night alone in the soft grasses. They had returned very early the next morning before the castle was fully awake. It had been a night of rapture and whispered love words. She remembered every word Jocelin had ever spoken to her.

Gradually, her thoughts became lazier. It was almost as if she went to sleep. Constance closed her eyes and smiled slightly, the sun on her face, the breeze in her hair, and thought no more.

"Boy! Are you all right?" a voice called down to Jocelin in a hoarse whisper.

He was dazed and had trouble understanding the words. "Oubliette" meant chamber of forgetfulness, and it earned its name.

"Boy!" the voice demanded again. "Answer me!"

"Yes," Jocelin managed.

A heavy sigh answered him. "He is well," a woman's voice said. "Put this around you and I will pull you up."

Jocelin was too dazed to fully realize what was happening to him. The woman's hands guided his body through the neck and up to the cool night air. The

air—the first real breath he'd had in many hours—
began to clear his mind. His body was cramped and
stiff. When his feet touched the ground, he unbuckled
the pulley strap.

The stableman and his fat wife stared at him.
"Love," she said. "you must leave at once." She led
the way through the darkness to the stable.

With each step, Jocelin's head cleared more. As he
had never before in his life experienced love until
recently, neither had he known hate. Now, walking
across the courtyard, he looked up at Edmund's dark
window. He hated Edmund Chatworth, who now lay
with Constance.

When they were in the stables, the woman spoke
again. "You must go quickly. My husband can get you
over the wall. Here—I have packed a bundle of food
for you. It will last you a few days if you are careful."

Jocelin frowned. "No, I cannot go. I cannot leave
Constance with him."

"I know you won't go until you know," the old
woman said. She turned and motioned for Jocelin to
follow her. She lit a candle from another one on the
wall and led Jocelin to an empty stall. A cloth was
draped over several bundles of hay. Slowly she pulled
the cloth away.

At first Jocelin did not believe what he saw. He had
seen Constance once before when he thought her to be
dead. He knelt beside her and took the frigid body in
his arms. "She is cold," he said with authority. "Fetch
blankets so I can warm her."

The old woman put a hand on Jocelin's shoulder.
"All the blankets in the world won't help. She is dead."

"No, she is not! She was like this before and—"

"Don't torture yourself. The girl's blood is gone. She
has none left."

"Blood?"

The woman moved the cloth back and held up
Constance's lifeless wrist, the vein exposed, severed.

Jocelin stared at it silently. "Who?" he finally whispered.

"She took her own life. No one else did it."

Jocelin looked back at Constance's face, finally realizing that she was gone. He bent and kissed her forehead. "She is at peace now."

"Yes," the woman said, relieved. "And you must go."

Joss pulled away from the woman's clutching hand and walked purposefully toward the manor house. The great hall was covered with sleeping men on straw pallets. Jocelin was silent as he slipped a sword from the wall where it hung amid a mixture of many weapons. His soft shoes made no noise as he went up the stairs to the fourth floor.

A guard slept in front of Edmund's door. Jocelin knew he would have no chance if the guard was to waken, for Jocelin's wiry strength was no match for a seasoned knight's. The man never uttered a sound as Jocelin rammed the sword through his belly.

Jocelin had never killed a man before and this one gave him no pleasure.

Edmund's door was not locked. He felt safe in his own castle in his own room. Jocelin pushed the door open. He didn't enjoy what he did, nor did he wish to linger over it as some would have done. He grabbed Edmund's hair in his hands. Chatworth's eyes flew open—and then widened as he saw Jocelin.

"No!"

It was the last word Edmund Chatworth spoke. Jocelin pulled the sword across the man's throat. In death, the earl disgusted Joss as much as when alive. Jocelin tossed the sword to the side of the bed and walked to the door.

Alice could not sleep. She had not been able to sleep properly for weeks—not since the jongleur had stopped coming to her bed. She had threatened him repeatedly, but to no avail. He had just looked at her through those long lashes of his and said nothing. Truthfully, she was a bit intrigued by a man who treated her so badly.

She threw the curtains of her bed back and pulled on a bedrobe. Her feet were soundless on the rush-covered floor. Once in the hall, Alice sensed something was wrong. Edmund's door was open, the guard before it sat in an odd position. Curious, she walked toward him. Her eyes were accustomed to the dark, and the hall was lit only patchily by the torches along the wall.

A man left Edmund's room, looking neither right nor left but walked straight toward her. She saw the blood on his doublet before she saw his face. Alice gasped and put her hand to her throat. When he stopped before her, she hardly recognized him. Here was no laughing boy, but a man who looked at her with boldness. A small chill of fear went up her spine. "Jocelin."

He walked past her as if he had not seen her or did not care that he had. Alice stared after him, then slowly walked to Edmund's room. She stepped over the dead guard, her heart pounding. When she saw Edmund's body, the blood still running from the slashed throat, she smiled.

Alice went to the window, her hand on the sill, covering a stain made by another's innocent blood on the day before. "A widow," she whispered. A widow! Now she had it all—wealth, beauty and freedom.

For a month she had been writing letters, begging for an invitation to King Henry's court. When it had come, Edmund had laughed at her, saying he refused to spend the money on such frivolities. In truth, he would not be free at court to toss serving girls from windows as he was in his own castle. Now, Alice thought, she could go unencumbered to the king's court.

And there would be Gavin! Ah yes, she had arranged that also. That red-headed whore had had him too long. Gavin was hers and he would remain so. If she could get rid of that wife of his, then he would be hers entirely. He would not deny her gowns of gold cloth. No, Gavin would deny her nothing. Had she not always gotten what she wanted? Now she wanted Gavin Montgomery again, and she would get him.

Someone walking across the courtyard caught her attention. Jocelin made his way to the stairs leading to the top of the wall, a leather sachel over his shoulder.

"You have done me a great favor," she whispered. "And now I will repay you." She did not call the guards. Instead, she stood silently, planning what she would do now that she was free of Edmund. Jocelin had given her much—access to great wealth—but most of all, he had given her Gavin.

Chapter Twenty-three

IT WAS HOT IN THE TENT. GAVIN COULDN'T SLEEP. HE stood and looked down at Judith, sleeping peacefully, one bare shoulder exposed above the linen sheet. Quietly, he drew on his clothes, smiling at his wife's still form. They'd spent a good part of the evening making love, and now she was exhausted. But he was not. No, far from it. Loving Judith seemed to set a spark to him and light a fire that was unquenchable.

He took a velvet mantle from a chest, then pulled the sheet from her and wrapped her in the cloak. She snuggled against him like a child—never waking, sleeping the sleep of the innocent. He carried her out of the tent, nodded to the guards on duty and walked toward the forest. He bent his head and kissed her sleep-softened mouth.

"Gavin," she murmured.

"Yes, it's Gavin."

She smiled against his shoulder, her eyes never opening. "Where are you taking me?"

He chuckled and held her closer. "Do you care?"

She smiled broader, her eyes still closed. "No, I do not," she whispered.

He laughed, deep in his chest. At the side of the river he sat her down and she gradually began to wake. The coolness of the air, the sound of the water and the sweetness of the grasses added to the dreamlike quality of the situation.

Gavin sat beside her, not touching her. "You once said you broke a vow to God. What vow was it?" He tensed for her answer. They had not spoken again of the time at Demari's, yet Gavin wanted to know what befell her there. He wanted her to deny what he knew to be true. If she loved Demari, why had she killed him? And if she did go to another man, wasn't it Gavin's own fault? He knew the vow she broke was the one she made before a priest and hundreds of witnesses.

The darkness covered Judith's blushes. She was unaware of Gavin's train of thought. She remembered only that she had gone to him before he left for battle.

"Am I such an ogre that you cannot tell me?" he asked quietly. "Tell me this one thing, and I'll ask nothing more of you."

It was a private thing to her, but it was true; he had asked her little. There was a full moon and the night was bright. She kept her eyes turned away from his. "I made a vow to you at our wedding and . . . I broke it."

He nodded; it was as he feared.

"I knew I broke it when I came to you that night," she continued. "But that man had no right to say we didn't sleep together. What was between us was ours to deal with."

"Judith, I don't understand you."

She looked at him, startled. "I speak of the vow. Didn't you ask me of it?" She saw he still didn't understand. "In the garden, when I saw you and—" She broke off and looked away. The memory of Alice in his arms was still vivid to her, and much more painful now than it was then.

Gavin stared at her, trying to remember. When it finally came to him, he began to chuckle.

Judith turned on him, her eyes blazing. "You laugh at me?"

"Yes, I do. Such a vow of ignorance! You were a virgin when you made it. How were you to know what pleasures were to be had in my bed, and that you couldn't keep yourself away from me?"

She glared at him, then stood. "You are a vain and insufferable man. I give you my confidence, and you laugh at me!" She threw her shoulders back, the mantle wrapped tightly about her, and arrogantly started to walk away from him.

Gavin, with a lecherous grin on his face, gave one powerful tug to the cloak and pulled it off her. Judith gasped and tried to cover herself. "Will you go back to camp now?" he taunted, rolling the velvet mantle and placing it behind his head.

Judith looked at him, stretched out on the grass, not even looking at her. So! he thought he had won, did he?

Gavin lay quietly, expecting any moment that she would return and beg him for her clothes. He heard a great deal of rustling in the bushes and smiled confidently. She was too modest to return to camp without her clothes. There was silence for a moment, then he heard a rhythmic movement of leaves, as if . . .

He was on his feet in an instant, following the sound. "Why you little minx!" he laughed as he stood before his wife. She wore a very concealing gown of tree leaves and the branches of several shrubs. She smiled up at him in triumph.

Gavin put his hands on his hips. "Will I ever win an argument with you?"

"Probably not," Judith said smugly.

Gavin chuckled devilishly. Then his hand swept out and tore away the fragile garment. "You don't think so?" he asked as he grabbed her by the waist and picked her up. The nude curves of her body were made silver by the moonlight. He swung her high in his arms, laughing at her gasp of fright. "Don't you know a good wife does not argue with her husband?" he teased.

He sat her on the branch of a tree, her knees at eye level. "I find you particularly interesting this way." He looked at her face, his own smiling, then he froze when he saw the sheer terror in her eyes.

"Judith," he whispered. "I forgot your fear. Forgive me." He had to pry her hands loose from the tree limb, the knuckles white. Even when she was loose, he still had to drag her across the limb, scraping her bare bottom on the rough bark. "Judith, forgive me," he whispered as she clung to him.

He carried her back to the edge of the river and wrapped the mantle about her, holding her in his lap and cuddling her close. His stupidity infuriated him. How could he have forgotten something so important as her terrifying fear of heights? He lifted her chin and kissed her sweetly on the mouth.

Suddenly her kiss turned to passion. "Hold me," she whispered desperately. "Don't leave me."

He was struck by the urgency in her voice. "No, sweet, I won't."

Always she had been a woman of passion but now she was in a frenzy. Her mouth clung to his; then her lips ran along his neck. Never had she been so aggressive.

"Judith," he murmured. "Sweet, sweet Judith." The mantle fell away and her bare breasts pushed against him, insolently and demanding. Gavin's head began to swim.

"Do you leave these garments on?" she asked in a

harsh whisper as her hands ran under the loose tabard. Gavin could hardly bear leaving the nearness of her body for even a few moments to remove his clothing. His doublet was quickly tossed over his head, then his shirt. He hadn't bothered with underwear when he left the tent.

Judith pushed him to the ground and leaned over him. He lay very still, scarcely able to breathe. "It is you who looks to be frightened," she laughed.

"I am." His eyes twinkled. "Will you have your way with me?"

Her hand moved over his body, delighting in his smooth skin, the thick mat of hair on his chest. Then it moved lower and lower.

He gasped, his eyes turning black. "Do what you wish," he said hoarsely. "Only do not take your hand away."

She laughed throatily, feeling a surge of power course through her. She had control of him. But the next moment, feeling his hardness in her hand, she knew he had as much power over her. She was insensible with desire. She climbed on top of him, leaned over and hungrily sought his mouth.

Gavin lay still as she moved on him but soon he could lay still no longer. He grabbed her hips and guided her—faster, harder, his fierceness beginning to match her own.

And then they exploded together.

"Wake up, you hussy," Gavin laughed and slapped Judith's bare buttocks. "The camp wakes and will search for us."

"Let them," Judith murmured and pulled the mantle closer to her.

Gavin towered over her, her body between his feet. Never had he experienced such a night as the one just past. Who was this wife of his? An adulteress? A woman who went from one loyalty to the next, as the wind carried her? Or was she good and kind, as his brothers thought? Whatever she was, she was a demon when it came to lovemaking. "Shall I call your maid to dress you here? Joan will have a few words to say, no doubt."

When Judith sleepily thought of Joan's smirks, it took little time for her to come fully awake. She sat up and looked at the river, then took a deep breath of cool, morning air. She yawned and stretched, the mantle falling away, exposing one full, impudent breast.

"God's teeth!" Gavin swore. "Cover yourself, or we will never reach London and the king."

She smiled at him enticingly. "Maybe I would rather stay here. Court couldn't be half as pleasant."

"Yes," Gavin laughed, then bent and wrapped her in his mantle and swooped her into his arms. "Come, let's return. Miles and Raine leave us today, and I wish to speak with them."

They were silent as they returned to the tent. Judith snuggled against Gavin's shoulder. Would that it could always be like this, she thought. He could be kind and tender when he wanted. Please God, she prayed, let this last between us. Don't let us quarrel again.

An hour later, Judith walked between Raine and Miles, each man holding her hand. They looked to be an incongruous group: two large men dressed in heavy wool traveling clothes, Judith between them, barely reaching to their shoulders.

"I will miss you both," Judith said, squeezing their hands. "It's good having all my family near, though my mother rarely leaves John Bassett's side."

Raine laughed. "Do I hear jealousy in that?"

"Yes," Miles said. "Aren't we enough for you?"

"Gavin seems to be enough," Raine teased.

Judith laughed, her cheeks turning pink. "Is there ever anything that one brother does that the others don't know about?"

"Not much," Raine said then looked over her head to Miles. "There is the question of course of where our little brother spent last night."

"With Joan," Judith said before she thought.

Raine's eyes danced in laughter while Miles's were, as usual, unreadable.

"I . . . know because Joan had a lot to say about him," said Judith, stammering.

Raine's dimples deepened. "Don't let Miles scare you. He is very curious as to what the woman said."

Judith smiled. "I will tell you the next time I see you. Perhaps I can encourage you to visit sooner than you planned."

"Well said!" Raine laughed. "Now, in truth, we must go. We wouldn't be welcome at court unless we paid our own way, and I cannot afford the extra expense."

"He is rich," Miles said. "Don't let him fool you."

"Neither of you fool me. Thank you both for all your time and concern. Thank you for listening to my problems."

"Shall we all cry, when we could be kissing this delicious woman?" Miles asked.

"You are right for once, little brother," Raine said as he lifted Judith from the ground and planted a hearty kiss on her cheek.

Miles took her next and laughed at his brother. "You don't know how to treat a woman," he said as he gathered Judith in his arms and gave her mouth a very unbrotherly kiss.

"You forget yourself, Miles," came a deadly voice.

Judith broke away from her brother-in-law to see Gavin staring at them, his eyes dark.

Raine and Miles exchanged looks. It was the first time that Gavin had ever shown any real jealousy. "Put her down before he draws a sword on you," Raine said.

Miles held Judith for a moment longer and looked down at her. "She might be worth it." He set her gently on the ground.

"We will see you again soon," Raine told Gavin.

"Perhaps at Christmas we can get together. I should like to see that Scottish lady Stephen is to marry."

Gavin placed a possessive hand on Judith's shoulder and drew her close to him. "At Christmas," he said. His brothers mounted their horses and rode away.

"You aren't really angry?" Judith asked.

"No," Gavin sighed. "But I didn't like seeing a man touch you—even my own brother."

Judith took a deep breath. "If they come at Christmas, the baby will be born then."

The baby, Gavin thought. Not "my baby" or "our baby," but "the baby." He didn't like to think of the child. "Come, we must break camp. We have stayed here too long."

Judith followed him, blinking back tears. They didn't mention the time at Demari's castle nor did they talk of the baby. Should she tell him that the child could only be his? Should she plead with him to listen to her, to believe her? She could count days and tell him how far along she was, but once Gavin had hinted that she might have slept with Demari at her wedding. She returned to the tent to direct the maids in the packing.

They made camp early that night. There was no hurrying to reach London, and Gavin enjoyed the time on the journey. He had begun to feel close to his wife. They often talked as if they were friends. Gavin found himself sharing childhood secrets with her, telling her of the fears he'd had when his father died and left him with so much land to manage.

He sat now at a table, a ledger open before him. Every penny spent must be recorded and accounted for. It was a tedious job, but his steward had fallen ill with some fever, and Gavin could not trust one of his knights' ciphering.

He took a drink from a mug of cider and looked across the room to his wife. She sat on a stool by the open tent flap, a ball of blue yarn in her lap. Her hands struggled with a long pair of knitting needles. As he watched, she made more and more of a mess. Her lovely face was contorted with the effort, the tiny tip of her tongue showing between her lips. He looked again at the books and realized that her attempt at knitting was an effort to please him. He had told her often enough of his displeasure when she interfered in the castle business.

Gavin smothered a laugh as she snarled at the yarn and muttered something beneath her breath. He calmed himself. "Judith," he said, "perhaps you can help me. You don't mind setting that aside?" he asked with all the seriousness he could muster. He tried not to smile as she eagerly tossed the yarn and needles against the tent wall.

Gavin pointed to the ledger. "We've spent too much on this journey, but I don't know why."

Judith pulled the ledger around. Here at least was something she understood. She ran her fingers down the columns, her eyes moving from one side to another. She stopped suddenly. "Five marks for bread! Who has been charging so much?"

"I don't know," Gavin said honestly. "I only eat the stuff, I don't bake it."

"You have been eating gold! I shall tend to this straightaway. Why didn't you show me this before?"

"Because, dear wife, I thought I could run my life on my own. Pity any man who thinks so." ⌐

She stared at him. "I will find this baker!" she said as she started to leave the tent.

"Shouldn't you take your knitting? Perhaps you won't find enough to occupy you."

Judith looked over her shoulder at Gavin and saw he was teasing her. She returned his smile, then picked up the ball of yarn and tossed it to him. "Perhaps *you* are the one who needs occupation." She glared pointedly at the ledgers, then left the tent.

Gavin sat and held the yarn for a moment, turning it around in his hands. The tent was too empty when she was gone. He went to the open flap and leaned against the pole, watching her. She never screamed at a servant, but somehow she got more work out of them than he ever had. She took care of the food, the laundry, the setting up of camp, everything, with ease. Yet she never showed any strain and one would never guess she managed six things at once.

She finished talking to the man whose cart was loaded with bread. The short, fat man went away, shaking his head, and Gavin smiled in amusement. He knew just how the baker felt. How many times had Gavin been right yet felt he'd lost the argument? Judith could twist words around until a person couldn't remember his own thoughts.

Gavin watched her walk about the camp. She stopped to taste the stew in a pot, spoke to Gavin's squire where the boy sat on a stool polishing his master's armor. The boy nodded and smiled at her, and Gavin knew there would be some small change made in the simple procedure. And the change would be for the better. Never had he lived or traveled in such comfort—and with such little effort made on his part. He remembered the times he left his tent in the morning and stepped into a pile of horse manure. Now he doubted if Judith allowed the muck to hit the ground. His camp was the cleanest he had ever seen.

Judith felt him staring at her and turned and smiled, looking away from the chickens she inspected. Gavin felt his chest tighten. What did he feel for her? Did it matter that even now she carried another man's child? All he knew was that he wanted her.

He walked across the grass and took her arm. "Come inside with me."

"But I must—"

"You would rather stay outside?" he asked, one eyebrow raised.

She smiled delightedly. "No, I don't think so."

They made love leisurely, savoring each other's bodies until their passion mounted. This was what

Gavin loved about making love to Judith. The variety. She never seemed to be the same twice. One time she would be quiet and sensual, the next aggressive and demanding. At other times she would be laughing and teasing, another acrobatic, experimental. But no matter how she was, he loved loving her. Even the thought of·touching her excited him.

Now he held her close, his nose buried in her hair. She moved against him as if she could get closer to him; it was not possible. He kissed the top of her head drowsily and fell asleep.

"You are falling in love with him," Joan said the next morning as she combed her mistress's hair. The light through the tent walls was soft and dappled. Judith wore a dress of soft green wool, a braided leather belt about her waist. Even in the simple, unadorned traveling garment, her skin glowed and her eyes were all the jewels she needed.

"I assume you refer to my husband."

"Oh, no," Joan said nonchalantly. "I meant the pie man."

"And how . . . can you tell?"

Joan didn't answer.

"Isn't it right for a woman to love her husband?"

"It is if the love is returned. But be careful and don't fall so hard for him that you are torn apart if he is untrue."

"He has hardly been out of my sight," Judith said in his defense.

"True, but what of when you are at the king's court? You won't be alone with Lord Gavin then. There will be the most beautiful women in England. Any man's eyes would stray."

"Be quiet!" Judith commanded. "And tend to my hair."

"Yes, my lady," Joan said mockingly.

All day, as they traveled, Judith thought of Joan's

words. Was she beginning to fall in love with her husband? She had seen him once in another woman's arms. She had been angry then but angry at the fact that he paid her so little respect. But now the idea of seeing him with another woman made her feel as if little slivers of ice were being driven through her heart.

"Judith, are you well?" Gavin asked from the horse beside her.

"Yes . . . no."

"Which is it?"

"I am worried about King Henry's court. Are there many . . . pretty women there?"

Gavin looked across her to Stephen. "What do you say, brother? Are the women at court lovely?"

Stephen looked at his sister-in-law, unsmiling. "I believe you will hold your own," he said calmly, then reined his horse away, going back to his men.

Judith turned to Gavin. "I didn't mean to offend him."

"You didn't. Stephen keeps his worries to himself but I know he dreads his coming marriage. And I don't blame him. The girl hates the English and is sure to make his life hell."

Judith nodded and looked back at the road.

It was when they stopped for dinner that she was able to escape for a few moments. She found a wild raspberry bush outside the camp and set to filling the skirt of her tunic.

"You shouldn't be here alone."

Judith gasped. "Stephen, you startled me."

"If I were an enemy, you could be dead now—or else taken and held for ransom."

Judith stared up at him. "Are you always so full of gloom, Stephen, or is it just this Scottish heiress who worries you so?"

Stephen let out his breath. "Am I so transparent?"

"Not to me, but to Gavin. Come and let's sit awhile. Do you think we could be thoroughly selfish and eat all these berries ourselves? Have you seen your Scottish lady?"

"No," Stephen said, plopping a sun-warmed berry in his mouth. "And she is not mine yet. Did you know that her father made her laird of the MacArran clan before he died?"

"A woman who inherits on her own?" Judith's eyes had a faraway look.

"Yes," Stephen said in disgust.

Judith recovered herself. "Then you don't know what she looks like?"

"Oh yes, I know that. I'm sure she is as small and dark and shriveled as a pine cone."

"Is she old?"

"Maybe she is a young, fat pine cone."

Judith laughed at his air of doom. "All four of you brothers are so different. Gavin is so quick-tempered—icy one moment, fire the next. Raine is laughter and teasing, and Miles is . . ."

Stephen smiled at her. "Don't attempt to explain Miles to me. That boy tries to populate all of England with his children."

"And what of you? Where do you fit? You are a middle son, and you seem to me the least easy to know."

Stephen looked away. "It wasn't easy when I was a boy. Miles and Raine had each other. Gavin had the worry of the estates. And I . . ."

"You were left alone."

Stephen looked at Judith in astonishment. "You have bewitched me! In only moments I have told you more than I have ever told anyone else."

Judith's eyes sparkled. "If this heiress of yours is not kind to you, let me know and I will scratch her eyes out."

"Let's just hope she has both of them to begin with."

They burst into laughter.

"Let's hurry and eat these or we'll have to share them. If I'm not mistaken, Elder Brother approaches."

"Do I ever find you except in the company of men?" Gavin frowned down at them.

"Do you ever greet me with anything except criticism?" Judith retorted.

Stephen snorted with laughter. "I think I should return to camp." He leaned over and kissed Judith's forehead. "If you need help, little sister, I too can find another's eyes."

Gavin grabbed his brother's arm. "Has she enticed you, too?"

Stephen looked back at his sister-in-law, her lips stained dark pink with berry juice. "Yes. If you do not want her . . ."

Gavin gave him a look of disgust. "Raine has already asked."

Stephen laughed and walked away.

"Why did you leave the camp?" Gavin asked as he sat beside her and took a handful of berries from her lap.

"We reach London tomorrow, don't we?"

"Yes. The king and queen don't frighten you, do they?"

"No, not them."

"What then?"

"The . . . women of the court."

"Are you jealous?" he laughed.

"I don't know."

"How could I have time for other women when you're near? You keep me so tired, I do well to stay on my horse."

She did not laugh with him. "There is only one woman I fear. She has separated us before. Don't let her—"

Gavin's face was hard. "Don't speak of her. I have treated you well. I don't pry into what happened at Demari's; yet you seek my soul."

"And she is your soul?" Judith asked quietly.

Gavin looked at her, her eyes warm, her skin soft and fragrant. The past nights of passion flooded his memory. "Don't ask me," he whispered. "I'm sure of one thing only, and that is that my soul is not my own."

The first thing Judith noticed about London was the stench. She thought she knew all the smells humans could create having spent summers in castles overrun with heat and humanity. But nothing prepared her for London. Open gutters ran on each side of the cobbled streets, overflowing with all manner of waste. From the heads of fish and rotting vegetables to the contents of the chamber pots, it all lay in the streets. Pigs and rats ran freely, eating the refuse, spreading it everywhere.

The houses, half-timbered and stone structures were three and four stories high, and so close together that little air and no sun reached between them. The horror Judith felt must have showed on her face, for both Gavin and Stephen laughed at her.

"Welcome to the city of kings," Stephen said.

Once inside the walls of Winchester, the noise and stench were less. A man came to take their horses, and as soon as Gavin helped Judith from hers, she turned to see to the ordering of the carts of baggage and furniture.

"No," Gavin said. "I am sure the king has heard of our arrival. He won't appreciate waiting while you set his castle to rights."

"My clothes are clean? They aren't too mussed?" Judith had dressed carefully that morning in a tawny silk undertunic and a bright yellow velvet dress. The long, hanging sleeves were lined with the finest Russian sable. There was also a wide border of sable along the hem of the gown.

"You are perfect. Now come and let the king look at you."

Judith tried to still her beating heart at the idea of meeting the king of England. She didn't know what she expected, but the rather ordinary great hall was not it. Men and women sat about, playing chess and other games. Three women sat on stools at the feet of a handsome man who played a psaltery. Nowhere did she see any man who could be King Henry.

Judith was astonished when Gavin stopped before a plain middle-aged man with small blue eyes and thin white hair. He looked very tired.

Judith recovered herself and quickly curtsied.

King Henry took her hand.

"Come to the light and let me look at you. I have heard much of your beauty." He led her away, towering over her, for he was six feet tall. "You are as pretty as I have heard. Come here, Bess," King Henry said, "and see the Lady Judith, Gavin's new bride."

Judith turned and saw a pretty middle-aged woman behind her. She had been surprised that Henry was the king, but there was no doubt that this woman was queen. She was a regal woman, so sure of herself, that she could be kind and generous. Her eyes held welcome for Judith. "Your Majesty," Judith said and curtsied.

Elizabeth held out her hand. "Countess," the queen said. "I'm so glad you could come to stay with us for a while. Have I said something amiss?"

Judith smiled at the woman's sensitivity. "I haven't been called 'countess' before. It has been such a short time since my father's death."

"Yes, that was tragic, wasn't it? And the man who did the deed?"

"He is dead," Judith said firmly, remembering too well the feel of the sword sinking into Walter's spine.

"Come, you must be tired after your journey."

"No. I'm not."

Elizabeth smiled fondly. "Then perhaps you would like to come to my chambers for some wine."

"Yes, Your Majesty, I would."

"You will excuse me, Henry?"

Judith suddenly realized she had turned her back on the king. She turned, her cheeks flushed pink.

"Don't mind me, child," Henry said in a distracted

manner. "I am sure Bess will put you to work on the wedding plans for our oldest son, Arthur."

Judith smiled and curtsied to him before she followed the queen up the wide stairs to the solar above.

Chapter Twenty-four

ALICE SAT ON A STOOL BEFORE A MIRROR IN A LARGE ROOM on the top floor of the palace. All around her were a profusion of bright colors. There were purple and green satins, scarlet taffetas, orange brocades. Each cloth, each garment had been chosen as an instrument to call attention to herself. She had seen Judith Revedoune's gowns at her wedding and Alice knew that the heiress's taste ran to simple colors of lush, finely woven fabrics. Alice meant to draw attention away from Gavin's wife with her brilliant clothes.

She wore an undertunic of pale rose, the arms embroidered with black braid swirling round and round. Her crimson velvet dress was cut in deep scallops at the hem and the skirt was appliquéd with enormous wildflowers of every known color. The capelet about her shoulders was her pride. It was of Italian brocade, and in the fabric were colored animals, each one as large as a man's hand, woven in green, purple, orange and black. She was sure no one would outshine her today.

And it was very important that Alice draw attention to herself today because she was to see Gavin again. She smiled at herself in the mirror. She knew she needed Gavin's love after that awful time she'd spent with Edmund. Now that she was a widow, she could look back on Edmund almost fondly. Of course, the poor man was only jealous.

"Look at this circlet!" Alice suddenly commanded her maid, Ela. "Do you think that blue stone matches my eyes? Or is it too light?" Angrily, she snatched the golden circle from her head. "Damn that goldsmith! He must have used his feet to do such clumsy work."

Ela took the headdress from her angry mistress. "The goldsmith is the king's own, the best in all of England, and the circlet is the most beautiful one he has ever created," Ela soothed. "Of course the stone looks light—no stone could match the rich color of your eyes."

Alice looked back at the mirror and began to quiet. "Do you truly think so?"

"Yes," Ela answered honestly. "No woman could rival your beauty."

"Not even that Revedoune bitch?" Alice demanded, refusing to use Judith's married name.

"Most assuredly. My lady, you don't plan something . . . that goes against the church, do you?"

"How could what I do to her be against the church? Gavin was mine before she took him, and he will be mine again!"

Ela knew from experience that it was impossible to reason with Alice once her mind was set on something. "Do you remember that you mourn your husband as she mourns her father?"

Alice laughed. "I imagine we feel the same about those two men. I have heard that her father was even more despicable than my late beloved husband."

"Don't speak so of the dead."

"And don't you reprimand me, or I will see you go to someone else." It was a familiar threat—one Ela no longer paid any attention to. The worst punishment Alice could imagine was to deny a person her company.

Alice stood and smoothed her gown. All the colors

and textures flashed and competed with one another.
"Do you think he will notice me?" she asked breathlessly.

"Who could not?"

"Yes," Alice agreed. "Who could not?"

Judith stood silently by her husband's side, overawed
by the king's many guests. Gavin seemed at ease with
them all, a man respected, his word valued. It was good
to see him in another setting besides a highly personal
one. For all their quarrels and disputes, he took care of
her, protected her. He knew she was not used to
crowds, so he kept her close to him, not forcing her to
go to the women, where she would be among strangers.
He took much ribbing about this but he smiled
good-naturedly with no embarrassment, as most men
would have shown.

The long trestle tables were being set for supper, the
troubadors organizing their musicians, the jongleurs,
the acrobats rehearsing their stunts.

"Are you enjoying yourself?" Gavin asked, smiling
down at her.

"Yes. It's all so noisy and active, though."

He laughed. "It will get worse. Let me know if you
get tired, and we'll leave."

"You don't mind that I stay so near you?"

"I would mind if you didn't. I wouldn't like you to be
free amid these people. Too many young men—and old
men, for that matter—look at you."

"They do?" Judith asked innocently. "I hadn't
noticed."

"Judith, don't tease these men. The morals at court
are very loose, and I wouldn't like for you to be trapped
in some web of your own innocent making. Stay by me
or Stephen. Don't venture too far away alone. Unless"—his eyes hardened in memory of Walter Demari,
—"you wish to encourage someone."

She started to speak, to tell him what she thought of

his insinuations, but an earl of somewhere—she could never keep them straight—came to talk to Gavin. "I will go to Stephen," she said and walked along the edge of the enormous room to where her brother-in-law leaned against the tapestried wall.

He, like Gavin, was dressed in a rich garment of dark wool, Stephen's brown, Gavin's gray. The form-fitting doublets were also of finely woven dark wool. Judith couldn't help but feel a shiver of pride at being associated with such magnificent men.

Judith noticed a pretty, freckle-faced young woman with a turned-up nose who kept looking at Stephen from around her father's back. "She seems to like you," Judith said.

Stephen didn't look up. "Yes," he said dejectedly. "But my days are numbered, aren't they? A few weeks from now, and I'll have a bit of brown woman on my arm, screeching at my every movement."

"Stephen!" Judith laughed. "She surely couldn't be as bad as you think she is. No woman could be. Look at me. Gavin hadn't seen me before our marriage. Do you think he also worried that I was ugly?"

He looked down at her. "You don't know how much I envy my brother. You are not only beautiful, but wise and kind as well. Gavin is the most fortunate of men."

Judith felt her cheeks turning pink. "You flatter me, but I like to hear it."

"I am no flatterer," Stephen said bluntly.

Suddenly the congenial atmosphere in the hall changed, and both Stephen and Judith looked toward the people around them, feeling that some of the tension was directed toward them. Many people looked at Judith—some in apprehension, some smiling snidely, others in bewilderment—not understanding what the current carried.

"Judith," Stephen said, "have you seen the garden? Queen Elizabeth has some beautiful lilies, and her roses are magnificent."

Judith frowned at him, knowing he wanted her out of the hall for some reason. Several people moved aside and she saw the reason for the tension. Alice Chatworth walked regally into the hall, her head high, a smile of great warmth on her face. And the smile was for one person alone—Gavin.

Judith stared at Alice, her gown seeming gaudy and ill-matched. Alice's pale skin, her obviously artificially darkened eyes did not seem at all beautiful to Judith.

The crowd grew quieter as the "secret" of Alice and Gavin was whispered from one person to the next. Judith turned from the woman to look at her husband. Gavin regarded Alice with an intensity that was almost tangible. His eyes were mesmerized by hers, and nothing seemed likely to break the contact. He watched her make her way slowly toward him and when she was close, she held out her hand. He took it and kissed it lingeringly.

The king's laughter was heard above the small sounds of the hall. "You two seem to know each other."

"We do," Gavin answered, smiling slowly.

"Most assuredly," Alice answered, giving him a demure, closed-lip smile.

"I think I should like to see the garden now," Judith said quickly and took Stephen's extended arm.

"Judith," Stephen began when they were alone in the lovely garden.

"Don't speak to me of her. There is nothing you can say that will give me comfort. I have always known of her. Since the day of our wedding." She looked down at a rose bush, the air heavy with fragrance. "He has never been false to me on her account. He hasn't hidden from me that he loves her or tried to pretend he cares for me in any way."

"Judith, stop this! You can't accept the woman."

Judith turned to Stephen. "And what else can I do? Pray tell me what. He believes me wicked at every turn.

If I go to him when he is held captive, he believes I go to my lover. If I carry his child, he believes it belongs to another."

"The child is Gavin's?"

"I see he has told you that he thinks that my baby is Demari's."

"Why don't you tell him the truth?"

"And have him call me a liar? No, thank you. This child is mine, regardless of the father."

"Judith, it would mean a lot to Gavin to know the child was his."

"Will you run and tell him?" she asked heatedly. "Will you knock his mistress down to get close to him? The news will make him quite happy, I'm sure. He has the Revedoune lands, an heir on the way, and his blonde Alice to love. Forgive me if I am selfish enough to want to keep some small thing for myself for a while."

Stephen sat on a stone bench and stared at her. He knew better than to confront his elder brother at this moment when he was so angry. A woman like Judith didn't deserve such neglect and ill treatment as Gavin heaped upon her.

"My lady," a woman called.

"Here, Joan," Judith answered. "What is it?"

"The tables are set for supper and you must come."

"No, I will not. Please say that I am indisposed. Plead my condition as the cause."

"And let that whore have him!" Joan screeched. "You *must* attend."

"I agree, Judith."

Joan whirled, not previously aware of Stephen's presence. She flushed becomingly. She never quite got over the striking handsomeness of the men in her mistress's new family. Even the way they moved set her to trembling with desire.

"Do you plan to attack him here?" Judith demanded. "You forget yourself at times, Joan."

"It's the man who makes me do so," the maid murmured. "Lord Gavin has asked for you."

"I'm pleased he remembers me," she said sarcastically.

"Yes, I remembered you," Gavin said from the gateway. "Go," he said to the maid. "I would like to speak to my wife alone."

Stephen stood. "I too will go." He gave his brother one hard look, then left.

"I don't feel well," Judith said. "I must go to my room."

Gavin caught her arm and drew her close to him. Her eyes looked at him coldly. How long had it been since she'd looked at him like that! "Judith, don't hate me again."

She tried to twist away from him. "You humiliate me, and I'm not to show anger? I didn't know you thought I was a saint. Perhaps I should make an application for canonization."

He chuckled at her sharp wit. "I did nothing but look at her and kiss her hand. I haven't seen her for a while."

Judith sneered at him. "*Look* at her!" she spat. "The rushes were nearly set on fire."

He looked down at his wife in wonder. "Are you jealous?" he asked quietly.

"Of that blonde who lusts for my husband? No! I would find a worthier candidate if I were to feel jealousy."

Gavin's eyes flared for a moment. He had never before allowed anyone to say anything against Alice. "Your anger says you lie."

"Anger!" she said, then quieted. "Yes, I am angry because you display your passion for everyone to see. You have embarrassed me before the king. Didn't you see how the people stared and whispered?" She wanted to hurt him. "As for jealousy, one must love another for that emotion to occur."

"And you bear me no love?" he asked coldly.

"I have never said so, have I?" She couldn't read his expression. She didn't know whether she hurt Gavin or not; but even if she had, her cruel words gave her no pleasure.

"Come, then," he said, taking her arm. "The king waits supper for us, and you will not insult him with your absence. If it is indeed your wish to stop the gossip, you must play the loving wife."

Judith followed him docilely, her rage strangely gone.

As newly arrived guests and ones to be especially honored, Gavin and Judith were seated by the king and queen; Judith to the king's right, Gavin to the queen's left and beside Gavin, Alice.

"You seem distraught," King Henry said to Judith.

She smiled. "No, it's only the journey and the child that weary me."

"A child, so soon? I'm sure Lord Gavin is especially pleased with that."

She smiled but could give no answer.

"Gavin," Alice said softly so no other ears would hear her words, "it has been so long since I've seen you." She was cautious with him, for she sensed things had changed between them. He had obviously not forgotten his love for her or he couldn't have looked at her as he had earlier. But he had only just finished kissing her hand when his eyes drew away from her and searched the hall. They settled when he saw his wife's retreating back. Moments later, he had deserted Alice and followed Judith.

"My condolences on your husband's early demise," Gavin said coldly.

"You will think I'm heartless, but I grieve very little for the man," Alice murmured sadly. "He was . . . unkind to me."

Gavin looked at her sharply. "But wasn't he your choice?"

"How can you say that? I was forced into the marriage. Oh Gavin, if you had only waited, we could have been together now. But I'm sure the king would allow us to marry." She put her hand on his arm.

He looked at her hand, so thin and pale, then back at her eyes. "Do you forget that I'm married? That I have a wife?"

"The king is a sympathetic man. He would listen. Your marriage could be annulled."

Gavin turned back to his food. "Don't speak to me of annulment. I have heard the word enough to last me a lifetime. She carries a child. Even the king wouldn't dissolve such a marriage." Gavin gave his attention to the queen and began asking questions about the forthcoming marriage of Prince Arthur to the Spanish Catherine.

Alice sat quietly, thinking of Gavin's words. She meant to find out why he was sick of the word "annulment" and why he referred to his wife's baby as "a child"—almost as if he hadn't fathered it.

An hour later, the tables were cleared and stacked against the wall, making room for any who cared to dance. "Would you dance with me?" Gavin asked his wife.

"Should I ask permission?" she asked, looking at Alice where she sat amid several young male admirers.

Gavin's fingers bit into Judith's arm. "You are unfair to me. I didn't arrange the seating for supper. I'm doing all in my power to pacify you, but there are some things I cannot control."

Maybe I am unreasonable, she thought. "Yes, I will dance with you."

"Or perhaps a walk in the garden," he smiled. "It's a warm night."

She hesitated.

"Come with me, Judith." They had no more stepped through the gate when he pulled her into his arms and kissed her hungrily. She clung to him desperately. "My sweet Judith," he whispered. "I don't know that I can bear any more of your anger. It hurts me deeply when you look at me with hatred."

She melted against him. It was the closest he'd ever come to saying he cared for her. Could she trust him, believe in him?

"Come upstairs with me. Let's go to bed, and don't let us quarrel again."

"Are you saying soft words to me in hopes that I won't be cold in bed?" she asked suspiciously.

"I say soft words because I feel them. I don't wish them thrown back at me."

"I . . . apologize. It was unkind of me."

He kissed her again. "I will think of some way for you to apologize for your hasty temper."

Judith giggled and he smiled warmly at her, his hand caressing her temple. "Come with me—or I'll take you in the king's garden."

She looked about the dark place, as if considering.

"No," he laughed. "Don't tempt me." He took her hand and led her up the stairs to the top floor of the manor house. The enormous room had been divided into small bedrooms for the night by folding oak screens.

"My lady," Joan said sleepily when she heard them approach.

"You won't be needed tonight," Gavin said in dismissal.

Joan rolled her eyes and slipped away through the maze of screens.

"She has her eye on your brother," Judith said.

Gavin raised one eyebrow. "Why should you care what Stephen does with his nights?"

Judith smiled up at him. "You waste ours in needless talk. I'll need help with these buttons."

Gavin was becoming quite efficient at undressing his wife. When he started to fling his own clothes away, Judith whispered, "Let me. I will be your squire tonight." She unbuckled the belt that held the doublet over his hard, flat stomach and slipped it over his head. The long-sleeved tunic came next, baring his chest and the upper part of his thighs between the hose and the brief undergarments.

A fat candle burned by the bed and she pushed Gavin toward it, looking at his body with interest. Judith had explored him with her hands but never so thoroughly with her eyes. Her fingertips ran over the muscles of his arm, and his rippling stomach.

"Do I please you?" he asked, his eyes dark.

She smiled at him. At times he could be a little boy, worried whether he pleased her or not. She didn't answer but moved down on the bed and untied the hose, pulling them away from his heavily muscled legs. He lay very still, as if afraid to break the spell. She ran her hands from his feet to the sides of his hips, and deftly untied the linen braies. Her hands roamed over his body.

"You please me," she said as she kissed him. "Do I please you?"

He couldn't answer but pushed her to the bed and moved on top of her. His passion was such that he could not wait for her long, but Judith also needed him as fiercely as he needed her.

Later, Gavin held her closely in his arms as he heard her quiet, even breathing of sleep. When had he fallen in love with her? he wondered. Perhaps he was in love with her when he'd first taken her home and left her on the doorstep. He smiled in memory of how angry he'd been because she'd dared defy him. He kissed her sleeping forehead. Judith would defy him when she was ninety, he thought, looking forward to the idea.

And what of Alice? When had he ceased to love her? Had he ever loved her? Or had it been a young man's passion for a beautiful woman? She was beautiful, it was true, and tonight he'd been startled when he saw her again, somewhat overwhelmed by her radiance.

Alice was a kind and gentle woman, as sweet as Judith was acid, but in the last few months he'd grown to love a bit of vinegar with his food.

Judith moved in his arms and he pulled her closer. He accused her of dishonesty but he didn't really believe his own words. If she carried another man's child, then she had conceived it while trying to protect her husband. Misguided, surely, but her heart was always good. She would give up her own life to save her mother, and even a husband who abused her.

He held her so tightly that she woke, fighting for breath.

"You are strangling me!" she gasped.

He kissed her nose. "Have I ever told you that I like vinegar?"

She gave him a blank look.

"What sort of wife are you?" Gavin demanded. "Don't you know how to help a husband sleep?" He rubbed his hips against hers and her eyes widened. "To sleep so would cause me much pain. You wouldn't want that, would you?"

"No," she whispered, her eyes half-closed. "You shouldn't have to bear such pain."

Gavin was the one who was aroused and Judith lay still in a coma of red and silver light as he ran his hands over her body. It was as if he'd never touched her before, and her body was completely new to her. After his hands became familiar with her soft, smooth skin, he started exploring again with his eyes.

Judith cried out in desperate longing for him, but he only laughed at her and pushed her hands away from his shoulders. When she was trembling with desire, he entered her and they came together almost instantly. They fell asleep, joined, Gavin still on top of her.

When Judith woke the next morning, Gavin was gone and the bed felt cold and empty. Joan helped her dress in a gown of maroon velvet, the neckline square and cut very low. Her sleeves were lined with fox. Across her breast and around her waist were gold cords, fastened at the shoulder with a diamond brooch. At supper there'd been talk of a day's hawking, and she wished to join the hunt.

Gavin met her at the foot of the stairs, his eyes dancing in delight. "You're a sleepy one. I'd hoped to find you still in bed, and perhaps join you there."

She smiled teasingly. "Shall I return?"

"No, not now. I have some news for you. I have spoken to the king, and he agrees to allow John Bassett to marry your mother." King Henry was a Welshman, a descendant of commoners.

She stared at him.

"Doesn't that please you?"

"Oh, Gavin!" she said and launched herself from the steps into his arms. Her arms were so tight about his neck, that he nearly choked. "Thank you. Many thousands of times, thank you."

He laughed and hugged her closer to him. "If I'd thought your reaction would have been like this, I would have talked to the king last night."

"You couldn't have handled more last night," Judith said flatly.

He laughed and squeezed her until she cried for release, her ribs nearly breaking. "You don't think so?" Gavin challenged. "Goad me some more and I'll take you upstairs and keep you there until you are too sore to walk."

"Gavin!" she gasped, her face red. She looked around to see if anyone was listening.

He chuckled and kissed her lightly.

"My mother knows of her marriage?"

"No, I thought maybe you'd like to tell her."

"I'm ashamed to say I don't even know where she is."

"I sent John to look after the lodging of my men. I would imagine your mother to be somewhere near him."

"True, she doesn't often leave his side. Gavin, thank you. It was very kind of you to grant me this favor."

"I wish I could grant you everything that you wanted," he said softly.

She looked at him in wonder.

"Go then," he smiled. "Tell your mother, then join me in the courtyard for the hunt." He set her down, then gazed at her with concern. "You are well enough to ride?"

It was the first time that he had mentioned the child in any way but anger. "Yes," she smiled. "I'm quite well. Queen Elizabeth says the exercise will do me good."

"Just be sure you don't overdo," Gavin cautioned.

She smiled and turned away, her mind warm from his concern. She felt light with happiness.

Judith walked down the stairs and out of the great hall. The enormous castleyard that stood inside the guarded walls was filled with people. The noise was nearly deafening as men and women shouted to servants and servants yelled at each other. Everything seemed so disorganized that Judith wondered how anything got done. A long building stood at the end of the courtyard. Horses pranced about outside, held by their grooms. It was obviously the stables.

"Ah, if it isn't little Miss Red-Hair," came a purring voice that halted Judith instantly. "Are you on your way to some tryst with a lover, perhaps?"

Judith stopped and stared at Alice Chatworth. Her enemy—face to face.

"I'm sure you must remember me," Alice said sweetly. "We met at your wedding."

"I'm sorry I was not able to attend yours, although Gavin and I shared your message of undying love," Judith returned in kind.

Alice's eyes shot blue fire, her body stiffened. "Yes, it is too bad it all ended so soon."

"Ended?"

Alice smiled. "Haven't you heard? My husband,

poor dear, was murdered in his sleep. I'm a widow now, and free. Oh yes, very free. I assumed Gavin told you. He was most interested in my . . . ah . . . new status."

Judith turned on her heel and stalked away. No, she hadn't known Alice was no longer married. Now all that stood between Alice and Gavin was herself. No Edmund Chatworth hindered them.

Chapter Twenty-five

JUDITH CONTINUED TO WALK TOWARD THE STABLES, BUT she had no idea where she was going. Her mind was only aware of the fact that Alice Chatworth was a widow.

"Judith."

She looked up and managed to smile at her mother.

"Will you ride in the hunt today?"

"Yes," she said, the joy gone from her day.

"What's wrong?"

Judith tried to smile. "I lose my mother—that's all. Did you know that Gavin has given permission for your marriage to John Bassett?"

Helen stared at her daughter. She neither spoke nor smiled. Slowly, the color drained from her face. She fell forward into her daughter's arms.

"Help!" Judith managed to gasp.

A tall young man who was nearby ran to her and quickly lifted Helen.

"To the stables," directed Judith, "out of the sun."

Once in the shade, Helen began to recover almost instantly.

"Mother, you are well?"

Helen looked meaningfully at the young man.

He understood the look. "I'll leave you alone," he said and walked away before Judith could even thank him.

"I . . . didn't know," Helen began. "I mean I didn't know Lord Gavin even knew of my love for John."

Judith stopped herself from laughing aloud. "I asked him some time ago for permission, but he wanted to consult the king. Yours will be an unusual wedding."

"And soon enough," Helen murmured.

"Soon—? Mother!"

Helen smiled like a child caught in some mischief. "It's true—I bear his child."

Judith sank into a pile of hay. "Shall we deliver together?" she asked in wonder.

"Close."

Judith laughed. "Arrangements must be made quickly, so the baby will be able to claim a name."

"Judith!" She looked up to see Gavin coming toward them. "A man said your mother took ill."

She rose and took his arm. "Come, we must talk."

Moments later, Gavin shook his head in disbelief. "And to think I believed John Bassett to be a sensible man!"

"He's in love. Men and women do unusual things when they're in love."

Gavin looked at her eyes, the gold especially brilliant in the sunlight. "I'm well aware of that."

"Why didn't you tell me she was a widow?" Judith asked quietly.

"Who?" he asked, honestly puzzled.

"Alice! Who else?"

He shrugged. "I didn't think to tell you." He smiled. "I find I have other thoughts when you are near me."

"Are you trying to change the subject?"

He grabbed Judith by the shoulders, lifting her from

the ground. "Damn you! It's not I who am obsessed with the woman, but you. If I cannot reason with you, I'll try to shake some sense into you. Would you like to be shaken in public?"

He shook his head in wonder when she smiled at him sweetly. "I would rather attend the hunt. Perhaps you could help me mount my horse?"

He stared at her a moment, then set her down. He would *never* understand women.

The hunt was exhilarating to Judith, the little tiercel hawk on a perch on her saddle. Her hawk brought down three cranes, and she was well pleased with the day's hunting.

Gavin wasn't as lucky. He was barely in his saddle when he received a whispered message from a maid. Stephen wished to meet with him on some private matter when they were two miles outside the castle walls. His brother asked that he tell no one about the meeting—even his wife. Gavin was puzzled by the message as it didn't sound like Stephen. He left the hunting party while Judith was engrossed in the flight of her tiercel, cursing his brother under his breath for taking him away from such a lovely sight.

Gavin didn't ride directly to the place indicated but tied his horse some distance away and approached cautiously, sword drawn.

"Gavin!" Alice said, her hand to her breast. "You gave me a terrible fright."

"Where is Stephen?" Gavin asked, still looking about the place warily.

"Gavin, please put your sword away. You frighten me!" Alice smiled, but her eyes didn't look fearful.

"You have called me, and not Stephen?"

"Yes, it was the only way I knew to get you here." She lowered her eyes. "I thought you wouldn't come for me alone."

Gavin sheathed his sword. It was a quiet and

secluded place, much like the one where she used to meet him.

"Ah, so you think of that time also. Come, sit by me. We have a lot to talk about."

He stared at her and without wanting to he began to compare her to Judith. Alice was pretty, yes, but her little mouth with its closed-lip smile seemed ungenerous—stingy, almost. Her blue eyes rather reminded him of ice rather than sapphires. And the red, orange and green she wore seemed gaudy instead of brilliant, as he used to think of her clothes.

"Have things changed so much that you sit so far away from me?"

"Yes, they have." Gavin didn't see the brief frown that crossed her pale brow.

"Are you still angry with me? I've told you over and over that I was married against my will to Edmund. But now that I am a widow we—"

"Alice," he interrupted, "please don't talk of that again." He had to tell her, and he dreaded hurting her. She was so soft and delicate, so unable to take the pain of life. "I will not leave Judith, neither through annulment nor divorce nor any other unnatural means."

"I . . . don't understand. There is a chance for us now."

He put his hand over hers in her lap. "No, there is not."

"Gavin! What are you saying?"

"I have grown to love her," he said simply.

Alice's eyes blazed at him a moment before she recovered her temper. "You said you would not. On your wedding day you *promised* me that you wouldn't love her."

Gavin almost smiled in memory. Two vows had been made that day. Judith had vowed to give him only what he took. How deliciously she had broken that vow! And he, too, had broken his. "Don't you remember that you threatened to take your own life? I would have done or said most anything to keep you from doing that."

"But now you no longer care what I do with my life?"

"No! It's not that. You know you will always have a place in my heart. You were my first love, and I will never forget you."

Alice looked up at him, wide-eyed. "You talk as if I were already dead. Tell me, has she taken all your heart that I can have none?"

"I told you that you had a part, Alice, don't do this to us. You must accept what has happened."

Alice smiled, her eyes beginning to fill with tears. "Should I accept it with the fortitude of a man? But Gavin, I'm a woman—a frail and fragile woman. Your heart may be cold to me, but mine is only warmer at seeing you again. Do you know what it was like being married to Edmund? He treated me like a servant, locked me in my room continually."

"Alice—"

"And can you guess why? Because at your wedding he had me watched. Yes, he knew when we went alone to the garden. He knew the times when I was alone with you in your tent. Remember the time you kissed me with such feeling, the morning after your wedding?"

Gavin nodded, not wanting to hear her confession.

"During our marriage, he never lost a moment to remind me of the time I had spent with you. Yet I bore it all, willingly—gladly almost—for I knew you loved me. Each and every lonely night I lay awake and thought of you, of your love for me."

"Alice, you must stop."

"Tell me," she said quietly, "didn't you once think of me?"

"Yes," he answered honestly. "I did at first. But Judith is a good woman, kind and loving. I never thought I would love her. It was a marriage for estates, as you know."

Alice sighed. "What am I to do now? My heart is yours—has always been, will always be."

"Alice, this won't help. It's over between us. I'm married and I love my wife. You and I must part ways."

"You are so cold to me." Alice touched his arm, then moved her hand up to his shoulder. "Once you were not so cold."

Gavin clearly remembered making love to Alice. Then he had been blinded by his love for her, and he believed anything she did was the way it should be done. But now, after months of passion with Judith, the idea of bedding Alice almost repulsed him. The way she could not stand to be touched before or after lovemaking. No, with Alice it was sex—a pure animal drive, nothing else.

Alice saw the expression on his face but didn't understand it. She continued with her hand until she touched his neck. He stood immediately. Alice stood also, but she took his reluctance at her touch as a sign of his growing desire for her. She stood boldly against him, her arms going around his neck. "I see you do remember," she whispered, raising her face to be kissed.

He gently pulled her arms from his neck. "No, Alice."

She glared at him, her hands clenched into fists at her sides. "You are so unmanned by her that you are afraid of her?"

"No," Gavin said, surprised, both at Alice's reasoning and her outburst. Anger was unnatural to Alice, who was always so sweet-tempered.

Alice quickly realized she'd made an error in revealing her true emotions. She blinked her eyes until great jewellike tears formed. "This is good-bye," she whispered. "May I not have even one last kiss? You would deny me that, after all we've meant to each other?"

She was so delicate and he'd loved her so much once. He wiped a tear from her cheek with his fingertip. "No," he whispered. "I wouldn't deny myself one last kiss." He took her gently in his arms and kissed her sweetly.

But Alice wanted no sweetness. He had forgotten her violence by half. She thrust her tongue in his mouth, grinding her teeth against his lips. He felt no building ardor as he once would have, but only a faint sense of distaste. He wanted to get away from her. "I must go," he said, concealing his revulsion.

But Alice could feel that something was very wrong. She thought to bring him under control through that kiss but she knew she hadn't. If anything, he was more remote than before. She bit her tongue over her sharp words and managed to look properly sad as he made his way through the trees to his waiting horse. "Damn that bitch!" Alice said through clenched teeth. That red-haired she-devil had taken her man!

Or at least she thought she had. Alice began to smile. Maybe that Revedoune woman thought she had Gavin, that she could crook her little finger and he would come to her. But she was mistaken! Alice would not allow someone to take what was hers. No, she would fight for her property and Gavin was hers . . . or he would be again.

She had done so much to get where she was now, at the king's court near Gavin; she had even allowed her husband's murderer to escape. She would watch the woman and find her weakness. Then Alice would regain what was hers. Even if she decided to cast Gavin aside, it was to be her decision and not his!

Gavin rode back to the hunting party quickly. He had been gone a long time, but he hoped no one had missed him. He sent up a silent prayer of thanks that Judith hadn't seen him kissing Alice. No amount of explaining in the world would have pacified her. But all that was over. As difficult as it had been, he had told Alice, and now he was forever free of her.

Gavin saw his wife ahead, swinging her lure to bring her tiercel back to the perch. Suddenly his desire for her was boundless. He urged his mount forward until he was almost galloping by the time he reached her horse. He bent forward and jerked the reins.

"Gavin!" Judith called as she grabbed the pommel of the saddle, her tiercel flapping its wings in fright.

The people around them hooted in laughter. "They have been married how long?"

"Not long enough," came the reply.

Gavin stopped both horses when they were some distance away in a secluded glade.

"Gavin! Have you lost your mind?" Judith demanded.

He slid from his horse then lifted her from hers. He didn't speak to her but began kissing her hungrily. "I was thinking of you," he whispered. "And the more I thought of you, the more my need . . . arose."

"I can feel your need." She looked about her. "This is a pretty place isn't it?"

"It could be prettier."

"Yes, it could," she answered as he kissed her again.

The sweet outdoor summer air added a great deal to their passion as did the slightly naughty idea that they were doing something somewhere they shouldn't. Judith giggled when Gavin made a comment on King Henry's numerous children. He stopped her laughter with his lips.

They fumbled with each other's clothing hurriedly and made love as if they'd not seen each other for years. Later, they cuddled close together, wrapped in warm sunlight and the delicate scent of wildflowers.

Chapter Twenty-Six

ALICE LOOKED OVER THE HEADS OF THE MANY MEN around her to the slim, blond, handsome man leaning against the wall. He had a pensive expression on his face that she recognized as that of someone in love. She smiled sweetly at a man nearby but Alice didn't really hear him. Her mind was completely on that afternoon, when Gavin said he was in love with his wife. She watched as Gavin held his wife's hand and led her through the intricate steps of a dance. It didn't matter that Alice had several young men at her feet. Being scorned by Gavin only made her want him more. Had he sworn he loved her still, perhaps she would have considered one of the many marriage proposals offered to her. But Gavin had rejected her, and now she knew she must have him. Only one thing stood in her way, and that she planned to remove.

The young blond man stared at Judith with fascination, his eyes never leaving her. Alice had noticed him at dinner when he looked up at the high table, not even blinking as he stared at Judith. Alice realized that the woman was too stupid to even be aware of an admirer, for Judith's eyes never left Gavin.

"Will you excuse me?" Alice murmured demurely and dismissed the men around her as she walked toward the man against the wall.

"She is lovely, isn't she?" Alice asked, gritting her teeth against the words.

"Yes," he whispered, the word coming from his soul.

"It's sad to see a woman such as that so unhappy."

The man turned and looked at Alice. "She doesn't look to be unhappy."

"No, she makes a good show, but the unhappiness is there."

"You are Lady Alice Chatworth?"

"Yes. And you?"

"Alan Fairfax, my beautiful countess," he said as he bowed and kissed her hand. "At your service."

Alice laughed gaily. "It is not I who need your service, but the Lady Judith."

Alan looked back at the dancers. "She is the most beautiful woman I have ever seen," he whispered.

Alice's eyes glittered like blue glass. "Have you told her of your love?"

"No!" he said, frowning. "I am a knight, sworn to honor, and she is a married woman."

"Yes, she is, though most unhappily."

"She doesn't look to be unhappy," he repeated as he watched the object of his affections look up at her husband with great warmth.

"I have known her a long time and she is indeed miserable. Only yesterday she was crying to me that she desperately needed someone to love, someone who would be sweet and gentle with her."

"Her husband is not?" Alan was concerned.

"It's not common knowledge"—Alice lowered her voice—"but he beats her often."

Alan looked back at Judith. "I don't believe you."

Alice shrugged. "I didn't mean to spread gossip. She is my friend and I would like to help her. They won't stay at court for long, and I'd hoped that before they left dear Judith could find just a few moments of pleasure."

It was true that Lady Judith was lovely; her radiant

coloring saw to that. Her auburn hair was visible
beneath a veil of transparent gauze. The silver tissue of
her dress hugged lush curves. But what Alan thought
was even more striking than her beauty was the vitality
she seemed to emanate. She looked at everyone, from
king to serf, with a calm level look that said she cared.
She never giggled or flirted or played the coy maiden.
Alan was truly fascinated by her. He would give a lot to
have her once turn those warm golden eyes on him.

"Would you like to see her alone?"

Alan's eyes sparkled. "Yes, I would."

"Then I will arrange it. Go to the garden and I'll send
her to you. We're great friends and she knows she can
trust me." Alice stopped and put a hand on Alan's arm.
"She'll worry that she is safe from her husband's
finding her. Tell her he is with me—then she'll know
that she has no fear of being discovered."

Alan nodded. It wouldn't hurt to spend some time
with the lady, and since her husband rarely let her out
of his sight, Alan would use this opportunity.

Judith stood close to Gavin, drinking a mug of cool
cider. She was warm from the dancing, and it was
pleasant to lean against the cool stone and watch the
others. A man came with a message for Gavin, which
he repeated quietly, for Gavin's ears alone. Gavin
frowned.

"Have you had bad news?" she asked.

"I don't know. Someone says I must meet them."

"No name?"

"No. I asked a horse merchant about a mare—
perhaps it's only that." He turned and caressed her
cheek. "There is Stephen. Go and stay by him. This
won't take long."

"If I can find a way through the women around
Stephen!" she laughed.

"You will do as I say."

"Yes, my lord," she said mockingly.

He shook his head at Judith, but smiled, then turned
and left.

She went to stand by Stephen who strummed on a lute and sang for a group of pretty and adoring young women. Stephen had told her that he meant to use his last days of freedom to advantage.

"Lady Judith?"

"Yes." She turned to a maid, one she did not recognize.

"There is a man waiting for you in the garden."

"A man? My husband?"

"I don't know, my lady."

Judith began to smile. No doubt Gavin planned some moonlight tryst. "Thank you," she said, leaving the hall to go to the garden. The garden was dark and cool, with many secret shadows that told of several couples locked together in each other's arms.

"Lady Judith?"

"Yes." It wasn't possible to see clearly but she saw a tall, slim young man with bright eyes, a prominent nose and lips a little too full.

"Allow me to introduce myself. I am Alan Fairfax of Lincolnshire."

She smiled at him as he took her hand and kissed it.

"Are you looking for someone?"

"I thought my husband would be here."

"I haven't seen him."

"You know him then?"

He smiled, showing even white teeth. "I have seen you. It is more that I know you and am aware of who is near you."

She looked at him in wonder. "A very pretty speech, sir."

Alan held his arm out for her. "Shall we sit here a moment while we wait for your husband?"

She hesitated.

"As you see, the bench is in plain view. I ask nothing of you but that you sit and talk to a lonely knight."

The bench was directly under a bright torch held in the garden wall. Judith could see him more clearly. His lips were sensual, his nose thin and aristocratic. His

eyes were almost black in the darkness. Judith was
wary of him. The last man she had sat and talked with
was Walter Demari, and that had led to disaster.

"You seem ill at ease, my lady."

"I'm not used to courtly ways. I've spent very little
time with men who aren't related to me."

"But you wish to spend more?" he encouraged.

"I hadn't thought about it. I have my husband and
his brothers. They seem to be enough."

"But here at court a lady may be freer. It's accepta-
ble to have many friends, both men and women." Alan
took her hand from her lap. "I should very much like to
be your friend."

She jerked away from him, frowning, then rose. "I
must return to the hall and my husband."

He stood beside her. "There's no need to fear him.
He is safely away. He is with your friend Alice
Chatworth."

"No! You insult me!"

"No," Alan said, bewildered. "I didn't mean to.
What have I said?"

So! Gavin was with Alice. Perhaps he arranged that
she should spend this time with another man in the
hope that she would be occupied. But she had no desire
to stay with a stranger. "I must go," she said quickly,
turning on her heel.

"Where have you been?" Gavin demanded, meeting
her before she reached the hall.

"With my lover," she said calmly. "And you?"

His hands tightened on her arms. "Are you teasing
me?"

"Perhaps."

"Judith!"

She glared at him. "Wasn't the Lady Alice especially
lovely tonight? Gold cloth goes well with her hair and
eyes, don't you think?"

Gavin loosened his hold somewhat, smiling slightly.
"I didn't notice. Are you jealous of her?"

"Do I have cause?"

"No, Judith, you do not. I have told you she is gone from my life."

She sneered at him. "Next you will be telling me your love is now mine."

"And if I did?" Gavin whispered with such an intensity she was almost frightened.

Her heart fluttered. "I don't know if I would believe you," she said quietly. Or was she afraid that if he said he loved her that she would return the words? Would he laugh at her? Would he and his Alice lay in each other's arms and make light of what to Judith was life and death?

"Come inside, then. It grows late."

What was there in his voice that made her want to comfort him?

"You leave tomorrow?" Gavin asked as he wiped sweat from his brow. He had been training since sunup on the king's long sand-covered field. There were many knights and squires present from all over England.

"Yes," Stephen said with an air of gloom. "I feel as though I'm going to my death."

Gavin laughed. "It won't be so bad. Look at my marriage. It has turned out quite well."

"Yes, but there is only one Judith."

Gavin smiled and scratched at the heavy armor he wore. "Yes, and she is mine."

Stephen returned his smile. "All is well between you then?"

"It's coming along. She is jealous of Alice and forever accuses me of all manner of happenings with her, but Judith will come round."

"And what of your Alice?"

"I'm no longer interested. I told her so yesterday."

Stephen gave a low whistle. "You told Alice, whom you once loved, that you now prefer another? I would fear for my life if I were you."

"Perhaps from Judith, but not from one as sweet as Alice."

"Alice Chatworth? Sweet? You are truly blind, my brother."

As always, Gavin was angered when someone spoke ill of Alice. "You don't know her as I do. She was very hurt when I told her, but she accepted it regally, as I knew she would. If Judith hadn't captured me so completely, I would still think of Alice as a choice for my wife."

Stephen thought it was better not to comment further. "Tonight I plan a splendid drunk. I will drink the castle dry. Then, when I see this bride of mine, I'll be better able to stomach her. Would you care to join me? We shall celebrate my last moments of freedom."

Gavin smiled in anticipation. "Yes, we haven't celebrated our escape from Demari's. Stephen, I didn't tell you my thanks."

Stephen hit his brother on the back. "You must return the favor when I need you."

Gavin frowned. "Maybe you can find me a man to replace John Bassett."

"Ask Judith," Stephen said, his eyes twinkling. "Perhaps she can run your men also."

"Don't even hint such an idea to her. She complains now that she has too little to do here."

"That's your fault, brother. Don't you keep her busy?"

"Have a care! I may begin to hope that your Scottish heiress is as ugly as you think she is."

Judith sat in the great hall amid a group of women. All of them, including the queen, sat behind beautiful rosewood and brass embroidery frames. Their hands flew deftly and swiftly over the fabric, beautiful colors of silk streaming from their needles. Judith sat quietly in a chair, a piece of embroidery before her, too; but she merely stared at it, feeling awkward, not knowing what else to do with herself. At least Gavin could do his work even when he was away from home. But he had threatened her against cleaning the king's fishpond . . . or his pantry or anything else, for that matter.

"I think that sewing is the most feminine of arts. Don't you agree, Your Majesty?" Alice said quietly.

Queen Elizabeth didn't even look up. "I believe it would depend upon the woman. I have seen some women use a crossbow, yet retain their femininity, while another who looked sweet and performed all the female arts to perfection, could underneath be cruel."

Judith looked up in surprise as a giggle escaped from a pretty young woman next to her.

"You don't agree, Lady Isabel?" Queen Elizabeth asked.

"Oh yes, Your Majesty, I most certainly do." The two women exchanged understanding glances.

Alice, furious at being set down, continued. "But would a true woman wish to use a crossbow? I cannot see that there would be a need. Women are always protected by men."

"May a woman not help her husband? I once took an arrow meant for John," Lady Isabel said.

Several of the women gasped in horror.

Alice looked at the green-eyed woman with disgust. "But a true woman could not do violence. Could they, Lady Judith? I mean, a woman couldn't kill a man, could she?"

Judith looked down at the empty canvas on the stretcher.

Alice leaned forward. "Lady Judith, you couldn't kill a man, could you?"

"Lady Alice!" Queen Elizabeth said sharply. "I believe you pry into matters that are not your concern."

"Oh!" Alice feigned surprise. "I didn't know the Lady Judith's handiness with a sword was a secret. I won't speak of it again."

"No, you won't," Lady Isabel lashed out, "now that you have told everything."

"My lady!" Joan announced loudly, "Lord Gavin requests you immediately."

"Is anything wrong?" Judith asked, rising quickly.

"I don't know," Joan said, an odd, blank expression on her face. "You know how he cannot bear for you to be out of his sight for very long."

Judith gave her a look of astonishment.

"Come quickly. He won't wait long."

Judith refrained from reprimanding her maid before the queen. She turned and excused herself from the women, glad to see that Alice's eyes smoldered in anger. When they were away, Judith turned back to her maid. "You forget yourself."

"No! I only helped you. That cat would tear you to shreds. You're no match for her."

"She doesn't frighten me."

"Then perhaps she should. She is an evil woman."

"Yes," Judith agreed. "I am aware of that. I am grateful though that you took me from that place. I almost prefer Alice's company to sewing, but the two together are more than I can bear!" She sighed. "I suppose Gavin didn't send for me."

"Why must he send for you? Don't you think he will be pleased to see you?"

Judith frowned.

"You are a foolish woman," Joan said, risking harsh words from her mistress. "The man wants you, yet you don't see it."

Once outside in the bright sunlight, Judith forgot all thoughts of Alice. Gavin leaned over a large trough of water, bare from the waist up as he washed himself. Judith crept silently behind him then leaned over and gave him a nipping kiss on his neck. The next moment she found herself gasping for breath as Gavin swung round and knocked her into the trough. Both of them were very surprised.

"Judith! Are you hurt?" Gavin asked as he put his hand out to her.

She knocked it away, wiping water from her eyes, looking at her soaked and ruined gown, the crimson velvet plastered to her body. "I am not, you clumsy oaf. Do you think I'm your war-horse, that I may be treated as an animal? Or perhaps you think I'm your squire?" She put her hand to the side of the trough to lift herself, but her feet slipped and she went under again. She gasped as she looked up at Gavin. His arms were folded across his chest and he wore a broad smile.

"You are laughing at me!" she hissed, enraged. "How dare—"

He grabbed her shoulders and lifted her dripping body. "May I offer my apologies? I'm not exactly calm since Demari's. I was too late in recognizing your kiss as a kiss. You shouldn't sneak upon me, but give me some warning."

"You needn't fear such happening again," Judith said grimly.

"Only you, my little wife, would be so saucy while being held over a body of water. I could drop you in again."

"You wouldn't dare!"

He grinned then lowered her slowly until her toes came near the water again.

"Gavin!" she cried, half-pleading.

He drew her to him, then gasped as her cold body touched his skin.

"You are well repaid," she laughed. "I hope you freeze."

"Not with you near." He swung her into his arms. "Let's go to our room and remove these wet clothes."

"Gavin, you can't think—"

"Thinking, while you are in my arms, is a waste of time. If you don't want to cause more attention drawn to yourself, be quiet and let me have my way."

"And if I don't?"

He rubbed his cheek against her wet one. "You will find those pretty cheeks will turn very red."

"Then I am a captive?"

"Yes," he answered firmly and carried her up the stairs.

Queen Elizabeth walked beside her husband. They stopped when they saw Gavin knock Judith into the water. Elizabeth would have gone to help Judith, but Henry stopped her.

"Look at their love play. It pleases me when I see a couple so in love. It isn't often that a marriage of estates turns to happiness."

Elizabeth sighed. "I'm glad to see them each loving the other. I wasn't sure there was love there. Lady Alice seems to think the Lady Judith isn't a fit match for Lord Gavin."

"Lady Alice?" King Henry asked. "She is that blonde woman?"

"Yes. Edmund Chatworth's widow."

Henry nodded. "I would like to see her married soon. I have watched her. She plays with men, rather like a cat with a mouse. She seems to care for one, then the other. The men are in love with her beauty and will take much from her. I wouldn't like to see them come to blows. But what has the woman to do with Lord Gavin and that lovely wife of his?"

"I'm not sure," Elizabeth said. "There is some gossip that Gavin was once in love with Lady Alice."

Henry nodded toward Gavin as he lifted his wife into his arms. "He is not so now, as everyone can see."

"Maybe not everyone. Lady Alice baits Lady Judith constantly."

"We must stop this," Henry said.

"No," Elizabeth put a hand on her husband's arm. "We can give no orders. I fear it will only make Alice more angry, and she is the kind of woman who would find a way to say what she wanted no matter what orders were given her. I think your idea of marriage to be the best. Can't you find a husband for her?"

Henry watched Gavin carrying his wife toward the manor house, teasing and tickling her, causing Judith's laughter to ring through the yard. "Yes, I will find Lady Alice a husband, and quickly. I wouldn't like to see anything come between those two."

"You are a good man," Elizabeth said and smiled up at her tall husband.

Henry chuckled. "Only to a few, my dear. You should ask the French who is a good king or not."

Elizabeth waved her hand. "You are too soft on them, too good to them."

He bent and kissed her forehead. "And if I were a French king, I'm sure you'd say the same of the English."

She smiled lovingly up at him and he laughed and squeezed her arm.

There was someone else who took a special interest in the play of the Montgomeries. Alan Fairfax had started forward, his hands on his sword when he saw Gavin knock Judith into the trough. Then he looked about guiltily. A man could treat his wife in any manner he wished, and Alan had no right to interfere.

As Alan watched, he saw Gavin's concern for Judith, how he took her from the water, held her and kissed her. This was no man who beat his wife! Alan frowned as he began to realize that he had been played for a fool.

He went back into the manor house where he found Alice Chatworth crossing the great hall. "I would like a word with you, my lady," he said, his fingers tightening on her arm.

She gasped at the pain, then smiled. "Of course, Sir Alan. My time is yours to command."

He drew her to the side of the room, into the shadows. "You have used me, and I don't like that."

"Used you? Pray, how so, sir?"

"Don't play the coy virgin with me. I know of the men who frequent your bed. You are a woman of some intelligence, I am sure, and you have manipulated me for your own purpose."

"Release me or I will scream!"

His hand dug deeper into her arm. "Don't I please you? My friends tell me you're not averse to pain."

Alice glared at him. "What is it you wish to say to me?"

"I don't care to be used. Your lies could have given Lady Judith great trouble, and I would have been the cause."

"Didn't you say you wished a few moments alone with her? I gave you that time—that's all."

"By trickery! She is a good woman and happily wed, and I'm no villain to resort to rape."

"Then you do desire her?" Alice smiled.

He released her quickly. "What man wouldn't? She is beautiful."

"No!" Alice hissed. "She's not as beautiful—" She stopped herself.

Alan smiled. "As you, Lady Alice? No, you are wrong. I have watched Lady Judith for days, and I have come to know her. She is not only beautiful on the outside, but inwards as well. When she is old and not so lovely, she will be well loved. But you! Your beauty is on the outside alone. If it were taken away from you, only a querulous, evil-minded, vicious woman would remain."

"I shall hate you for this!" Alice said in a deadly voice.

"Someday every second you have spent hating will show on your face," Alan noted calmly. "Whatever your feelings for me, don't think I can be used again." He turned his back on her and left her alone.

Alice watched his retreating back but her vengeance was for Judith rather than for Alan. The woman had been the cause of all her problems. Nothing had been the same since Gavin had decided to marry the bitch. Now Alice was insulted by a young man because of the deviousness of that Revedoune woman. Alice was even more determined to put an end to a marriage that she considered wrong.

"Judith, sweet. Stay in bed," Gavin murmured against her sleepy cheek. "You need rest, and the water may have given you a chill."

Judith didn't answer. She was sated with their lovemaking and feeling drowsy and languid.

He nuzzled his face against her neck once more and slipped from the bed. He dressed quickly, watching her all the while. When he was dressed, he smiled at her, kissed her cheeks and left the room.

Stephen met him at the foot of the stairs. "I can't walk through a room that I don't hear more gossip of you!"

"What now?" Gavin asked suspiciously.

"Only that you beat your wife and throw her in troughs of water, then flaunt her before everyone."

Gavin smiled. "It's all true."

Stephen returned his brother's grin. "Now we understand each other. I thought you didn't know how to treat a woman. Is she asleep?"

"Yes. She will stay there the night." Gavin lifted one brow. "I thought you would have a hogshead of wine ready."

"I do," Stephen grinned. "I didn't want you to feel the lesser man by my drinking twice as much as you."

"You!" Gavin snorted. "My younger brother? Didn't you know I got drunk the first time before you were born?"

"I don't believe you!"

"It's true. I'll tell you the story though it is a very long one."

Stephen slapped his brother on the back. "We have all night. The morning is when we'll repent what we've done."

Gavin chuckled. "You shall repent with your ugly Scottish bride, but I will wearily lay my head in my beautiful wife's lap and kindly allow her to cosset me."

Stephen groaned. "You are a cruel man!"

For both brothers, the night was a special time of closeness. They celebrated their release from Demari. They celebrated Gavin's good fortune in his marriage, and they commiserated together on the prospect of Stephen's forthcoming one.

"I'll give her back to her people if she disobeys me," Stephen said. The wine they drank was so bad that they had to strain it through their teeth, but neither of them noticed.

"Two disobedient wives!" Gavin said in a slur as he raised his mug. "If Judith were to obey me, I would think a devil had stolen her mind."

"And left only her body?" Stephen leered.

"I will call you out for that," Gavin said as he fumbled for his sword.

"She wouldn't have me," Stephen responded as he refilled his cup.

"You don't think so? She certainly seemed pleased with Demari." Gavin changed from happiness to sadness in moments, as only a drunk could.

"No, she hated the man."

"But she bears his child!" Gavin said, sounding like a little boy about to cry.

"You have no sense, brother! The child is yours, not Demari's."

"I don't believe you."

"It's true. She told me."

Gavin sat at the thick table silently for a moment then started to rise, but his head swam. "You're sure? Why didn't she tell me?"

"She said she wanted to keep some small thing to herself."

Gavin sat down heavily. "She considers my son a small thing?"

"No. You don't understand women."

"And you do?" Gavin asked archly.

Stephen refilled his brother's mug. "No more than you do, I'm sure. Perhaps even less, if that is possible.

Raine could explain what she said better than I. She said you already had the Revedoune lands and Alice, and she would give you no more."

Gavin's face blackened as he rose. Then suddenly he calmed and sat down again, a slight smile on his face. "She is a witch, isn't she? She swings her hips before me until I am blind with desire. She curses me when I merely talk to another woman."

"One you have freely admitted you loved."

Gavin waved his hand as if that didn't matter. "And yet she holds the key that would unlock all secrets and free us both from the strain that is between us."

"I don't see any reluctance on your part," Stephen said.

Gavin chuckled. "No, none on mine, but I have been reluctant to . . . force myself on her. I thought that Demari meant something to her."

"Only a means to save your unappreciative neck."

Gavin smiled. "Pass me that wine. We have more to celebrate tonight than a mere Scots princess."

Stephen grabbed the jug before Gavin could touch it. "You are a cruel brother."

"I learned it from my wife," Gavin smiled and filled his own mug.

Chapter Twenty-Seven

"I CANNOT ALLOW THIS!" ELA SAID, HER BACKBONE HELD rigid. She stood beside Alice in a little partitioned chamber in the castle.

"Since when do you allow or disallow what I want?" Alice sneered. "My life is my own and all you do is help me dress."

"It isn't right that you throw yourself at this man. There isn't a day that some man doesn't ask to marry you. Can't you content yourself with one of them?"

Alice turned on her maid. "And let *her* have him? I would die first."

"Do you really want him for your own?" Ela persisted.

"What does that matter?" Alice demanded as she adjusted her veil and circlet. "He is mine and will stay mine."

The stairway was dark when she left the room. Alice had soon discovered that the court of King Henry was an easy place to find out what she wanted to know. There were many who were willing, for a price, to do anything that she asked. Her spies had told her that Gavin sat below with his brother, away from his wife. Alice knew how befuddled a man could get with drink, and she planned to use the opportunity to the best advantage. He wouldn't be able to resist her when his mind swam from drink.

She cursed when she reached the great hall and neither Gavin nor his brother were in sight. "Where is Lord Gavin?" Alice asked harshly of a yawning servant girl. The floor was cluttered with sleeping retainers on straw pallets.

"He left—that's all I know."

Alice grabbed the girl's arm. "Where?"

"I have no idea."

Alice pulled a gold coin from her pocket and watched the girl's eyes gleam. "What would you do for this?"

The girl came fully awake. "I would do anything."

"Good," Alice smiled. "Then listen to me carefully."

Judith woke from a sound sleep to a faint scraping at the door. She stretched out her arm before she opened her eyes, only to find Gavin's side of the bed empty. She sat up, knitting her brows, then remembered he'd said something about saying good-bye to Stephen.

The scratching at the door continued. Joan, who often stayed with her mistress when Gavin was away, wasn't in the room. Reluctantly, Judith threw the covers back and slipped her arms into the emerald-green velvet of her bedrobe. "What is it?" she asked as she opened the door to a servant girl.

"I don't know, my lady," the girl said with a smirk. "I was told that you were needed and must come straightaway."

"Who said this? My husband?"

The girl shrugged in reply.

Judith frowned. The court crawled with anonymous messages, and all of them seemed to lead to places she did not care to be. Yet perhaps her mother needed her. More likely Gavin was too drunk to mount the stairs and she must help him. She smiled at the thought of the tongue-lashing she would give him.

She followed the girl down the dark stone stairs to the floor below. It seemed darker than usual; some of the torches on the walls hadn't been lit. Cut within the twelve-foot-thick walls were dreary rooms, not favored by the nobler guests. The servant girl stopped before one of these rooms that lay near the steep circular stairwell.

The girl gave Judith a look that she didn't understand, then disappeared into the darkness. Judith was aggravated at this skulking about and meant to say so when a woman's voice caught her attention.

"Gavin," the woman whispered loudly.

It was a whisper of passion. Judith could only remain frozen in place. Tinder was struck and a candle lit. Judith could see clearly then. Alice, her thin, bony body nude from the waist up, lay half under Gavin. The candlelight revealed his bronze skin to advantage—there was none of it hidden. He lay on his stomach, his bare legs covering Alice's.

"No!" Judith whispered, her hand to her mouth, her eyes blurring with tears. She wanted it to be a nightmare, but it was not. He had lied to her, over and over again. And she had come so close to believing him!

She backed away from them, Gavin not moving, Alice holding the candle, watching Judith, smiling at her from her position under Gavin. "No!" was all Judith could say. She moved farther and farther back, unaware of the staircase with no railing.

Her feet unsteady, Judith was not even conscious at first that she stepped into midair. She screamed as she fell down one step, then two, then five. Frantically, she clawed at the air, screaming again as her body fell sideways and missed the stairs altogether. Judith hit the floor below with a horrible thud, her fall finally cushioned by the pallet of one of King Henry's knights.

"What was that?" Gavin asked in a slurred voice as he raised his head.

"It was nothing," Alice murmured, her heart beating quickly with pure joy. Perhaps the woman had killed herself and Gavin would truly be Alice's once again.

Gavin raised himself on one elbow. "My God! Alice! What are you doing here?" His eyes roamed over her nude body. The only thought that occurred to him was that he had not realized she was so scrawny. There was no desire for that body he had once loved.

Alice's joy was killed by the look in Gavin's eyes. "You do . . . not remember?" Her words were halting. She was truly stunned by Gavin's reaction. She had been so certain that once she held him again, he would be hers.

Gavin frowned at her. He had been drunk, true—but not so drunk that he didn't remember the night. He knew full well that he hadn't gone to Alice's bed, nor had he asked her to his.

His accusations were ready, but suddenly the great hall on the floor below them was alive with light and noise. Men shouted to each other. Then a bellow that fair shook the rafters rose: "Montgomery!"

Gavin was out of the bed in one swift movement, hastily throwing his tunic over his head. He took the steps two at a time, but he stopped at the last turn of the spiral staircase. Judith lay just below him on a pallet, her auburn hair in a tangled mass about her head, one leg bent under her. For a moment, his heart stopped.

"Don't touch her!" he said with a low growl as he leaped the last steps and knelt beside her. "How?" he murmured as he touched her hand, then felt for the pulse at her neck.

"She seems to have fallen down the stairs," Stephen said as he knelt next to his sister-in-law.

Gavin looked up and saw Alice on the landing, her robe clutched about her, smiling slightly. Gavin felt there was something missing in the puzzle but he had no time to search for it.

"The physician has been sent for," Stephen said as he held Judith's hand. She didn't open her eyes.

The physician came slowly, dressed in a rich fur-collared robe. "Give me room," he demanded. "I must look for broken bones."

Gavin moved back and watched the man run his

hands over Judith's limp body. Why? How? Gavin kept wondering. What was she doing on the stairs in the middle of the night? His eyes went back to Alice. The woman stood quietly, avid interest on her face, as the doctor examined Judith. The room where Gavin awakened to find himself in bed with Alice was at the head of the stairs. He felt the blood drain from his face as he glanced again at his wife. Judith had seen him in bed with Alice! She had backed away, probably too upset to look where she was going, and had fallen. But how had she known where he was? Only if someone had told her where to look.

"No bones seem to be broken," the physician said. "Take her to her bed and let her rest."

Gavin murmured a prayer of thanksgiving, then bent and lifted his wife's limp form. The crowd of people around them gasped when he held her. The pallet and her gown were soaked with blood.

"She miscarries the child," Queen Elizabeth said at Gavin's elbow. "Carry her above. I will have my own midwife look at her."

Gavin could feel the warmth of Judith's blood on his arm through the sleeves of his tunic. A strong hand was placed on his shoulder, and he knew without looking that Stephen was there.

"My lady!" Joan gasped when Gavin entered the room carrying Judith. "I just now returned and she was gone. She has been hurt!" Joan's voice showed the love she had for her mistress. "Will she be all right?"

"We don't know," Stephen answered.

Gavin gently put his wife on the bed.

"Joan," Queen Elizabeth said. "Fetch warm water from the kitchen and clean linen."

"Linen, Your Majesty?"

"For absorbing the blood. She miscarries the baby. When you have the linen, fetch Lady Helen. She will want to be with her daughter."

"My poor lady," Joan whispered. "She wanted this

child so much." There were tears in her voice as she left the room.

"Go now," Elizabeth urged as she turned back to the two men. "You must leave her. You are of no use. We will see to her."

Stephen put his arm around his brother's shoulders but Gavin shrugged it away. "No, Your Majesty, I won't go. Had I been with her tonight, she wouldn't have been hurt."

Stephen started to speak but Elizabeth stopped him. She knew it would be no use. "You may stay." She nodded to Stephen and he departed.

Gavin stroked Judith's forehead as he looked up at the queen. "Tell me what to do."

"Take her robe off."

Gavin carefully untied the garment, then gently lifted Judith and took her arms from the sleeves. He was horrified to see the blood on her thighs. He stared at it for a moment, not moving.

Elizabeth watched him. "Birthing is not a pleasant sight."

"This is not a birth, but a . . ." He could not finish.

"She must have been far along to show so much blood. This will indeed be a birth, though with less pleasant results."

They both looked up as the midwife, a fat, red-faced woman burst into the chamber. "Do you intend to freeze the poor girl?" she demanded. "Here! We need no men," she said to Gavin.

"He will stay," Queen Elizabeth said firmly.

The midwife looked at Gavin for a moment. "Go then and fetch the water from the maid. She takes too long to carry it up the stairs."

Gavin reacted immediately.

"Her husband, Your Majesty?" the midwife asked when Gavin was gone.

"Yes, and their first child."

The fat woman snorted. "He should have taken

better care of her, Your Majesty, and not let her roam about the halls at night."

As soon as Gavin set the water down inside the room, the woman snapped more orders at him. "Find her some clothes and keep her warm."

Joan, who had entered behind Gavin, rummaged in a chest and handed him a warm woolen gown. Gavin carefully dressed Judith, all the while watching the blood slowly seep from her. Perspiration appeared on her forehead and he wiped it away with a cool cloth. "Will she be all right?" he whispered.

"I can't answer that. It depends on whether we can get all the birth out of her and if we can get the bleeding to stop." Judith moaned and moved her head. "Keep her quiet or she'll make our work harder."

"Judith," Gavin said quietly. "Be still." He took her hands in his when she began to move them about.

She opened her eyes. "Gavin?" she whispered.

"Yes. Don't talk now. Be still and rest. You will be well soon."

"Well?" She did not seem fully aware of her state. Then a violent cramp shot through her. Her hands clutched at his. Judith looked up at him, bewildered. "What happened?" she gasped then her eyes began to focus clearly. The queen, her maid and another woman knelt over her, looking at her with concern. Another spasm rocked her.

"Come," the midwife said. "We must knead her stomach and help her."

"Gavin!" Judith said in fright, panting after the last pain.

"Quiet, my love. You will soon be well. There will be other children."

Her eyes opened in horror. "Child? My baby? Am I losing my baby?" Her voice rose almost hysterically.

"Judith, please," Gavin said, soothing her. "There will be others."

Another pain shot through Judith as she stared at Gavin, her memory returning. "I fell off the stairs," she said quietly. "I saw you in bed with your whore and I fell from the stairs."

"Judith, this is not the time—"

"Don't touch me!"

"Judith," Gavin said, half-pleading.

"Do I disappoint you that I'm not dead? As my child is now dead?" Her eyes blinked back tears. "Go to her. You wanted her so badly, and you are welcome to her!"

"Judith—" Gavin began, but Queen Elizabeth took his arm.

"Perhaps you should go."

"Yes," he agreed as Judith refused to look at him Stephen waited outside the door for him, his brows raised in question. "The child is lost and I don't know yet if Judith will live."

"Come below," Stephen said. "They won't allow you to stay with her?"

"Judith wouldn't allow it," Gavin said flatly.

Stephen didn't speak again until they were outside the manor house. The sun was just beginning to rise, the sky gray. The commotion caused by Judith's fall made the castlefolk rise earlier than usual. The brothers sat on a bench by the castle wall. "Why was she walking about the hall at night?" Stephen asked.

"I don't know. When you and I parted, I fell into a bed—the nearest one at the top of the stairs."

"Perhaps she woke and found you were gone and came to search for you."

Gavin didn't answer.

"There is more to this that you aren't telling me."

"Yes. When Judith saw me, I was in bed with Alice."

Never before had Stephen offered a judgment of his brother. Now his face blackened. "You may have killed Judith! And for what? That bitch—" He broke off when he saw Gavin's bleak profile. "You were too drunk to want a woman. Or if you wanted one, Judith waited above for you."

Gavin stared across the courtyard. "I didn't take her to bed," he said quietly. "I was asleep and I heard a noise which woke me. Alice lay beside me. I wasn't so drunk last night that I would have taken her to my bed and not remembered."

"Then how?"

"I don't know."

"I do!" Stephen said through clenched teeth. "You are a sensible man except when it comes to that witch!"

For the first time, Gavin didn't defend Alice.

Stephen continued. "You have never been able to see her for what she is. Don't you know she sleeps with half the men at the court?"

Gavin turned and stared at him.

"You may look at me in disbelief, but she is the jest of all the men—and I'm sure most of the women. From stableboy to earl, she doesn't care, so long as they have the equipment to pleasure her."

"If she's like that, then I have made her that way. She was a virgin when I first took her."

"Virgin, hah! The Earl of Lancashire swears he had her when she was only twelve years old."

Gavin's expression was one of disbelief.

"Look at what she has done to you. She has controlled you and used you—and you have allowed it. No, you have begged for more. Tell me, what method did she use to keep you from loving Judith straightaway?"

Gavin stared with sightless eyes. He was reliving the scene in the garden on his wedding day. "She vowed to kill herself if I loved my wife."

Stephen leaned his head back against the stone wall. "God's wounds! And you believed her? That woman would willingly kill thousands before she would endanger one hair on her own head."

"But I asked her to marry me," Gavin persisted. "Before I ever heard of Judith, I asked her to marry me."

"Yet she chose a rich earl instead."

"But her father—"

"Gavin! Can't you look at her with clear eyes? Do

you think that drunkard of a father of hers ever gave anyone an order? Even his servants don't obey him! Were he a strong man, would she have had such freedom to slip about the countryside with you at night?"

It was hard for Gavin to believe all this of Alice. She was so pink and blonde, so delicate, so shy. She looked up at him with great tears in her eyes and his heart melted. He remembered how he felt when she threatened to take her own life. He would have done anything for her. Yet even then his attraction to Judith had been enormous.

"You aren't convinced," Stephen said.

"I'm not sure. Old dreams die hard. She is a beautiful woman."

"Yes, and you fell in love with that beauty. You never questioned what else was there. You say you didn't take her to your bed. How did she get there then?"

When Gavin didn't answer, Stephen continued. "The slut stripped her own clothes off and planted herself there. Then she sent someone to summon Judith."

Gavin rose. He didn't want to hear any more. "I must go and see if Judith is well," he murmured and walked back to the manor house. All his life, since he was sixteen, Gavin had been responsible for property and men. He had never had the carefree time of his brothers to court women and learn of their natures. True, there had been many women in his bed, but always they were gone quickly. No woman had spent time close to him, laughing and talking with him. He had grown up believing all women were like he remembered his mother—pretty, sweet-tempered, gentle. Alice had always seemed to be the epitome of those traits, and as a result, he had become infatuated with her almost immediately.

Judith had been the first woman he had really known. At first she had infuriated him. She was not obedient, as a woman should be. She would rather concern herself with his household account books than the colors used in a piece of embroidery. She was breathtakingly beautiful, but she seemed unaware of her beauty. She did not spend hours on her clothes. In truth, Joan often chose her mistress's attire. Judith seemed to be everything undesirable, unfeminine. Yet Gavin had fallen in love with her. She was honest, brave, generous—and she made him laugh. Never once had Alice shown even a touch of humor.

Gavin stood outside the door of Judith's chamber. He knew he no longer loved Alice, but could she be as treacherous as Stephen said? As Raine and Miles also said? How did she come to be in his bed except for the reason Stephen gave?

The door opened and the midwife stepped into the hall. Gavin grabbed her arm. "How is she?"

"Sleeping now. The child was born dead."

Gavin took a deep, calming breath. "Will my wife recover?"

"I don't know. She has lost much blood. I don't know if it was from the infant, or perhaps something inside was damaged in the fall."

Gavin's face drained of color. "Didn't you say she lost blood from the child?" He didn't want to believe that something else could be wrong.

"How long have you been wed to her?"

"Nearly four months," he answered, surprised.

"And she was a virgin when you took her?"

"Yes," he said, remembering the pain he had caused her.

"She was quite far along. The child was well formed. I would say she conceived that first night or the next. No later. Perhaps there is so much blood because the child was so well advanced. It's too early to tell."

She turned to go, but Gavin grabbed her arm. "How will you know?"

"When the bleeding stops and she is still alive."

He released her arm. "You say she sleeps. May I go to her?"

The old woman chuckled. "Young men! They never seem to deny themselves. You bed one woman while another waits for you. Now you hover over the first one. You should choose one or the other."

Gavin swallowed his reply, but his scowl made the smile leave her face.

"Yes, you may go to her," the woman said quietly, then turned and went down to the stairs.

The rain came down in slashing sheets. The wind bent the trees almost in half. Lightning flashed and far away a tree split and crashed. But the four people who stood around the tiny coffin that the workers had just lowered into the ground, were unaware of the cold torrent. Their bodies swayed with the gale, but they did not notice it.

Helen stood by John, her body limp, leaning heavily against the strength of him for support. Her eyes were dry and hot. Stephen stood close to Gavin, ready if his brother should need him.

It was John and Stephen who exchanged looks, the rain running down their faces, dripping into their clothes. John gently led Helen away from the little gravesite and Stephen guided Gavin. The storm had started suddenly, after the priest had begun to read the words over the tiny coffin.

Stephen and John looked as if they were leading two blind and helpless people across the graveyard. They led Helen and Gavin into a mausoleum and left them there while they went to get the horses.

Gavin sank heavily onto an iron bench. The child had been a son. His first son, he thought. Every word he'd said to Judith about the child not being his rang in his ears. And the baby was dead because of him. He dropped his head into his hands.

"Gavin," Helen said as she sat beside him and put

her arm about his shoulders. They'd had so little to do with each other since Helen screamed she wished she'd killed her daughter before allowing her to marry him. But over the months many things had changed. Helen had found out what it was like to love someone, and now she recognized love in Gavin's eyes. She saw the pain he suffered over his lost child, the fear he had of losing Judith.

Gavin turned to his mother-in-law. He never thought of any hostility between them. He saw and remembered only that Helen was close to the woman he loved. He put his arms about her, but he did not hold her. No, it was Helen who held her son-in-law, and Helen who felt the hotness of his tears through her rain-soaked gown. And finally Helen found release for her own tears.

Joan sat by her sleeping mistress. Judith's color was gone, her hair damp with perspiration. "She will soon be well," Joan said to Gavin's unasked question.

"I'm not so sure." He touched his wife's hot cheek.

"It was a nasty fall she took," Joan said, staring intently at Gavin.

Gavin only nodded, more concerned with Judith than with any talk.

"What do you plan to do to her?" Joan continued.

"Do to her?" Gavin demanded. "I hope only to see her well once again."

Joan waved her hand. "No, I mean to Lady Alice. What punishment do you plan for the trick she played? Trick!" Joan snorted. "A trick that may cost my lady her life!"

"Don't say that," Gavin growled.

"I ask you again: what punishment do you plan?"

"Hold your tongue, woman! I know nothing of a trick."

"No? Then I will speak my piece. There is a woman below, in the kitchen, who cries her eyes from her head. She has a gold coin which she says Lady Alice gave her to lead my lady to you while you were in bed with that whore. The girl says she thought she would have done anything for the coin, but she didn't mean murder. She says Lady Judith's baby's death and maybe the lady's own death are her fault and that she will go to hell for their murders."

Gavin realized it was time to face the truth. "I would like to see this woman and speak with her," he said quietly.

Joan rose. "I will fetch the girl if I can find her."

Gavin sat with Judith, watching, noting that her natural color was returning.

It was some time later when Joan came back, pulling a frightened and cowering girl behind her. "This is the slut!" Joan said and gave the servant a vicious push. "Look at my mistress as she lies there. You have killed a baby, and now you may kill my lady. And she never hurt a soul. Do you know she often lectured me for mistreating scum like you?"

"Quiet!" Gavin commanded. The girl was obviously very frightened. "Tell me what you know of my wife's accident."

"Accident, ha!" Joan snorted, then quieted at Gavin's look.

The girl, her eyes darting from one corner of the room to the other, told her story in disjointed, hesitant sentences. At the end, she threw herself at Gavin's feet. "Please, my lord, save me. Lady Alice will murder me!"

Gavin's face showed no pity. "You ask me for help? What help did you give my wife? Or our child? Shall I take you to where they have buried the child?"

"No," the girl cried desperately, her head touching the floor.

"Get up!" Joan commanded. "You dirty our floor!"

"Take her away," Gavin said. "I cannot bear the sight of her."

Joan grabbed the girl's hair and viciously pulled her up, then gave her a hard kick toward the door.

"Joan," Gavin said. "Take her to John Bassett and tell him to see that she is safe."

"Safe!" Joan exploded then her eyes hardened. "Yes, my lord," she said in a falsely submissive voice. She closed the door, twisting the girl's arm behind her back. "She kills my lady's baby, and I am to see her safe!" she muttered. "No, I will see that she gets what she deserves."

At the top of the spiral stairs, Joan's hand bit into the terrified girl.

"Here! stop that!" John Bassett growled. He had never been far from Judith's room over the last several days. "Is this the one Lady Alice paid?" There wasn't a person in the castle who wasn't aware of the story of Alice's treachery.

"Oh please, sir," the girl begged, falling to her knees. "Don't let her kill me. I won't do anything like that again."

John started to speak. Then he gave Joan a look of disgust and lifted the maid. Joan stood for several minutes, watching their retreating backs.

"Too bad he took her. You could have saved me some work," said a quiet voice behind her.

Joan whirled to face Alice Chatworth. "I would rather see you at the bottom of the stairs," Joan sneered.

Alice's blue eyes blazed. "I will have your life for that!"

"Here? Now?" Joan taunted. "No, that's not your way. You hire people to do your work for you—then you simper as if you were an innocent maid."

No one had ever dared say such things to Alice!

"Come," Joan taunted. "Why do you hesitate? I stand on the brink of the stairs."

Alice was tempted to try to give the maid one hard push, but Joan looked to be strong, and Alice couldn't risk losing such a struggle. "You will look to your life for this," Alice sneered.

"No, I will look to my back, where such as you would

strike." Joan stared at the woman, then began to laugh. She laughed all the way up the stairs until she reached her mistress's room.

The midwife and Gavin hovered over Judith. "The fever has begun," the old woman said quietly. "Now prayers will help as much as anything else."

Chapter Twenty-Eight

JUDITH WAS DREAMING. HER BODY WAS HOT AND SORE, and she had trouble concentrating on what was happening. Gavin was there, smiling at her, but his smile was false. Behind him stood Alice Chatworth, her eyes glowing in triumph. "I have won," the woman whispered. "I have won!"

Judith woke slowly, coming fretfully from the dream that seemed real as she felt the ache of her body, as if she'd slept for days on a board. She moved her head to one side. Gavin sat sleeping in a chair by the bed. Even asleep he looked tense, as if he were ready to spring to his feet. His face was haggard, his cheekbones prominent under his skin. He wore several days' growth of beard, and there were dark circles under his eyes.

Judith was puzzled for a few moments, wondering why Gavin should look so tired and she should ache so badly. Her hand moved under the covers and touched her stomach. It had once been hard and slightly rounded, but now it was sunken and soft. And oh so horribly empty!

She remembered everything then, remembered

Gavin in bed with Alice. He had said he no longer cared for her and Judith had begun to believe him. She had started to think of a good life together, of when their child would be born and they would be happy. What a fool she had been!

"Judith!" Gavin said in a strangely harsh voice. He quickly sat beside her on the bed, his hand feeling her forehead. "The fever is broken," he said with relief. "How do you feel?"

"Don't touch me," she whispered. "Get away from me!"

Gavin nodded, his lips set in a firm line.

Before either of them could speak again the door opened and Stephen entered. The worried expression on his face gave way to a broad smile when he saw she was awake. He quickly went to the side of the bed opposite Gavin. "Sweet little sister," he murmured. "We thought we might lose you." He touched her neck gently.

At the sight of a familiar and loved face, Judith felt tears come to her eyes.

Stephen frowned and looked to his brother but Gavin shook his head. "Here, sweet," Stephen said, gathering Judith in his arms. "Don't cry," he whispered as he stroked her hair.

"Was it a boy?" she whispered.

Stephen could only nod.

"I lost him!" she cried desperately. "He didn't even have a chance of life before I lost him. Oh, Stephen, I wanted the baby so much. He would have been good and kind and so very beautiful!"

"Yes," Stephen agreed. "Tall and dark like his father."

Judith's sobs tore through her. "Yes! At least my father was right about getting a grandson. But he is dead!"

Stephen looked over her head to his brother. He didn't know who was the most grief-stricken, Gavin or the woman he comforted.

Gavin had never seen Judith cry. She showed him hostility, passion, humor, but never this horrible racking grief. He felt a deep sadness that she did not share her grief with him.

"Judith," Stephen said. "You must rest. You have been very ill."

"How long have I been ill?"

"Three days. The fever nearly took you from us."

She sniffed, then abruptly drew away from him. "Stephen! You were to leave. You will be late for your own wedding."

He nodded grimly. "I was to wed her this morning."

"Then you have left her at the altar."

"I would hope she heard that I didn't arrive and would not go so far."

"Did you send a message?"

He shook his head. "If the truth were told, I forgot. We have all worried greatly about you. You don't know how close you came to death."

She did feel weak and extremely tired.

"Now you must sleep again."

"And you will go to your bride?" Judith asked as he helped her lie down.

"I can go now that I know the fever is broken."

"Promise me," she said tiredly. "I wouldn't wish you to start your marriage as mine was. I want better for you."

Stephen glanced quickly at his brother. "Yes, I promise. I will leave within the hour."

She nodded, her eyes closing. "Thank you," she whispered and fell asleep.

Gavin rose from the bed as his brother did. "I too forgot your marriage."

"You had other things on your mind," Stephen answered. "Is she still angry with you?"

Gavin gave his brother a cynical look. "More than angry, I would say."

"Talk to her. Tell her how you feel. Tell her the truth about Alice. She will believe you."

Gavin looked across the room at his sleeping wife. "You must pack now. That Scots bride will have your hide."

"If that were all she wished, I would give it to her gladly."

Both men left the room, closing the door behind. Gavin clasped his brother to him. "Christmas," he said smiling. "Bring that wife of yours to us at Christmas."

"Yes, I will. And you will speak to Judith?"

Gavin nodded. "When she is better rested and I am bathed."

Stephen smiled. Gavin had not left his wife's side for the three days of her fever. Stephen cuffed his brother affectionately and turned and left the hallway.

When Judith woke again, it was dark in the room. Joan was sleeping on a pallet near the door. Judith's head was clearer and she felt stronger and very hungry. "Joan," she whispered.

The maid was on her feet instantly. "My lady," she said and grinned happily. "Lord Gavin said you were well again, but I didn't believe him."

"I would like some water," Judith said through parched lips.

"Yes," Joan laughed merrily. "Not so fast," she said as Judith greedily drank from the cup.

The door opened and they both turned to see Gavin entering with a tray of food.

"I don't want to see him," Judith said firmly.

"Go!" Gavin commanded Joan.

The maid put down the cup and left hastily.

Gavin set the tray down on a small table by the bed. "You are feeling better."

She stared at him but wouldn't answer.

"I brought you some broth and a bit of bread. You must be very hungry."

"I don't want anything from you. Neither food nor company."

"Judith," he said with great patience, "you are acting like a child. We'll speak of this again when you're well."

"Do you think time will change my mind? Will time give me back my baby? Will time let me hold him, love him, even let me see the color of his eyes?"

Gavin took his hands away from the tray. "He was my child, too, and I have lost him also."

"So, you have learned that much! Should I feel pity for your sorrow? You didn't even believe him to be yours. Or did you lie about that also?"

"I haven't lied to you, Judith. If you will only listen, I'll tell you everything."

"Listen?" she said calmly. "When have you ever listened to me? I have tried from the moment we married to please you, yet there was little I could do that didn't make you angry. Always, I felt I was compared to someone else."

"Judith," he said and took her hand from her lap.

"Don't touch me! I am fouled by your touch."

His eyes turned from gray to black. "I have something to say, and I will say it even though you try hard to prevent me. Much of what you say is true. I did love Alice, or I thought I did. I fell in love with her before I even heard her speak. I created a woman for her to be, and she became that woman. We never spent much time together, only swift moments here and there. I never knew what she was really like, only what I wished her to be."

Judith didn't answer. Gavin couldn't read her thoughts.

"I fought against loving you," he continued. "I thought my heart belonged to Alice. But now I know that was not so. Judith," he said quietly, "I have loved you for a long time. Perhaps I have loved you from the first. I do know that now I love you with all my heart and soul."

He stopped and watched her, but her expression didn't change.

"Shall I fall into your arms now and declare my great love for you also? Is that what is expected of me?"

Gavin was stunned. Perhaps he had expected her to say she loved him.

"Your lust killed my child!"

"It was not my lust!" Gavin said passionately. "I was tricked. Stephen and I drank too much together. A leopard could have climbed into bed with me and I wouldn't have known it!"

Judith smiled icily. "And did you enjoy the leopard's claws? You have before."

Gavin gave her a cold look. "I have tried to explain my actions to you, but you won't listen. I have told you of my love—what more can I do?"

"You don't seem to understand. I don't *care* that you love me. Your love is worthless, given freely to whoever requests it. Once I might have done much to hear those words, but they are no longer sweet to me. It has taken the death of my child to clear my mind of such fairy tales as love."

Gavin sat back, staring at her. He didn't know what else to say. "I have been wrong on all counts. You are right to be angry."

"No," she smiled "I'm not angry. Neither do I hate you. I merely find life with you intolerable."

"What do you mean?"

"I shall beg the king to ask the pope for a divorce. I don't believe that even the pope would wish me to live with you after this. You shall keep half my land and—" She broke off as Gavin stood.

"I will send Joan to you. You must eat," Gavin said, then left the room.

Judith lay back against the pillow. She felt drained. How could she believe he loved her when all she could see was Alice rising from under his nude body?

For three more days, Judith didn't leave her bed. She slept a great deal and ate dutifully. Her spirits were so low that food meant little to her. She refused to see anyone, most especially her husband. Preferring to keep her opinions to herself, Joan hardly spoke to her mistress.

On the morning of the fourth day, Joan pulled the covers from Judith. "You will not lie in bed today. There is work to be done and you must exercise." Joan took a new robe from the foot of the bed—a robe to replace the bloodstained one of green velvet. The robe was of a deep gray velvet with a wide mink collar, a mink edge along the front and around the hem. Intricate gold embroidery ran around the shoulders.

"I don't want to get up," Judith said and turned over.

"You will!"

Judith was still too weak to resist. Joan easily pulled her mistress from the bed and helped her into the velvet robe. She led Judith to a deep window seat. "Now you will stay there while I get clean linen."

The summer breeze did feel good on Judith's face. She had a wonderful view of the garden. She leaned back against the embrasure and watched the people below.

"Gavin?" someone said quietly at his side. He sat alone in the garden, a place where he'd spent a lot of time lately. He whirled quickly at the familiar voice. It was Alice, her skin radiant in the early morning light. He had purposely put off dealing with her; he didn't trust his own reactions. "Do you dare show yourself to me?"

"Please, allow me to explain—"

"No. You cannot explain."

Alice looked away, her hand at her eye and when she looked back, there were great, glittering tears present. Gavin looked at her and wondered how her tears had once had the power to move him. How different Judith's were! Great wrenching sobs that tore through her. She cried from grief, not to enhance her beauty.

"I did it only for you," Alice said. "My love for you is so strong that—"

"Don't speak to me of love! I wonder if you know

what it is. Do you know that I talked to the girl you paid to bring Judith to you? You planned well, didn't you?"

"Gavin, I—"

He grabbed her arms and shook her. "You killed my child! Does that mean nothing to you? And you nearly killed my wife—a woman I love." He pushed Alice away from him. "I could have you before a court for this, but I blame myself as much as you. I was a fool not to have seen through you."

Alice drew her hand back and slapped him across the cheek. He allowed it for he felt he deserved it.

"Get out of my sight and don't tempt me to wring that pretty neck of yours."

Alice turned on her heel and fled from the garden.

Ela crept from the shadows. "I told you not to go to him. I told you to wait. He is very angry with you and well you deserve it." Ela was puzzled when her mistress walked behind the kitchen, into an alley.

Alice leaned against the wall. Her shoulders shook.

Ela went to her mistress and pulled her head to her ample bosom.

This time, Alice cried genuinely. "He loved me," she said through painful sobs. "He did love me once and now he doesn't anymore. I have no one else left."

"Hush, sweetheart," Ela soothed. "You have me. You have always had me." Ela held her as she had when Alice was a child and the lovely little girl had cried at the neglect of her mother. "Lord Gavin is only one man. There are others. You are so very beautiful. There will be many men to love you."

"No!" Alice said with such violence that it shook her body. "I want him—I want Gavin! Another man will not do!"

Ela tried to calm her mistress, but couldn't. "You shall have him then," she said finally.

Alice raised her head, her eyes and nose red and swollen. "Do you promise?"

Ela nodded. "Haven't I always given you what you want?"

"Yes," Alice agreed. "You have. And you will get Gavin for me?"

"I swear it."

Alice gave a small smile. Then, in a rare burst of affection, she gave Ela a swift kiss on the cheek.

The maid's old eyes misted. Of course she would do anything for this sweet girl who was so misunderstood by the people around her. "Come upstairs," she said sweetly. "We will plan a new gown."

"Yes," Alice smiled, sniffing loudly. "A merchant brought some Frankish wools this morning."

"Let's go and see them."

Judith had watched from the window only long enough to see her husband speak to his mistress. "Joan, I would like to see the king," she said, turning away from the sight.

"My lady, you cannot ask King Henry to come here."

"I don't intend to do so. You must help me dress, and I will go below to see him."

"But—"

"Don't argue with me!"

"Yes, my lady," Joan said in a hard voice.

An hour later, Judith appeared in the great hall, leaning heavily on her maid's arm.

A young man came to her side. "Alan Fairfax, my lady, if you don't remember."

"Of course I do." She managed a small smile "You are kind to help me."

"It is a pleasure. You wish to see the king?"

She nodded gravely. She took Alan's arm and he led her to the king's chamber. It was an elegant room with a hammer-beam ceiling, linenfold paneling, and oak floors covered with Persian carpets.

"Countess!" the king said when he saw her. He had an illuminated manuscript in his lap. "You should not have left your bed so soon." He put the book aside and took her other arm.

"You are very kind, both of you," she said as Alan and Henry helped her into a chair. "I would like to speak to you, Your Majesty, on a private matter."

Henry nodded toward Alan and the knight left them. "Now, what matter is so important that you must weary yourself to seek me?"

Judith looked down at her hands. "I would like a divorce."

King Henry was silent for a moment. "Divorce is a grave undertaking. Do you have cause?"

There were two types of divorce and three reasons for each. The best Judith could hope for was a separation, allowing her to live apart from her husband for the rest of her life. "Adultery," she said quietly.

Henry considered this. "If such grounds were allowed, neither of you could remarry."

"I do not wish to. I will enter a convent, as I was trained for."

"And what of Gavin? Would you deny him the right of a new wife and of sons to follow him?"

"No," she whispered. "He has his rights."

Henry was watching her intently. "Then we must look to a divorce which declares your marriage null and void. You are not related?"

Again she shook her head, thinking of Walter Demari.

"What then of Gavin? Was he pledged to another?"

Judith lifted her chin. "He did ask another woman to marry him."

"And this woman is?"

"Lady Alice Chatworth."

"Ah," Henry sighed and leaned back in his chair. "And now the lady is a widow and he wishes to marry her?"

"Yes, he does."

King Henry frowned. "I don't like divorce, but I also don't like my earls and countesses so unhappy. This will cost you a great deal. I am sure the pope will require that you endow a chapel or a nunnery."

"I will do that."

"Lady Judith, you must let me think about this. I must speak to the others involved before I make a decision. Alan," he called, "take the countess to her room and see that she is made to rest."

Alan smiled broadly as he helped Judith to her feet.

"The Lady Judith looked to be very sad," Queen Elizabeth commented as she entered the room just as Judith was leaving and took a seat next to her husband. "I know how she feels after having lost a child."

"It's not that, or at least the child is not all that weighs upon her. She asks for a divorce from Gavin."

"No!" Elizabeth said, dropping her knitting to her lap. "I have never seen two people more in love. They argue, true, but I have seen Lord Gavin lift her in his arms and kiss her."

"It seems that Lady Judith is not the only woman Gavin kisses."

Elizabeth was silent. Not many men were faithful to their wives. She knew that even her husband at times . . . "Lady Judith asks for a divorce for this reason?"

"Yes. Gavin seems to have asked Lady Alice Chatworth to marry him before he married Judith. It is a verbal contract and grounds for divorce. That is, if the woman will accept Gavin."

"She will!" Elizabeth said angrily. "She will be glad to take Gavin—she has done so much to obtain him."

"What are you talking about?"

Elizabeth quickly told her husband of the castle gossip how Lady Judith had fallen and miscarried her child.

Henry frowned. "I do not like such happenings between my subjects. Gavin should have been more discreet."

"There is some doubt whether he asked the woman to his bed, or whether she placed herself there."

Henry chuckled. "Poor Gavin. I wouldn't want to be in such a state as he."

"Have you talked to him? I do not think he wants this divorce," Elizabeth stated.

"But if he were pledged to the Lady Alice before his marriage . . ."

"Then why did she marry Edmund Chatworth?"

"I see," Henry said seriously. "I think I will investigate this further. There is more here than appears on the surface. I will talk to both Gavin and Lady Alice."

"I hope your talks take a long while."

"I don't understand."

"If Judith is allowed to separate from her husband, their marriage will indeed end; but if they were forced to stay near one another, they might realize they do care for each other."

Henry smiled fondly at his wife. She was a wise woman. "I will indeed take a long time before I send a message to the pope. Where are you going?" he asked as she stood.

"I would like to talk to Sir Alan Fairfax. I wonder if he would be willing to help a lady in distress."

Henry gave her a puzzled look, then picked up his manuscript. "Yes, my dear. I am sure you will handle all of this without me."

Two hours later the door to Judith's chamber was thrown open. Gavin stalked into the room, his face blackened with fury.

Judith glanced up from the book in her lap.

"You asked the king for a divorce!" he bellowed.

"Yes, I have," she replied firmly.

"Do you plan to tell the world of our differences?"

"If that is what it takes to rid myself of you."

He glared at her. "You are a stubborn woman! Do you ever see anything but one side? Do you ever listen to reason?"

"Your idea of reason is not the same as mine. You want me to forgive you for adultery time and again. I have done so many times, yet now I can no more. I plan to rid myself of you and enter a convent, as I should have done long ago."

"A convent!" he said in disbelief, then smiled mockingly. He took one swift step toward her and threw an arm around her shoulders. He lifted her from the bed and his mouth covered hers. He was not gentle, but even his harshness set Judith afire. Her arms went around his neck, pulling him to her violently. Abruptly, he released her, letting her fall onto the feather mattress. The sides of the soft mattress rose around her.

"Make up your mind that you'll never be rid of me. When you are ready to admit that I'm the man you need, come to me. Perhaps I'll take you back." He turned and stalked from the room before Judith could say a word.

Joan stood in the open doorway, a look of adoration on her face.

"How dare he—" Judith began then stopped at Joan's look. "Why do you look at me so?" she demanded.

"Because you are wrong. That man loves you, has told you so, yet you won't listen to him. I have been on your side throughout your marriage, but now I'm not."

"But that woman—" Judith said in a strange, pleading voice.

"Can't you forgive him? He thought he loved her once. He would be less of a man if he were willing to forget her when he first saw his beautiful wife. You make great demands of him."

"But my baby!" Judith said, tears in her voice.

"I told you of Alice's treachery. How can you hold him responsible?"

Judith was silent for a while. The loss of the child hurt her so badly. Perhaps she wanted someone to blame and Gavin was a convenient person to inflict it on. She knew what Joan said of Alice was true. That night, things had happened so quickly; but now, days later, she knew that Gavin's body on Alice's had been too inert.

"He says he loves you," Joan continued in a quieter voice.

"Do you do anything besides listen at doors?" Judith snapped.

Joan smiled. "I like to know what happens to those I care for. He loves you. What do you feel for him?"

"I . . . I don't know."

Joan uttered an oath that made Judith's eyes widen. "Your mother should have taught you something besides accounts. I don't believe I have seen a woman love a man as you love Lord Gavin. Your eyes have not left him since he lifted you from that white horse at your wedding. Yet you have fought him on every count . . . as he has you," she added before Judith could interrupt. "Why don't the two of you stop fighting and make some more babies? I should like one near me."

Judith smiled even as her eyes filled with tears. "But he doesn't love me, not truly. Even if he did, he is furious with me. Should I go to him and tell him that I don't want a divorce, that I . . . I . . . ?"

Joan laughed. "You can't even say it. You love him, don't you?"

Judith was very serious before she answered. "Yes, I do."

"Now, we must plan. You cannot go to him. He would gloat over it for years to come, and besides you would make a poor job of it. You would no doubt be cold and logical when you should weep and sigh."

"Weep and—!" Judith was offended.

"See you what I mean? Once you said I make too much of a person's appearances, and I said you make too little of them. For once you are going to use your beauty to its best advantage."

"But how? Gavin has seen me in every way. My appearance will have no affect on him."

"You think not?" Joan laughed. "Listen to me and in a few days I will have Lord Gavin groveling at your feet."

"It would be nice for a change," Judith smiled. "Yes, I would like that."

"Then leave it to me. There is an Italian cloth merchant downstairs and—"

"I need no more clothes!" Judith said, glancing at the four large trunks in the room.

Joan smiled in a secret way. "Let me handle the men. You just rest. You're going to need your strength."

The news of Judith's desire for a divorce spread throughout the court like a fire. Divorce was not uncommon, but Judith and Gavin had been married only a short while. The reaction of the people of the court was unusual. The women—orphaned heiresses, young widows—flocked to Gavin. They sensed that his long love affair with Alice Chatworth was over. Obviously his lovely wife had no hold on him. They saw Gavin as an unattached man who would soon need to choose one of them for a wife.

But the men did not run to Judith. They were not given to acting first and thinking later. The queen kept Judith at her side, giving her preferential treatment, or, as the men saw it, guarding her as a bear with her cubs. The men also knew that it was unusual for King Henry to keep the warring couple at court. The king didn't like divorce and usually sent the couple away. True, the Lady Judith was lovely and very rich, but too often a man felt Gavin's eyes on him when he stayed too long at the golden-eyed beauty's side. More than one man voiced the opinion that a good beating would have kept Judith from making their differences public.

"My lady?"

Judith looked up from her book and smiled at Alan Fairfax. The new gown she wore was extremely simple. It had a plain square neck and long, tight sleeves. It hung past her feet so it made a small pool of fabric when she stood. She had to throw part of it over her arm in order to walk. The sides were laced tightly. But what was truly unusual about the gown was its color. It was black—solid, midnight black. There was no belt, no mantle. About her neck was a collar of gold filigree set with large cabochon rubies. Her hair was uncovered, left loose to hang down her back. She'd objected when Joan showed her the black dress and she wondered at how appropriate it was. She had no idea that the black made her skin glow like a pearl. The gold of the collar reflected her eyes and the rubies took second place to the blaze of her deep, rich auburn hair.

It was all Alan could do to keep from staring with his mouth agape. Judith obviously had no idea she was driving the men of the court wild, as well as her husband. "You sit inside on such a lovely day?" he finally managed.

"It would seem so," she smiled. "If the truth were known, I haven't been very far outside these walls in several days."

He held his arm out. "Then perhaps you would like to walk with me?"

She rose and took his arm. "I would indeed enjoy that, kind sir." Judith held his arm firmly. She was glad to talk to a man again. For days they had all seemed to shy away from her. The thought made her laugh aloud.

"Something amuses you?" Alan asked.

"I was thinking that you are a brave man. For the last week, I had begun to fear that I had the plague—or perhaps even worse. If I only look at a man, he scurries away as if in mortal fear."

It was Alan's turn to laugh. "It's not you but your husband who sends them into the shadows."

"But he may . . . soon be my husband no longer."

"May?" Alan asked, one eyebrow raised. "Do I hear a note of uncertainty?"

Judith was quiet a moment. "I fear I am transparent."

He covered her hand with his. "You were very angry

and rightly so. The Lady Alice—" He stopped when he felt her stiffen. "It was unkind of me to mention her. You have forgiven your husband then?"

Judith smiled. "Can one love another without forgiveness? If it's possible, then that is my fate."

"Why don't you go to him and end this estrangement?"

"You don't know Gavin! He would gloat and lecture me on my waywardness."

Alan chuckled. "Then you must make him come to you."

"That is what my maid says, though she gives me no lessons on how to return my husband to my side."

"There is only one way. He is a jealous man. You must spend some of your time with another, and Lord Gavin will soon see his mistake."

"But what man?" Judith asked, thinking that she knew so few people at court.

"You wound me sorely," Alan laughed, raising his hand to his breast in mock despair.

"You? But you have no interest in my cause."

"Then I must force myself to spend time with you. Surely, it will be a most difficult task. But truthfully, I owe you a favor."

"You owe me nothing."

"No, I do. I was used to play a trick on you, and I would like to repay you."

"Trick? I don't know what you mean."

"It's my secret alone. Now, let's talk no more of serious matters. This is a day for pleasure."

"Yes," she agreed. "We know little of each other. Tell me about yourself."

Alan smiled teasingly. "I have had a long and interesting life. I'm sure my story will take the entire day."

"Then we should start," Judith laughed.

Chapter Twenty-Nine

ALAN AND JUDITH LEFT THE NOISE AND CONFUSION OF the king's manor and strolled toward the wooded park outside the castle walls. It was a long walk, but one they both enjoyed.

It was an interesting afternoon for Judith. She realized how few men she had known in her life. Alan was entertaining and the day passed quickly. He was fascinated that she was so well educated. They laughed together over Judith's confession of how her maids sneaked romantic tales to her and how she read to them aloud. Alan was certain Judith was not fully aware of how unorthodox her childhood had been. Only late in the afternoon did she speak of her married life. She told of her reorganizing of Gavin's castle, briefly mentioned her talks with the armorer. Alan began to see the cause of Gavin's outbursts of temper. It would take great strength in a man to be able to stand aside and let his wife's word take precedence over his.

They talked and laughed until the sun was low in the sky. "We must return," Alan said. "But I hate to end this day's enjoyment."

"I agree," Judith smiled. "It has indeed been enjoyable. I'm pleased to get away from court. There's too much gossip and backbiting there for me."

"It's not a bad place—unless you're the object of the abuse."

"As I am now?" Judith winced.

"Yes. No one has had so much to talk of for years."

"Sir Alan," she laughed. "You are cruel to me." She tucked her hand around his arm and smiled up at him.

"So!" a voice hissed close to them. "This is where you hide?"

Judith whirled to see Alice standing close to them.

"He will be mine soon!" Alice sneered and moved closer to Judith. "When he rids himself of you, he will come to me."

Judith stepped back. The light in Alice's blue eyes was unnatural. Her lips curled and showed her uneven teeth, which she usually was so careful to hide.

Alan put himself between Alice and Judith. "Get away from here!" he said in a low, threatening voice.

"Are you hiding behind your lover?" Alice screeched, ignoring Alan. "Can't you wait for the divorce before you take other men?"

Alan's hand clamped onto Alice's shoulder. "Go and don't return. If I see you near Lady Judith again, you'll answer to me."

Alice started to speak but Alan's hand digging into her shoulder prevented her. She turned on one heel and stalked away.

Alan turned back to Judith, to see her staring after the woman. "You look almost frightened."

"I am," she said and rubbed her arms. "The woman gives me chills. Once I thought her to be my enemy, but now I almost pity her."

"You are kindhearted. Most women would hate her for what she has done to you."

"I did once. Maybe I still should. But I can't blame her for all of my problems. Many have been caused by myself and—" She stopped and looked down at the ground.

"And your husband?"

"Yes," she whispered. "Gavin."

Alan stood very close to her. The darkness was rapidly gathering, and he had spent the whole day with her. Maybe it was the delicate light on her hair and eyes, but he knew he couldn't keep himself from kissing her. He took her chin in his hand and lifted her face. Her lips met his. "Sweet, lovely Judith," he whispered. "You are too often concerned with others and yourself not enough." He bent and pressed his lips to hers.

Judith was startled, but she didn't find Alan's caress offensive. Nor did she find it particularly exciting. Her eyes stayed open, and she noticed Alan's lashes on his cheek. His lips were soft and pleasant, but they set no fire in her.

The next moment, the world had opened up and emitted hell. Judith was violently pushed away from Alan, her back slamming into a tree, her senses leaving her briefly. She looked about her dazedly. Alan was on the ground, blood trickling from the corner of his mouth. He rubbed his jaw, flexing it. Gavin stood over him, then bent as he went for the man again. "Gavin!" Judith screamed and flung herself at her husband.

Gavin carelessly tossed her aside. "Do you dare touch what is mine?" he growled at the knight. "I will take your life for this!"

Alan was on his feet instantly, his hand going for his sword. They glared at each other, not speaking, their nostrils flared in anger.

Judith placed herself between the two men, facing Gavin. "You want to fight for me after you have willingly turned me aside?"

At first Gavin didn't seem to hear her or even be aware of her presence. Slowly, he pulled his eyes away from Alan to look at his wife. "It wasn't I who set you aside," he said calmly. "It was you."

"It was you who gave me just cause!" she stormed. "It was you who throughout our marriage fought me when I tried to offer you love."

"You never offered me love," he said quietly.

Judith stared at him, the anger leaving her. "Gavin, I have done nothing else since we were married. I have tried to do and be what you wanted of me, but you wanted me to be . . . her! I could be no one but myself." Judith bent her head to hide her tears.

Gavin took a step toward her, then looked back at Alan with hatred.

Judith felt the tension and glanced up. "If you touch one hair on his head, you will regret it," she warned.

Gavin frowned and started to speak, then gradually began to smile. "I had begun to think that my Judith was gone," he whispered. "She was only hidden under a cloak of sweetness."

Alan coughed to cover the laughter that threatened to escape.

Judith straightened her spine and held her shoulders back as she started to walk away from both men. It disgusted her that both of them were laughing at her.

Gavin watched her for a moment, torn between his fight with Alan Fairfax and his desire for his wife. Judith easily won the tug-of-war. Gavin took three long strides, then pulled her into his arms, sweeping her from the ground. Alan quickly left the two of them alone.

"If you're not still, I will set you in a tree until you can no longer move." The horrible threat quieted her. Gavin sat down on the ground with her and pinned her arms between their bodies. "That is better," he said when she was calmer. "Now I will talk and you will listen. You have humiliated me publicly. No!" he interrupted himself. "Don't speak until I'm finished. I can withstand your fun of me in my own castle, but I've had enough of this in front of the king. By now all of England laughs at me."

"At least I have some pleasure in that," Judith said smugly.

"Do you, Judith? Has any of this given you pleasure?"

She blinked rapidly. "No, it hasn't. But it wasn't my fault."

"That's true. You have been innocent of most of it, but I've told you I loved you and I have asked for your forgiveness."

"And I told you—"

He put two fingers over her lips and smothered her words. "I'm tired of fighting you. You are my wife and my property, and I plan to treat you as such. There will be no divorce." His eyes blackened. "Neither will there be more afternoons spent with young knights. Tomorrow we'll leave this gossip-ridden place and return home. There, if need be, I will lock you in a tower room and only I will have a key. It will take a long time to still the laughter throughout England, but it can be done." He paused but she didn't speak. "I'm sorry about the trick Alice played, and I shed my own tears over our lost son. But a divorce now won't change the past. I can only hope that soon I will get you with another child and that will heal your wound. But if you think it won't, it will not matter, for I am to have my own way."

Gavin had said all of this in a deliberate manner. Judith didn't answer, but lay quietly in his arms. "Don't you have anything to say?" he asked.

"And what would I say? I don't believe I'm allowed an opinion."

He didn't look at her but stared across the green countryside. "Is the idea so repulsive to you?"

Judith could contain herself no longer. She started laughing and he stared at her in wonder. "You say you love me, that you will keep me apart from everyone but you, locking me in a tower room where we spend nights of passion. You admit the woman you swore you loved has played you false. You say all these things to me and ask if I am repulsed. You have given me what I have most wanted since I first saw you at the church."

He continued staring at her. "Judith . . ." he began, hesitating.

"I love you, Gavin," she smiled. "Is that so difficult to understand?"

"But three days ago—the divorce—"

This time she put her fingers to his lips. "You ask for forgiveness from me. Can't you forgive me?"

"Yes," he whispered as he bent and kissed her. He drew away abruptly. "And what of that man who kissed you? I will kill him!"

"No! It was but a token of friendship."

"It didn't look—!"

"Are you getting angry again?" she demanded, her eyes shooting sparks. "I have stood by for several days and watched woman after woman paw you."

He chuckled. "I should have enjoyed it, but I didn't. You have ruined me for all time."

"I don't understand you."

"The women talked of nothing but clothing and"— Gavin's eyes twinkled—"face creams. I had more trouble with the ledgers, and not one woman could I find who could help me!"

Judith was instantly concerned. "Do you again allow some baker to rob us?" She started to push away from him. "Come on, let's go. I must see to this straight-away."

Gavin tightened his arms about her. "You will not leave me now! Damn the ledgers! Can't you think of anything else to do with that sweet mouth of yours but talk?"

She smiled at him innocently. "I had thought I was but your property and you the master."

He ignored her jibe. "Come then, slave, and let's find a secret den in this dark wood."

"Aye, my master. Most willingly." They walked hand in hand into the forest.

But Judith and Gavin were not alone. Their words of love, their play, had been witnessed by Alice. She watched them with feverish blue eyes.

"Come, love," Ela said as she forcibly steered her mistress away. She looked with hate at the couple who walked through the trees, their arms and bodies intertwined. Those devils played with Alice! she thought. They teased and laughed at her until the sweet and lovely child nearly lost her mind. But they would pay, she vowed.

"Good morning," Judith whispered and snuggled closer to her husband. He kissed the top of her head but didn't speak. "Are we really going today?"

"If you wish."

"Oh yes, I do. I've had enough of gossip and sly looks and men asking me improper questions."

"What men?" Gavin frowned.

"Do not bait me," she answered, then suddenly sat up in the bed, the covers falling away. "I must speak to the king! Now! He cannot keep believing that I want the divorce when I don't. Perhaps the messenger can be overtaken."

Gavin pulled her down in the bed beside him. He ran his teeth along the cord of her neck. He'd made love to her in the forest yesterday and most of last night, but he wasn't anywhere near satiated. "There's no need for such haste. No message will reach the pope."

"No message?" Judith asked as she moved away from Gavin. "What are you saying? It's been days since I talked to the king about a divorce."

"No message was ever sent."

Judith pushed forcibly away from him. "Gavin! I demand an answer. You speak in riddles."

He sat up in the bed. "King Henry told me first of your request and asked if I wanted a divorce. I told him it was an absurdity you had dreamed of while you were so angry with me. I told him you would repent it in a short while."

Judith's mouth opened to speak, her eyes wide. "How dare you!" she finally gasped. "I had every right—!"

"Judith," he interrupted. "A divorce cannot be granted to every wife who is angry at her husband. Soon there would be no marriages left."

"But you had no right—"

"I have every right! I'm your husband and I love you. Who else has rights if I don't? Now come back here and let's stop talking."

"Don't touch me! How can I face the king after what you have said."

"You have been facing him for days, and you seem to have come to no harm." Gavin leered at her bare breasts.

She snatched the covers under her arms. "You have laughed at me!"

"Judith!" Gavin said in a low, threatening voice. "I have taken a great deal from you over this. I have been laughed at, ridiculed, all in an attempt to appease you. But all that is at an end. If you don't behave now, I will turn that pretty bottom of yours over my knee and spank you. Now come here!"

Judith started to defy him, but then she smiled and snuggled against his chest. "What made you so sure I wouldn't divorce you?"

"I guess I knew I loved you enough to forbid it. I would truly have locked you in a tower before I let another man have you."

"Yet you bore the laughter about the divorce."

Gavin gave a derisive snort. "I had no intentions of doing that. I didn't know your tantrum would leak into public knowledge. But then I had forgotten what gossip there was at court. No one does anything that everyone else doesn't know of it."

"How did the news spread?"

Gavin shrugged. "A maid, I guess. How did the knowledge of Alice's trick spread?"

Judith's head came up. "Don't speak that woman's name to me!"

He pulled Judith back to his chest. "Have you no forgiveness in your heart? The woman loves me, as I once believed I loved her. She has done everything for that love."

Judith gave a sigh of exasperation. "You still don't believe any wrong of her, do you?"

"You are still jealous?" he asked, smiling.

She looked up at him, her eyes very serious. "In a way, I am. She will always be a perfect woman to you. What she did, you believe she did out of love for you. She is a pure, perfect woman to you and will always be. While I am . . ."

"You are what?" he teased.

"I am earthy. I am the woman you have and can have, while Alice represents an ethereal love to you."

He frowned. "You say I'm wrong, yet why else would she have done what she did?"

Judith shook her head at him. "Greed. She believes you are hers and I have taken you. She loves you no more than she loves me—except that you have the wherewithal to give her body some pleasure . . . however brief."

He raised one eyebrow. "Do you insult me?"

"No, but I listen to gossip. The men complain of her penchant for violence."

Gavin drew his breath in sharply. "Let's not speak of this again," he said coldly. "You are my wife and I love you, but even so I'll not listen to you malign such an unhappy woman. You have won and she has lost. That should be enough for you."

Judith blinked back tears. "I love you, Gavin. I love you so much, but I fear that all your love will not be mine as long as the disease of Alice Chatworth eats at your heart."

Gavin frowned, tightening his hold on her. "You have no reason to be jealous of her."

Judith started to speak but of what use would her words be? She knew she would always share a tiny bit of her husband's love with an icy blonde beauty. And no words would ever change those feelings.

Saying good-bye to the people Judith liked at court was not easy. The queen especially had become her friend. As Judith curtsied before the king, she felt her face grow hot. She regretted the publicity of her seeking a divorce, but if she had not realized her mistake, she and Gavin would not be together now. As she lifted her head to the king, she smiled. Knowing that Gavin loved her and that she loved him was worth all the embarrassment and teasing.

"We will miss your lovely face," King Henry smiled. "I hope you come to see us again soon."

Gavin put an arm possessively about his wife's shoulders. "Is it her face or the amusement she provides?"

"Gavin!" Judith gasped in horror.

The king threw back his head and roared with laughter. "It's true, Gavin," he said after a while. "I vow I've not been so entertained in years. I'm sure no other marriages will be half so fascinating."

Gavin returned his king's smile. "Then you might watch Stephen. I've just heard that that Scots bride of his took a knife to him on his wedding night."

"Was he harmed?" Henry asked, concerned.

"No," Gavin grinned. "Though I imagine his temper wasn't so well controlled. But then perhaps the woman had some reason for her anger—Stephen was three days late for his own wedding."

King Henry shook his head in disbelief. "I don't envy the man." He smiled again. "At least all is well with one of the Montgomery brothers."

"Yes," Gavin said as he stroked Judith's upper arm. "All is indeed well."

They finished their last good-byes and left the great hall. It had taken most of the day to complete the packing for the journey home. Truthfully, they should have waited until the next day, but everyone seemed as ready to leave as Judith and Gavin. What with the time at Demari's and at court, they had been away a long while.

As they mounted their horses and waved good-bye to the several people who gathered to see them off, only one watched with concern. Alan Fairfax hadn't been able to find a moment alone with Judith as he had hoped. Early that morning Alice Chatworth had left the castle with her servants and household goods. All of the castlefolk seemed to believe that the woman accepted defeat when Judith and Gavin were reconciled. But not Alan. He felt he knew Alice better than that. Alice had been humiliated. He knew that she would seek revenge.

When the bailey was cleared and the Montgomery group well outside the castle walls, Alan mounted his horse and followed at a discreet distance. It wouldn't hurt to be cautious—at least until the Lady Judith was safe inside her own castle walls. Alan smiled and flexed his sore jaw where Gavin had struck him the day before. He hadn't openly voiced his fears of Alice; he knew Lord Gavin believed him to have an unchivalrous concern for his wife. Perhaps it was true, Alan thought. Perhaps at first; then he had come to know her and began to look on her as a little sister. He sighed and then nearly laughed aloud. At least he could tell himself that. With the way she looked at Lord Gavin, there was no hope for anything else.

Chapter Thirty

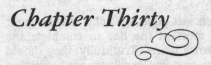

THE WARM WATER FELT HEAVENLY AGAINST JUDITH'S BARE skin. But better than the water was the freedom. There were no court gossips watching them, commenting on their improper behavior. For their behavior now was very improper for an earl and his countess, the rulers of vast estates. They'd traveled for three days when they saw the lovely blue lake, a corner of it hidden and secluded by overhanging willow trees. Now Gavin and Judith frolicked about like children.

"Oh, Gavin," Judith said in a voice that was half giggle and half whisper.

Gavin's laugh rumbled deep in his throat as he lifted her out of the lake then threw her back in again. They had been playing in the water for an hour, chasing each other, kissing and touching. Their clothes lay in a heap on the bank as they moved through the water unencumbered.

"Judith," Gavin whispered as he drew her close, "you make me forget my duties. My men aren't used to such neglect."

"Nor am I used to so much attention," she said, nipping at his shoulders.

"No, don't start again. I must return to camp."

She sighed but knew he was right. They walked ashore where Gavin quickly dressed, then stood and waited impatiently for his wife.

"Gavin," she smiled, "how can I dress when you glower so? Go back to camp and I will follow in a few moments."

He frowned. "I don't want to leave you alone."

"I am within sound of the camp. I won't come to any harm."

He bent and gave her a fierce hug. "You must forgive me if I'm too protective. I came too close to losing you after the child."

"It wasn't that that nearly caused you to lose me," she retorted.

He laughed and smacked her on her bare wet bottom. "Get dressed, you saucy wench, and return to camp quickly."

"Yes, my lord," she smiled.

When Judith was by herself, she dressed slowly, feeling that it was good to have some solitude for a moment of reflection. The last few days had been bliss. Gavin was at last hers. No more did they hide their love from each other. When she was dressed, she didn't return to the camp, but sat quietly under a tree, enjoying the peaceful place.

But Judith wasn't alone. Not far away stood a man who had hardly left her side since they left court; yet she had not seen him and had no idea he stayed so nearby. Alan Fairfax remained a discreet distance away, where he could see the emerald-green of Judith's gown, yet far enough away that he didn't interfere in her privacy. After these days of following her, he'd begun to relax. Several times he'd wondered just what he was doing when she had her husband who had hardly left her side.

Alan was cursing himself for his stupidity and didn't hear the footsteps so close behind him. A sword came down on the side of his head with brutal force. He slumped forward, his head on his chest and then fell heavily into the leaves of the forest floor.

Without warning, a hood was thrown over Judith's head and her arms pinned behind her when she started to struggle. The suffocating fabric muffled her screams. She was thrown across a man's shoulder, the air nearly forced from her lungs.

The man walked past Alan's inert body, and looked up in question to the woman on the horse.

"Leave him. He will tell Gavin that she's gone. Gavin will come to me then, and we'll see which of us he chooses."

The man's face gave no betrayal of his thoughts. He merely collected his money and performed the tasks. He slung his bundle across the saddle and followed Alice Chatworth through the forest.

Alan awoke some time later, his thoughts confused, his head splitting. He put his hand against a tree to steady himself as he stood. As his eyes began to focus again, he remembered Judith and knew that he must find Gavin so they could search for her. He stumbled awkwardly toward the camp.

Gavin met him halfway. "What are you doing here?"

he demanded. "Isn't it enough that you touch my wife at court? Do you think I'll allow you your life again?"

"Judith has been taken!" Alan said, his hand to his pounding head.

Gavin grabbed the smaller man by the neck of his clothes, lifting him from the ground. "If you so much as harm her, I—!"

Alan gasped, forgetting his head and jerking from Gavin's grasp. "It's you who may have hurt her. You wouldn't believe Lady Alice capable of any wrongdoing, so you left Judith unprotected."

"What are you saying!"

"You are a dense man! Alice Chatworth has taken your wife prisoner—and you stand here talking."

Gavin stared at him. "Alice . . . my wife . . . I don't believe you!"

Alan turned away. "Believe me or not, but I'll not waste any more time talking. I'll ride after her alone."

Gavin didn't speak again but turned and went back to the camp. Within moments, he and several of his men were saddled and quickly reached Alan's side. "The Chatworth manor?"

"Yes," Alan answered gravely.

Those were the only words exchanged as the noblemen rode side by side following Judith's captors.

"Welcome to my home," Alice said when the hood was taken from Judith's face. Alice watched the younger woman gasp for breath. "You didn't like the ride? I'm very sorry. A woman such as yourself is used to only the best, I'm sure."

"What do you want of me?" Judith asked, trying to ease the soreness of her shoulders as the ropes on her wrists nearly pulled her arms from their sockets.

"Of you I want nothing," Alice stated. "You have what is mine and I wish its return."

Judith's chin came up. "Do you mean Gavin?"

"Yes," Alice sneered. "I mean Gavin. My Gavin. Always my Gavin."

"Then why didn't you marry him when he asked you?" Judith asked calmly.

Alice's eyes widened, her lips curled into a snarl, exposing her teeth, and her hands formed claws as she lunged for Judith's face.

Judith turned away and the claws didn't reach her.

Ela forcibly grabbed her mistress's arm. "Now, sweet, don't upset yourself. She's not worth it."

Alice seemed to relax.

"Why don't you go and rest?" Ela soothed. "I'll stay with her. You must look your best when Lord Gavin arrives."

"Yes," Alice said quietly. "I must look my best." She left without looking at Judith.

Ela placed her large, soft form in a chair close to the one Judith was tied to and took out some knitting.

"Whose house is this?" Judith asked.

Ela didn't look up. "The Chatworth estate, one of them that my Lady Alice owns," she responded proudly.

"Why am I here?"

Ela paused briefly in her knitting, then resumed. "My lady wishes to see Lord Gavin again."

"Do you believe that?" Judith demanded, her composure leaving her. "Do you believe that crazy woman wants only to see my husband?"

Ela threw down the knitting to her lap. "Don't you call my lady crazy! You don't know her as I do. She's not led an easy life. There are reasons . . ." She stomped across the room toward the window.

"You know, don't you?" Judith asked quietly. "She's insane. Gavin's rejection of her has driven her to madness."

"No!" Ela began, then calmed. "Lord Gavin wouldn't reject my Alice. How could any man deny her? She is beautiful, has always been beautiful. Even as a baby, she was the loveliest anyone had ever seen."

"And you have been with her since she was a child?"

"Yes. I've been with her always. I was past the age for children of my own when she was born. She was given into my care, and she has been a gift of heaven to me."

"Is there nothing you wouldn't do for her?"

"No," Ela said firmly. "I would do anything for her."

"Even killing me so she can take my husband."

Ela looked back at Judith, her old eyes worried. "You won't be killed. It's just that my Lady Alice needs time again with Lord Gavin and you won't allow her that. You are a selfish woman. You have taken what was hers, yet you have no pity or sympathy for my lady's pain."

Judith could feel her temper rising. "She has lied to me, tricked me, done everything she could to take my husband. One of her pieces of treachery cost me the life of my child."

"A child!" Ela hissed. "My lovely lady can have no children. Don't you know how much she has wanted one? Lord Gavin's child! The one you stole from her. It's only fitting that you should lose what should have been my Lady Alice's."

Judith started to speak, then stopped. The maid was as mad as her mistress. No matter what anyone said, Ela would defend Alice. "What are your plans for me?"

Ela realized Judith was calmer and she resumed knitting. "You will be our . . . guest for a few days. Lord Gavin will come, and he will be allowed to spend some time with Lady Alice. Once they are together again, he'll see how much he loves her. It will only take a few days—perhaps only hours—for him to forget you. For in truth he loved her long before he even met you. Theirs is a *true* love match—not one of estates, as is your marriage. Now my Lady Alice is a wealthy widow. She too can bring vast lands to the Montgomery family."

Judith sat quietly and watched Ela knitting. The old

woman had a contented look on her face. There were many questions Judith would like to have asked—such as how Alice planned to free Gavin so they could marry. But Judith wisely didn't put any more questions to the maid. It would have been useless.

All through the hard and fast ride to the Chatworth manor, Gavin was silent. He couldn't believe he would find Judith held prisoner by Alice. He knew of Alice's deception at court and what others said of her, but he truthfully could find little wrong with her. He still considered her a sweet-natured woman driven to great lengths through her adoration of him.

The front gate was standing open. Gavin gave Alan a glance of triumph. This was no place that held an heiress captive.

"Gavin," Alice said as she rushed into the inner bailey to meet him. "I hoped you would come to see me." She was exceptionally pale in a blue silk gown that matched her eyes.

Gavin dismounted and held himself stiffly away from her. "Is my wife here?" he asked coldly.

Alice's eyes widened. "Your wife?" she asked innocently.

Alan's hand swept out and grabbed the woman's upper arm. "Where is she, you bitch? I haven't time to play your games!"

Gavin gave Alan a vicious shove and knocked the young man against his horse. "Don't you touch her again!" he warned. He turned back to Alice. "I want an answer to my question."

"Come inside," Alice began, then stopped when she saw Gavin's face. "She is not given to visiting me."

"Then we must leave. She is taken captive and we must find her." He turned to mount his horse again.

"No! Gavin, don't leave me," she cried as she flung herself at him. "Please don't leave me!"

Gavin turned to set her aside.

"Your wife is here."

He turned to see Ela standing in the doorway.

"The woman is kept here, safe now, but she won't be so safe if you spurn my Lady Alice."

Gavin was next to the fat woman in seconds. "Do you threaten me, old hag?" He turned back to Alice. "Where is she?" he demanded.

Alice's eyes spilled over with great, lovely tears. She didn't speak.

"You waste time!" Alan said. "We'll tear this place apart to find her."

Gavin took a step toward the manor house.

"You won't find her!"

Gavin whirled. The voice was a distorted version of Alice's—high and screeching. Her little mouth was pulled back in a snarl, and he saw that her teeth were badly crooked. Why hadn't he seen that before?

"She is where you nor any man will find her," Alice continued, for the first time dropping her facade of sweetness before Gavin. "Do you think I would give that whore my best room? She deserves only the bottom of the moat!"

Gavin took a step toward her, disbelieving the drastic change in Alice. She didn't seem even remotely kin to the woman he once loved.

"You didn't know she gave herself to many men, did you? Did you know the child she lost was not even yours, but Demari's?" Alice put her hand on his arm. "I could give you sons," she leered, her face and voice a caricature of the woman he thought he knew.

"This is what you have neglected Judith for," Alan said quietly. "Can you see now what everyone else does?"

"Yes, I see it," Gavin said in disgust.

Alice backed away from the men, her eyes wild. She picked up her skirts and turned and ran, Ela following her.

When Alan started in pursuit, Gavin said, "Leave

her. I would rather have my wife back than punish Alice."

Alice ran from one building to the next, hiding, skulking, furtively looking about. Gavin had looked at her as if she repulsed him. Somewhere in her mind she knew Ela followed her, but her mind didn't seem to be able to think of more than one thing at a time. Right now all she could think of was the fact that another woman had taken her lover from her. Quickly, she climbed the tower steps making sure no one was after her.

Judith looked up at Alice as she stood in the doorway. The woman's hair was disarranged, her veil askew.

"So!" Alice said, her eyes glinting wildly. "You think you will get him back?"

Judith cringed against the ropes, her throat raw from calling out. But the walls were too thick for her to be heard.

Alice swept across the room grabbing a pot of hot oil from the brazier. A wick floated on top of the oil, ready to be lit. Alice held the oil carefully as she walked toward her prisoner. "He won't think you are lovely once this eats away half of your face."

"No!" Judith whispered and drew back as far as she could.

"Do I frighten you? Do I make your life hell as you have made mine? I was a happy woman before I knew of you. My life hasn't been the same since I first heard your name. I had a father who loved me. Gavin worshiped me. A rich earl asked to marry me. Yet you have taken them all away from me. My father hardly recognizes me now. Gavin hates me. My rich husband is dead. And all because of you."

She moved away from Judith and buried the pot of oil deeper into the coals. "It must be hot, very hot. What do you think will happen when your beauty is gone?"

Judith knew it was impossible to reason with the woman, but she still tried. "What you do to me won't bring back your husband, and I don't even know your father."

"My husband!" Alice sneered. "Do you think I want him back? He was a swine of a man. Yet he once loved me. He changed after he went to your wedding. You made him believe I wasn't worthy of him."

Judith couldn't speak. Her eyes stared at the heating oil.

"My lord," Ela said nervously. "You must come. I'm afraid."

"What is it, you old hag?" Gavin demanded.

"My lady. I fear for her."

Gavin would have gone to great lengths to keep from hurting a woman. Even seeing Alice as she truly was, he couldn't demand that she tell him where Judith was. Now he grabbed Ela's arm. "What are you saying? I grow tired of this game of hide-and-seek. Where is my wife?"

"I meant no harm," Ela whispered. "I only tried to get you back for my lady. It was what she wanted so much. I always try to get her what she wants. But now I'm afraid. I wish the Lady Judith no harm."

"Where is she?" Gavin demanded, tightening his grip.

"She has locked the door and—"

"Go!" Gavin said and pushed the woman. He and Alan followed her across the courtyard to the tower. Please, God! Gavin prayed, let nothing happen to Judith.

At the first pounding on the door, Alice jumped. She knew the bolt wouldn't hold long. She took a long, sharp knife from her side and held it to Judith's throat as she untied the binding ropes. "Come," she said as she grabbed the oil in the other hand.

Judith felt the blade at her throat and the heat from

the pot of oil near her cheek. She knew that the slightest movement could startle the nervous Alice and release the oil or push the knife into her throat.

"Up here!" Alice commanded Judith as they slowly made their way up a narrow wooden stairway to the rooftop. Alice stood back, away from the edges, her arm around Judith, holding the knife closely to her neck.

Gavin, Ela and Alan burst through the doorway seconds later. When they saw the empty chamber, they followed Ela up the stairs. They all froze at the sight of the wild-eyed Alice holding Judith.

"My sweet Lady Alice—" Ela began.

"Don't you talk to me!" Alice said, tightening her grip. "You said you'd get him back for me. But he hates me—I know he does!"

"No!" Ela said, taking a step forward. "Lord Gavin doesn't hate you. He protects his wife because she's his property. No other reason. Now come and let's talk. I'm sure Lord Gavin will understand why this has happened."

"No!" Alice sneered. "Look at him. He despises me! He snarls at me and looks as if I were the lowest form of life. And all for this red-haired slut!"

"Do not harm her!" Gavin warned.

Alice cackled. "Harm her! I will more than harm her. See this?" She held the pot of oil aloft. "It is very, very hot. It will scar her face. What will you say when she's no longer so lovely?"

Gavin took a step forward.

"No!" Alice screeched. "Get up there!" she commanded Judith, pushing her closer to the edge near a chimney pot.

"No!" Judith whispered. She was very frightened but her terror of heights was even greater.

"Do as she says," Gavin said in a low voice, realizing finally that Alice was not sane.

Judith nodded and stepped up on the edge of the

roof. In front of her was the upward thrust of the chimney. She grabbed it, her arms tightly rigid.

Alice began to laugh. "She fears this place! She is a child, and you wanted this bitch over me. I am a true woman."

Ela put her hand on Gavin's arm as he started forward. The two women were in a precarious position. Judith's eyes were glazed with fright, her knuckles white as she held onto the bit of brick in front of her. Alice waved the knife and the pot of boiling oil about wildly. "Yes," Ela said. "You are truly a woman. If you will come down, Lord Gavin will soon be sure of that."

"Are you trying to trick me?" Alice asked.

"Have I ever tricked you?"

"No," Alice said and smiled down at the old woman for a moment. "You are the only one who has always been good to me."

The momentary lapse of concentration caused Alice to stumble. Ela grabbed frantically at her beloved mistress, catapulting her body from the slate roof of the manor. Alice grabbed at her maid at the same time as Ela pushed her mistress to safety. Ela fell over the side of the house, taking several seconds before she hit the stones below. Alice fell backward, away from the edge, thanks to the sacrifice of her maid. But the pot of oil in her hand fell with her, spilling across her forehead and cheek. She began to scream horribly.

Gavin made one leap across the roof to where Judith still clung. Her extreme fear of heights and her resulting iron grip on the chimney had saved her life.

Alice's screams filled the air as Gavin pried Judith's fingers loose from the brick. He held her close, feeling her body tighten, her heart pounding.

"Look what you've done to me!" Alice screamed through her pain. "And Ela—you have killed my Ela! She was the only one who ever truly loved me."

"No," Gavin answered, looking at Alice's mutilated face with great pity. "It was not I nor Judith who has harmed you, but only yourself." He turned to Alan as he picked Judith up in his arms. "See to her. Don't let her die. Perhaps that scar will be a fitting reward for her lies."

Alan looked with distaste at the cringing woman, then walked toward her.

Gavin took Judith down the stairs to the room below. It was some moments before she was able to relax. "It's over now, my love," Gavin whispered. "You are safe now. She will harm you no more." He held her very tightly.

Alice's screams, now little more than hoarse groans, came closer. Gavin and Judith watched as Alan led her below. She stopped and gave Judith one last vicious look, then turned away when she saw the sorrow in Judith's eyes. Alan led her from the room.

"What will happen to her now?" Judith asked quietly.

"I don't know. I could give her to the courts, but I think perhaps she's been punished enough. No longer will her beauty ensnare men."

Judith looked up at him in surprise and studied his face.

"You look at me as if you're seeing me for the first time," he said.

"Maybe I am. You're free of her."

"I have told you before that I no longer loved her."

"Yes, but there was always a part of you that was hers, a part I couldn't touch. But now she no longer possesses you. You are mine—totally and completely mine."

"And that pleases you?"

"Yes," she whispered. "It pleases me greatly."